Praise for the novels of
New York Times Bestselling Author

DEBBIE MACOMBER

"Fans are certain to take to the Dakota series
as they would to cotton candy at a state fair."
—*Publishers Weekly* on *Dakota Born*

"Ms. Macomber provides the top
in entertaining relationship dramas."
—*Reader to Reader*

This Matter of Marriage
is "so much fun it may keep you up till 2 a.m."
—*The Atlanta Journal*

"Macomber's storytelling sometimes yields a tear,
at other times a smile."
—*Newport News, (VA) Daily Press*

"Popular romance writer Macomber
has a gift for evoking the emotions
that are at the heart of the genre's popularity."
—*Publishers Weekly*

"*Can This Be Christmas?* will enchant and entertain
readers for generations to come...a beautifully told story."
—*Harleysville, PA Bucks-Mont Courier*

"Well-developed emotions and appealing characters."
—*Publishers Weekly* on *Montana*

Dear Friends,

A universal question for writers is "Where do you get your story ideas?" The answer is as varied as the stories themselves. Some of my best ideas have been inspired by old movies. Who couldn't fall in love with heroes like Humphrey Bogart? Other than *The African Queen,* my favorite Bogart movie is *Sabrina,* starring Bogart, Audrey Hepburn and William Holden. (The film has since been remade starring Harrison Ford.) I loved the idea of two brothers—one dedicated to his professional career while life passes him by. A man who's so completely out of balance that he wouldn't recognize love until it stared him in the face. Meet Damian Dryden in "Ready for Romance," my version of the Humphrey Bogart character. It takes a woman falling in love with his brother to wake him to what's really important in life.

Then there's Evan Dryden, Damian's younger brother, the playboy who's wasting his life on wine, women and song— well, not exactly, but close. Everything's a joke to him, a party waiting to happen. At least, that's what Evan wants his family to believe. Only, he's using the easy lifestyle to hide a deep pain, one he refuses to confront, until the woman he loved reenters his life. This time the younger brother gets a starring role—in "Ready for Marriage."

Just think, a bowl of microwave popcorn and a rented video of a fifty-year-old movie inspired two books. Not a bad way to spend a Friday night, is it? One night soon, curl up with a bowl of popcorn and my book, and enter the world of Damian and Evan Dryden.

Enjoy!

Debbie Macomber

DEBBIE MACOMBER

READY FOR LOVE

MIRA®

ISBN 1-55166-792-4

READY FOR LOVE
Copyright © 1999 by MIRA Books.

The publisher acknowledges the copyright holder
of the individual works as follows:

READY FOR ROMANCE
Copyright © 1993 by Debbie Macomber.

READY FOR MARRIAGE
Copyright © 1994 by Debbie Macomber.

Visit us at www.mirabooks.com

Printed in U.S.A.

CONTENTS

Ready for Romance

For Jessica,
who caught the wedding bouquet first

Prologue

Jessica Kellerman looked both ways, then slipped around the corner of the Dryden four-car garage. She flattened her body against the wall and moved cautiously, one infinitesimal step at a time. It was vital no one see her.

Evan's vehicle, a fancy sports car, was parked just outside the garage—and in direct view of the house. She needed to be quick.

Squatting down by the side mirror, she withdrew a bright red tube of lipstick from her pocket, opened it and heavily outlined her lips. Taking a soft white rag from the pocket of her jeans, she wiped his mirror clean and then kissed it several times. The imprint of her mouth was left in bold red.

Jessica sighed with satisfaction as she carefully opened the door on the driver's side and crawled into the front seat. The mirror over the dash was next. Her heart was pounding hard and fast, but it wasn't entirely due to her fear of being discovered. Her heart rate tended to accelerate whenever she thought about Evan.

There wasn't a man in all of Boston who could compete with Evan Dryden. To think she'd lived next door to him all these years and hadn't noticed until recently what a gorgeous hunk he was! As far as Jessica was concerned, he was the handsomest man in the universe.

She remembered the exact moment she had realized her destiny. She hadn't been the same since. The Dryden estate, Whispering Willows, was next to her own family's, and she'd often spent time in the huge oak tree spying on the two brothers. Damian was in law school now and Evan in college. Being an only child, Jessica was left to invent her own amusement, and spying on the Dryden brothers had always been great fun.

Jessica had been sitting in the tree one day when Evan had

walked to the pond and stood on the footbridge tossing rocks into the water. His back was to her and she held her breath, wondering if he'd seen her hiding in the thick foliage.

She must have made a sound, because he turned abruptly and stared into the tree.

"Jessica?"

She didn't dare move or even breathe.

He stared upward and the sun cut across his shoulder, highlighting his handsome features. It was then that she realized Evan wasn't just an ordinary boy. He was an Adonis. Perfect in every way.

After that she started having dreams about him. Wonderful dreams about him falling in love with her. Dreams about them marrying and having a family. It seemed so...so right. It came to her about a week later that fate had thrown them together. They were meant for each other. The only problem was that Evan had yet to make this discovery for himself.

Jessica had recently turned fourteen and Evan was much older. Six whole years, but it might have been a hundred for all the notice he gave her.

That was when Jessica decided she had to take matters into her own hands. She was a woman of the world, and when a woman knew what she wanted, she went after it. It, in this case, was Evan Dryden.

Jessica soon discovered she wasn't nearly as dauntless as she would have liked. She must have phoned him ten times or more, and each time he answered, she lacked the courage to so much as speak, much less tell him about her undying love. Each call had ended with her replacing the receiver and stewing in frustration.

She'd always been better at expressing herself with the written word, so she'd taken to writing him love notes, pouring out her devotion. She let her best friend read one such note, and the girl claimed it was the most beautiful love letter she'd ever seen. Unfortunately, Jessica hadn't found the courage to sign her name.

This latest trick, planting kisses on his rearview mirror, was sure to accomplish what nothing else had. He'd know it was Jessica and he'd finally come for her, and together they'd ride into the sunset in his sports car.

Outlining her lips with a fresh coat of brilliant red, Jessica was about to kiss the interior mirror when the car door was flung open.

"So it *is* you."

Her heart sank all the way to her knees. Slowly she looked over and her eyes connected with Damian Dryden's. He was taller than his younger brother, dark and handsome in his own way. She was certain the day would come when some girl would feel as strongly about him as she did about Evan.

"Hello," she said, pretending it wasn't the least bit out of the ordinary for her to be sitting in his brother's car kissing the mirrors.

"You're the one, I bet, who's been phoning at all hours of the night."

"I've never called past ten," she denied heatedly, then realized her mistake. It probably would have been best to pretend she didn't know what he was talking about.

"The notes on Evan's windshield have been from you, too, haven't they?"

She could have denied that, but it wouldn't have done any good. Feeling trapped in Evan's car, she swung her legs around and gingerly climbed out. "Are you going to tell him it was me?"

"I don't know," Damian said thoughtfully. "How old are you now?"

"Fourteen," she said proudly. "I know Evan's older, but I was hoping he'd be willing to wait for me to grow up so we could get married."

"Married!"

Damian made the word sound ludicrous and Jessica bristled. "Just wait until you fall in love," she challenged. "Then you'll know."

"You aren't in love with Evan," he said gently. "You're too young to know about things like that. You're infatuated with him because he's older and—"

"I most certainly do love Evan," she flared, stuffing the lipstick tube in her pocket. She wasn't about to stand there and let him ridicule her. She might only be fourteen, but she had the heart of a mature woman and she'd made her decision. Someday she would marry Evan Dryden, and nothing Damian could say or do would stand in her way.

"I'm sure my brother's flattered by your devotion."

"He should be. The man who marries me will see himself as the luckiest man in the world." Her words were fed by pure bravado.

Damian laughed.

Jessica had been willing to overlook his earlier statements, but this was unforgivable. Hands braced against her hips, she glared at him with all the indignation she could muster, which at the moment was considerable.

"You might be older than Evan, but you don't know a thing about love, do you?"

Her question appeared to amuse him, and that only served to irritate her further.

"When a woman makes up her mind about a man, nothing can change the way she feels. I've decided to marry your brother, and not a thing you say or do will have the least effect, so save your breath. Evan is my destiny."

"You're sure about this?"

At least he had the courtesy to wipe the grin off his face.

"Of course," she said confidently. "Mark my words, Damian Dryden. Time will prove me right."

"Does my brother have a say in this?"

"Naturally."

"What if he decides to marry someone else?"

"I...I don't know." Damian had zeroed in on her worst fear— that Evan would get married before she had a chance to prove herself.

"There's something else you haven't considered," Damian said.

"What's that?"

He grinned. "I just might want to marry you myself."

One

Jessica Kellerman's time of reckoning had arrived. For the first time in eight years she was about to face the Dryden brothers. Evan didn't concern her. She suspected he wouldn't even remember what a nuisance she'd made of herself. Then again, he just might. But Damian was the brother who worried her most. He was the one who'd caught her red-handed. He was the one who'd mocked her and suggested her devotion to his brother was a passing fancy. Now she was forced to face him and admit he'd been right. She sincerely hoped Damian would have the good grace not to drag up the past.

Swallowing her dread, Jessica walked into the high-rise office building in the most prestigious part of downtown Boston. The building was new, with a glistening black-mirrored exterior that towered thirty stories above the ground. The Dryden law firm was one of the most distinguished in town, and in Boston that was saying something.

Jessica's footsteps made tapping sounds against the marble floor in the lobby. Although she'd been in this part of town often—the university wasn't far from the business section—this was the first time she'd been inside the impressive building.

She was nervous, and rightly so. The last time she'd spent any time with either of the Dryden brothers she'd been caught kissing rearview mirrors.

Looking back, she knew she'd been a constant source of amusement to the brothers and their respective sets of parents, as well. Young love, however, refused to be denied. Risking her family's censure, Jessica had diligently sought Evan's heart all through high school. It wasn't until Benny Wilcox asked her to the graduation dance that she'd realized there were other fish in the sea. Sweet, attentive, good-looking ones, too. Yes, Evan had been the man of her dreams, the one who'd awakened her to womanhood. She held her love for him in a special place in her heart, but was more than willing to forget the way she'd embarrassed herself over him, praying he did, too.

Although Jessica had let her infatuation with Evan die gracefully, neither set of parents had. Particularly, Lois and Walter Dryden. They thought the way Jessica felt about Evan was "cute," and they mentioned it every now and again, renewing her embarrassment.

When Walter Dryden heard that Jessica had recently graduated from business college with a certificate as a legal assistant, he'd insisted she apply with the family firm. In the beginning Jessica had balked, but jobs were few and far between just then, and after a fruitless search on her own, she'd decided to swallow her pride and face the two brothers.

She was warmly greeted by the receptionist, who gave her a wide smile. Jessica smiled back, hoping she looked composed and mature. "I have an appointment with Damian Dryden," she said.

The woman, who appeared to be in her early thirties, with large blue eyes and a smooth complexion, glanced at the appointment book. "Ms. Kellerman?"

"That's right."

"Please have a seat and I'll let Mr. Dryden know you're here."

"Thank you." Jessica sat in one of the richly upholstered chairs and reached for a *People* magazine. She'd dressed carefully for this interview, choosing a soft dove gray suit with a double-breasted jacket. The silver-dollar-size buttons were made from mother-of-pearl with flashes of deep blue and white. She wore high heels, hoping to seem not only professional, but sophisticated. Her glossy brown hair was sophisticated, too, cut in a flattering pageboy. She'd grown up, and it was important Damian know that.

Jessica hadn't even scanned the magazine's contents page when the elder Dryden brother appeared. She'd seen Damian often, from a distance, but this was the first time they'd spoken in months, possibly years. She'd forgotten how tall he was, with broad shoulders that tapered to slim hips. She remembered how much he enjoyed football as a teenager, and how good he was at tackling the opponent. From what she remembered about Damian, he preferred to tackle problems head-on, too. She knew him to be aggressive, hardworking and ambitious. He'd taken over the leadership of the law firm upon Walter Dryden's retirement three years earlier, and the firm, which specialized in corporate law, had thrived under his leadership.

"Hello, Jessica. It's good to see you again," Damian said, stepping forward.

"It's good to see you, too." She stood and offered him her hand.

He clasped it with both of his own. He wasn't an especially large man, and at five eight she wasn't especially small, but her hand was dwarfed in his. His grip was solid and strong, like the man himself.

"I've come to talk to you about a position as a legal assistant," she said. The direct approach would work best with Damian, she felt.

"Great. Let's go to my office, shall we?"

She was struck by the rugged timbre of his voice. It exuded confidence, sounding deep and firm. Little wonder Damian was one of the most sought-after corporate attorneys in Boston.

He motioned her to be seated, then walked around behind the deep mahogany desk and claimed the black leather chair. He tilted it back slightly, conveying ease and relaxation.

Jessica wasn't fooled. She sincerely doubted that Damian knew how to relax. His mother, Lois, had often voiced her concern about her elder son, complaining that Damian worked too many hours.

"Thank you for seeing me on such short notice," Jessica said, crossing her legs.

"It's my pleasure." He rolled a pen between his palms. "I understand you recently graduated from college."

She nodded. "I have a degree in early-American history."

The motion of the pen between his palms froze and a frown creased his brow. "Unfortunately we don't have much call for historians here at the firm."

"I realize that," she said quickly. "About halfway through my senior year, I realized that although I love history, I wasn't exactly sure what I planned to do with my degree. I toyed with the idea of teaching, then changed my mind."

"And you want to be a legal assistant now?"

"Yes. I was dating a law student and I discovered how much I enjoyed law. You see, we often did our homework together. But rather than register for law school and invest all that time and effort, I decided to work as a legal assistant—sort of get my feet wet and then decide if becoming an attorney is what I want to do. So I went to business college and got a certificate." She said all this in an eager rush. "Your father suggested I come and talk to you," she added, winding down. She opened her purse and produced her certificate for his inspection.

"I see." The pen was in motion again.

"I'm a hard worker."

Damian smiled fleetingly. "I don't doubt that."

"I'll work any hours you wish, even weekends. You can put me on probation if you want." She hadn't meant to reveal how much she wanted the position, but despite her resolve, she couldn't keep the anxiety out of her voice.

"This job means a great deal to you, doesn't it?"

Jessica nodded.

"I think," Damian said casually, "you're still infatuated with my brother."

He spoke as if it had been only a few days since she'd all but thrown herself at Evan. Heat radiated from her cheeks. "I...I don't believe that's a fair statement."

Damian smiled shrewdly. "You've had a crush on Evan for years."

"Perhaps, but that has nothing to do with my applying for a position here." She closed her mouth and collected her composure as best she could. She should have known Damian wouldn't conveniently forget their encounter all those years ago.

"It's true, though, isn't it?" Damian seemed to take delight in teasing her, which infuriated Jessica. She clamped her mouth shut, rather than argue with the man she hoped would employ her. "I was there the day you put kisses all over his rearview mirror, remember?"

Not trusting herself to speak, she nodded.

"I watched you look at him with those big worshipful eyes. I've seen plenty of other women do the same thing since, all gazing at my younger brother as though he were an Adonis.''

Jessica's eyes widened at the use of the term. That was exactly the way she'd viewed Evan. A Greek god.

''It's true isn't it, or are you going to deny it?''

Jessica's mouth refused to work. She opened and closed it a number of embarrassing times, not knowing how to respond, or if she should even try.

Cathy Hudson, her best friend, had claimed it wasn't a good idea to apply for work with a family who knew her so well. Jessica was about to concede that Cath was right.

''I did have a schoolgirl crush on your brother at one time,'' she confessed, ''but that was years ago. I haven't seen Evan in...heavens, I don't remember. Certainly not any more often than I've seen you. If you believe my past feelings for Evan would hinder my performance as a legal assistant, then there isn't anything more I can say—other than to thank you for your time.''

Damian's smile was slightly off kilter, his eyes bemused as if, despite himself, he'd admired her little speech. Slowly a look of sadness crossed his face. ''Evan's changed, you know. He isn't the man you once knew.''

''I'd heard from my mother that he's been unhappy recently.'' She didn't know the details and hoped Damian would fill in the blanks.

''Do you know why?''

''No.''

Damian gave a soft regretful sigh. ''I might as well tell you, since you'll find out soon enough yourself. He was in love possibly for the first time in his life, and it didn't work out. I don't know what caused the rift, and neither does anyone else, not that it matters. Unfortunately, though, Evan can't seem to snap out of his depression.''

''He must have loved her very much,'' she whispered, watching Damian. He was genuinely concerned about Evan.

''I'm sure he did.'' Damian frowned, apparently at a loss as to how to help his brother, then shook his head. ''We've ventured far from the subject of your employment, haven't we?''

She straightened and folded her hands in her lap, wondering if Damian would take a chance and hire her. She was a risk, too, fresh out of school, with no job experience.

"You're sure you want to work here?" he asked, studying her with a discerning eye.

"Very much."

Damian didn't immediately respond. His silence made her uncomfortable enough to want to fill it with something, even useless chatter. "I know what you're thinking," she said breathlessly. "In your eyes I'm a love-struck fourteen-year-old, convinced your brother and I are meant for each other." She shook her head. "I don't know what to say to convince you I've grown up, and that nonsense is all behind me, but I have."

"I can see that for myself." A glint of appreciation sparked in his eyes. "As it happens, Jessica, you're in luck, because the firm could use another legal assistant. If you want the job, it's yours."

Jessica resisted vaulting out of the chair and throwing her arms around Damian's neck to thank him. Instead she promised, "I won't let you down."

"You'll be working directly with Evan," he replied, still studying her closely.

"With Evan?"

"Is that a problem?"

"No... No, of course not."

"Just remember one thing. It doesn't matter how many years our parents have been friends. If you don't do your job and do it well, we don't have room for you here."

"I wouldn't expect you to keep me on if I didn't pull my weight," she said, trying hard not to sound defensive.

"Good." He reached for the intercom and glanced at her. "When would you like to start?"

"Now, if you want."

"Perfect. I'll ring Mrs. Sterling. She's Evan's secretary, and she'll show you the ropes."

Jessica stood and extended her hand. "You won't be sorry, I promise you." She pumped his hand enthusiastically until she realized she was overdoing it.

Grinning, Damian walked around to the front of his desk. "If there's anything I can help you with, let me know."

"I will. Thank you, Damian."

She hadn't meant to call him by his first name. Theirs was a professional relationship now, but it *was* difficult to think of him as her boss. A personal bond existed between them, but until this interview Jessica hadn't realized it was there. To her surprise she found she had no such problem regarding Evan.

She and Damian walked out of the office together and down the corridor to a door with Evan's name engraved on a gold plaque.

Damian opened the door for her and allowed her to precede him. Jessica's gaze fell on Evan's secretary. The woman was middle-aged, with sharp, but not unattractive, features. She seemed to breathe efficiency. One look and Jessica was confident this woman could manage Evan's office and the entire law firm if necessary.

"Mrs. Sterling," Damian said, "this is Jessica Kellerman, Evan's new legal assistant. Would you show her around and make her feel at home?"

"Of course."

Damian turned to Jessica. "As I said earlier, come to me if you have any problems."

"Thank you."

"No, Jessica," he said cryptically on his way out, "thank *you*." The door made a small clicking sound as it shut.

Mrs. Sterling rose from her chair. She was a small woman, barely five feet, a stark contrast to tall and slender Jessica. Her salt-and-pepper hair was cropped short, and she wore a no-nonsense straight skirt and light sweater.

"I'll show you where the law library is," Mrs. Sterling said. Jessica glanced toward the closed door, wondering if Evan was in. Apparently not, otherwise Damian would have made a point of letting his brother know Jessica would be working for him.

The secretary led the way out of the office and down the hall. The library was huge, with row upon row of thick dusty volumes. Long narrow tables with a number of chairs were scattered about the room. Jessica knew she'd be spending the majority of her research time here and was pleased by how pleasant it was. She noticed the faint scent of lemon oil and smiled as she saw various types of potted plants set here and there, including a speckled broad-leaved ivy that stretched across the top of one large bookcase.

"This is very nice."

"Mr. Dryden has worked hard to make sure our work environment is pleasing to the eye," the woman remarked primly.

"Damian's like that," Jessica murmured.

"I was speaking about the younger Mr. Dryden," came the surprised response.

"Oh, of course," Jessica said quickly.

By the end of the first day, Jessica felt as though she'd put in a forty-hour week. She'd been assigned a small desk in the corner of the room and her own phone. Mrs. Sterling seemed to feel it was her duty to keep Jessica occupied with a multitude of tasks which included taking lunch orders, organizing file cabinets and hand-delivering messages throughout the office.

Just when she was about to think she wouldn't even lay eyes on Evan her first day, he breezed into the office, stopping abruptly when he saw her. He was as tall as Damian, at least six-two, with chestnut hair and dark soulful eyes. To Jessica's way of thinking, it wasn't fair that any one man should be so breathtakingly handsome.

"Julia," he whispered, as though he'd stumbled upon a treasure chest. His eyes suffused with delight. "What are you doing here?"

"It's Jessica," she corrected him, refusing to be offended by his failure to remember her name. "I'm here because I'm working for you now."

"Your brother hired Ms. Kellerman as your new legal assistant," Mrs. Sterling explained.

Evan stepped forward, gripping Jessica's hand in his own. "This must be Christmas in July! Why else would Damian present me with such a rare gift?"

"Christmas in July," Jessica repeated, having a difficult time not laughing. What she'd heard about Evan was true, she decided. He was a flirt, but such a pleasant lighthearted one that it didn't seem to matter. She knew he wasn't serious.

"There are several matters here that need your attention," Mrs. Sterling said stiffly from behind Evan.

"I'll be with you in a few minutes," he said.

"I know you will," Mrs. Sterling said. "Just don't leave before these letters are signed, and while we're at it, there are a few items we need to discuss—when you have the time."

"I promise to get to the letters first thing," he said as if he had no interest beyond studying the young woman who stood before him. "Just put everything on my desk and I'll look through it before I leave."

"You won't forget?"

Evan chuckled. "My, my, how you love to mother me."

"Someone has to look after you," his secretary said, her eyes crinkling above a bright smile.

Jessica watched in amazement as Evan charmed the older woman. Mrs. Sterling had been the picture of cool efficiency until Evan walked in the door. The minute he did she turned into a clucking mother hen. Before Jessica had a chance to analyze this reaction, Evan grinned. "You love me, Mary, and you know it."

"It's just that you've been a bit forgetful of late," Mrs. Sterling said with a concerned frown. She reached for a stack of letters and leafed through them. "It doesn't hurt to offer you a little reminder now and then, does it?"

"I suppose not," Evan said and, taking the letters with him, walked into his office as if he hadn't a care in the world.

"Have you been working on the brief for the Porter Corporation?" Mrs. Sterling asked, following on his heels.

"The Porter Corporation," Evan repeated as if he'd never heard the name before. "It's not due anytime soon, is it?"

"Yes, it is," the secretary said, and Jessica heard a hint of panic in her voice. "First thing Friday morning."

"I'll have it ready by then. What day is this, anyway?"

"Mr. Dryden, you've got to start coming into the office before closing time!"

"Don't you fret. I'll have everything ready the way I always do,'' he said as he ushered his secretary out the door. He paused when his gaze fell on Jessica and he winked. Then the door closed and Evan disappeared.

Mrs. Sterling shook her head and glanced toward Jessica. ''Mr Dryden's been going through some rough times lately,'' she explained.

''How long has he been without a legal assistant?''

''Quite a while now. He didn't seem to think he'd need one. Damian's cut his work load and, well, things just haven't been the same around here for quite a while.''

Jessica was leaving for the day when she happened upon Damian. Looking dignified and businesslike, he was talking to his secretary. A few silver hairs at his temple added a distinguished air. He made a striking figure, and she wondered briefly why he hadn't married. Tagged onto that thought came another. One that took her by surprise. She realized she was *happy* Damian hadn't married.

He must have seen her in his peripheral vision, because he straightened, smiled and walked toward her. ''Well, Jessica, how'd your first day go?''

''Really well.''

''Mary isn't working you too hard, is she?''

''Oh, no, she's great.''

''Mary's one of the best secretaries I've ever worked with. She may be a bit abrupt, but you'll get used to that.'' He was walking with Jessica now, their steps matching, his hands clasped behind his back. Mary was abrupt perhaps, Jessica mused, but not with Evan.

''I'll always be grateful to you for being willing to take a chance on me,'' she said conversationally.

Damian's smile was rueful. ''You may not be thanking me later. My brother can be a handful, but if there was ever someone who could get him back on the straight and narrow, it's you.''

''Me?'' she asked, not understanding.

Damian broke eye contact and looked away. ''Everybody needs to be looked at with wide worshipful eyes now and then, don't you think?''

"Ah…" Jessica didn't know how to respond. One thing was becoming abundantly clear. Damian hadn't hired her because of her high test scores at business college.

Two

"You actually got the job?" Cathy Hudson said over the telephone line, her voice raised with astonishment. "You were hired, just like that, by one of the city's most prestigious law firms?"

"It helps to have friends in high places." Jessica was excited about this job, but she felt mildly guilty knowing the only reason she'd been hired was that their families were such good friends. However, Damian had made it plain she'd need to pull her own weight. Jessica was determined to prove herself; she'd be the best legal assistant the firm had ever hired. It was a matter of pride.

"Why is it everything comes so easy for you?" Cathy lamented. "You set your sights on something that would give Norman Vincent Peale second thoughts and—"

"Me? You're the one trying out for a lead in *Guys and Dolls.* Talk about setting your sights high."

"All right, all right," Cathy said with a dramatic sigh, "you've made your point."

"So how did the tryouts go today?"

"I...don't know. It's so hard to tell. I would kill for the part of Adelaide, but then I watch the others, and they're all so good. I came away today thinking it's just a pipe dream. David, the director, is wonderful. Working with him would be one of the highlights of my career, but I don't dare hope I'll get the part."

"I have faith in you. You're a natural, Cath." It was true, her friend had a knack for the dramatic, and that had always made their friendship so interesting.

Cathy laughed softly. "How can I fail, when both you and my mother are convinced I'm destined for stardom? Now, before we get off the subject, how did the interview with Damian go?"

"Really well, I think." Damian had dominated her thoughts all afternoon. He'd changed, she decided, or perhaps she was the one who was different. Whichever, she found herself enthralled by the man. The thought of working with him excited her.

"What about the younger brother?"

"Actually I'll be working directly for Evan."

Cathy must have noticed the hesitation in her voice because she asked, "Does that worry you? What's the matter? Do you think you're going to make an idiot of yourself over him—again?"

So much for Jessica's delicate ego. "No way. I was fourteen years old, for heaven's sake."

After she'd hung up, Jessica slipped a CD into the player, choosing an invigorating medley of jazz hits, and set about fixing her dinner. She whipped together a hot chicken-and-spinach salad and stood barefoot in her kitchen, humming along to the music, her heart singing its own melody.

Later that evening, she relaxed with the paper. Despite her best efforts, her thoughts drifted to Damian. The last thing she wanted was to make a fool of herself over another Dryden.

To the best of her knowledge, the source of which was her mother, Damian wasn't currently involved in a relationship. Joyce Kellerman said that Lois Dryden had complained that her elder son didn't take enough time for fun in his life. What Damian needed, Jessica decided now, was to fall in love with a woman who would take his mind off his work. Someone fun. Someone who would make him laugh and enjoy life. Someone who appreciated him.

An hour later, as she was getting ready for bed, Jessica realized she'd spent most of the evening thinking about Damian. Well, quite understandable, she rationalized. After all, he was head of the firm she was working for.

The following day, Evan didn't show up at the office until well after eleven. As she had previously, Mrs. Sterling fussed over him as though he were the prodigal son the moment he waltzed in the door.

"Good morning, Mr. Dryden." Mrs. Sterling gushed, nearly leaping from her chair. "It's a beautiful day, isn't it?"

Evan seemed to need time to think about this. "I hadn't noticed, but you're right, it is a gorgeous day," he said as he reached for his mail and leafed through the envelopes.

He was on his way into his office when he noticed Jessica sitting at her desk. She felt his scrutiny and was pleased that she'd dressed carefully, choosing a smart-looking flowered silk dress with a blue jacket. In her heels, she was nearly as tall as he was.

"Good morning, Mr. Dryden," she offered.

"Evan," he insisted. "You can call Damian Mr. Dryden if you insist, but I'm Evan."

"All right. Good morning, Evan,"

"It is a good morning, isn't it?" he asked, giving her a roguish grin. Jessica couldn't help but respond with a smile of her own. She hadn't noticed it so much the day before, but there were definite changes in the Evan she remembered. He was thinner and his smiles didn't quite reach his eyes. Another thing she couldn't help noticing was the way everyone walked on eggshells around him. Mrs. Sterling had made a point of letting her know Evan's work load had recently been cut, and Damian had said Evan hadn't yet recovered from a broken relationship. It must have been pretty serious, she mused.

"It's been a long time since we've had a chance to talk, hasn't it?" Evan asked, walking over and sitting on the edge of Jessica's desk.

"A very long time," she agreed, praying with all her heart he wouldn't resurrect her girlish antics. It'd been embarrassing enough to have Damian do it.

"I think we should make up for lost opportunities, don't you? Tell you what—I'll treat you to lunch." He checked his watch and seemed surprised at the time. "We'll leave in half an hour. That'll give me enough time to clear whatever's on my desk."

"You want to take me to lunch?" Jessica asked. "Today?"

"It's the least I can do," Evan said with a shrug. "I'll have Mary make reservations."

"But—"

"That's an excellent idea," Mrs. Sterling interjected, clearly pleased.

"I...I've only just started work," Jessica said. "I'd enjoy lunch, perhaps in a week or so, after I've settled into the job." The last thing she wanted was to give Damian the impression she was already slacking in her duties.

Evan pressed his thumb to her chin and gazed deeply into her eyes. "No buts, and no arguments. We're going to lunch and you can fill me in on what you've been doing for the last five or six years."

Mrs. Sterling followed Evan into his office, looking inordinately pleased with the turn of events. She returned a few minutes later, casting a delighted look in Jessica's direction as she picked up her phone and called the restaurant to make reservations. Evan chose Henri's, one of Boston's finest, well-known for its elegant dining. It also happened to be a good fifteen-minute drive from the office, which meant they were going to be out for lunch much longer than usual.

"I doubt we'll be back in an hour if we have lunch at Henri's," Jessica felt obliged to say.

"Don't worry about it. You'll make it up another time, I'm sure."

"But this is only my second day. I don't want to give the wrong impression."

"My dear, Mr. Dryden is your boss. If he wants to take a leisurely lunch with you, don't argue. You should be counting your blessings, instead."

"I know but—"

"From what I understand, you two are old family friends," Mrs. Sterling interrupted. "It's only natural for him to want to personally welcome you into the firm."

It seemed the reservation had barely been made when Evan reappeared. "Are you ready?"

Jessica blinked back her surprise. "Yes, of course, if you'll give me just a moment." She finished typing her notes into the computer, stored the information and pushed back her chair.

Evan took her elbow and told his secretary, "We'll be back in a couple of hours."

They were on their way through the corridor leading to the front of the office when Damian appeared. His gaze shifted from Evan to Jessica.

"Jessica and I are on our way out to lunch," Evan explained. "Do you need me for anything?"

"No. You two go on ahead. I'll talk to you later."

Damian nodded, and it was all Jessica could do not to blurt out that this lunch date hadn't been her idea, but there wasn't the opportunity and she doubted it was necessary anyway. Damian must have known she hadn't invited herself out to lunch. Nevertheless, she didn't want him to think ill of her.

"We'll probably be late getting back," Evan said to his brother, guiding Jessica out of the office.

They arrived at the restaurant by taxi and were seated immediately. The ambience was formal, with soft chamber music playing unobtrusively in the background. The waiters, who dressed like diplomats, were attentive, the tables were well spaced, and the meal was served with a good deal of ceremony.

Evan seemed disinclined to talk about himself, asking her a series of questions about school, her friends and activities. He appeared attentive, but she suspected his thoughts were far removed from her and their lunch. At least he didn't dredge up the past and her infatuation with him. She could have kissed him for that.

After their dishes were cleared away, Evan took out a pad and pen. "I'm going to be working on a civil suit that'll demand a fair amount of research," he told Jessica. His eyes were bright with an enthusiasm she hadn't seen before. "The case involves Earl Kress—you might remember reading about him."

"Of course." The unusual details of the case had filled the local news for weeks. The twenty-year-old former athlete was suing the Spring Valley School District for his education.

Jessica wished she'd brought along a pad and pen herself. She listened, enthralled, as Evan explained the details of the suit. It seemed Earl was a gifted athlete and the key figure in three of the school's biggest sports—football, basketball and track. In order for him to participate in these sports he had to maintain a C average. Unfortunately Earl had a learning disability and had never mastered reading skills. Although he'd graduated from high school and been awarded a full scholarship, he was functionally illiterate.

Evan explained that the school district had pressured Earl's teachers, and they'd been forced to give him passing grades. After he graduated from high school, he went on to college, but a severe knee injury suffered during football training camp effectively ended his career. And within the first two months of school, Earl flunked out.

"That's so unfair," Jessica said when Evan finished. If Damian was concerned about his brother, she thought, then offering Evan this groundbreaking case was sure to take his mind off other things. It would give Evan purpose, a reason to come to work in the morning, the necessary incentive to look past his personal problems.

"There've been a number of similar suits filed in other parts of the country," Evan continued. "I'm going to need you to do extensive research on the outcome of the cases previously tried."

"I'll be happy to help in any way I can."

Evan grinned his appreciation. "I knew I could count on you."

So this was the real reason for their lunch. The case clearly meant a good deal to Evan, and consequently to Jessica. She was grateful for the opportunity to prove herself.

By the time they returned to the office, their lunch hour had stretched to three. It seemed everyone in the office was staring at them, and Jessica felt decidedly uncomfortable.

She walked directly to her desk, keeping her face averted when she passed Damian's office. His door was open, and when he saw her walk by he stood up, called her name and then glanced pointedly at his watch. It was all Jessica could do not to tell him it had been a *business* lunch.

Damian had made it painfully clear that he expected her to do her job. He wasn't paying her to romance his brother during three-hour lunches, and Jessica didn't want him to have that impression. She longed to explain, but she'd look ridiculous doing so in front of Evan. The only thing she could do was stay late that evening in an effort to make up for the time spent over lunch.

Although it was after seven when she started out of the office, a number of others were still there. With her sweater draped over her arm, she was on her way down the long corridor when Damian stopped her.

"Jessica."

"Hello, Damian," she said. He was standing just outside his office.

He relaxed, crossed his arms and asked, "How'd your lunch go with my brother?"

"Very well, but..."

"Yes?" he prompted when she didn't immediately finish.

"I want you to know it was a working lunch," she said, rushing the words in her eagerness to explain. "We discussed the Earl Kress case. I didn't want you to think we'd spent three hours socializing."

"It wouldn't have mattered."

"But it does!" she insisted fervently. "The lawsuit was the reason Evan asked me out. He wasn't interested in renewing an old friendship."

Damian's frown was thoughtful. "Did he seem pleased with the assignment?"

"Very much so," Jessica recalled Mrs. Sterling's saying that "things just haven't been the same around here for quite a while," implying *Evan* hadn't been the same. She wondered if Damian realized the extent of his brother's unhappiness.

Damian grinned; Jessica had the feeling he didn't do that often, which was a shame. The grooves in his cheeks and the sparkle in his gray eyes were very attractive. "I thought he might need a change of pace. Did you two have a chance to talk about old times?"

This was a casual way of asking if she'd noticed the changes in his brother, Jessica guessed. "A little. Evan really was hurt, wasn't he?"

Damian nodded. "Generally he disguises it, but I wondered if you'd detect the changes in him."

"I couldn't help noticing." She'd seen it almost from the first moment. Even though she hadn't seen Evan for years she could see how hard he was struggling to hide his misery. No wonder his parents and brother were so concerned.

Damian glanced at his watch and arched his brows. "It's late. We'll talk again some other time. Good night, Jessica."

"Good night, Damian."

As she waited for a train in the subway station, Jessica at last understood what Damian had meant when he'd told her that everyone needed to be looked at with wide worshipful eyes sometimes. It made perfect sense now that she thought about it. Damian still viewed her as that teenage girl infatuated with his younger brother. If ever there was a time that Evan needed a woman to idolize him, it was now. She'd been hired, not for her legal skills, but to help his brother forget the woman he'd loved and lost. Damian was looking to her to heal Evan's pain.

The following morning around ten, Evan, his smile bright enough to rival the sun, breezed into the office and presented Jessica with a bouquet of a dozen bloodred roses. Their perfume filled the room.

Jessica was speechless. "For me?" The flowers took her completely by surprise. Mrs. Sterling, too, from the look the secretary cast her.

"I need a favor," Evan said, leaning against the edge of her desk, his face scant inches from her own.

"Of course." She was holding the flowers against her like a beauty queen, inhaling their heavenly scent.

Evan reached into his jacket pocket and withdrew a folded sheet of yellow paper. "I need you to do some last-minute research for me."

"Certainly."

"There're some statutes I need you to look up and report back to me on as soon as possible. This stuff is as dry as old bones—I'm sorry about that."

"Don't worry about it." Jessica looked at the items Evan wanted her to research and her heart sank at the number. "How soon do you need this?"

"Yesterday," was his frank reply.

Mrs. Sterling made a small tsk-tsk sound in the background, which made Jessica smile. Evan's eyes twinkled and he whispered,

"There's nothing worse than a woman who can't let 'I told you so' pass. Remember that, Jessica."

"I will," she said with a small laugh. "I'd best get started. I'll have the information for you before I leave tonight."

"Good girl."

Mrs. Sterling produced a vase for the roses, and after setting them on the edge of her desk Jessica got down to work. She ensconced herself in the library and kept at her research straight through the lunch hour. She didn't notice the time until it was after three, when her stomach rumbled in protest. Even then she didn't take the time to sit down to eat, but grabbed an apple and munched on it while she continued to search for the required data.

The next time she looked up, the clock on the wall said seven forty-five. She'd heard the others leave, but that seemed like only minutes ago. She stood up and, placing her hand at the base of her spine, arched her stiff back and breathed in deeply.

Her eyes felt tired and her back sore as she carried her paperwork into the office. She stopped, surprised to find the room dark. She flicked on the lights and looked around, certain Evan had left a note for her.

He hadn't.

Picking up one of the roses, she held it to her nose and closed her eyes as she tried to battle down the weariness—and the disappointment.

"Jessica, what are you doing here?"

"Damian." She could ask the same question of him.

"It's nearly eight o'clock."

"I know." She rotated her overworked shoulders. "I guess time got away from me."

"So I see. I had some reading I was catching up on, but I assumed I was here alone. There was no reason for you to stay this late."

She glanced toward Evan's office. "What time did Evan leave?" she asked casually, not wanting him to know how abused she felt.

"A couple of hours ago. Why?"

"He said he needed this information right away." She'd been in a frenzy attempting to finish the task as quickly as possible. She'd assumed he would wait until she'd collected the data he seemed to need so desperately.

"I believe he had a dinner engagement," Damian explained.

"I see," she muttered. In other words, he'd cheerfully abandoned her.

"You sound angry," Damian said.

"I am. I worked through my lunch hour getting this stuff for him." And dinner hour, too, she thought, feeling even angrier. She realized too late that she probably also sounded jealous.

"I'm sorry, Jessica."

Evan's thoughtlessness wasn't Damian's fault and she said so, then asked bluntly, "Is there anything to eat around here?" She blinked back unexpected tears. Hunger always had a strange effect on her emotions, but it was embarrassing, and she tried not to let Damian see.

"You mean you haven't eaten since lunch?"

"Not since breakfast, unless you count an apple, and if I don't eat soon I'm going to cry and you really wouldn't want to witness that." The words rushed out and she felt a sniffle coming on. "Never mind," she muttered, turning away from him. She wiped her nose with her forearm and returned to the library. Several ponderous law volumes were spread open across the tables. She closed them and began lugging them back to the shelves.

"I found a package of soda crackers," Damian said, coming into the room.

"Thanks," she said, ripping away the clear plastic wrapper and sniffling again. "I'm sorry, I don't mean to act like this." She ate a cracker quickly and managed to hold back a sob. "Don't look so concerned. I just needed to eat."

"Let me take you to dinner." Damian lifted a couple of the volumes and replaced them for her.

"That isn't necessary." A second cracker had made its way into her mouth and she was beginning to feel more like herself.

"We owe you that much," Damian countered. "Besides, I'm half-starved myself."

"The least he could have done was waited," Jessica fumed.

Ignoring her comment Damian suggested a popular seafood restaurant nearby.

"He made it sound like it was a matter of life and death, and
then he doesn't even bother to tell me he's leaving," she continued
to fume. "You're right," she said as Damian cupped her elbow
and led her out the door. "Evan *has* changed."

Damian didn't respond to this comment either.

They walked the three blocks to the restaurant. It wasn't too
crowded, and they were given immediate seating at a wooden table
near one of the windows. Even better, the waitress brought hot
bread and chowder no more than a minute after it was ordered.
Damian must be a regular here to get such service, Jessica thought,
her good mood restored now that her stomach had something warm
and filling.

"This is excellent," she said. "Thank you." She sighed in con-
tentment as she spooned up the last of her chowder.

Grinning, he finished his own soup, then reached for another
piece of bread.

"What's so funny?" she demanded. How like a man to keep
something humorous to himself and then feel superior about it.

"I think I might just have averted a lawsuit. Can't you hear it?
'Woman Sues Boss over Lost Meals.'"

"I'd get a huge settlement." The corners of her mouth twitched
with a smile. Her eyes met Damian's and soon their amusement
had blossomed into full-blown grins.

He had very nice eyes, Jessica mused. They were a dark gray
and revealed his keen intelligence, his sharp insight. She wanted to
clear away any lingering misconception he had about her and Evan,
but she couldn't think of a way to do it without sounding as if she
was jealous of whatever person Evan spent his personal time with.

Jessica wondered what Damian saw when he looked at her. Did
he see the woman she'd become, or did he view her as the pesky
kid next door who'd adamantly declared that his younger brother
was her destiny?

The waitress arrived then with their main courses. Damian had
ordered oysters and Jessica baked cod, which was delicious. By the
time they'd finished, she felt completely restored.

"I said some things I shouldn't have back at the office," Jessica began, feeling self-conscious now but eager to explain. "You see—"

"You'd worked far longer than necessary and were starving to boot," he interrupted. "Don't worry about it."

"I just wanted to be sure I hadn't provoked you into firing me."

"It'll take more than a demand for food to do that," he assured her, hardly disguising his amusement.

The June sky was dark and overcast and the temperature cooler as they came down the stairs and into the street. "It looks like rain," Damian said. No sooner had he spoken when fat raindrops began to fall. Taking Jessica by the elbow, he raced across the street. Neither had thought to bring an umbrella.

"Here," Damian said, running toward an alcove in front of a bookstore. The business had closed hours earlier, but the covered entrance was a good place to wait out the cloudburst. Jessica was breathless by the time they stopped. A chill raced over her and she rubbed her arms vigorously.

Damian's much larger hands replaced hers, then he stopped and peeled off his jacket, draping it over her shoulders.

"Damian, I'm fine," she protested, fearing he'd catch a chill himself.

"You're shivering."

The warmth of his coat was more welcome than she cared to admit. No doubt about it, Damian was a gentleman to the very core.

The downpour lasted a good ten minutes. Jessica was surprised at how quickly the time passed. When the storm dwindled to a drizzle and eventually stopped, Jessica discovered she was almost sorry. She was talking books with Damian and discovered they both shared an interest in murder mysteries. Damian was as well-read as she was, and they tossed titles and authors' names back and forth without a pause.

"Did you drive to work this morning?" he asked.

She shook her head. She'd taken the subway.

"I'll give you a lift home, then."

"Really, Damian, that isn't necessary. I don't mind using public transit."

"*I* mind," he said in a voice that brooked no argument. "It's too late for you to be out on the streets alone."

How sweet of him to worry about her, she thought. "But I already have enough to thank you for."

"What do you mean?"

"I was just thinking—I seem to be continually in your debt. You've got a heart of gold."

He chuckled. "Hardly, little Jessica."

"You hired me without any real job experience, then you fed me dinner, and now you're driving me home."

"It's the least I can do."

They returned to the office building, walking directly to the underground parking garage. Damian opened the car door for her and she nestled back in the leather seat.

One thing she'd learned during their time together was the fact that Damian was protective of his younger brother, though she doubted Evan appreciated that.

"You're worried about him, aren't you?" she asked, without clarifying her question. Damian knew who she was talking about.

"Yeah," he admitted.

"Evan's the real reason you hired me, isn't he? You think I might be able to help him through this…difficult time." It wasn't a responsibility she welcomed or wanted. She was about to explain that when she noticed the way his mouth quirked into an amused smile.

Instead, she told him sharply, "I'm not a silly fourteen-year-old infatuated with an older man. What I felt for your brother was just a crush. It was over years ago." That was the simple truth.

His shrug was noncommittal.

"Nevertheless," she forged on, "you hired me because of Evan?"

It took Damian a long time to answer. "Sometimes I wonder," he finally said. "Sometimes I wonder."

Three

Jessica arrived early the following morning, hoping to have an opportunity to thank Damian again for dinner and more importantly to let him know how much she'd enjoyed the time they'd shared. But when she passed his office, the door was closed and his secretary was searching urgently through a file drawer. It didn't look like the time to pop in unannounced.

Not surprisingly, Evan was nowhere to be seen. Mrs. Sterling arrived ten minutes after Jessica, greeting her with a small approving smile, and set about sorting through the mail.

Jessica spent the first part of the morning organizing the material she'd researched the day before and typing up her notes. That way, Evan wouldn't be forced to waste time deciphering her hasty scrawl.

She'd just completed printing out the results when a breathless Evan entered the office. From the look of him, he'd raced all the way up from the parking garage. Briefcase in hand, he marched up to her desk.

"Do you have those notes ready?" he asked, reaching for the file before Jessica had a chance to present it. She stood up, intending to discuss a number of points with him, but he brushed past her and hurried into his office without a word. She would have followed him, but he closed the door.

Jessica was taken aback; unsure of what to do, she looked at Mrs. Sterling. The secretary sighed and shrugged. "Working for Mr. Dryden can be a real trial," she muttered, then grinned and added, "No pun intended."

No sooner had Mrs. Sterling finished chuckling over her own little joke than Evan reappeared, looking composed and confident. He'd removed his raincoat and was leafing casually through the file. He looked over at Jessica and his face relaxed into a broad smile.

"You're an angel," he said, kissing her cheek as he walked past. Jessica had seen him kiss Mrs. Sterling in the same affectionate way.

"I'll be in a meeting with Damian this morning," Evan announced on his way out the door.

As the morning progressed, Jessica found herself wondering exactly what her role in the office was. Although Evan had recently been assigned the Earl Kress case, his work load had been light in the past few months. Now that she'd finished the research project, there was barely enough to keep her busy.

From various bits and pieces, Jessica had learned that Evan's interest in corporate law had waned recently. Surely Damian hadn't hired her expecting miracles! Since he was so closemouthed about Evan's troubles, Jessica wondered if Mrs. Sterling could fill in some details. She didn't want to be obvious about asking, which could prove tricky since the woman was so clearly devoted to her employer.

"That Evan's a real charmer, isn't he?" Jessica began conversationally.

"He always could charm the birds right out the trees," Mrs. Sterling answered proudly.

"He's different now from the way I remember him. More...intense."

Evan's secretary nodded and muttered, "I'd like to shoot that woman."

Jessica's heart leapt with excitement. "What woman?" she asked, hoping to hide her eagerness. She was about to learn what had happened to change Evan so drastically from the man she'd known.

Mrs. Sterling glanced up, as if surprised that Jessica had heard her mumbling. "Oh...it's nothing."

"But it *must* be something. Evan isn't anything like he was a few years back. Oh, he's charming and sweet, but there's an edge to him now. A sharpness, I guess. Something I can't put my finger on." She looked expectantly at the other woman.

"That's true enough," Mrs. Sterling reluctantly conceded.

"You say a woman's responsible for the changes in Evan?"

"Isn't it always a woman?"

"What happened?" Might as well try a more direct approach, Jessica thought. Tact wasn't getting her anywhere.

"It's a pity, a real pity."

"Yes, Evan just isn't the same," Jessica said, hoping to encourage the other woman to continue.

"It shouldn't come as any surprise, really. Yet it does, Mr. Dryden being the charmer he is. Plain and simple, he fell in love with someone who didn't feel the same way about him." Then she clamped her mouth closed as though she'd already said far more than she should—far more than was circumspect for a secretary to say about her boss.

But this much she already knew. What she was looking for were the particulars. Who was this woman who'd hurt Evan so badly? Her back stiffened at the thought of someone rejecting him. The man she'd worshiped from afar during her tumultuous teenage years. Whoever this woman was, Jessica decided, she was a fool.

About eleven Evan walked into the office. He smiled as he strolled past Mrs. Sterling's desk to hers. "The research you did was wonderful, Jessica. Thank you."

His appreciation caught her off guard. She wondered if Damian had said something to him and was momentarily speechless.

"I appreciate the effort that went into your report," he continued. "I'm very pleased by the quality of your work."

"I...I was happy to do it. That's my...my job." The words stumbled off the end of her tongue. Jessica was amazed that his praise could fluster her so. She was embarrassed now by the way she'd overreacted last night when she'd learned he'd left the office. It was her own fault for not taking time to eat lunch. Evan's disappearance wouldn't have bothered her in the least if she had....

"Damian said you were here till almost eight."

So Damian *had* mentioned that. "As I said earlier, I was only doing my job."

"Mom and Dad are having a barbecue this weekend," Evan

continued, "Saturday, around four. I'd like you to attend it with me."

His invitation threw her. She wasn't sure what to say. Although she hadn't had a lot of work experience, she knew that dating the boss could lead to problems.

"This shouldn't be a difficult decision," Evan said, grinning.

His pride had already suffered one blow, and Jessica discovered she was unwilling to deliver a second, no matter how slight. "I'd enjoy that very much," she said. "Thank you for thinking of me."

He smiled affectionately. "You always were a sweet thing."

As a teenager, Jessica's daydreams had been filled with such scenarios. She'd close her eyes and pretend Evan had asked her out. Now her dream had come true, but Jessica was left wishing it had been Damian issuing the invitation, instead of his brother.

"I'll pick you up. You are living in the city, aren't you?"

Jessica nodded. "Wouldn't it be simpler if we met at the party? As it happens, I'm spending the weekend with my parents, and I can walk over with them."

Evan seemed a bit surprised by her suggestion. "You're sure?"

"Positive."

"Then that'll be fine. I'll look forward to seeing you there."

There'd been a time in her life when she would have gladly walked across a bed of hot coals to attend a party with Evan. Any party. Anywhere. Hadn't Damian been counting on that when he hired her—even if he claimed to know she was long over her crush?

"The festivity's in honor of some dignitary," Evan went on. "Mom's worked herself into a tizzy for the event. I can guarantee this will be the most elaborate barbecue Boston has ever seen. The last I heard, Mom hired a country-and-western band."

"It sounds like fun."

"Considering all the effort that's going into it, I'm sure it will be. You can do the two-step, can't you, sweet Jessica?"

"Of course." How easy it was to stretch the truth. In fact, she'd only done the two-step once or twice before. "Well, I'm pretty rusty," she amended.

"Me, too. We'll leave the fancy footwork to Damian."

Damian, she thought with a sigh. There was definitely something wrong with her, something psychological, something rooted deep in her childhood, she guessed, if she could agree to date one brother while longing for the other.

The hours flew by and before Jessica knew it, the workday had come to an end. Mrs. Sterling had just stepped out of the office when Damian strolled casually in.

"Evan's left for the day," Jessica said, a little flustered to find him standing in front of her desk. Especially since she'd again been thinking how much she'd have preferred to attend the family barbecue with *him.*

"I'm not here to see my brother."

"Mrs. Sterling will be right back."

"I came to see you," Damian explained, his eyes dark and intense as they settled on her.

Jessica tensed. Did he have some complaint with her work?

"Don't look so worried. I came to tell you my parents are holding a party this weekend. A barbecue."

"Yes, I know. Evan mentioned it earlier."

Jessica swore Damian's eyes brightened with interest. He crossed his arms and leaned against her desk. "What did he say about it?"

"Not much. Apparently it's in honor of some dignitary."

"I see." He hesitated as if he was unsure, which Jessica knew was completely out of character for Damian. "I was wondering…" he began, then straightened and buried his hands deep in his pants pockets. "Would you like to come to the party with me?"

Her shoulders sagged as she opened her mouth to explain that Evan had already invited her, but before she could respond, Damian added, "I realize it's short notice, but I didn't hear the details myself until this morning." A hint of a smile turned up the corners of his mouth. "Mother phoned, wanting to be sure I'd be there. She seems to be taking her duties very seriously."

"Ah…"

"There's a problem," he guessed.

She nodded glumly. "Evan's already invited me to the party— as his date." She wanted to tell Damian she'd much prefer to attend with him, but she couldn't. "I'm sorry," she added.

"He did?" Instead of looking displeased at this turn of events, Damian sounded positively delighted. "Don't be sorry."

His reaction annoyed her.

"It isn't like a real date," she said, wanting to make that clear. "At least, that wasn't the impression Evan gave me. The invitation was his way of thanking me for working so hard on the research project."

"My brother wouldn't invite you if he wasn't interested in your company," Damian insisted. "Besides, I wouldn't want my brother to think I was cutting in on his territory."

His territory.

Damian must have guessed her feelings, because he said, "Evan asked you first."

He was right about that, she thought, but little else.

Damian turned away, and it suddenly became important to Jessica to explain herself. "I don't think you should put much stock in Evan's invitation. It really *was* just a way of thanking me."

"It's a start, though, don't you think?" Damian said over his shoulder. "A good start, at that." He left her then before she could say anything more.

Jessica was upset, and it wasn't until she got home that she figured out why. Damian hadn't invited her to the party out of any real desire for her company. He'd assumed that Evan hadn't asked her—and he was looking for an opportunity to throw her and his brother together socially.

Jessica arrived at her parents' house early Saturday afternoon, after spending all morning shopping for the perfect outfit. Cathy had come along to offer encouragement and advice.

She might not be attending the barbecue with Damian, but when she showed up looking like a movie star, he'd wish she was. This was her mission, plain and simple.

Evan had casually mentioned the country-and-western band, but he'd also said the barbecue was in honor of some dignitary. These somewhat contradictory snippets of information served to confuse her about how to dress. Nothing in her closet seemed suitable, but then little in the shops did, either.

In one outfit she resembled Annie Oakley, and in another Jackie Kennedy. There didn't seem to be much of a middle ground—until she found a long denim skirt, a red shirt decorated with rainbow-colored fringe sewn about the yoke and white cowboy boots. A white silk scarf tied around her neck lent a touch of elegance.

Her mother's eyes widened with approval when Jessica modeled the outfit. "I wish now I'd gone shopping, too, and bought something new myself. You look great."

"Thanks." Her mother's praise gave Jessica confidence. Cathy, who tended to dress like a character in a sci-fi movie, had also said she looked great, but Jessica wasn't sure she trusted her friend's fashion sense.

"It was so sweet of Evan to include you," Joyce Kellerman went on to say. "Not that I'm surprised, his being your boss and all. Life is certainly full of little twists and turns, isn't it?"

"It sure is," Jessica said without elaborating.

"I'm thrilled that you're working with Evan."

"He's a nice person."

"He's *wonderful*. It's always been my dream, I know it's silly, but well, we're such good friends with the Drydens... I've hoped you'd grow up to marry one of Lois's boys."

"Whatever you do," Jessica said quickly, "don't say that in front of Damian or Evan."

"Why not, dear?"

"Mom, it'd embarrass me to death!"

"But you were so keen on Evan a few years back, and I thought... I hoped..."

"Mother, I was only fourteen!" Her old infatuation with Evan was turning into the proverbial albatross around her neck—thanks to Damian and her mother. If it wasn't for them, the whole thing would have been forgotten by now.

"You'll make a beautiful bride," her mother said, adding the finishing touches to her own outfit. Suddenly she changed the subject. "Lois has worried herself sick over this silly barbecue."

"But why?" Mrs. Dryden had thrown a hundred parties more elaborate than this.

Her mother sat on the bed and leaned back on her hands. "I

don't suppose there's any reason to keep it a secret. Walter's been approached about running for the Senate.''

Walter Dryden had been active in community affairs for years. Although he'd never held public office, he'd often managed the successful campaigns of others. He'd taken an early retirement from the law firm, and, from what Jessica understood, had grown restless with inactivity. Running for office would doubtless come as a welcome challenge.

"Has he decided he's going to run?"

"Your father and I think so. He hasn't declared his candidacy yet, but we're confident he will. He's testing the waters with this barbecue tonight. Several people from the political arena will be present. This is probably the most important party of Lois's marriage. Little wonder she's a nervous wreck.''

Even before Jessica and her parents arrived for the barbecue, the pungent smells of tomato sauce, spices and roasting meat mingled with the afternoon sunshine and drifted over the fence.

As they were greeted at the front door, Jessica was reminded, by the way Lois hugged her mother, what very good friends the two women were. Their friendship had spanned twenty years, and they were like sisters. Jessica felt the same way about Cathy. They'd met in college, where they'd been roommates for three years.

When Jessica didn't immediately see Evan or Damian, she wandered outside. A series of round tables decorated in red checked tablecloths were scattered across the lush expanse of lawn. The day was perfect, warm but not hot, and the sky was cloudless. A soft breeze ruffled the leaves of the large shade trees that lined the property. This was New England summer at its best. The smells of food were heavenly, too, reminding her how hungry she was. Shopping and preparing for the party hadn't left time for lunch.

Several dozen guests had arrived, and Jessica scanned the crowd. She spotted Evan standing next to a lovely blonde in a chic white fringed dress with a turquoise belt and silver buckle. Jessica didn't recognize the woman, and a few discreet inquiries got her nowhere. She became all the more curious. She attempted to make her way to Evan, since she was officially his date, but in actuality, she was seeking an introduction to the lovely blonde. Perhaps this was

Evan's new romantic interest, she thought hopefully. But before she could reach Evan, she was waylaid by some family friends. Most of the Drydens' guests were older people, established names Jessica had known or heard all her life.

"Hello, Jessica," Damian said from behind her. She turned to find him in the sort of suit he wore at the office. He'd made an attempt to dress to the theme with a black Stetson, which, Jessica thought, looked entirely out of place on his very Bostonian head.

His eyes glimmered with appreciation. "You look—" he hesitated as though he didn't know what to say "—good."

Jessica wagered that it wasn't often Damian was at a loss for words. It lifted her spirits considerably.

"I imagine you're wondering who that blonde is, the one draping herself all over Evan," he suggested casually.

Jessica pretended she was, although she couldn't help being grateful to this unknown woman for keeping Evan occupied. Otherwise he might feel obliged to pay attention to her, and she'd much rather spend her time with Damian.

"Who is she?" Jessica asked, playing his game.

"Do I detect a small hint of jealousy?"

"Of course not." The question irritated her.

"That's Romilda Sidonie."

"Who?"

"The European dignitary's daughter."

That explained it. Naturally Evan considered it his duty to make Romilda feel welcome. Jessica was pleased to see him apparently enjoying himself.

"Would you like me to introduce you?" Damian asked.

"No," Jessica said, noticing Evan and Romilda moving toward the dance area. "Evan's having a good time. I don't see any reason to interrupt him."

"You're his date."

"But only because you prompted him into asking me."

Damian's eyes narrowed. "What makes you say that?"

"I'm not completely naive, you know. I think the reason you came into my office to invite me was that you didn't think Evan had—you wanted to make sure the two of us were together in a social situation so you could see what happened. Am I right?''

He joined his hands behind his back and took two small steps away, then turned to face her again. She saw a hint of a smile in his eyes. "If you're right—though I'm not saying you are—I'd never admit it.''

"You must wreak havoc on a jury.''

"That's what my clients pay me for.''

Jessica looked toward the dance area again and couldn't see Evan and the European woman. When she glanced over at the picnic area, she found the pair sitting at a table beneath a large elm tree munching on barbecue sandwiches.

"She's lovely," Jessica murmured, watching the couple. "No wonder Evan's forgotten me.''

"Romilda may be lovely, but so are you," Damian returned quickly, then looked as if he regretted speaking.

"Thank you.''

"I shouldn't have said that.''

"Why not? That makes me think you didn't mean it.''

"I shouldn't be the one saying such things to you," Damian replied. "You're Evan's date.''

"He seems to have forgotten, which is just as well. I'd rather spend my time with you.''

"With me?" Damian repeated, sounding appalled by the mere suggestion. "Have you eaten?" he asked hurriedly. They were standing next to the dessert table. It was laden with an enormous chocolate cake decorated with fresh strawberries, a lemon torte that would have tempted a saint and a fresh blueberry cobbler, which Jessica knew from years past was the caterer's specialty.

"I'm not hungry just yet," she said, thinking Damian might have used her desire to eat as an excuse to squire her away to one of the tables and conveniently leave her.

Damian eyed her speculatively. "You're sure about that? I'd hate to see a repeat of what happened the other night.''

"Well, yes, I guess I will have a bite…but may I sit with you?''

"If you insist.''

She did. Damian handed her a plate. Together they walked along the buffet table. Jessica helped herself to potato salad, baked beans and a generous rack of spareribs.

The band started to play a popular tune, and her foot tapping to the beat, Jessica enjoyed the culinary feast. She was content to sit on the sidelines. Evan seemed to have forgotten her, but far from being offended, she felt only a sense of relief.

Damian's invitation to dance came as a surprise. "Why do you want to dance with me?" she asked. She had a sneaking suspicion it somehow involved his brother.

"Do I need a reason?"

Jessica hesitated, then nodded. "If you're thinking it's a way to get Evan to notice me, then I'd rather sit out."

"What if I said it was because I wanted to see how you felt in my arms?"

Her heart gave a flutter. "Then I'd agree." She met his gaze directly. "So, what's it to be, Damian?"

He took a long time deciding, much longer than should have been necessary. Slowly he pushed back his chair and stood. "Why don't we find out together," he suggested, leading her by the hand toward the farthest reaches of the dance area.

The party was in full swing by now, with a good number of couples two-stepping around the area. When several old family friends stopped to chat with Jessica and Damian as they made their way toward the other dancers, Jessica could sense Damian's impatience.

They reached the outskirts of the crowd, and Damian turned Jessica in his arms. They fit together nicely, thigh to thigh, hip to hip. Damian was an excellent dancer, his steps easy to follow, his movements smooth and assured. He held her loosely about the waist and gazed down at her as if they'd been dancing together all their lives.

"You're good at this." Her surprise must have been obvious, because he threw back his head and laughed. It was the first time she could ever remember hearing Damian really laugh.

"That amazes you, doesn't it?" he said.

"Yes." It was pointless to deny it. She was discovering that Damian was full of surprises. Just then Jessica felt someone brush against her. She turned to see Evan, partnered with the dignitary's daughter.

"Well, well, if it isn't Damian and Jessica." Evan said with a smile, not sounding jealous in the least.

It hadn't taken long to attract Evan's attention, and Jessica groaned inwardly, wondering if Damian had planned it this way.

"You haven't met Romilda, have you?" Evan murmured. Without waiting for a response, he made the introductions.

Jessica could see that the blonde had fallen under Evan's spell, just like most women did when he'd decided to charm them. His magnetism was lethal. Jessica nearly felt sorry for the unsuspecting woman. Evan did have a bit of a reputation as a playboy.

The two couples moved off to get something to drink. They were making small talk and sipping punch when Damian suddenly asked Romilda to dance. The woman glanced anxiously at Evan, obviously reluctant to leave him. Jessica smiled softly to herself, recognizing Damian's ploy. He'd all but thrown her and Evan together.

Damian and Romilda joined the throng of dancers. "It's a wonderful party," Jessica said to Evan. "I've been having a good time."

"Glad to hear it," Evan commented distractedly, his eyes following the other couple. "Shall we?" he asked, holding out his hand to her.

It became apparent as they moved into the dancing area that Evan was more interested in keeping an eye on Romilda than dancing with Jessica. She and Evan made polite conversation, but his attention wandered as often as her own. The dance couldn't end soon enough for either of them.

When it did, she was grateful Damian and Romilda were on the far side of the dance area, because she needed time and space to put order to her thoughts. When the number ended, Evan was corralled by an older couple who wanted to talk to him privately. He cast Jessica an apologetic look and moved away.

She strolled to the far reaches of the property, near the fence that bordered her parents' home. A white footbridge spanned a good-size pond. She stood in the middle of the bridge, dropping small rocks into the still water and watching the ripples radiate to the shore one after another.

Thus absorbed, she didn't hear Damian approach and was startled to hear him speak. "I wondered if I'd find you here," he said.

"I used to come here a lot when I was growing up," Jessica admitted. "I guess you could have charged me with trespassing."

"Not too likely."

"I know, that's why I used to come. It was so peaceful. So safe." A duck glided past, disturbing the water in the pond, and Jessica wished she'd thought to bring some bread crumbs. The ducks had often been beneficiaries of her trips here.

Damian was silent for a moment, then he said, "You're discouraged, aren't you?"

"About what?"

"It's over, you know," Damian assured her softly. "It was over a long time ago—more than six months now. I thought Evan would get over her, but I was wrong."

Oh, dear, Jessica thought. Apparently Damian believed she was here at the pond brooding about Evan, when in fact nothing could have been farther from the truth. She'd been standing on the bridge thinking about her relationship with Damian.

"Who was she?" Jessica was still curious.

"Someone he met on a beach. No name the family had ever heard of before, not that it mattered. Mary Jo Summerhill."

"What happened."

"I don't think anyone really knows for sure. Whatever it was devastated Evan. He hasn't been the same since. My brother isn't one to burden others with his problems. He's like that duck down there on the pond—everything seems to roll off him like water. He'd been in and out of a dozen relationships, and I assumed he was never going to really fall for any woman, but I was wrong."

"You haven't a clue what happened between him and Mary Jo?"

"No. He changed abruptly after the breakup, started working odd hours. But his heart clearly wasn't in it, so I cut back his work load. That helped for a time, but now I'm not sure it was the right thing to do. I've never seen him more miserable."

"Have you tried to talk to him?"

"A dozen times," Damian admitted, "but it hasn't helped. If anything, he's resented my prying. This broken relationship seems to have cut him more deeply than he's willing to admit."

"He'll get over her," Jessica said reassuringly. "It just takes time."

"I thought so, too." Damian shrugged. "But now I wonder. It's been more than six months." He paused, gazing down at the water. "He needs you, Jessica. You might be the only one able to reach him."

"Me?"

"I knew the minute Dad mentioned you were coming in to apply for a job that you could well be the answer to our prayers." She started to say something, but Damian wouldn't let her. "You're just going to need a lot of patience."

Jessica sighed in frustration. "If I'm going to need patience, it's with *you*. You and your family seem to think I'm still a kid with a crush on Evan."

Damian's eyes darkened. "All right, all right, I didn't mean to offend you. You're old enough to make up your own mind."

"Thank you for that," she said. Turning away from him, she rested her hands on the railing and stared into the serene waters below. "I remember once when I was about six coming to this bridge and crying my eyes out," she murmured.

"What hurt you so badly then?"

"You," she said, turning and jabbing a finger at his chest.

"Me?" Jessica had never seen such an expression of outraged innocence. "What did I do?" Damian demanded.

"Your father was taking you and Evan to the roller coaster at Cannon Beach. My dad was out of town on business, and our mothers were taking the shopping cure. They weren't keen on having to drag me along, and I can't remember who, but one of them suggested I go to the carnival with you and Evan."

"And I didn't want you with us," Damian finished for her.

"Not that I blame you. No fifteen-year-old wants a six-year-old girl tagging along."

Damian chuckled. "Times change, don't they?"

Her mother had said the same thing earlier. *Indeed, times do change.*

To Jessica's astonishment, Damian reached for her hand. He linked their fingers and tugged her off the bridge. "Where are we going?" she protested. He looked at her in surprise, as though she hadn't already guessed. "Where else? The beach. From what I understand the same roller coaster is still running. The party here is starting to wind down, and I don't think we'll be missed, do you?"

She couldn't help but agree.

Four

Carrying a sticky ball of pink cotton candy in one hand and a purple stuffed elephant under the other, Jessica strolled leisurely with Damian down the long pier. The tinny music of the merry-go-round played behind them, mingling with children's laughter. The scent of the bay and fresh popcorn swirled around them like smoke from a cooling fire. The night was perfect. The sun had set, and clusters of bright stars blinked approvingly down on them.

"I don't think I've ever enjoyed myself more," Jessica said to Damian. She tipped the cotton-candy cone toward him and he helped himself to a handful. Taking another bite herself, she savored the way the sugary sweetness melted on her tongue.

"We still haven't gone on the roller coaster," Damian reminded her.

"That's because you spent all that time trying to win that silly stuffed elephant." She hugged it against her, belying her words.

"Are you game?" Damian asked, looking toward the huge steel structure.

Jessica hedged. "I...I don't know if that's such a good idea after all the junk we've eaten."

"Trust me." He looped his arm through hers and pulled her along, not giving her a chance to protest.

"Great, first you fill me up with popcorn and cotton candy, then you insist on dragging me onto one of the biggest roller coasters in the country. That's not smart, Damian, not smart at all."

The crowds were thicker than ever, and Damian reached for her hand as he led her toward the ride. The line was long, and the wait was sure to be at least thirty minutes. A list of possible arguments crowded Jessica's mind, but she knew it wouldn't do any good. The determined set of Damian's jaw told her that much.

"What am I supposed to do with the elephant?" she asked, clinging to it tightly, as they edged closer.

"Hold it."

"If I'm holding the elephant, who's going to hold me?"

"I will," he assured her calmly. "Stop looking so worried."

"I should tell you, Damian Dryden, the last time I rode on this thing I had a near-death experience. I don't suppose you know when this ride had a safety inspection."

"Thursday."

"You don't *know* that!"

He laughed, seeming to enjoy her unease. "True, but it sounded good. Listen, this roller coaster has been running for twenty years without a single mishap. Well, there was that one time..."

"Damian!"

"I was joking."

"Don't tease," Jessica muttered furiously. She flattened her palm against her stomach and sighed loudly. "My stomach doesn't feel right."

"You won't be sick."

"How can you be sure?"

"Experience. Anticipation's the worst part. The ride itself is fun. The only problem is that it doesn't last long enough. The whole thing is over in no time."

For all her complaining, as the minutes passed, Jessica found herself beginning to anticipate their turn. At last the silver cars came to an abrupt halt right in front of them.

"Just promise me you won't fling your arms up in the air in that bizarre descent ritual," Jessica murmured as the bar fell into place, securing them in the seat.

"I wouldn't dream of it," Damian said, "not when I promised to hold on to you."

Jessica colored slightly, but didn't respond. She dared not look down. Heights were something she generally avoided, which meant she was trapped into closing her eyes. The stuffed elephant was cradled in her arms, much the same way Damian was cradling her.

The cars slowly made their ascent, chugging up the steep incline, making a straining noise as if the weight was too much to bear.

The line of cars topped the peak and started its rapid descent. A scream of excitement froze in her throat as they plummeted downward. Damian's arm tightened around her shoulders. Her free hand gripped his, her nails digging into his fingers, but if she was hurting him, he gave no indication. Just when it seemed they were about to break the sound barrier, they started up another steep grade, which slowed the momentum, but once they reached the top they were cast on a crazy twisting, turning journey that left her stomach far behind. Her eyes were closed so tightly her face ached.

When at last they rolled to a halt, Jessica's shoulders surged forward, righted and then sagged with a twinge of disappointment as she realized the ride was over.

"Well?" Damian asked, taking her hand to help her climb out of the cramped car. "Did you or did you not have fun?"

Her legs felt a little shaky once she started walking. "Give me a minute—I don't know what I'm feeling." Confessing he'd been right was too much to ask.

Damian laughed. "Admit it. Don't be shy. It was fun, wasn't it?"

"Yes," Jessica said with ill grace.

Damian laughed again and tucked his arm around her waist. His action seemed so natural, especially since it was evident that her knees had yet to right themselves. Although his touch was automatic, it had a curious effect on Jessica. She enjoyed being linked with Damian, enjoyed having his body close to hers. She'd experienced it while they were dancing, too.

"You ready to head back?" Damian asked as they neared the brightly lit arched entryway to Cannon Beach.

She agreed with a nod, but in fact she didn't want the night to end. Their time together had been perfect. Perhaps now Damian would understand that it was *his* company she sought and not his brother's. Perhaps now he'd view her as a woman and not the pesky girl next door.

And maybe Evan's obvious attraction to Romilda would blossom into something more, and the Drydens would stop looking to Jessica for solutions. She sincerely hoped that was the case. A man always enjoyed a challenge, and the dignitary's daughter might be just the thing Evan needed.

Damian and Jessica walked along the sawdust-covered ground of the parking lot until they reached his car. The lights from the carnival lit up the night sky, and the sounds droned on behind her.

"I had a marvelous time," she told Damian as he started the engine.

"Me, too," he said. "It's been years since I've been to Cannon Beach. Years since—" He stopped abruptly.

Jessica was reminded of what she'd heard about Damian's working too hard and not taking time to enjoy life. It felt good to know that Damian had enjoyed her company. The memory of his laughter produced a sudden smile. He didn't laugh often enough, and when he did she felt as if she'd been rewarded with a priceless gift.

Damian drove Jessica to her apartment building. It was after eleven by then, but she was keyed up with excitement. Somehow she felt it would all end when Damian left, and she wasn't ready to let that happen.

"Do you want to come up?" she asked, not really expecting he would, hoping she could change his mind.

He glanced her way as though judging the sincerity of her offer. "All right."

"I'll put on a pot of coffee, and you can gloat over how much I enjoyed the roller coaster."

"I'll gloat, coffee or not." He found a parking spot on the street, got out of the car and then went around to open her door. A true gentleman, she thought not for the first time.

Laughing and joking they strolled toward her building. The doorman held the door for them and smiled at Jessica and the purple elephant.

The laughing and teasing continued as they stepped into the elevator for the ride up to the tenth floor. The doors glided shut and Jessica sagged against the mirrored wall in mock exhaustion.

"You sure you don't want to close your eyes?" he said.

"Why?"

"This elevator is moving at death-defying speeds. Who knows the last time it was checked for safety."

"Thursday," came her glib reply.

Damian laughed delightedly.

"I don't know," she teased. "You might be right." Jokingly she squinted her eyes closed, but when she did, Damian kissed her.

It took Jessica a moment to realize what had happened. Damian had actually kissed her. It was a simple, uncomplicated kiss, the kind a brother gives a sister. One pair of lips touching another.

Only it didn't *feel* simple.

If anything, it left her longing for much, much more. Dumbstruck, she blinked up at him, not knowing how to respond.

"Don't look so shocked," Damian muttered.

"I..." She closed her mouth to stop herself from asking him to kiss her again.

"It was just a kiss."

"I know," she muttered. She realized he regretted the impulse and wished she knew of some way to tell him how thoroughly she'd enjoyed it. But before she could find the words, the elevator stopped.

Jessica led the way to her apartment and unlocked the door. Turning on the light, she moved into the cheery yellow kitchen and, as was her habit, flipped the switch to her answering machine. Cathy Hudson's voice greeted her.

"Jess. Hi, it's me. I haven't heard from you in days, and of course I want to know how the barbecue went with Lover Boy today. Give me a call when you can."

"So your friend knows about Evan?" Damian asked casually, making himself comfortable at her round oak table. He leafed through a newsmagazine she'd been reading that morning.

"I might have mentioned him, but certainly not as Lover Boy, if that's what you're asking."

"That's not what she said."

"She's teasing," Jessica insisted. She hadn't talked to her friend about her new feelings for Damian and was sorry now, because Cathy, like everyone else, it seemed, was intensely curious about the relationship between Jessica and Evan. "I made the mistake of telling her I once had a crush on Evan and she assumed... Well, you just heard." Jessica took out the coffee canister and poured some grounds into the paper filter. The rich coffee aroma filled the room. "This will only take a minute," she promised.

"Listen, don't bother. It's later than I realized."

"You're sure?" Jessica said, disappointed.

"Positive." He set aside the magazine and stood. Pausing in front of her, he drew his hand against the side of her face. "Thank you for a wonderful day, Jessica."

"Thank *you*," she whispered back.

The apartment seemed unnaturally empty when Damian was gone. She'd hoped he'd kiss her again before he left. He'd been tempted, she could see it in his eyes, but he'd resisted, apparently wanting to keep an emotional distance from her.

Jessica wasn't at all tired and, needing to talk, dialed her friend's number.

A groggy Cathy answered on the fourth ring.

"I didn't wake you, did I?" Jessica said with a giggle, delighted to pay back her friend for all the times Cathy had phoned her in the middle of the night.

"From the dead. What are you doing calling so late and sounding so damned cheerful? There should be a law against that. Let me guess. You were with Evan."

"No! Damian and I went to the—"

"Damian? You're dating Evan's brother?" Cathy sounded wide-awake now and interested. Very interested.

"I know in that silly romantic heart of yours you figured once I was working with Evan, all the unrequited love I'd stored up years ago would suddenly blossom."

"Those were my thoughts exactly," Cathy said.

"Cathy, listen to me. Evan Dryden is a terrific guy, but he isn't the man for me."

"How can you be so sure?"

"Because…well, because I just am." Even now it was difficult to talk about her feelings for Damian. She wasn't sure how to describe them. "For one thing, Evan's in no emotional shape to get involved in another romance, which is fine by me."

"What happened?" Cathy demanded. "I thought he asked you to his family's barbecue."

"He did, but only because Damian prompted him. By the time I arrived he'd met a lovely European woman and the two were inseparable."

"How rude!"

If she'd had her heart set on Evan it would have been devastating, but she didn't, and as a consequence she'd spent a glorious night in Damian's company. She wouldn't have traded the evening for anything. "No, not at all," she said.

"You aren't disappointed?"

Apparently Cathy wasn't as awake as Jessica had believed. "Not in the least. Damian and I drove out to Cannon Beach and rode the roller coaster."

"You? The original wimp on that monster ride? You didn't really, did you?"

"Yes, I did," she announced proudly, "and it was fabulous." She spent the next few minutes relaying the highlights of the evening—Damian's winning the stuffed elephant for her and their walking along the pier and sharing cotton candy. When she finished there was a short silence.

"Hmm," said Cathy thoughtfully. "This could be *very* interesting."

Jessica arrived bright and early at the office Monday morning. Evan had apparently been to work at some point during the weekend, for he'd left her a list of instructions. His notes included a series of laws he needed her to research. Jessica got to the task right away.

Damian found her in the library some time later. "So you *are* here," he said, sounding surprised. "Mrs. Sterling didn't think you'd come in for the day. I phoned your apartment and got the answering machine."

Jessica straightened in her chair and arched her back, hoping to relieve the tension in her tired muscles. A glance at her watch told her it was nearly eleven. She'd been so involved in her research she hadn't noticed the time.

"I've been in here all morning," she explained, pinching the bridge of her nose. The words were beginning to blur in front of her eyes. Some of the reading was dull, but there were several cases she found intriguing.

Damian left and returned a moment later with a steaming cup of coffee. "Here," he said, handing it to her. "Take a break before you go blind."

"Has Evan shown up yet?" The coffee tasted like ambrosia.

Damian sighed. "Not yet. But Evan comes and goes at will, or at least he has for the past several months."

"Well, he left me some work to do, so he must have been in yesterday." She paused. "What about him and Romilda?" She sincerely hoped those two were enthralled with each other.

"It's too soon to tell, but maybe there's some hope there." Good. Damian sounded as if he really meant it.

"I want Evan to be happy," she said, not exactly sure why it was important Damian know that.

"Exactly." Damian smiled and got up to walk over to the polished bookcase. He pulled down a well-used volume. "Take some advice," he said tucking the book under his arm.

"Sure."

"Don't skip lunch."

"I won't," she promised.

He left then and Jessica smiled and closed her eyes. After a moment she returned to her research. A long time passed before her smile faded.

As promised, Jessica took her lunch hour and returned to find Evan searching for her. He sat down next to her in the library and reviewed her notes, asked a series of intelligent questions and made comments every now and then about her progress. Several times he praised her efforts. He made a few notations himself, and they spent the better part of an hour discussing different aspects of the Earl Kress case.

After Evan left, Jessica was exhilarated. Damian had revealed a keen insight into his brother's personality by assigning Evan to this important case. Representing Earl Kress had given Evan the challenge he needed; had given him a purpose, a cause. Evan was no slouch. He was dynamic, sharp and dedicated to representing this former athlete to the best of his ability and to the full extent of the law.

Several hours of research remained, and although it was late, Jessica decided to trudge on until she was finished.

"It's six o'clock and time for you to go home," Damian said from behind her in the tone she recognized. It was the one he used when he wouldn't listen to a word of argument. The kind that swayed juries.

"I'll be finished in a bit."

"You're finished now."

"Damian."

"Don't argue with me, Jessica. It won't do any good."

She closed the book she was reading and stood up. Every small movement of her lithe body spelled reluctance.

"Did you take time for lunch?"

"You're beginning to sound like my guardian!"

"I see you didn't eat, otherwise you wouldn't be snapping at me."

"I did so—and I'm not snapping!"

"That does it!"

Was he about to fire her for insubordination? Jessica wondered. She stared up at him, wondering what would happen next.

"We're going to dinner," he muttered.

"Dinner! But Damian, you've already—"

"Pizza," he said, "the deep-dish variety. There's a small Italian restaurant around the corner. I swear it's one of the best-kept secrets in Boston."

"Pizza," Jessica repeated slowly and her stomach growled in anticipation. "Well, if you insist, and it seems that you do." She reached for her purse.

They walked to the restaurant, which was nestled in the basement of one of the older buildings. The marble floors were badly worn, and the architecture showed that the structure had been built in the early thirties. Jessica had passed the building a hundred times and barely given it a second's notice.

"How'd you hear about this restaurant?" she asked.

"From the security guard. He eats here regularly and recommended it to me. I've never tasted better Italian food."

The proprietor greeted Damian as if he were a long-lost cousin, kissing him on both cheeks and speaking in Italian as he looked approvingly at Jessica.

"What did he say?" she asked when they were seated at a table covered with a red-and-white-checked cloth. A candle flickered from inside a small red vase, and shadows danced across the opposite wall.

"I'm not entirely sure. I only know a few words myself."

"In that case you did a good job of faking it."

"All right, if you must know, Antonio assumed we're lovers," Damian said casually, opening the menu.

"You corrected him, didn't you?" she demanded, putting a hand to her chest. She could feel the color rush into her face.

"No."

"Damian, you can't let that man believe you and I..."

"You're probably right, I shouldn't. Especially when it's my brother you're in love with, not me."

Jessica set the menu aside and leaned forward until her stomach pressed against the edge of the table. They needed to get this straight between them once and for all. "I'm not in love with Evan," she whispered heatedly.

"All right, all right."

"You don't sound convinced."

"I'm convinced," he said, without looking at her. Whatever was offered on the menu had apparently captured his full attention.

"Good," she said, reaching for her own menu. She was about to suggest the sausage pizza when a basket of warm bread was brought to their table. The lovely dark-haired woman who'd delivered it caught Damian's face between her hands and kissed him soundly on both cheeks. Jessica must have looked shocked, because the older woman laughed delightedly. "You don't need to worry— I won't steal Damian away from you," she said, then added something in Italian.

Damian seemed to go pale at the woman's words. Jessica's own knowledge of Italian was scant, but she knew what *bambino* meant.

"Damian, tell me what she said."

He was silent while the same woman poured them each a glass of wine and brought a plate of antipasto. Then he sighed. "Nona says you seem good and sturdy."

"*What?* Anyway, she said more than that."

"Jessica, I already explained I only know a few words of Italian."

"You know more than me. She said *bambino.* Doesn't that mean 'baby'?"

Damian sighed again. "Yes. If you must know, Nona said you'll make a good mother to my children."

"Oh." Jessica glanced at the woman, who was standing on the other side of the room, busy ladling minestrone soup into two ceramic bowls, which she then brought.

"I guess we aren't going to get that pizza," Damian muttered after the soup was served.

Antonio returned with the bottle of Italian wine and replenished their glasses with many exclamations of pleasure. Damian thanked him in Italian, then they spoke for a minute or two.

"When did you learn to speak Italian?" Jessica asked.

"I didn't. I picked up a smidgen here and there over the years. I spent a couple of months in Italy before I entered law school and muddled my way through the country. That's about it."

"You're a man of many talents," she said, picking up her spoon and sampling the soup. It was rich and flavorful. In fact, everything was excellent—the meal, the smooth red wine, the cappucino and dessert. Each time she was convinced she couldn't swallow another bite, Nona would bring them something else she insisted they try.

"Either we leave now, or you'll have to roll me out of here," Jessica said.

Damian chuckled, settled the bill, and together they walked back to the office high rise. The evening was glorious, and Jessica felt wonderful. She wasn't sure if it was the result of the weather, the delicious food and wine or the company—or maybe all of them.

"Thank you," she said in the elevator.

"You're welcome." Damian fell strangely quiet as they walked to the law library. Before she left for the night, Jessica wanted to shelve the volumes she'd been studying. Damian worked silently with her. When they were finished, he preceded her from the room, automatically turning off the light.

The room was suddenly dark and Jessica bumped into a table.

"Jessica."

"I'm fine," she assured him, walking toward the hall light.

"That's the problem," he muttered, reaching for her. She was in his arms before she realized it. "I'm not." With that his mouth came down on hers.

Five

This kiss wasn't brotherly, nor was it uncomplicated. Damian's mouth fit over hers, warm and coaxing. Jessica sighed and relaxed against him, giving herself up to the sensation. It felt *right* to be in his arms, that was all there was to it.

Her hands gripped the lapels of his jacket, her fingers crushing the soft wool as his mouth moved against hers. Damian's hand curved around the side of her neck, his touch tender as though he feared hurting her.

The kiss was unlike any Jessica had ever experienced. She felt the sensual power of it all the way to her toes, the impact stealing her breath. She moaned and Damian did, too. When they broke apart, neither spoke. Jessica wished he'd say something, anything, to break the silence. She needed him to explain what was happening, because she was lost, taken by surprise, yet delighted to the very depths of her being.

Instead, Damian turned and walked away.

She couldn't believe it. A tear slipped unnoticed down her cheek and dropped onto her silk blouse, the droplet bleeding into a small circle. She raised her hand to her face, surprised by the tear.

Funny that when she couldn't find the words to say what she felt, a tear would speak for her. She'd learned that lesson years earlier. Her mother's tears had fallen onto her grandmother's casket, and they had said far more than a whispered farewell. Tearstains on a letter revealed more than its words.

A tear on her cheek now, after she'd shared a kiss with this man, spelled out volumes. Only to Jessica the language was one she couldn't fully understand.

The sudden need to escape overwhelmed her. Collecting her purse, she stepped out of the library and proceeded down the hallway. She paused outside Damian's open door. She saw him standing in front of his window, looking into the night. His hands were clasped behind his back.

"Good night," she called softly.

He turned and smiled briefly. "Good night, Jessica. See you in the morning."

She wished they could sit down and discuss what had happened, but one look told her Damian was confused and not nearly as delighted as she was. He seemed troubled, burdened somehow. She wondered if he regretted having kissed her.

"Thank you for dinner," she said. "You were right. It's the best Italian food I've ever had." She didn't want to leave, but didn't have an excuse to stay.

"I'm glad you enjoyed it."

Jessica headed for the elevator. Her thoughts remained so muddled that she nearly missed her subway stop on the ride home. The first thing she did when she walked into her apartment was reach for the purple elephant Damian had won for her. She wrapped her arms around it and hugged it tight. It made her feel close to Damian. All she needed to do was shut her eyes and the memories of their night together at Cannon Beach filled her mind. She could almost hear the sound of the carousel, the echo of her own laughter when Damian insisted on winning her the elephant. She could hear the roller coaster as the riders shrieked past and smell the popcorn, candy apples and hot dogs.

Keeping the elephant pressed to her, Jessica slumped into the overstuffed chair and reached for her phone, dialing the number of her best friend. Cathy was far more insightful in these matters than she was. She would help her make sense of Damian's kiss.

"Hi," Jessica murmured when her friend answered.

Her greeting was met with a slight hesitation. "What's wrong?"

It didn't surprise her that her friend knew her so well. "What makes you think anything's wrong?"

"I recognize that tone of voice."

Smiling to herself, Jessica brought up her knees and rested her chin there as she assembled her thoughts. There didn't seem to be an easy way of explaining what had happened. Best just to blurt it out. "Damian kissed me tonight."

"And you liked it, didn't you?"

Cathy sounded gleeful, as though tempted to break into song. Jessica supposed this was what she got for having a theater-arts major for a best friend.

"Yeah—but I'm totally confused," Jessica admitted quietly. This jumble of mixed feelings was the main source of her troubles.

"Surprises you, doesn't it?" Cathy asked, then chuckled softly, again with that note of delight. "I've seen the handwriting on the wall ever since you mentioned Damian Saturday night. The guy sounds perfect for you."

"Don't be ridiculous. "

"What's ridiculous about it?"

"I haven't thought of him…that way. Well, I have recently, and frankly, it frightens me to death. I've already made a fool of myself over one Dryden. I'm not anxious to make the same mistake with another one."

"You were a kid the first time. There's a world of difference between what happened then and what's happening now."

"Maybe," was all Jessica was willing to concede.

"Think, woman," Cathy said dramatically. "The man's obviously attracted to you, too. Otherwise he wouldn't be kissing you."

"I don't know that, and you don't, either. We kissed, and then he acted as if it was the worst thing he could have done. He didn't say a word and he just walked away. I don't know what to think. I'm so confused." She pressed a hand to her forehead.

"So you think he regretted it?"

"He must have. Otherwise…otherwise everything would have turned out differently. He looked at me as if I were a stranger, as if he didn't want to see me again."

"What was he supposed to do? Confess undying love? Didn't you tell me you had the whole situation figured out? The only reason Damian hired you in the first place was to bolster his brother's spirits. Think about it, Jess—the man has integrity. He can't very well start dating you himself if he believes you might still have some feeling for his younger brother."

"It drives me crazy that he'd think that!"

"I know, but you've got to look at it from his point of view."

"At the cost of my own sanity?"

"For now," Cathy said sympathetically.

"I don't know what to do!" Jessica cried, amazed at the amount of emotion that spilled into the words.

"There's more," Cathy said, warming to the subject. "If you're interested in Damian, it makes perfect sense that you're going to have to be the one to make the first move. Damian's hands are tied as long as he thinks there's the least chance you're interested in his brother. The guy's in a real bind here."

"Him! This whole thing with Evan's gotten out of hand. The poor guy's suffocating with everyone's concern. I actually feel sorry for him. He got the raw end of a deal in a relationship, and all he needed was some time to work out his pain," Jessica lamented. "Instead, Damian cut his work load until he's bored out of his mind. His parents, especially his mother, are dishing out sympathy by the truckload, and it's all Evan can do to stay afloat."

She paused for breath, then went on, "The only reason Damian hired me was that he thought I'd pull Evan out of the doldrums. I haven't talked to Evan, but I'm sure he resents all this nonsense. And I don't blame him."

"What about you and Damian?"

"I don't know what to think," Jessica admitted. "I wish I did. If he's interested in me, then surely it's his place to say or do something. Regardless of how he thinks I feel about Evan."

"Oh, come on, Jess!"

"I know Damian."

"Huh. You thought you knew Evan, too."

"I do, or rather, I did," she argued. The conversation was frustrating her more by the minute. "Besides, like I said earlier, I'm not interested in making a fool of myself over another Dryden. I learned my lesson the last time. Good grief, that was years ago and my parents and his *still* talk about it. Just this last weekend my own mother mentioned how pleased she'd be if I married Evan!"

"I have an idea," Cathy said slowly as though the scheme was taking shape in her mind as she spoke. "Introduce me to Damian."

"What possible reason do you have to meet him?" Jessica didn't like the sound of this.

"I just want to. Things aren't going well with David...."

"David?" Jessica cried. "Who's David?"

"The director for *Guys and Dolls*. Now listen, I know this sounds crazy, but trust me, it could work."

"What could work?" Jessica was fast losing what remained of her patience.

"Our meeting. I'll turn on the charm, do what I can to enchant him, and—"

"Just a minute, Cath, you're talking about the man *I'm* interested in."

"I know," she replied as if all this was perfectly logical. "But you want to know how serious he is about you, don't you? Also, maybe watching him with another woman will help you sort out *your* feelings for *him*.

"Yes, but—"

"Come on, Jess. You said yourself you weren't willing to make a fool of yourself a second time. This way you'll know."

"This sounds silly to me."

"Not only that," Cathy went on as though Jessica hadn't spoken, "it'll give me a chance to practice some of my best lines. Just introduce us, and I promise I won't do anything to embarrass you."

"All right," she agreed without any real enthusiasm. "How do you propose we do this?"

"I could stop by the office one day soon and suggest lunch. It'd be natural for you to introduce me around, wouldn't it?"

"I...suppose, but doesn't that seem a bit obvious?"

"Perhaps. Do you have a better idea?"

"No." She sighed. "Okay. Do you want me to invite Damian to join us? I'm coming into the office this Saturday to catch up on a few things, before Evan's big court case starts next week. My guess is that Damian will be there, as well."

"All the better, then. I'll see you Saturday around noon."

Jessica hedged. "You're sure about this?"

"Absolutely! I have ways of getting a man to talk."

"That sounds like something out of a movie."

Cathy laughed. "It is."

"That's what I thought," she mumbled.

Precisely at noon Cathy arrived at the office. Jessica envied her petite friend her pixie good looks, short dark hair and big blue eyes. Cathy looked striking in her pants, which were black with huge white dots, and multicolored striped suspenders. Her blouse was white with small black dots and she was wearing black high heels. One thing was certain—no one would miss seeing her walk down the street. If Evan had been in the office, he doubtless would have begged an introduction.

"You must have forgotten about our lunch," Cathy said more loudly than necessary, standing outside Jessica's office. Loudly enough for Damian to hear.

Her friend's ploy worked because a minute later he wandered out of his office.

"Damian, this is my friend Cathy Hudson," Jessica said. "I might have mentioned her in passing."

Damian and Cathy shook hands. "Jessica forgot we were supposed to meet for lunch today." Cathy said.

"It isn't a good idea for Jessica to skip meals," Damian said. His eyes twinkled and the effort to suppress a smile caused the corners of his mouth to quiver.

"So you've seen what happens when Jessica's stomach growls. Wounded bears are easier to reason with than Jess when she's hungry."

"Hey, that's not true!" Jessica flared. They were speaking as if she wasn't there. She braced her hands on her hips and glared at the two of them. She hadn't been keen on this idea of Cathy's from the first and her instincts were proving to be right.

Her former roommate eased closer to Damian and was gazing soulfully into his eyes. He didn't seem to mind in the least; in fact, he seemed to lap it up.

"I'll get my purse," Jessica said stiffly, leaving Cathy and Damian gazing at each other while she went behind her desk and dug in the bottom drawer. The whole charade irritated her, and she was furious she'd allowed herself to be talked into it.

Cathy managed to tear her eyes away from Damian long enough to throw visual spikes at her friend. It took Jessica a moment to realize what was being signaled. Oh, yes—she was supposed to invite him to tag along.

"Would you care to join us for lunch?" she asked Damian, managing to sound polite, if unenthusiastic.

"Please, do," Cathy said, her words like warm honey.

Damian looked at Jessica as if seeking her confirmation, and to her credit, she did produce a smile. She didn't know why she'd ever agreed to this.

"I'll be happy to join you," Damian surprised her by saying. She'd never dreamed he would. The man was *full* of surprises.

"Great, just great," Jessica muttered under her breath.

"Fabulous," came Cathy's melodious response.

Jessica rolled her eyes, and together the three of them headed out of the office. Damian suggested a well-known expensive restaurant, and before Jessica could comment one way or another, Cathy had agreed. Jessica snapped her mouth closed before she said something she'd regret. It irked her that Damian would so easily fall into Cathy's snare. It might be just a charade, but she was left more than a little confused.

Outside the building, Damian waved down a cab, and Cathy managed to have Damian in the back seat with her. Jessica sat in the front while her best friend giggled her way through the streets of Boston. They drove past the Boston Common and the Freedom Trail, the winding yellow path that led history buffs and tourists from one historic monument to another.

She was acting like a jealous fool, Jessica realized with a start. Jealous of Damian and Cathy? The fog that had clouded her thinking for the past several days cleared.

She was falling in love with Damian Dryden. It couldn't have been any more obvious. It was one of the things Cathy had set out to prove, and her friend was right—she'd needed this blunt lesson.

Of course she loved Damian. From the minute she'd walked into his office and asked about the job. From the minute he'd stood on the footbridge that forged the pond on his parents' property and insisted on taking her to Cannon Beach.

From the minute he'd kissed her.

This was what Cathy had been trying to tell her.

When they arrived at the restaurant, Cathy excused herself and Jessica. With her arm wrapped around her friend's, she dragged her to the ladies' room.

Before Jessica could open her mouth, Cathy burst out, "Damian's wonderful!"

"I know."

"I haven't met Evan, but I'm telling you right now if you're not interested in his big brother, I am. He's got a great wit, he's gorgeous, and—"

"I know all that." And a lot more.

"Listen," Cathy said, "I want you to make some excuse and leave."

Jessica was stunned. "You want me to *what?*"

Cathy was refreshing her makeup in front of the mirror, her eyeliner in hand. "You heard me. Remember an urgent appointment, something that will call you away so the two of us can be alone together. Only don't make it sound phony, or Damian will know what we're doing."

"*I* don't know what we're doing," she protested.

"I want you to give me some time alone with him."

"Why?" Jessica demanded. "Listen, you've already proved your point. I do care about Damian. And I'm not interested in sharing him with you."

"I know how you feel about him," Cathy said slowly as if that much had been understood from the beginning. "But my being alone with him will tell us both how he feels about *you,* which was the main purpose of my plan."

"You're sure about this?"

"How many times are you going to ask me? Of course I'm sure."

"I can't help thinking we're both good candidates for psychoanalysis!"

Cathy laughed outright at that. "Don't worry, I'm not going to steal him away from you, although heaven knows I'm tempted. The guy's a hunk. Why hasn't he ever married?"

"How am I supposed to know?"

"Have you tried asking?"

Cathy had a way of making everything sound perfectly straight-forward. "Don't worry about it. I'll find that out, along with everything else."

Jessica hesitated. She trusted Cathy—most of the time. She also knew it wasn't beneath her best friend to say or do something sneaky. That was what worried Jessica.

"Go back to your apartment," Cathy instructed, before outlining her lush full mouth with a glossy shade of lipstick.

"I still don't understand what you're doing."

Cathy patiently closed the tube and shook her head as though to suggest the answer was obvious. "You don't need to. When Damian and I've finished lunch I can report my findings to you. Is everything clear now?"

"As mud."

Cathy rolled her eyes. "I'm trying to be a help here. The least you can do is cooperate."

"All right, all right," Jessica muttered, but she didn't like it.

"Let's not keep Prince Charming waiting any longer," Cathy said, taking Jessica's elbow. "Just remember to come up with something brilliant to excuse yourself."

Jessica was feeling anything but brilliant at the moment. "All right," she promised.

Jessica did manage to come up with a plausible excuse. They were seated and given elaborate menus decorated with gold tassels. Jessica set her purse on the floor, and it promptly fell over. When she leaned down to right it, she pulled a small appointment card from the outside pocket. Straightening, she studied the card.

"What's the date today?"

"The twelfth. Why?" Cathy's eyes had never been rounder, or more guileless.

"It says here I've got a dentist's appointment this afternoon." She made a show of looking at her watch. "In half an hour."

"On a Saturday?" Damian asked casually.

"Lots of dentists are keeping Saturday hours," Cathy explained conversationally, spreading the linen napkin across her lap. "I went in for a checkup myself no more than a month ago, and my appointment was on a Saturday.''

"It's too late to call and cancel,'' Jessica said with a defeated air. ''It took me months to get this appointment as it was. The Saturday schedule fills up quickly.''

"If you made it months ago, it isn't any wonder you forgot.'' Cathy seemed all too willing to offer Jessica an excuse.

"I'd better see if I can catch a cab,'' Jessica mumbled. She wouldn't be able to keep up this charade much longer. It'd be a miracle if Damian didn't see through their plot. It had more holes than a golf course.

"I'm so sorry you have to go,'' Cathy said with enough sincerity to sound believable.

Damian said nothing. If Cathy's theory was true, Damian would reveal some regret at her leaving. Instead, he smiled at her and nodded as if he welcomed the time alone with her friend. Jessica's hands closed tightly around her purse strap as she stood and made her farewells.

Once she was outside, the doorman's whistle hailed her a cab. Jessica climbed into the back seat and gave the man the address of her apartment, thinking this was going to be the longest afternoon of her life.

She was right.

She paced her living room munching on pretzels for a good two hours. Most of the large bag had disappeared before her doorbell chimed. Cathy. In her eagerness to hear what she'd achieved, Jessica nearly jerked the door off its hinges.

Nothing could have surprised her more than to find Damian standing on the other side. She must have looked as dumbstruck as she felt, because he grinned and let himself in without waiting for an invitation.

"How was the dentist's appointment?''

"Ah… I didn't have one.''

"I know.'' He walked over to her bookcase and was examining the titles as if he'd come for that purpose alone.

"You knew?''

"You're not nearly as good an actress as your friend,'' he said, turning to face her. Jessica tried to read his expression, but found it impossible. She felt rooted to the carpet, unable to move and hardly able to breathe. She wondered if he was angry with her. Perhaps he was amused. She couldn't tell which.

She should have known he'd see through their ploy. "It was a stupid plan," she admitted. Her shoulders sagged with a burden of regrets. She'd allowed Cathy to talk her into this crazy scheme, and she'd followed like a lamb to the slaughter.

"I...we didn't offend you, did we?"

A hint of a smile touched his eyes. "No, it was a very sweet thing to do, but unnecessary."

She blinked, not knowing what to say because she wasn't sure she understood.

Damian walked over to her and reached out a hand to press against her cheek. His touch was gentle, his gray eyes as serious as she'd ever seen them. He spoke as though his words pained him. "I appreciate your efforts, Jessica, but I can find my own dates." Then he bent and gently placed his mouth on hers. The kiss was far too short to satisfy her. Instead, it created a need for more. When he lifted his head, everything within her wanted to beg him not to stop.

"I'll see you Monday morning," he said, turning and heading toward the door.

She opened her mouth to tell him to stay, but by the time she could get the words out he was gone. He actually believed she was setting him up with Cathy. No wonder. That was exactly what it looked like. Why hadn't she thought of this before? Jessica slumped onto her sofa, covered her face with her hands and resisted the urge to cry.

Damian hadn't been gone for more than five minutes when Cathy arrived. Jessica opened her door to find her friend leaning against the doorjamb as if she needed its support. She threw herself down on Jessica's couch and removed her high heels. "That man's a tough nut to crack."

Jessica folded her arms and asked, "What do you mean?"

"I mean he was so closemouthed about you, there's only one sensible conclusion."

"And what's that?"

Cathy stopped rubbing her toes and turned her big blue eyes on Jessica. "You're serious? You mean you really don't know?"

"I wouldn't be asking if I did!"

"He's in love with you."

Jessica didn't believe it. "He can't be."

"Why can't he? Is there a law posted somewhere that says it's a crime to fall in love with Jessica Kellerman?"

"No..."

"He wasn't interested in me, and trust me, I tried."

Jessica stiffened, remembering her reaction to Cathy's attempts to flirt with Damian. She hadn't liked it. None of the crazy stunts her friend had pulled over the years had put their friendship on the line. This one had. Damian was off-limits, and before Cathy left for home, Jessica wanted to make sure she knew it.

"He thought I was trying to set him up with you," Jessica muttered disparagingly.

"What's so tragic about that? That was exactly what I wanted him to think."

"But why?"

Cathy's smile was slow and confident. "This is the reason I'm your best friend. My little performance this afternoon was for both your benefits. You know how you feel about Damian, too. I'm right, aren't I?"

Jessica nodded reluctantly, hating to admit her friend's ploy had worked. But there was a problem. "Damian assumes I was setting him up with you because I'm not interested in him."

"What makes you think that?"

"'Think' nothing. He practically said so."

"When?"

"Just a few minutes ago. He was here. The whole experiment backfired, Cath."

"You straightened him out, didn't you?"

"No... I didn't get the chance." Jessica felt worse and worse. She had no one to blame but herself. She'd allowed Cathy to talk her into this crazy scheme, and now she was suffering the consequences.

Cathy went uncharacteristically quiet. "You'll talk to him, won't you?"

"I...I don't know. I suppose so."

"Good. Explain how you feel, otherwise he'll go right on thinking you're not interested."

Jessica closed here eyes and groaned.

"It won't be hard," Cathy assured her. "He's crazy about you, Jess."

When her former roommate left a few minutes later, Jessica realized what a good friend Cathy had always been—despite her penchant for theatrics.

Jessica considered Cathy's advice for what remained of the weekend and arrived at the office early Monday morning. To her surprise, Evan was sitting at his desk when she walked in. He smiled broadly in greeting. "Good morning, sweet Jessica." He seemed to be in an awfully good mood. His brown eyes were clear and lively, and his smile was warm. "You're just the person I was waiting to see."

She stowed her purse and moved into his office with a pen and pad, fully expecting him to give her another lengthy assignment.

"Sit down," he instructed, motioning her toward a chair on the other side of his desk. He leaned back in his own chair, looking relaxed. "Now tell me something."

"Sure." Her mind was churning with a possible list of requests.

"I've been something of a bad boy around here lately, not pulling my own weight and the like. You know that, don't you?"

"I...I've only been in the office a short time," she said, not wanting to speak out of turn. "It's not for me to say if you have or haven't been doing your share of the work."

"Really, Jess, there's no need to be shy."

"All right," she said, resenting the fact that she'd been put in this position. "I know you were hurt, but we all face disappointments in life. It's time to pull yourself up by your bootstraps."

Evan laughed delightedly, not the least bit offended. "By heaven, I like a woman who can speak her mind."

Jessica relaxed and uncrossed her legs. "Was that all?"

"No." He tipped back in his chair and rubbed the side of his face while studying her carefully. "There was a time when you were rather...keen on me, wasn't there?"

"Yes." She flushed. "Years ago."

"You worshiped me from afar, so to speak."

She lowered her gaze and nodded.

"You're right about my being disappointed," he went on. "I felt the need to prove myself. In looking back, I realize how shallow I've been. I'm not proud of my behavior these past few months, and I'm hoping to make up for it with the Earl Kress trial."

Jessica didn't know how to comment or even if she should.

"My father and I had a good long talk this weekend," Evan added thoughtfully.

"I understand he's considering running for the Senate."

"Yes, and he's decided to give it a shot. Damian and I will be spending a fair amount of time working on his campaign. The gist of our conversation was simple. He wants me to get my life straightened out and start dating again."

"I think he's absolutely right," she agreed readily, assuming Evan was referring to the diplomat's daughter.

"Great." He beamed her a killer smile. "I was hoping you'd feel that way."

Jessica blinked, not grasping what he meant. "Why's that?"

"Because, my dear Jessie, I've decided I'd like to get to know you better. You're very sweet and a hell of a good worker. Dad reminded me that you were keen on me a few years back, and I'm hoping to capitalize on your affection."

"Ah..." Now didn't seem the appropriate moment to bring up her feelings for Damian. Then again, she'd better before matters got out of hand.

"I don't mind telling you," Evan said before she could speak, "my confidence has been badly shaken. I feel safe and secure with you. Frankly, I don't know how I'd deal with any more rejection."

Six

"Aren't you seeing Romilda?" Jessica asked with a sinking feel-ing. She *had* to say something, set the record straight, but Evan was studying her with an eager intensity, and coward that she was, Jessica couldn't make herself do it. "You seemed to get along so well with her at the barbecue, and her political connections might help your father's campaign efforts."

"She's already returned to Europe."

"I see."

"Don't get me wrong, Romilda's a sweetheart, but she isn't the one for me," Evan explained. "I want an old-fashioned girl, who values the same things I do. Mom, home, apple pie—that sort of thing. A woman who knows what's really important in life. Some-one like you, Jessica."

Jessica didn't doubt for an instant that Evan was echoing his father's words. Maybe the sort of woman he described *was* right for him, but Jessica wasn't the one. She was about to explain dip-lomatically that there was already someone in her life—without telling him who—when he spoke again.

"I've got a ton of work waiting for me this morning, but my parents asked that we meet later, and I thought the five of us could have lunch together."

"Five?"

"Damian will be there, too. Would noon be convenient?"

"Ah..."

"Great." He returned his attention to the papers on his desk. Jessica waited a moment, then got up and went back to the outer office. She felt the blood drain out of her face as she reached her desk and sat down.

"Is Mr. Dryden here?" Jessica hadn't been aware of Mrs. Sterling's arrival.

Jessica looked up and nodded.

"But it's barely nine."

"I know," she murmured.

"What's come over that man?" the secretary murmured, unable to disguise her amazement. "Never mind, let's not question it. I'd rather count my blessings. I was about to lose heart with him. I was afraid Damian had given Evan too much slack the past few months."

Jessica managed a weak smile. Mrs. Sterling moved about the office with the efficiency that was her trademark. She brewed a pot of coffee and the aroma of the rich Colombian helped revive Jessica. When the coffee was ready, Mrs. Sterling poured Evan a cup and carried it into his office. Jessica couldn't hear what was being said, but apparently Evan was in top form, because his secretary returned grinning broadly.

Jessica sat at her desk, too numb to think clearly. She'd missed her golden opportunity, if indeed there'd been one, to tell Evan she was in love with Damian. Yet it didn't seem fair to make such a confession to his brother when she hadn't said a word to Damian. Nor was she convinced Damian felt the same way about her. All she had to go on was Cathy's faith.

Her theatrical friend had a tendency to exaggerate, to expand the truth and fill it with an enthusiasm that simply might not exist. Damian was fond of her, Jessica didn't doubt that, but as for his being in love with her, Jessica couldn't say.

There was nothing to do but sit by patiently and wait to see how matters developed. Evan was making this effort for his father; it didn't mean he intended their relationship to be anything but show. Certainly he wasn't serious about wooing her. Not when he'd cared so deeply for this unknown Mary Jo.

The morning passed quickly as they prepared for the Earl Kress trial, slated to begin the following day. The attention generated by the local television stations was sure to spark interest in the law firm and in Evan's father's bid for the Senate. In addition, the trial had the potential to affect the outcome of education in school districts across the country.

Close to noon, Evan emerged from his office, and with a warm smile at Jessica, said to his secretary, "I'm going to steal this lovely one away from you for a couple of hours."

Mrs. Sterling nodded approvingly.

Jessica reached for her purse and stood, hoping this lunch would afford her a few minutes alone with Damian so they could talk. She desperately needed to discuss things with him, to explain what had happened and seek his counsel.

To Jessica's disappointment, the opportunity never arose. The three met Evan's parents at the Hilton. The meal was pleasant and cordial, and everyone seemed to be in a good mood—with the exception of Damian, who practically ignored Jessica. She might have been invisible for all the attention he paid her.

She decided to make an effort to let her feelings for the older Dryden son be known, and she waited until there was a lull in the conversation.

"Damian and I were out to Cannon Beach recently," she announced brightly after their salads were served. Evan's parents exchanged meaningful glances.

"From here on out Evan will be the one taking you to the beach, isn't that right?" Damian said to his brother.

"You should have said something earlier, Jess," Evan said, picking up on Damian's cue. "I love Cannon Beach. We'll make a point of going there sometime, all right? As soon as the Earl Kress trial's over."

"All right," Jessica agreed, her heart in her throat. She looked to Damian, who was busy eating his salad. From all outward appearances, it made no difference to him whom she dated. Apparently the idea of Evan's holding her close while they rode on the roller coaster didn't trouble him. Not at all.

After lunch they made their way into one of the meeting rooms on the second level of the hotel, where a news conference was scheduled. There, Walter Dryden, surrounded by his wife and family, announced his intention to run for the Senate.

Mingling in the audience of newsmen, well-wishers and political-party members, Jessica was able to stand back and view the four Drydens. They were a handsome, wholesome family who believed in the American dream. She admired and loved them, and wished Walter Dryden every success.

Flashbulbs exploded around her as she wandered to the back of the room. She wasn't sure why Evan had insisted she attend this affair, other than to reassure his father he'd taken their father-son talk to heart.

Jessica knew that life was often filled with ironic twists such as this, but why did hers have to be so frustrating? She was pretty sure Evan's father had put the idea of dating her into his son's head. And why not? It was well-known she'd once had a crush on Evan. And their families were so close. She was the logical choice, and the fact that she now worked for Evan made it all the more convenient.

The younger Dryden hoped to enhance his image, assist his father in his campaign efforts and prove he was over a painful relationship. What better way to start than with a woman who'd once had stars in her eyes for him?

Except that those stars were focused in another direction now. On his older brother. A man who seemed determined to do the noble thing and step aside for his brother.

For the first time in months, Evan had revealed a willingness to put the past behind him and get on with his life. And Damian believed she was the reason he had. So he would do nothing to change that—even if he did love her himself.

Every day for the next week the Dryden name turned up in all the media. The television and radio stations followed the trial, and each afternoon the newspaper carried an account of what had happened in the courtroom. Jessica met Earl Kress the first time in the courtroom and was impressed with the young man's sincerity. He wasn't looking to cripple the school system with a huge monetary settlement; instead, he sought changes that would help other athletes. Evan had arranged for a private tutor for the young man. Earl hoped to return to college within a year and work toward a degree in education. His goal was to teach high school students himself.

The more she learned about Evan's generosity to Earl, the more impressed she was with the lawyer's generous heart. Earl had been cheated out of his education, and Evan had made it his mission to make sure this didn't happen to future generations.

At the same time, Walter Dryden was making a splash across the various media. It seemed there was a social engagement every night of the week having to do with the upcoming primary. Because of his involvement with the trial, Evan wasn't expected to attend these functions. For that Jessica was grateful, although she knew Damian had become actively involved in his father's campaign. She yearned to talk to him, but he seemed to be avoiding her. She rarely saw him, and when she did he was occupied with someone else.

On Friday the jury convened. Jessica returned to the office, preferring not to wait at the courthouse for the outcome of the trial. Evan had built a strong case and she was confident Earl would win his suit, but waiting for the jury's verdict was agony.

The office buzzed with activity, the way it generally did in the afternoons. There was the hum of computers, fax machines and photocopiers, and messengers zigzagged from one room to the next, crowding the hallways. The whole place was filled with an air of expectancy.

Jessica walked over to her desk, removed her shoes and rubbed her sore toes against her calves. Her muscles ached, and she was mentally and emotionally exhausted. This had been an incredibly hectic week. As soon as she got home, she was going to soak in a hot tub and curl up with a good book. Sleeping until noon the next day held irresistible appeal.

Mrs. Sterling had left on an errand and Jessica had just slumped down in her chair when Damian strolled into the office. He stopped abruptly when he saw she was alone.

Jessica froze, her breath trapped in her lungs.

"Hello, Jessica," he said stiffly.

"Hello," she managed.

"Where's Mrs. Sterling?" he asked, recovering first. He was brisk and businesslike, as if he'd never held her in his arms, as if she'd never been more to him than a friend, a casual one at that.

"Off on an errand," she answered, then added, "The jury's still out."

"So I understand." He walked over to Mrs. Sterling's desk and set a stack of papers in the secretary's in-basket.

"Have you been to that Italian restaurant lately?" she asked, desperate to make conversation. Desperate to remind him of the good times they'd shared—and what had happened afterward. She yearned with all her being that he understood her message—that those times had meant the world to her and that she hoped they'd been important to him, too. She prayed he'd realize how much she missed him.

"I haven't dined out lately." Then he turned abruptly and strode from the room.

Hurt and angry, Jessica wanted to shout at him to come back. But it wouldn't have done any good; she knew that. He'd sliced her out of his life without a second thought, and apparently without a single regret.

About an hour later, Evan burst into the office. He paused just inside the doorway, threw back his head and released a yell loud enough to sway the light fixtures.

"We did it!"

Startled, Jessica looked up from her desk. She stood to offer him her congratulations, and Evan rushed to her, lifting her high off the ground and whirling her around. "We won!" he shouted.

"Evan!" She laughed, bracing her hands on his shoulders. He was spinning so fast she was growing dizzy.

His cries of jubilation had attracted the attention of others in the office, but Evan didn't show any signs of releasing her. He set her back down on the ground and, looping his arm around her shoulders, kept her close to his side. Words of congratulations were enthusiastically offered.

"I couldn't have done it without Jessica," he announced to the gathering. "Her research was invaluable. Damian, too," Evan said, holding his free arm out to his brother. "A man couldn't ask for a better brother."

Jessica was looking at Damian, and whether he'd intended it or not—she suspected he hadn't—their eyes met. His guard had lowered, and his expression was one of such emotional intensity that nothing could have pulled her gaze from his. In him she read pride, loyalty and devotion. In him she saw that there was nothing on this earth he would do or say to hurt his brother, even at the sacrifice of his own happiness.

Tears clouded her vision. Gazing into the faces of those around her, she forced herself to smile, forced herself to look as though this was the happiest moment of her life, when on the inside, she'd never felt more miserable.

Evan insisted on taking her to dinner that night to celebrate. A victory gala, he told her. He chose a restaurant well known for its superb food and service, and Jessica knew when they were seated that she was the envy of every woman there. Evan had never looked more handsome or been more charming.

They were leaving the restaurant, waiting for the valet to bring around Evan's car, when a news photographer stopped them and took their picture. Jessica protested, but Evan told her that this was the price of fame and she might as well smile.

The next morning, Jessica's mother phoned before she'd had a chance to awake, and hours before she'd intended to. She was extremely depressed, and sleep was the perfect escape.

"Jessica, have you seen it?" Joyce demanded, her voice raised with excitement. "I've already called the newspaper and am having them make copies for Lois and me. You both look fabulous."

"Seen what, Mother?" was the groggy reply.

"The newspaper, sweetheart. There's a picture of you and Evan on the society page with a nice little write-up. In case you didn't see it, your name was mentioned in the gossip column, too, on Thursday, linking you with Evan. Oh, honey, I'm so pleased."

"Oh, Lord," Jessica whispered, her mind clouded with exhaustion. "I remember now. A photographer stopped us last night."

"Yes, I know, that's what I've been telling you. The picture's in this morning's paper. I'm thrilled and so is your father, not to mention Lois and Walter."

Jessica was anything but thrilled. "It's only a picture, Mom."

"It's more than that, Jessica. It's a dream come true for you, and for me, too. You've always felt so strongly about Evan and now, after all these years, he feels the same way about you.''

''Mother, you don't understand, Evan and I—''

''You don't know how pleased Lois and I are. We realize it's much too soon to be making wedding plans, but it's the sort of thing good friends love to do when their children are dating. You're our only daughter, and I can tell you right now this will be the gala event of the year. Your father and I insist.''

She only paused long enough to take a breath, then rushed on, ''We'd be so very pleased if you and Evan decided to have an autumn wedding. Lois has been my friend for so many years, and to think that someday we might share grandchildren! It does both our hearts good.''

Jessica rubbed a hand over her eyes, repressing the urge to weep. ''Mom...''

''I don't mean to pressure you.''

''I know you don't.''

''Good. I'm sorry I woke you, darling. I should have realized you'd be exhausted after this last week. Go back to sleep. We'll talk later.''

Sleep was impossible now. Jessica padded barefoot into the kitchen and made coffee, standing at the counter until the liquid had drained into the glass pot. Then she poured herself a mug, and cradling it in both hands, sat at her kitchen table. Balancing her feet against the edge of the chair, her knees propped up under her chin, she waited until the coffee had cooled enough for a first sip. It did little to revive her sagging spirits, settling unsatisfactorily in the pit of her stomach while she mulled over what she was going to do.

Already it had started, already she could feel the ropes tightening around her heart, binding her. She felt imprisoned by what everyone believed was right for her, what everyone believed she wanted herself, when in reality she loved Damian, not Evan.

The phone startled her, and she swore as she spilled coffee on her hands. ''Hello,'' she snapped, grabbing the receiver.

''What the hell's going on?'' Cathy demanded, sounding full of righteous indignation.

"Excuse me!" The last thing she needed was her best friend's accusations.

"I picked up the paper this morning, and there's your bright smiling face to greet me."

"So I understand," she muttered.

"There's something wrong with this picture, though. You're with the wrong brother. Care to explain?"

"No."

"Why not?"

Jessica sighed. "It's a long story."

"Condense it."

She sighed again. "Evan's decided to come out of his doldrums—"

"About time, wouldn't you say?"

"Yes, definitely, but he isn't doing this for himself. His father's running for political office and so Evan's making an effort to smile and put on a happy face."

"By dating you."

"It seems so."

"I know all about his father. Walter Dryden's name's been splashed across the headlines all week, right along with Evan's and Earl Kress's," Cathy said impatiently. "So cut to the chase and tell me why you were out on the town with Evan and not Damian."

A simple explanation was beyond Jessica. This was the most complicated misadventure of her life. "You were wrong, Cath," she said miserably. "Damian isn't nearly as fond of me as you assumed. Otherwise he would have said something long before now."

"Said something about what?" Cathy yelped.

"Caring about me," she whispered miserably. She felt as though she was standing chest deep in quicksand with no chance of getting free.

Cathy groaned. "All right, I can see this tale of woe isn't something you're going to be able to abbreviate. Start at the beginning and be sure you tell me everything."

To her credit, Cathy listened attentively to the events of the week, all that had ensued since Jessica's conversation with Evan on Monday morning. When Jessica finished, Cathy was uncharacteristically silent.

"I see what you mean," she said finally, sounding none too happy herself. "Damian's caught between a rock and a hard place. He's crazy about you, Jess. My instincts told me that the day we had lunch."

"But apparently not crazy enough." Jessica closed her eyes to the sharp pain the thought produced.

"Wrong," Cathy corrected defensively. "Damian's got a sense of family and duty so strong he'd sacrifice his own happiness. That's not loving you too little, my friend, that's loving you—and Evan—too damn much."

"If that's the case, then why do I feel like leaping off a bridge? My mother and Lois Dryden are talking about a wedding and grandchildren."

Cathy let the comment pass. "How often do you see Evan?"

"Every day—we work together, remember?"

"I meant socially."

That wasn't a fair question. Because of the trial they'd been together for the better part of each evening, as well as every day. Lunch and dinner had been haphazard affairs while they discussed different aspects of the case and their strategies. It was business, nothing more. He hadn't so much as held her hand.

"We've been seeing a good deal of each other," Jessica said, and then explained.

"I see, and how do you feel about Evan now?"

"I'm glad he's trying to get his life together. But he isn't attracted to me, and doesn't pretend to be, either."

"Then why haven't you said something to Damian? Why haven't you explained?"

"How could I?" Jessica protested tartly. It wasn't that she hadn't thought of doing so a hundred times. "First off, we were both heavily involved in the Earl Kress case. The timing was wrong. I might have said something over dinner last night if Damian had given me any encouragement, but he didn't. I can't help thinking you're wrong about us."

"We've already been through that," Cathy muttered in frustration.

"I know Evan is dating me for show. I wouldn't be surprised if he'd arranged for that photographer himself. It's the sort of thing he'd do."

"Aren't you afraid he'll fall in love with you?"

"No. His heart is so battered it'll be a good long while before he takes a chance on love again."

Cathy was uncharacteristically quiet. "His family's important to him, the same way yours is to you. So play this hand close to your chest, Jess. Vulnerable as he is just now, Evan might develop a deep...affection for you. That would be a disaster."

This was something Jessica had worried about earlier, and she was greatly relieved that their relationship had turned out to be strictly platonic. "You're certainly filled with happy suggestions."

Cathy ignored that, too. "When are you seeing him again?"

"Tomorrow afternoon. He's picking me up for a fund-raiser for his father. It's a picnic." She dreaded the entire affair. If it wasn't for the opportunity of seeing Damian, she'd have found an excuse not to attend.

"Have fun."

"Right," Jessica said, knowing fun would be impossible.

After she'd hung up the phone, Jessica took a shower. She stood under the hard spray, letting the water hammer at her face. When she'd finished she felt better—and filled with purpose.

Evan arrived to pick her up early the next day. He wore a white sweater with a blue braid along the V-shaped neckline. He looked stylish and debonair, very Ivy League casual. His eyes lit up when he saw her in her cheery summer dress with the short white jacket.

"I can't get over what a beauty you grew up to be."

"You always were a silver-tongued devil," Jessica teased. He was in a good mood, and he had a right to be after the success of the previous week.

Evan's sports car was parked right in front of her building. He held open the door for her and helped her inside. They chatted amiably on the ride to Whispering Willows, where the fund-raising picnic was being held. The area was decorated with banners and American flags, and there was even a small grandstand and a band.

Jessica was determined to find a chance to talk to Damian, to explain her feelings. He couldn't avoid her forever.

Jessica's parents were there, handing out small American flags to the guests. Rows of folding chairs were set up in front of the grandstand for Walter Dryden's speech.

Everyone was busy with one picnic task or another. Jessica helped where she could, keeping her eye out for Damian.

She was busy dishing up potato salad alongside Evan when she first saw Damian. He was talking to an older woman and happened to look in Jessica's direction. Their eyes met for the briefest of seconds before he quickly averted his gaze. Jessica swallowed the pain that constricted her throat.

After the food had been served, Walter Dryden strolled up to Jessica. He was a big man, strong in build and, she knew, equally strong in character. He hugged her and thanked her for all her help.

"You've grown into a beautiful young woman, Jessica." His deep voice echoed what Evan had said to her earlier.

"Thank you. I don't know if I've had a chance to tell you how pleased I am that you've decided to run for senator," she said.

"I wish I'd started my campaign much sooner. I'm going to be stuck playing catch-up the next couple of months, which means a lot of hard work."

"You're exactly what this state needs," Jessica said sincerely.

"Your confidence means a lot to me." They were strolling together side by side. "I've been doing some hard thinking along those lines myself. About how you're exactly what my son needs."

"I'm sorry?"

"You and Evan."

Jessica didn't know what to say. She should have explained then and there that it was Damian she loved, but her throat went dry and her tongue seemed glued to the roof of her mouth.

"He needs you," Walter Dryden repeated.

"He's going to be just fine, Mr. Dryden. I don't think you should worry about him."

Walter Dryden's nod was somber. "Lois and I believe you're responsible for that."

The taste of panic filled her mouth. "I'm sure that's not true."

"Nonsense. You have to learn how to accept a compliment, young lady. It'll serve you well later in life—Evan, too, for that matter." He paused, his look thoughtful. "I believe my son will eventually enter politics himself. He's a natural, but he isn't ready yet and probably won't be for several years. I've had to bite my tongue not to sway that son of mine, but Lois would never forgive me if I pushed him toward something he didn't want."

Jessica hoped he felt the same way about forcing Evan into an unwanted relationship.

"We're getting off the subject," Walter muttered, with a shake of his head. "I wanted to thank you, my dear, for helping Evan."

"But I haven't."

"Nonsense. You've made all the difference in the world to my son these last few weeks. I'd mentioned to Damian that you and I had talked and you'd be coming in for an interview. His decision to hire you was brilliant. I couldn't have thought of anything better for Evan myself."

"I have a lot to thank Damian for," Jessica said, so softly she doubted Walter heard her.

"Ah, here you are," Evan declared, coming up behind them. "Don't tell me my own father is stealing away my favorite girl."

Walter chuckled. "Not likely, son. You two enjoy yourselves now. You've both worked hard all afternoon. Take a break, sneak away and have fun."

"But your speech..." Jessica protested.

"No matter. You can hear me speak any day of the week. Now off with you."

Evan reached for her hand, and they walked along the outskirts of the grandstand area. They were moving toward a stand of weeping willow trees, and Jessica found that Evan's mood had changed subtly. He seemed troubled. She waited for him to broach the problem.

"Do you mind if we take a few minutes to talk?" he said after a moment.

"I'd like that." Her heart swelled with relief. What they needed was a healthy dose of honesty. She stopped and leaned against the trunk of a tree. They were partially hidden from view, and the privacy was welcome.

"I don't feel that you and I are connecting, Jessica."

"I know." She thought about her mother and all her talk about a wedding and grandchildren. Her mind drifted back to the conversation she'd had with Evan's father moments earlier. Everything had gone much too far.

"I've wanted to talk to you all week, but everything was so hectic, what with the trial and Dad announcing his candidacy."

"It was quite a week," Jessica agreed.

"Our names have been linked in the newspaper."

"Your name's often in the paper." He was from one of Boston's most prominent families, after all.

Evan chuckled. "That's true enough." He reached for her hand then, holding it between his own. "I'd like all that speculation about us to change. I'm ready to settle down with one woman."

Jessica's heart stopped beating. If he proposed marriage, she swore she was going to break down and weep. Everything and everyone seemed to be working against her, including her own parents.

"I...I've always been fond of you, Evan, but I think it's only fair for you to know—"

"'Fond' is such a weak word," he interrupted, frowning.

She didn't want to walk over his already bruised ego. "I know, but—"

"Do you realize we haven't even kissed?" He smiled, his eyes twinkling with boyish eagerness. "That's about to be corrected, sweet Jessica." He placed his hands on both sides of her face and, before she could protest, lowered his mouth to hers.

It was a gentle kiss, undemanding and tender. Jessica felt nothing, except an increasing desire to cry. How could she feel anything for Evan when she cared so deeply for Damian? When she *loved* Damian?

Evan lifted his head from hers and gazed down at her, his eyes now dark and unreadable. He studied her for a moment. "I won't pressure you, Jessica. We'll give this time.'' He brushed a stray curl from her cheek and kissed her there, his lips warm and moist against her face.

It was then that Jessica saw Damian. He was standing on the edge of the crowd that had gathered to hear Walter's speech. His eyes were on Jessica and Evan. When he realized she'd seen him, he turned and walked away. His steps were brisk and hurried as though he couldn't move fast enough.

For one wild moment, Jessica considered running after him, but Evan had put one arm possessively around her shoulders and was leading her back toward the grandstand.

It was too late.

Seven

"Well?" Cathy demanded without a word of greeting as Jessica opened the apartment door to her friend Sunday evening. Cathy swept her backpack from her shoulder and carelessly tossed it aside. "How'd the picnic go?"

"Politically it was a success. From what I understand, Mr. Dryden raised a lot of money for his campaign." She was avoiding the issue and knew it, but the subject of Evan and Damian had become too painful even to think about.

Cathy knew her well enough to recognize the signs. "Sit down," she instructed, pointing at the overstuffed chair that was Jessica's favorite spot. Her friend became downright dictatorial whenever she felt strongly about something; apparently, she did now.

Jessica followed Cathy's orders simply because she didn't have the force of will to argue. Settling into the chair, she waited while Cathy paced the carpet in front of her. Jessica could almost hear her friend's brain waves crackling.

"I've been giving this matter some thought," Cathy began.

"I can see that," Jessica returned, wondering what Cathy's feverish mind had concocted this time.

"I want you to develop a limp," Cathy said. She sounded as though this was a stroke of pure genius.

Jessica wanted to laugh out loud. "You're joking, right? Because heaven knows I can't take you seriously."

"I'm dead serious, but I only want you to limp when Damian's around, not Evan."

Jessica shook her head, as though that would improve her hearing. For sheer lunacy, this idea ranked right up there with the luncheon invitation. "What possible reason would I have to do something as stupid as fake a limp?"

"Just remember to limp on the same foot," Cathy said, ignoring Jessica's question and looking a bit worried. "This is just the type of thing you'd forget. It might be a good idea if you put a mark on the top of your shoe so you don't goof up."

Jessica held up her hands. "Cathy, have you OD'd on too much sugar or something? This is the craziest thing you've ever suggested!"

"Trust me," Cathy said impatiently. "I'm in theater—I know what I'm doing."

"Your self-confidence doesn't reassure me in the least."

"It should. I know about these things."

"Would it be too much to share the logic of your plan with me?"

"Not at all." Cathy's step was jaunty as she walked over to the sofa, dropped down and crossed her legs. "Sympathy. We want Damian to think you've hurt yourself—a twisted ankle, a trick knee, that sort of thing. If he cares about you half as much as I believe, he won't be able to stand by and do nothing. He'll come to your aid, and the minute he touches you, he won't be able to hide how he feels." She stopped abruptly. "Be warned, though. You should be prepared."

"For what?"

"He might just explode at you. Anger in a man is far more complicated than it is with us women. He'll think you aren't taking care of yourself, and he'll feel responsible for that. Men do that kind of thing, you know. He might even decide to blame Evan, so make sure you take that into account."

"Of course Damian'll get angry!" Jessica cried. "And he'll have every right to be mad once he discovers I'm faking an injury to gain his sympathy."

"Don't let him know that part," Cathy said simply.

"Cathy," Jessica said on the end of a long sigh. "I appreciate your efforts, I really do, but I can't pretend to be hurt. First of all, Damian would know in an instant. I'm not nearly as good an actress as you, and he'd figure out my ploy in no time. You seem to have forgotten Damian's an experienced attorney."

Cathy frowned, chewing on her lower lip as she thought. "Okay," she said after a while. "Forget the limp. The only other thing I can suggest is forthright honesty. You'd be amazed at how well it works sometimes. This might just be one of those times.''

"As it happens, I couldn't agree with you more," Jessica said. "This whole situation is preposterous. I'm not any good at charades. I'd like to help Evan, but not at the expense of my emotional well-being."

"Now you're talking." Cathy slid to the edge of the cushion. "What are you going to say to Damian?"

"I...don't know yet." A heaviness settled on her shoulders at the thought. "You know what my biggest fear is? That Damian will smile fondly at me and tell me how flattered and honored he is by my little confession."

"With sadness echoing in his voice," Cathy added, demonstrating her usual flair for the dramatic.

"Right. Then he'll sigh and add that unfortunately he doesn't share my feelings."

"That sounds just like a man," Cathy agreed. "Naturally he'll lie through his teeth, because he's being noble for his brother's sake. Just don't listen to him. Trust me, Jess, this guy loves you."

Jessica wished with all her heart that it was true. She looked over to her friend, realizing how much she treasured Cathy's support, and gave her a thumbs-up. Cathy grinned and returned the gesture.

Evan was in his office working when Jessica arrived Monday morning. "Good morning," he called out cheerfully. "I was hoping it was you."

"Would you like me to put on a pot of coffee?" she asked. Then she glanced toward the machine and noticed Evan had already done so.

He wandered out of his office, mug in hand, and sat on the corner of her desk, one leg swinging like a pendulum. He smiled down on her, his eyes twinkling. "Are you rested and ready to tackle the world?"

Jessica smiled. That didn't describe her even on her best Monday morning. "Not quite. Give me until Wednesday or Thursday for that."

"Then this should help brighten your day," he said casually, withdrawing two tickets from the inside pocket of his jacket and handing them to her. Jessica read the tickets and gasped. "Two box seats for the Red Sox game this evening!"

"I thought you might enjoy baseball."

"I love the Red Sox."

"So your mother told me. Be prepared, Jessica, my lovely, I'm planning to sweep you off your feet."

Her gaze shot up to his. He was sweeping her off her feet all right, but she didn't like where she was landing. She'd awakened that morning determined to resolve this matter between her and the Dryden brothers once and for all, only to be thwarted at the first turn. As if things weren't bad enough, Evan had been conferring with her mother, learning what he could about her.

"Evan, we need to talk," she said, keeping her gaze lowered. All the way into the office she'd practiced what she intended to say.

"I can't now, Jess. Sorry. I'm going to be in court all day with the Porter case. But don't worry, there'll be plenty of time for talking later. I'll come by for you at six-thirty, all right?"

"All right," she muttered, managing a weak smile.

By the time Evan arrived to pick her up that evening, Jessica was determined to have her say—after the game, she decided, when they were afforded some privacy.

Evan was determined, as well, only his determination was to lay on the charm. Their seats were situated directly behind home plate and their view was excellent.

They downed steaming hot dogs, salty peanuts and a glass of draft beer each. Evan was more relaxed than she'd seen him in a long while, cheering on his team and shouting at the umpire. When the Red Sox scored a home run, he placed his fingers in his mouth and let loose with a piercing whistle. In all the years she'd spied on Evan and his brother, she couldn't remember him once whistling like that.

"My mother would've had my hide," he explained when she asked. "Whistling isn't proper behavior," he said, sounding so much like Lois Dryden that Jessica laughed.

"When did that ever stop you?" she teased.

"I found that my yen to whistle was the one thing Dad wouldn't tolerate, either," Evan said, as though cheated out of a normal childhood.

Jessica was amazed. She'd assumed that Evan, who'd always been the fair-haired boy, had gotten away with everything.

In the seventh-inning stretch, Evan reached for her hand and squeezed her fingers. She'd always liked Evan and found it impossible to be irritated with him for any length of time. This was his gift, Jessica realized, what his father had referred to during their talk at the fund-raising picnic. Evan was a born leader. People had always been drawn to him. He'd always been accepted, admired and highly regarded. When uncomfortable situations arose, they viewed him as a problem solver.

Suddenly Jessica felt a change in him. He let her hand slip from his grasp. He stiffened and went utterly still. He gasped, and then seemed to stop breathing altogether.

"Evan?"

His smile was decidedly forced. At that moment the crowd roared and fans got to their feet. Jessica hadn't a clue what had happened in the play. Her eyes and mind were on Evan.

"What's wrong?" she asked when the noise died down.

"Nothing." He attempted to convince her with a smile, but failed. Something was very wrong, indeed, and she was determined to find out what.

"Come on," she said, standing and not waiting for him. "We're leaving."

"Jessica, no, it's all right. I'm fine."

"You're not, and don't even try to tell me otherwise, because I know better."

"It's nothing," he said once more, defensively.

She ignored him, gathered her things and left the box. He had no alternative but to follow her.

"Has anyone ever told you what a stubborn woman you are?" he muttered, racing after her. Their steps echoed against the concrete steps as they made their way out of the stadium. Every now and again they could hear shouts and cheers coming from inside. A couple of times Evan glanced regretfully over his shoulder.

"All right, tell me what happened to you in there," Jessica demanded, as they neared the parking lot.

"It was nothing."

"If you say 'nothing' again, I'm going to scream. Now, who'd you see?" But she already knew the answer. Only one person would have evoked such a pain-filled response in Evan, and that was the woman he'd loved and lost.

"What makes you think I saw anyone?" Evan tossed right back at her, irritated now and not bothering to disguise it.

"Was it Mary Jo?"

He stopped so abruptly she'd taken half a dozen steps before she realized he wasn't at her side.

"Who told you about Mary Jo?" His voice was hoarse.

"No one yet, but you're about to."

"Sorry, Jess, but—"

"Now listen here, Evan Dryden, you need to get this off your chest once and for all. You've nursed the pain she caused you long enough. It's time to let it go. Past time!" Jessica tucked her arm in the crook of his elbow as they wove their way toward his car.

He was silent, his mood dark and brooding by the time they arrived at Jessica's apartment. She wasn't sure if she was helping matters by insisting he tell her about this woman he'd once loved. She feared her insistence might well rip open a half-healed wound, but she also knew he couldn't hold this inside any longer.

Jessica led the way into her kitchen, turned on the light and brewed a pot of coffee. Evan sat down, but grew restless almost immediately and stood, prowling about her small apartment.

Soon Jessica was sitting in her favorite chair, watching Evan pace. She didn't pressure him to talk, didn't try to prompt him. When he was ready, he'd tell her what she wanted to know.

"We met by accident," he said, his voice low and intense, "although I've wondered since if it really was."

"You mean you think she arranged it?"

Evan's eyes widened with surprise. "No...not that. I was thinking that there's little in life that really *is* an accident."

"I see," Jessica murmured.

"I was at the beach with a few friends of mine. We'd played

volleyball and had a few beers and were enjoying ourselves—taking a real break from the grind of the office. We soaked up sunshine and laughter and got rid of a lot of pent-up energy.''

He stopped moving and turned to face her. ''Most of my friends had left and I was winding down by taking a walk along the beach, and that's when I met Mary Jo. She was walking her dog and good old Fighto—bad pun, eh?—anyhow, he got loose. She was chasing him down the beach and, being the heroic kind of guy I am, I caught the leash for her. She stopped to thank me and we got to talking. She's small and pretty with big brown eyes that... Well, none of that matters now.''

''You liked her right away?''

Evan nodded. ''There was a freshness about her, an enthusiasm that bubbled over. I knew immediately that I wanted to know her better, so I asked her out to dinner. It threw me for a loop when she refused.''

That must have been something of a novelty, Jessica mused. ''Did she give you a reason?''

''Several, as a matter of fact, but I was able to talk her out of her objections. She had the most marvelous laugh, and I found myself saying the most ridiculous things, just so I could hear it. Being with Mary Jo made me want to laugh myself. It was the most exhilarating day I'd had in years.''

''She did go out with you, though?''

''Not exactly.'' Caught in the memories, Evan didn't seem inclined to say anything more for a minute. Jessica watched silently as the emotions crossed his face. First she saw his eyes light up with the recollection, followed by a pain so deep she yearned to reach out and take his hand. The small movements of his mouth were telling, too. It quivered when he first mentioned meeting Mary Jo, as if that first conversation served to amuse him still. But a moment later, the corners sank as his pain took hold. Jessica longed to reassure him, but knew Evan wouldn't have appreciated it.

''As it happened,'' Evan continued at last, his tone wistful, ''I spent the rest of the day and nearly all of the night with Mary Jo. We built a fire on the beach and talked until morning.

''We started dating regularly after that. I found her refreshing and fun. Our lives were so different. Mary Jo was the youngest of a family of six. She's the only girl. I met her family one Sunday, and her mother insisted I stay for dinner. I'd never seen such a spread in all my life. There were kids running all over the place. Several of Mary Jo's sisters-in-law were pregnant at the time, as well. I've never known such a family, the joking and the teasing and fun. Don't get me wrong, I've got a great family myself, but Mary Jo's is different. I really loved being with them.''

"I'm sure they felt the same way about you."

He shrugged, his look doubtful. "I'd like to think so."

"What happened next?" Jessica prompted when he didn't immediately continue. She was eager now for the details.

"I knew I was going to fall in love with her that first day on the beach," he said, his voice so low it was a strain to distinguish the words. "Love isn't something I take lightly, but it hit me then—and I knew."

"I know what you mean," Jessica offered. She felt the same way about Damian.

"After I met her parents, I realized how much I wanted to marry her, how much I wanted us to have five or six children of our own. The Summerhills' home was full of love and I wanted that kind of happy free environment for my own children someday."

"Mary Jo sounds like a very special woman," Jessica said quietly.

"She is," Evan whispered softly. "Special enough to marry."

"You asked her to be your wife, didn't you?"

He gave an odd smile, one that was a blend of amusement and pain. "Yes. Afterward I took her to meet my parents. Mary Jo was intimidated by my family's wealth—I realized that from the beginning. Who wouldn't be, seeing Whispering Willows for the first time. My parents had some doubts about our being suited, but once Mom and Dad met Mary Jo, they changed their minds."

"I don't remember hearing about the engagement," Jessica said.

"I wanted to give her a diamond, but she preferred a pearl ring, instead. She'd recently completed her student teaching and been hired as a first-grade teacher. She wanted to delay making a formal announcement until she'd settled in to her job, but more importantly until after her parents' fortieth wedding anniversary celebration that October.

"I wasn't keen on waiting," Evan confessed, "but I agreed, because, well, because I was willing to do whatever Mary Jo wanted." He paused and drew a deep breath, holding it a moment as if he dreaded continuing. "I first suspected something was wrong the first part of October. She kept finding excuses why we couldn't see one another. In the beginning I accepted them—I was busy myself—and although I missed her, I didn't press the issue. I didn't like it, mind you, but I understood how busy she was with school and her family obligations. A couple of times I showed up at her parents' house. They seemed glad to see me, and her mother obviously assumed I was starving and made me stay for dinner." He smiled.

"They sound like wonderful people."

Jessica didn't think Evan heard her. "When Mary Jo mailed me back the ring, I was stunned. I've had some surprises in my life, both pleasant and unpleasant, but none that have shocked me more."

Jessica felt angry at Mary Jo for not having the courage to confront Evan face-to-face. If she wanted to break the engagement, even an informal one, then the least she could have done was have the consideration to tell him in person. Mailing Evan the ring was cowardly and cruel.

"So," Evan continued, "I drove over to her apartment in a fury."

"You had every right to be furious."

He shook his head. "I should have waited until I'd cooled down. I wish with everything in me that I had."

Life was filled with regrets, Jessica thought. She'd been carrying around a fair share of her own, especially in the past few weeks.

"When I confronted her, Mary Jo told me there was someone else," he whispered. "I didn't believe her at first. I refused to entertain the thought that a woman as fundamentally honest as Mary Jo would see another man behind my back. It didn't tally in my mind—but I was wrong." His voice dwindled to a whisper. "Apparently they met at the school where she teaches. He's a teacher, too. The agony of being engaged to me and in love with someone else must have torn her apart.''

Jessica dropped her gaze for fear he would read what was in her eyes. She wasn't engaged to Evan, but she continued to see him when she was in love with Damian. While Evan spoke, Jessica had been casting mental stones at Mary Jo, when she was guilty of essentially the same thing.

''You saw her tonight at the ball game?'' Jessica gently prodded.

Evan nodded. ''She was with him…at least I assume it was him.'' The pain was back in his eyes, and Jessica felt the urge to weep. For Evan, yes, but for herself, as well. What a couple they made, each in love with someone else, fighting hard to do the right thing and making themselves miserable in the process.

''Mary Jo's a special woman,'' Evan whispered. ''The man who marries her is a lucky man…'' He paused again, and that odd smile, the one of blended joy and pain returned. ''She'll be a wonderful wife and mother.''

''Under the circumstances, that's a generous thing to say.''

''You don't know Mary Jo, or you'd think the same thing yourself. In the months since we parted, I've come to realize that my ego played a substantial role in all this. Mary Jo was the first woman to break off a relationship with me.'' He smiled as he said it, as though it had served him right after all these years. ''I guess I'd gotten a bit cocky.''

''We're all guilty of that in one form or another,'' she offered.

He looked at Jessica then, and his gaze sobered. ''I've ruined our evening, haven't I?''

''No,'' she told him, hoping he heard the sincerity in her voice. She understood how passionately Evan had loved the woman, and how deeply the pain of their parting affected him still.

More than ever, after hearing Evan talk about losing the woman he loved, Jessica knew she couldn't allow the same thing to happen to her. She couldn't continue to mislead Evan by letting him believe their relationship would evolve into something it was never meant to be.

A week passed. Every time she was with Evan he told her more about his relationship with Mary Jo. She soon realized that every invitation to dinner or a show was an excuse to talk. Every outing was followed by coffee and a long heart-to-heart. It was as though a floodgate had opened inside him, and the need to release the pent-up emotion was too strong to ignore.

They were friends, nothing more, and Jessica was comfortable with their relationship. With their frequent talks, she was able to open up to him, as well, in little ways.

"Have you ever been in love, Jessica?" he asked her unexpectedly one night.

"I think so," she said hesitantly as they strolled through Boston Common. "Yes," she amended quickly. "And it isn't what you're thinking."

"Oh?"

"It's not you, so don't get a big head." She didn't realize until she spoke how insulting she sounded, and she immediately sought his pardon.

Evan laughed off her apology.

The night was lovely. The stars were like twinkling rows of sequins that hung so close they seemed draped over the upper limbs of the trees.

"You know when it's love, don't you?" he asked after a few moments.

"Oh, yes," she whispered.

"Does this mystery man feel the same way about you?"

"I...I don't know. I like to think so." Although there were more signs to the contrary.

For Damian continued to avoid her. Other than that brief moment when he'd come into her office, she hadn't talked to him once.

He arrived at the office promptly at eight each morning and left at five. She guessed that his involvement with his father's campaign dictated his hours. That meant if she wanted to see him, it had to be during working hours. With his hectic schedule it was easier getting an audience with the pope. Jessica didn't know how Damian managed to cram all he did into a single workday. She'd tried to talk to him, but hadn't found the opportunity when there weren't other people around.

Jessica was fast losing her patience. And then, just when she was about to throw her hands in the air and scream with frustration, it happened. Quite by accident, and where she'd least expected it.

Whispering Willows. His family's home.

Evan had learned from Jessica's mother that she'd played on her college tennis team; he'd been intrigued, and challenged her to a game. It had sounded like an entertaining way to spend a Saturday afternoon, and she'd agreed. Since he'd neglected to schedule time on the courts at the country club, they drove to his parents' home to play.

They smacked the ball back and forth for a solid hour, and Evan soundly defeated her. Not that his athletic ability surprised her, but in her effort to impress him she strained her knee. It wasn't anything serious, but Evan insisted they stop playing.

They made their way to the house, laughing and in a good mood, her knee long forgotten, to discover Evan's mother anxiously attempting to start her car, without success. She needed to be at campaign headquarters within the hour and was fretting about what she should do.

"Not to worry, Mom," Evan said, affectionately kissing his mother's cheek. "I'll drive you."

"Nonsense," Lois protested when she viewed Evan's two-seater sports car.

"Didn't you tell me you gave Richmond the day off?" Evan said, opening his car door. "No more excuses, Mom."

"But what about Jessica?"

"I'm perfectly capable of entertaining myself," Jessica assured her. She stood in the driveway until the car had disappeared, then wandered back into the house, wiping the perspiration from her brow with the back of her forearm. She walked into the kitchen and, finding a cold soda in the refrigerator, helped herself.

She was humming a show tune when the kitchen door swung open. "Mother, what in blazes are you doing here? You're supposed to be at—" Damian stopped when he saw her. "Jessica," he said, his surprise evident.

"Your mother's car wouldn't start, so Evan drove her over to campaign headquarters,'' she explained. Her face was red with exertion, and her hair fell in damp tendrils about her face.

"Evan drove her.'' Already Damian was physically withdrawing from her. "I'd better go see what's wrong with Mom's car.''

"Damian...'' Cathy's suggestion about faking an injury came into her mind like a stone from a slingshot. She was injured—well, only slightly—but there was no better time than the present to make use of it.

She concentrated her efforts on her right foot and limped toward him. She hated resorting to such an underhanded method but she was desperate to talk to him. Surely he'd forgive her once he learned the truth.

His gaze went to her knee, his concern immediate. She was wearing a white top and a short tennis skirt. "You hurt yourself,'' he said, moving toward her. The kitchen door swung in his wake.

"I'm fine,'' she whispered.

"Sit down,'' he ordered, his voice none too tender. "Does Evan know about this?''

"Yes, but it's not all that bad,'' she mumbled. He pulled out a kitchen chair and eased her into it. His hands at her shoulders were gentle but firm. She closed her eyes at his touch. Lord, how she'd missed him! For days she'd waited for the opportunity to be alone with Damian, and she wasn't about to waste it now.

"We need to talk,'' she said. "Listen, I—''

"We'll talk after I've seen to your knee. What in God's name possessed my brother to leave you like this?''

"Damian, please listen to me.''

"Later.'' He was busy at work packing ice into a bag.

She was irritated now and leapt off the chair. "My knee will be fine. I strained a muscle or something. It's no big deal.''

"You'd better have a doctor check it out,'' he insisted, positioning her back in the chair, raising her leg and resting it against the seat of a second chair, then balancing the ice pack on the knee.

"I need to talk to you about Evan and me,'' she said, refusing to be put off any longer. "I'm not in love with Evan and he doesn't love me. We're friends, nothing more. He's in love with Mary Jo and I'm in love with—''

"Keep that ice pack on your leg for a good twenty minutes, understand?"

Infuriated, Jessica rose to her feet and tossed the ice pack into the sink. "You're going to listen to me, Damian, if it kills me! I realize I'm making a mess of this. I should never have used my knee to keep you here, but I was desperate."

"Did you or did you not twist your knee?" he demanded.

"Yes, a little, but it's nothing. I want to talk about the two of us. About you and me."

"Jessica," he said with ill-concealed impatience. "You're dating my brother."

"Your brother and I are *friends,* nothing more. How many times do I have to say it?"

"There's a change in Evan," Damian insisted heatedly. "Do you think I haven't noticed? For the first time in months, he's his old self. My brother's back again and it's all due to you."

"Maybe, Damian, but not in the way you think."

"It doesn't matter what I think," Damian said angrily. "You're dating my brother, so there can't be a you and me. Do you understand?"

"No!" she cried. "No, I don't!"

"It has to be this way, Jessica."

"But why?" Hot tears blurred her vision.

He didn't answer her for several time-shattering seconds. "That's just the way it is."

"Is...is that the way you want it?" Swallowing became impossible. She knotted her hands into fists at her sides.

"Yes," he said after a moment, the longest moment of her life. "That's the way I want it."

Jessica turned away from him, grateful to the very depths of her soul that she hadn't declared her undying love for him. This humiliation was bad enough.

"Jessica." Her name was a plea on his lips.

She hung her head, knowing he would abandon her the way he always did—but he didn't. Instead, his arms came around her and turned her to face him. His touch was as if he had to experience holding her, as if the feel of her was the one thread keeping his sanity intact. And then his mouth came down on hers.

This kiss was hungry and hard, unlike the kisses they'd shared previously. Jessica clung to him, mindful only of this man and the sheer joy she experienced in his arms. She caressed his face with wondering fingers as the intensity of their need increased. He angled her head to one side for a series of short nibbling kisses down her cheek, her throat.

"No more," he moaned, then jerked his head away. But she refused to release him, hugging him around the neck and burying her face in his shoulder. "Jessica, please." When he tugged her hands free, she realized he was shaking as badly as she was. His hands closed around hers and his head fell forward.

The sound of the front door closing echoed like a clap of thunder. Damian moved away from her and had his back to her when Evan strolled into the kitchen, whistling. He stopped when he saw Damian.

"Damian, hello. I'm glad to see you kept my best girl company."

With something less than a curt nod to his brother, Damian strode out of the kitchen, muttering about seeing to his mother's car.

Jessica thought her heart would break.

Eight

"Thank you," Evan said when he dropped Jessica off at her apartment half an hour later. "By the way, there's a formal dinner with three hundred of my father's closest friends Monday night," he said casually. "I'd like you to attend it with me."

Jessica looked up at Evan, realizing she hadn't heard what he'd said. She hurt too much. Damian didn't love her, didn't want her. She'd all but blurted out her love for him, and he'd rejected her, insisted Evan needed her, and then walked away. As he always did.

"Jessica, are you all right?"

"I'm fine." How easily the lie came, even though she was falling apart on the inside.

"I was asking you about the dinner party."

She blinked. Dinner party?

"Monday night," he said slowly, waving a hand in front of her face. "You'd better tell me what's wrong."

"Would it be all right if I go in now?" she asked, instead. She wasn't in the mood to explain anything, least of all what had happened between her and Damian.

"Of course."

Evan insisted on escorting her into her apartment. He placed her tennis racket in the hall closet and stepped into her kitchen to get her a glass of ice water.

Jessica sat at the table and smiled her appreciation. "I'm fine," she said, and this time it was a little less of a lie. Yes, she hurt but it was a clean cut, deep and swift. She knew now what she'd suspected all along. Damian didn't want her, didn't love her.

"Thank you, Jess," Evan said again, and although his words were casual, Jessica sensed a deeper meaning.

"For letting you whop me in tennis?" she asked, knowing it was much more than that.

The smile faded from his eyes. "For that, too, but mostly for listening to me these last few days. Talking about Mary Jo has helped clear my head. It's shown me what went wrong between us and helped me realize how much I still love her." This was issued with a pain-filled sigh.

"That isn't a sin, Evan." Any more than her loving Damian was a sin.

"Talking is what's helped me. Perhaps you should take note and tell me what's troubling you. You can't fool me—those are tears glistening in your eyes."

Instinctively she lowered her gaze, focusing her attention on the water glass. "I...I'm not ready to talk just yet. Don't be upset with me. I have to sort through my own feelings first."

His hand covered hers. "I understand. You will attend the dinner party with me, won't you?"

Jessica's first inclination was to refuse. Instead, she nodded. "All right." Sitting home feeling sorry for herself would solve nothing. Nor would she give Damian the satisfaction. From here on out, she was going to kick up her heels and enjoy life. Even if it killed her, and that was what it felt like just now.

"Damian will be there," Evan said as if he expected her to comment.

She nodded. After this afternoon it made no difference.

"He'll be bringing someone, too," Evan added. "You won't mind if we share a table, will you?"

"I won't mind in the least," Jessica said brightly. "The more the merrier."

"I thought we'd look through your wardrobe before dinner," Cathy said as she entered Jessica's apartment. Jessica realized her mistake the moment she'd mentioned the dinner party to her friend. From that point on, Cathy had insisted she choose the dress.

"I've managed to dress myself without a problem for several years now," Jessica felt obliged to say.

Cathy was sorting through the dresses in her closet, shuffling them from one side to another as if this was a mission of great importance. She paused and tapped her foot impatiently. "I can't tell you how disappointed I am in Damian. You're sure you didn't misunderstand him?" She sounded as though the fault was Jessica's.

"There was no misunderstanding," Jessica said firmly, wishing she'd never mentioned the incident to Cathy. She wouldn't have except that her friend had been on virtually every phase of this...this mess. "He doesn't want anything to do with me. He couldn't have made it any plainer."

"I don't believe it. There's something very wrong here, and it's up to you to figure out what it is."

"I know what it is," Jessica protested. It wasn't necessary to dissect the problem when the answer was so simple. If Damian *did* care for her, he would have found a way to make things right. He didn't, and he hadn't.

"You're coming to my opening night, aren't you?" Cathy asked as she continued to examine the contents of Jessica's closet.

"I wouldn't miss it for the world." Jessica was proud of Cathy's big career break. She'd gotten the plum role of Adelaide, after all, in the local production of *Guys and Dolls*. Jessica also thought Cathy was sweet on the director, David Carson. Her friend had mentioned his name several times in passing, and Jessica thought there'd been a small catch in her voice each time.

"I think I'll invite Damian to my opening," Cathy suggested nonchalantly. "After all, I have met him."

Jessica wasn't likely to forget. Cathy's eyes shifted in her direction. "You don't have anything to say."

"Do what you want, Cathy."

Cathy's laugh was short and telling. "You can't fool me, Jess, I know you too well. I don't know what's wrong with Damian, but trust me, he'll soon come around."

"I sincerely doubt it." Jessica hated to be so pessimistic, but she couldn't stop herself.

Cathy took three dresses from the closet and laid them across her friend's bed. Her hands on her hips, she circled the bed, then returned two of the dresses to the closet.

Jessica studied Cathy's selection. It was a full-length black dress, sleek and shiny with silver highlights that sparkled in the overhead light.

"Try it on," Cathy insisted.

Mumbling her discontent, Jessica slipped out of her clothes and into the dress, lifting her hair so Cathy could close the zipper properly. Then she regarded herself in the full-length mirror. Her shoulders drooped as she released a slow, defeated sigh.

"I look like Natasha from the Rocky and Bullwinkle cartoon show," she muttered.

"Nonsense," Cathy said. "The dress is perfect."

"For consorting with spies maybe," Jessica muttered. But then again, maybe it *was* right. If she was destined to sit at the same table as Damian and his date, she wanted to be darn sure he noticed her—and knew what he was missing.

Evan arrived to pick her up for the dinner party five minutes ahead of schedule, just as Jessica was putting the finishing touches to her makeup. "Beautiful," he said, taking both her hands in his. "You're absolutely beautiful."

His appreciation lent Jessica confidence—until they reached the table where Damian and his date were sitting. The woman was tall, regal, blond and gorgeous. Every woman's basic nightmare. So much for the best-laid plans.

"Nadine Powell," Damian said. "My brother, Evan, and Jessica Kellerman."

Jessica's gaze moved to Damian, and she was gratified to discover he was staring at her the way a child gazes into a store window at Christmastime. Cathy had been right—the dress was perfect. Damian abruptly looked away as if angry with himself for being so obvious.

"Nadine," Evan said, taking the other woman's hand and holding it several moments longer than necessary.

Dinner was a drawn-out affair, with speeches from several long-winded politicians. Jessica lost count of the number of speakers and the number of courses served, but they seemed to be running neck and neck. The speeches made dinner conversation almost impossible, but Jessica did manage to learn that Nadine was a longtime friend of Damian's. Friends and nothing more, Nadine went on to explain, reading the situation with amazing accuracy. As for Damian, well, he pretended she wasn't there. He didn't say one word to her the entire meal.

When the dessert dishes were removed, a ten-piece orchestra began to play on a low stage behind the polished oak dance floor.

"You game?" Evan asked, holding out his hand to Jessica. The music was from the forties, the big-band sound she particularly loved. Evan was tapping his foot and swaying his shoulders.

Jessica declined. She wasn't keen on being one of the first ones on the floor. "I think I'd prefer to sit out a few of the numbers, if you don't mind."

"Nonsense. I won't take no for an answer." Evan all but pulled her out of her chair. He led her onto the dance floor, and although the number was fast, he brought her into his arms and held her close.

"Evan," she hissed, acutely aware of the impression they were creating. It looked as if they were madly in love and couldn't bear to be separated.

"Shh," he whispered close to her ear.

"What's wrong with you?"

"Me?" he asked, then threw back his head and laughed as if she'd said something uproariously funny.

"Nothing. I'm having a good time, that's all."

"At my expense," she told him in an angry whisper. "Soon everyone will be talking about us."

"Let them."

"Something is very wrong," Jessica insisted.

He laughed again. "Not exactly, but soon everything should be just right."

Jessica hadn't a clue what he meant, but she wasn't going to continue with this farce any longer than necessary. As soon as the number finished, she broke away from him and returned to their table.

"Jessica's knee is bothering her," Evan explained, and before she realized what was happening, Evan had asked Nadine to dance and the pair stood and left the table. Damian looked unnerved.

"Well," Jessica said dryly, "I guess you can't keep a good man down."

Damian frowned darkly. "He might have asked someone other than my date." His hand closed around his water glass, and he seemed intent on studying the dancing couples. Intent on not making conversation with her, Jessica thought, which was fine. Just fine. Everything had already been said as far as she could see, and apparently Damian felt the same way.

"How's your knee?" Damian asked unexpectedly.

"It's okay. Evan was using it as an excuse to dance with Nadine."

The music circled them in a warm halo of melody. Soon Jessica was tapping her foot, wishing she hadn't been so quick to insist she leave the dance floor.

"Come on," Damian said with a decided lack of enthusiasm. He stood and offered her his hand.

Stunned, Jessica looked up at him.

"There's nothing worse than sitting with a woman who obviously wants to dance."

"I..." She intended to tell him there was nothing worse than dancing with someone who obviously didn't want to be her partner. But before she could speak, he'd taken her hand. He was muttering something under his breath, which she couldn't quite make out. She did hear Evan's name, and she guessed he wasn't pleased with his brother.

Jessica wanted to kick Evan for leaving her alone with Damian. The orchestra had been playing fast-paced songs, but when Damian and Jessica moved onto the floor, the band began a slow dreamy number. The lights lowered and Jessica groaned inwardly.

"Let's sit this one out," she suggested.

"Not on your life," Damian said, easing her into his arms. She didn't understand why he felt obliged to dance with her. He held her stiffly in his arms as though afraid to bring her close. His back was rigid and he stared straight ahead.

"Relax," he whispered impatiently. "I won't bite."

"Me?" she said. "I might as well be waltzing with a manne-quin."

"Okay, let's both make an effort."

Jessica hadn't realized she was so tense. Determined to do as he suggested, she closed her eyes and released a slow sigh. She felt the tension ease from Damian, and when she opened her eyes he'd brought her closer, close enough for her to rest her temple against the side of his jaw. The solace she found, as their bodies swayed gently to the rhythm, was worth every minute she'd waited to feel his arms around her.

This was where she belonged, Jessica mused sadly, where she'd always belonged. Surely Damian felt it too. Why else would he be holding her as if she was the most precious thing in his world? Why else would his lips be moving against her hair as if he longed to kiss her.

Neither spoke, she realized, because they feared words would destroy the moment. She clung to him even when the music stopped, not wanting this blissful time to end.

"We should get back to the table," Damian said, and the reluc-tance she heard in his voice gave her hope.

"I don't see Evan or Nadine. Do you want to dance one more number?" she asked.

He didn't answer her for a long moment, and then said gruffly, "Yes."

"I do, too."

"Jessica, listen…"

She chanced raising her face and looking at him, her eyes filled with a longing so great she couldn't hide it. Pressing her finger over his mouth, she smiled. "Please, Damian, not now."

He briefly closed his eyes, sighed and nodded.

Jessica lost track of time. She knew they danced far longer than they should have, for more numbers than she could count. Every once in a while she glanced at their table, but neither Nadine or Evan were in sight.

It wasn't until the music sped up again, that he revealed any signs of regret. She knew something was wrong the minute he eased her from his arms. His face hardened. She looked up at him and blinked, not understanding.

"I'll have my brother's hide for this," Damian muttered.

"For what?" she asked softly.

A muscle in his jaw jerked as he reined in his temper, but that was the only answer she got.

They left the dance floor and sat like strangers at the table. Jessica couldn't bear it any longer. She stood, excused herself and moved from table to table to greet several old family friends. She returned only when she saw that Evan had joined his brother. Nadine was nowhere in sight. The two brothers seemed to be having a rapid intense exchange of words, but when she approached, Damian clamped his mouth closed and looked the other way.

"I've neglected you," Evan said contritely, claiming her hand between both of his. "I'm sorry, Jessica. Can you forgive me?"

"Of course." What else could she do? Demand that he immediately take her home? That would have been silly. Especially as she wasn't interested in him as anything other than a friend. Besides, his neglect had given her all that time with Damian.

A breathless and laughing Nadine returned to the table a few moments later, and the four of them ordered drinks. The waitress had just brought their order when Walter and Lois Dryden approached their table.

"I hope you four are enjoying yourselves."

Evan said that they certainly had been.

Lois smiled benevolently down on Jessica, then gently placed her hands on Jessica's shoulders, leaning forward so that their heads were close together. "We owe you so much," she said, kissing her cheek.

"Nonsense." The words embarrassed her.

"It's true. Tell her, Walter," Lois insisted. "We were about to despair over what was happening with Evan, and that all changed the minute you started working for the firm."

"Mother..." Evan didn't seem to appreciate this, either.

"It's true. You have no idea how pleased Joyce and I are that the two of you are seeing so much of each other," Lois continued.

"I have to agree with your mother," Walter said in his deep, vibrant voice. "You're a good man, Evan, with a bright future. It was a damn shame to watch you waste your life over a woman you couldn't have. It's much better now that you're seeing Jessica."

A stilted uncomfortable silence followed his father's praise. Within a few minutes of the elder Drydens' visit to their table, Damian made an excuse, and he and Nadine got up and left. After that, Evan didn't seem too keen to stay, either. As for Jessica, she was more than happy to get home. Enough was enough.

She lay awake most of the night thinking, and by daybreak, she'd made her decision. With purpose driving her steps, Jessica walked into the office the next morning, her eyes burning from lack of sleep.

"I need to see Mr. Dryden for a moment," she told Damian's secretary.

The woman, doubtless noting the determination in Jessica's voice, reached instantly for the intercom and announced her.

Jessica strode into Damian's office and stood before him. He was sitting behind his desk reading a file. He glanced up, his expression, as always, inscrutable. "What can I do for you, Jessica?"

Her heart pounding, she said flatly, "I'm resigning from my position with this firm, effective immediately." It was an impulsive thing to do, Jessica realized, considering how difficult it was these days to find a job. But her sanity was more important. She'd do temporary work if she had to. Or work in another field.

If Damian was surprised by her announcement, he didn't reveal it. He leaned back in his chair, calm and composed. "This is rather sudden, isn't it?"

"Yes…but it's necessary." She avoided eye contact by studying the painting on the wall behind him. It was a seascape with the ocean crashing against the jagged edge of a protruding rock. A bird was perched on the uppermost point of the rock, undisturbed by the raging sea. Jessica wished she could be more like that bird.

"Does Evan know?"

"Not yet," she replied. "Since you were the one to hire me, I felt obligated to tell you first."

He paused as if gathering his thoughts. "If you could work out your two-week notice, I'd appreciate it."

Jessica wasn't sure what she'd expected. Nothing, she'd told herself, but she realized now that wasn't true. In the deepest part of her, she was praying Damian would ask her to reconsider, that he'd make at least one attempt to change her mind. Perhaps a raise or some other inducement. Instead, he calmly accepted her resignation as if he was almost pleased to see her go.

That hurt. She held the pain to herself for as long as she could, before turning and walking toward the door.

"Jessica."

She stopped, but didn't turn around.

"You've been a valuable asset to this firm, and we'll miss you."

That was all he was willing to offer. It was damn little.

"Thank you," she whispered, then walked out the door.

She was trembling by the time she sat down at her own desk. After taking a moment to compose herself, she reached for the phone and dialed Cathy's number.

"You did *what?*" her friend cried.

Jessica had never used the office phone for personal calls before, but she made this day the exception. "You heard me. I quit."

"But why?"

"It's a long story," she murmured, "but suffice to say, I'm tired of this whole ridiculous charade."

"Damian loves you."

"No," she whispered, "he doesn't." She'd been swayed by Cathy's comments and her own foolish heart, because she so desperately wanted to believe it was true.

"Jessica, Jessica, Jessica," Cathy said in an impatient singsong, "don't be so hasty."

It was either leave the firm or lose her sanity, Jessica mused. It'd been a mistake to contact Cathy; her friend simply didn't understand.

"What did Evan say?"

"He doesn't know yet," she admitted reluctantly. Not that it would make any difference. No argument Evan offered could convince her to change her mind.

"Keep me informed, will you? Following what's going on in your life is more interesting than my soap operas."

Mrs. Sterling came into the office and stared at Jessica, looking as if she were about to burst into tears. "You're leaving!"

This office had an information network the CIA would envy. Jessica didn't bother to ask where Evan's secretary had heard the news; it didn't matter.

"But you can't go now, not when Mr. Dryden's back to his old self."

"I apologize for leaving you in the lurch."

"You won't reconsider?"

Jessica shook her head.

"Personally," said Mrs. Sterling, "I think it makes for bad politics when men and women from the same office date one another. These things have a way of turning sour."

"What does?" Evan asked, stepping into the room, carrying a leather briefcase and looking very much the professional he was. He paused at his secretary's desk and reached for his mail.

"Jessica's resigned," Mrs. Sterling said baldly.

Evan dropped the mail and turned to stare at Jessica. His mouth fell open with disbelief. "Is it true?"

She nodded. Until she saw the look of dismay on his face, she hadn't believed he held any real affection for her.

"Come into my office," he commanded, leading the way and clearly expecting her to follow. When she was inside, he closed the door.

"What's this all about?" he demanded.

To the best of her memory, Jessica had never seen this side of Evan. He looked and acted like Damian. "It's time I moved on," she said weakly, not knowing exactly how much to say, if anything, about the real reason.

"After less than two months?"

She crossed her arms and shrugged.

"Are the hours too long?"

"No."

"We're not paying you enough?"

"I'm receiving an adequate salary," she returned. She didn't like the way he was putting her on the defensive, and she stiffened her resolve. There was a side of her he hadn't seen, either—her stubborn side.

"There must be a reason you find it so repugnant to work for me."

"I never said I found it repugnant to work for you." She dropped her hands and formed tight fists at her sides. Evan was acting every inch the attorney.

"So it's the firm you don't like. Have we done something to offend you?"

"No!" she cried, hating this interrogation. Evan's reaction was certainly the opposite of Damian's. Evan was clearly upset at the idea of losing her.

"Then why? You owe me an explanation," he insisted.

"I don't feel I do..." She hesitated, her stomach in knots.

"Is it something I've done?" His voice was gentler now, as if he was trying to soothe her, to gain her confidence.

"No," she assured him. "You've been wonderful...a good friend. I'll treasure the times we've had together, Evan, but you don't love me and I don't love you. It seems to me that we should appreciate what we do share and not try to make something of it that isn't there." Or allow their parents to do so, either, she added mentally.

He looked puzzled. "That's no reason to quit working for the firm."

"Perhaps not, but it's the right thing for me. Damian asked me to work out my two-week notice, which I'll gladly do, but I'm not going to change my mind."

"All right," he agreed reluctantly. "In the meantime, you don't mind if we continue to see one another, do you?"

"I'm...not sure it would be wise."

Evan jerked back his head as though her answer amazed him. "You aren't serious, are you?"

"Yes, Evan, I am. I enjoy your company and consider you a friend, but..."

"What about coffee to talk over old times?"

"Perhaps."

Evan grinned then, that devilishly handsome grin guaranteed to stir the heart of any woman. "I'm not letting you back out of our sailing date, though. I've been counting on that. You aren't going to let me down, are you?"

"No, I won't let you down." Nevertheless, Jessica's heart sank as she remembered her promise to go out with Evan on his sailboat in three weeks' time. He'd made the date *before* the formal dinner event. *Before* she'd known she wanted out of the Drydens' sphere.

He beamed her a wide smile.

Jessica stayed late that night, wanting to clear her desk before she headed back to her apartment. Undaunted by her stated reluctance to continue seeing him socially, Evan had asked her to dinner, and Jessica had declined. Besides, she'd been out late the night before, hadn't slept well and was anxious to finish up at the office and head back to her apartment.

She was leaving just as Damian came out of his office.

"Good night," she said cordially, moving down the corridor to wait for the elevator. Damian joined her there.

The doors opened and they stepped inside together. They stood like strangers while the elevator made its descent. Jessica stared at the numbers above the door as they lighted up one by one. Only a week earlier, she would have been thrilled to have these few seconds alone with Damian, and now she would have given anything to avoid him. Being this close to him physically and so far apart emotionally was agony in its purest form.

The elevator doors silently slid open, and Jessica stepped into the lobby, glad to make her escape. Damian would go about his life, and she would go about hers.

"Jessica." Damian sounded impatient, but she didn't know if it was with her or himself. "Are you taking the subway?"

"Yes, it's right around the corner." She began to move away.

"I'll give you a ride home."

"No, thank you."

"I insist," Damian said in steel tones. "It's time we talked."

If Jessica had thought her heart was beating hard that morning when she entered his office, it didn't compare with the way it thundered against her ribs now.

Silently he led her into the parking garage to his car. He unlocked the passenger-side door and held it open for her, then went around to the driver's side and climbed in. As he inserted the key into the ignition, he asked, "Have you spoken to Evan about your resignation?"

"Yes."

"What did he have to say?"

She gestured weakly with her hands. "He asked me to reconsider."

"Have you?"

"No. I'll work out my two-week notice, since you asked me to, but my decision stands."

Damian's hands tightened around the steering wheel. "Why, Jessica?"

"Why should you care, Damian?" she returned, losing patience with him. "This morning, you couldn't wait to be rid of me."

"That's not true," he said sharply.

"I don't think discussing this will solve anything," she said, reaching for the door handle, intent on letting herself out.

The air was electric. "Jessica, stay for a few minutes. Please." His words were soft, without emotion, and yet filled with it.

Jessica hesitated. "All right." She dropped her hand.

"Did you give your notice because of what happened at the dinner?" he asked.

Confused, Jessica turned to study Damian. "Last night?"

"Evan virtually abandoned you. I know your feelings must have been hurt, but—"

"Just a minute," she said, twisting in her seat to look at him directly. "You don't honestly believe that, do you?"

A puzzled look crowded his features. "Yes. My brother was rude in the extreme to abandon you the way he did."

She was angrier than she could remember being in a long time. When she let things fester inside her this way, her anger took the form of hiccups when she released it.

"Do you think *hic* I'm so shallow I'd quit *hic* my job in a fit of *hic* jealousy? Is that *hic* what you're saying, Damian?"

He blinked when she was finished, as though he expected more.

Jessica threw open the car door, climbed out and slammed it. "I *hic* don't think this *hic* conversation is getting us anywhere."

With that she marched away. She thought she heard Damian's car door close, but she didn't bother to look back.

"Jessica!" he called storming into the empty lobby.

She hesitated. The hiccups hadn't subsided, and she was having a hard time breathing properly.

"I'm sorry," he said after a tense moment.

She understood then. He was apologizing for much more than their argument. He was telling her how much he regretted not loving her.

Nine

Other than brief glimpses Jessica didn't see Damian at all during the next two weeks. A new legal assistant, Peter McNichols, was hired, and Jessica helped train the conscientious young man.

On her last day, Damian sent word that he wanted to see her in his office. Mrs. Sterling issued the summons. "I hope you'll change your mind," Evan's secretary said wistfully. "You're an excellent worker and I hate to see you go." She cast a speculative eye toward Evan's closed office door. "I'm sure Mr. Dryden's going to miss you, too."

Evan had made several attempts in the past two weeks to bribe her into staying, but Jessica had stood steadfastly by her decision. Although it had been made impulsively, it was the right thing to do.

Jessica reached for her pad and pen before starting toward Damian's office, although she doubted he expected her to take notes. She was promptly shown in by his secretary.

She found Damian standing at the window, his back to her. His hands were clasped behind him, the pose he assumed when he was thinking or when he was troubled about something. She wondered if he found her departure distressing, then decided if that was the case he'd have said so long before now.

"You wanted to see me?" she asked quietly.

He turned around and offered her a reassuring smile. "Yes, please sit down." He motioned toward the chair, then claimed the seat behind his desk. He reached for an envelope on the corner and handed it to Jessica.

"It's your paycheck," he explained. "I took the liberty of adding a small bonus."

"That wasn't necessary," she said, surprised by the gesture.

"Perhaps not, but I wanted you to know how much the firm appreciated the extra time and effort you put into the Earl Kress case."

"I stayed late because I wanted to."

"I realize that. Now," he said, leaning back in his chair, his posture casual, his eyes curious, "have you found another position yet?"

"No." Working every day had made searching for a job almost impossible. There would be time enough for that later, in the days and weeks to follow.

"I see," he said unemotionally. "If you like, I'd be happy to write you a letter of recommendation."

The offer was generous in light of the fact she'd worked for the firm such a short while.

"I'd appreciate that very much." She'd given considerable thought to the consequences of being out of a job. A letter of recommendation would help.

"There are a number of firms I know who might be interested in obtaining a top-notch legal assistant. I could make a few calls on your behalf."

Damian was being more than generous, she thought. "Thank you. I'd be grateful."

He nodded and she got to her feet. Saying goodbye to Damian was much more difficult than she'd ever expected. When she walked out the door she didn't know how long it'd be before she saw him again. Their families might be close, but Jessica and Damian led very separate lives. It could well be months or even years before they ran into each other. But perhaps that would be for the best. She fidgeted with the yellow notepad. "I want you to know how much I've appreciated working for you and Evan," she said, barely managing to keep her voice steady. "You were willing to give me a chance when all I had was classroom experience."

"You've proved yourself in countless ways since then."

She backed away, taking small steps, until her back was against his door. She felt the wood pressing against her shoulder blades. "Thank you, too," she said, and her voice came out a hoarse whisper, "for everything else."

His brow creased with a frown.

"For the dinners and our time at Cannon Beach," she elaborated. The final words stuck in her throat, and she was sure that if she said what was really in her heart, it would embarrass them both.

His eyes revealed his sadness. "Goodbye, Jessica."

She turned then and opened the door, but before she walked out of his life, before she took that first step, she glanced over her shoulder to look once again, to grab hold of this last memory of him.

Damian was standing there, in the same spot he'd been when she first arrived, gazing out the window, his hands clasped behind his back.

"I can't believe you left it like that." Cathy was outraged, pacing Jessica's living room like a caged tiger. She hadn't been able to stand still from the moment Jessica had told her about her last meeting with Damian.

"What did you expect me to say to him?" Jessica demanded in irritation. The romantic part of her had been hoping Damian would come after her, but he hadn't. Even Evan had seemed resigned to her wishes. She'd spent one of the most emotionally draining days of her life, and the last thing she needed was chastisement from her best friend. "If he had a shred of feeling for me, this would have been a golden opportunity for him to say something, don't you think?"

"You don't want to know what I think about that man," Cathy muttered darkly.

"The best he was willing to do was a letter of recommendation. I don't need to be hit over the head, Cathy. Damian Dryden simply doesn't care about me." Kneeling before the coffee table, she jerked a piece of pizza from the box with such force the cheese slid off the top.

"Does he know you're not seeing Evan?"

"Of course he knows."

"How can you be so sure? Did you tell him?"

"No."

Cathy lifted her hands in abject frustration. "Then that's it. He thinks you're still dating his brother."

"Evan's gone out with Nadine Powell twice this week. Damian knows that. Besides, all Evan and I have ever been is friends. I told Damian that. Obviously he's not interested one way or the other, so there's no point in discussing it, is there?"

Cathy dropped onto the carpet and reached for a slice of pizza. "I'm really disappointed."

"So am I." That was a gross understatement, but Jessica had never been one to dwell on past mistakes. It would be a long time before she could consider loving Damian a mistake. She'd learned several lessons about herself, and love, in the process. When all was said and done she was going to miss him dreadfully.

"I thought you told me you and Evan were going sailing this weekend?" Cathy asked curiously.

"Not this weekend. Next."

"Aha!" Her friend slapped the end of the coffee table with her free hand. "So you *are* continuing to see Evan. Damian must know that, too. No wonder he's—"

"Cathy," Jessica said, cutting her off, "leave it. I probably won't be seeing Damian again, and apparently that's the way he wants it. Heaven knows I couldn't have been any more obvious about how I felt."

Cathy shook her head sadly. "I guess I must be more of a romantic than I realized. I was so sure he was in love with you. I was so confident I was right, I guess, because I wanted to be. I've waited all these years for you to fall in love, and now that you have..." Her voice faded as a frown ruled her features. "I was so very sure," she whispered, the puzzled expression growing more intense as though she didn't understand, even now, what could possibly have gone wrong.

"This is a treat," Jessica said, sitting across the table from her mother in their favorite seafood restaurant. They were given a table that looked out over Back Bay. The waters were green and peaceful, and fishing boats could be seen in the distance, bobbing up and down like corks.

Joyce Kellerman spread the linen napkin on her lap and smiled serenely.

Jessica groaned inwardly. She knew that look well. It was the one that spoke of pained disappointment. Her mother had given her that identical look when she'd learned Jessica had dropped out of piano lessons. The look was there again when Jessica had refused to go to Girl Scout camp when she was twelve; it hadn't helped that her mother had been the group leader. It was her mother's way of saying Jessica's behavior completely baffled her. Jessica didn't pretend not to know what this luncheon engagement was about.

"You think I made a mistake quitting my job, don't you, Mother?"

Joyce looked mildly surprised that Jessica had introduced the subject. "I just don't understand why, that's all. It was the perfect job for you, with old family friends. You and Evan seemed to be getting along so well, and then for no reason I can discern, you resigned."

"It was time for me to move on," Jessica said vaguely.

"But you'd barely worked there two months," Joyce protested. "It doesn't look good on a résumé for you to be hopping from one job to the next. You know what your father has to say about such behavior."

There it was, in black and white, with the emphasis on black. She'd disappointed her father, the man who'd devoted his life to the preservation of her happiness.

"Working for the Drydens had become...uncomfortable, Mom." Jessica didn't explain further. What could she say?

Her mother reached for the menu and focused her attention there. "Lois and I blame ourselves for this, you know. We were both so excited when you and Evan hit it off that we let our imaginations run away with us. Here we were talking about a wedding and grandchildren, and you two had barely started dating."

"Mom, it wasn't that."

Joyce set the menu aside and clutched the edge of the table, leaning toward Jessica. "I feel so badly about all this. I do hope you'll accept my apology, Jessica."

"Mom, listen to me. Evan and I were never romantically interested in each other. He's in love with someone else. We've had several long talks, and he's simply not ready to become involved in another relationship. That's perfectly understandable.''

"Oh, dear, I'm sorry I'm late.'' A flustered Lois Dryden approached their table, surprising Jessica. This was her first week away from the Dryden law firm, and when her mother had suggested lunch, it had sounded like a great way to kill a couple of hours between job interviews, the very ones Damian had arranged for her. Jessica hadn't realized Damian's mother had been invited to this luncheon, as well.

"With the primary less than three weeks away, I don't think I've ever been busier.'' Lois Dryden pulled out a chair and sat down next to her friend and neighbor.

"Mom didn't mention you'd be joining us,'' Jessica said, casting a mild accusatory glance at her mother. The last thing she needed now was another inquisition.

"I hope you don't mind,'' Lois murmured contritely. "It does look as though we're ganging up on you, doesn't it? We don't mean to, dear. It's just that we can't help being curious about what's going on between you and Evan.''

So, her mother wasn't the only one looking for answers. Lois Dryden, too. And the pair *were* ganging up on her.

"We're both far snoopier than we should be,'' Lois Dryden went on breathlessly, setting her small handbag next to her silverware, "but that's just part of being a mother.''

"Jessica was telling me that Evan's still in love with someone else,'' Joyce explained.

"Oh, dear,'' Lois said wistfully, "I was afraid of that. Is it that Summerhill girl he was so keen on a few months ago?''

Jessica looked out over the sun-brightened waters of Back Bay and sighed. "Please understand, I don't mean to be rude, but Evan and I are friends, and I don't feel comfortable sharing what he said to me in confidence.''

Joyce Kellerman beamed proudly at her friend. "My goodness, she sounds just like an attorney, doesn't she?''

"That's what she gets from hanging around my sons too long,'' Damian's mother replied. She crossed her arms and leaned on the table, her expression regretful. "I'm afraid I made a terrible mistake when Evan brought Mary Jo out to the house to meet Walter and me."

"I can't imagine your doing anything to offend anyone," Joyce said loyally.

"She was a shy little thing, and it was easy to see that Walter and I made her decidedly uncomfortable. After dinner, I tried to put her at ease, and I'm afraid I made a miserable job of it. You see, it's vital that Evan marry the…right kind of woman."

"Right kind of woman?" Jessica echoed, a little confused. She'd known the Drydens most of her life. They weren't snobs. They were two of the most generous conscientious people she'd ever met.

"Sometime in the future, Evan is destined to enter the political arena," Lois explained. "Being a politician's wife is like being married to a minister. I should know. After the last few weeks, I've been left with the feeling that *I* am the one running for the Senate, not Walter."

Jessica looked puzzled. "To the best of my knowledge Evan's never said anything about being interested in politics."

"Perhaps not recently, but he was keen on it before, and we've talked about it a lot in the past. It's only been in the past year or so that his interest has waned."

"You said all this to Mary Jo?" Joyce asked.

Lois nodded, her eyes betraying her remorse. "I've thought back on our conversation a hundred times, and I see now that I did more harm than good."

"Does Evan know what you said to her?" Jessica questioned.

"I'm fairly certain she didn't repeat it. I've thought of contacting her since then, thinking if I apologized she might find it in her heart to forgive me for being so terribly presumptuous."

Jessica groaned inwardly. This new information explained much of what had happened between Mary Jo and Evan, but it was too late. Mary Jo was married now, wasn't she? To that other teacher?

"I feel like I'm responsible for ruining things between you and Evan, as well," Lois went on. "I do try to stay out of my sons' lives, honestly I do, but I don't seem to have much success. I do hope you'll forgive Walter and me for pressuring you and Evan."

"Mrs. Dryden, please, you aren't at fault."

"You're such a dear girl, and Walter and I hoped it would work out between you and Evan." She paused to reach for the menu. "You make a handsome couple."

"Thank you."

The waiter came and took their order, and Lois fully relaxed. "Something's bothering Damian," she remarked. "I've tried to ask him about it, but you know Damian. He's as closemouthed as his father. Evan, bless his heart, is more like me. I've always known what Evan's thinking—well, until recently—because he's so open about his feelings. Not so with Damian."

"What about Damian?" Jessica asked, making the question sound as casual as she could.

"You could probably explain more to me than I can to you, dear," Lois said. "You see him far more often than I do, or at least, you did."

"I... Damian didn't make a practice of confiding in me."

Lois sighed noisily. "I figured as much. Mark my words, there's a woman involved in this. Damian may be as tight-lipped as his father, but I know my son. I think he might have fallen in love."

Jessica glanced back at the water, knowing that if Damian's mother was right, the woman was someone else. Not her.

"Once on board, you can go below and unload the groceries," Evan instructed, as they walked along the floating dock at the marina. When they reached the berth where the thirty-foot sailboat was moored, Evan helped Jessica aboard.

While she went below, Evan moved forward and busied himself with the sails, setting the jib and readying the spinnaker.

"It looks to me like you packed enough food for a week," Jessica shouted through the open stairwell that led to the deck above. The day was lovely, the wind perfect for sailing. Despite all his comments about being the captain while she was the crew, Evan seemed eager to do the majority of the work. Putting away a few bags of groceries seemed a paltry task.

"I'll probably set sail while you're below," Evan shouted down to her, "so don't be concerned if you feel the boat move."

Jessica's experience as a sailor was limited. Evan had insisted for weeks that he was going to change all that. Before the end of the day, he claimed she'd be a top-notch mariner. Apparently the lessons started in the galley.

Humming as she worked, Jessica unloaded the three large grocery bags. They were apparently going to eat well this weekend. She was busy cleaning radishes when she heard voices up above, but although she craned her neck to see who Evan was speaking to, she couldn't see anyone. It was probably someone standing on the dock, Jessica decided.

A few moments later came the sound of the sailboat's small outboard motor. The boat dipped slightly as Evan moved ahead and raised the sails. When the motor stopped, she knew they were a safe distance from the marina.

She finished her tasks and, bringing a couple of cans of cold soda with her, climbed up from the galley. It wasn't until she looked away from the helm that she realized someone else had joined them.

Damian.

She cast an accusatory look in Evan's direction, but it was nothing compared to the look Damian sent his way.

"I didn't know Evan had invited you," she said.

"I didn't know he'd invited *you*," Damian returned, his voice cut by the wind. The boat tilted to one side and sliced through the water.

"Evan?" Jessica glared at the man she'd once considered a friend.

Evan was grinning broadly, clearly pleased with his own cleverness. "Didn't I mention Damian would be coming along?" he asked innocently.

"No," she answered, handing each brother a can of soda and retreating to the galley. Evan was pretending the situation was the result of miscommunication, but she knew he'd purposely set it up.

Damian followed her below a few minutes later. She was sitting at the booth, her back against the side of the boat and her legs stretched out on the upholstered seat. Her arms were crossed over her chest as she tried to take in what was happening.

Damian didn't look any happier with this turn of events than she did. Walking over to the refrigerator, he replaced the can of soda she'd given him as though that had been his sole purpose in coming below.

"I think you should know I didn't arrange this meeting, if that's what you're thinking."

Jessica had nothing to say. She wasn't angry with Damian; he'd been just as manipulated as she had. She didn't know what game Evan was playing, but she wanted no part of it.

"I imagine having me around ruins your day with my brother," Damian said in what sounded strangely like an apology. He investigated the cupboards as if searching for something to eat. He brought out a bag of potato chips. "Have you found another job yet?"

"Not yet, but I've been called in for a second interview." She doubted this was news to Damian. From what she'd gathered at the new firm, he'd made her sound like God's gift to the legal profession, which was going to be one hell of a reputation to maintain.

"Do you mind if I ask you something?" she said.

"Of course not." He slipped into the narrow booth across from her.

"If you thought so highly of me, why'd you accept my resignation?" Not an entirely fair question, she realized, since she'd been the one to quit.

"Did you want me to ask you to stay?"

She smiled and shrugged. "I guess in a way I did, although it's difficult to admit that now."

"Why did you decide to quit?" He opened the bag of potato chips and offered it to her. Jessica took a handful of chips and dumped them on the tabletop, grateful for something to occupy her hands.

"Why did I decide to quit?" she said, repeating his question thoughtfully. He wasn't going to like her answer. "Mainly because of what happened at that dinner party."

Damian's dark eyes glittered with indignation. "Then it did have something to do with the attention Evan paid Nadine."

"No," she flared back. "I quit because of the pressure I felt from both sets of parents. They practically had me and Evan engaged.''

"You could do far worse than marrying my brother.''

"How can you even suggest such a thing?'' she demanded, her voice quavering. She'd never marry a man she didn't love. "What's the matter with you, Damian?''

"With me?''

"Did you or did you not hear me in the kitchen of your parents' home less than three weeks ago?''

He frowned. "Yes." The word was clipped and angry.

"Then how can you ask me something so stupid?''

Damian's eyes were furious. He wasn't the kind of man to take kindly to insults.

Jessica grabbed a potato chip and shoved it into her mouth. Crunching down on something crisp and salty seemed to help vent her frustration.

"But Evan—''

"If you so much as suggest that Evan's in love with me,'' she interrupted, "I swear I won't be responsible for what I say or do next.''

Damian looked taken aback by her angry retort. He closed his mouth and frowned heavily. Reaching for the potato chips, he munched on two or three, and for a moment this was the only sound in the galley.

"You know my problem, don't you?'' she said.

"You mean you only have one?'' Damian asked with honey-coated sarcasm.

Jessica ignored the comment. "It's that I assumed a man who had passed the bar and was one of the most brilliant minds in corporate law in Boston today, would—''

"How's everything going down there?'' Evan called down. "Are you two talking yet?''

Jessica looked up to find that the younger Dryden brother had opened the door to the galley and was sitting almost directly above them, his arm on the helm, steering the sailboat. The wind ruffled his hair and flattened his windbreaker to his chest.

"We're trading insults!'' Damian called back.

"That's a good place to start." Evan sounded disgustingly cheerful. "There's something you should know," he added. "I don't have any intention of turning this boat around until you two have reached an agreement."

"About what?" Jessica demanded.

"We'll get to that in a moment. Now, Damian, admit you're in love with Jessica and be done with it. Quit playing these ridiculous games."

"Damian in love with me?" she repeated incredulously. "Not a chance."

"So that's the way it's going to be," Evan called down. "Not to worry, I packed enough food to last us a good three or four days."

"Don't be absurd." Damian was beginning to sound impatient.

"Listen up, big brother," Evan shouted. "You didn't think I saw you the day you kissed Jessica in Mom's kitchen, but I did. You're crazy about her. What I can't figure out is why you insist on hiding it."

"You were the one dating her."

"So?"

"I don't get involved with women you're dating."

"There's always an exception to the rule. Jessica's a free woman. If you're in love with her, like I suspect, then why didn't you say something?"

Damian's mouth thinned. "You wouldn't understand."

"Try me," Evan insisted.

"Listen, you two," Jessica said, interrupting the exchange. "If you don't mind, I'd rather you didn't discuss me like I wasn't here."

Both men ignored her.

"Jessica's been crazy about you since she was a kid," Damian declared.

"So?" Evan returned. "She grew up and fell in love with you. A woman can change her mind if she wants. They've been known to do that."

"But you love her!" Damian insisted impatiently.

"You're right—like a sister. She'd make a terrific sister-in-law. We get along great."

Damian's eyes, which were now fixed on Jessica, grew dark and intense. "Were you about to tell me you love me?" he asked her in a husky murmur.

"Yes, you imbecile! What do I have to do—hit you over the head?"

"I don't mean to be offering you advice, big brother," Evan shouted down, "but this might be a good time to kiss her."

"I appreciate the help, *little* brother, but I can take it from here," Damian hollered back and slipped out of the booth. He shut the galley door and bolted it, then turned to Jessica.

He was grinning, she noticed, as if he'd just found out he was holding the winning ticket in the state lottery. "You must have thought I was a stubborn fool," he said, grasping her ankles and tugging her across the length of the upholstered bench. Then he gripped her around the waist and brought her upright and into his arms.

"Do you love me, Damian?" she asked.

"Heart and soul," he admitted as his hands framed her face.

"You might have said something sooner, you know," she murmured, thinking there'd been ample opportunity.

"I didn't dare. I assumed Evan loved you and needed you, but I was wrong, Jessica, very wrong. In the past few weeks I've discovered how very much I loved and needed you myself." He stroked her hair as though he couldn't believe even now that she was with him.

His mouth found hers. She wrapped her arms around him and leaned her weight into his. Damian kissed her again and again, until she was breathless with wonder. Until she marveled at how she'd managed to survive this long outside of his arms.

"I can't believe I'm holding you like this," he whispered between kisses. He couldn't seem to get enough of her, which was fine with Jessica, because she couldn't get enough of him, either.

"You're a fool, Damian Dryden."

"I know, but not any longer. I thought I was doing the noble thing by stepping aside for Evan. I was furious with him after the dinner party, but even more furious with myself.''

"Why?"

"For being unable to resist holding you.'' His grip around her tightened. She felt the even rise and fall of his chest and nestled closer.

"You let me walk out of your life,'' she said, remembering the pain of leaving the law firm.

"I let you walk out of my office,'' he said, pressing his jaw against her hair, "but not out of my life. Never that. I was waiting, rather impatiently, to see what developed between you and my brother.''

A loud knock from above finally separated them. Continuing to hold her, Damian raised one arm to unhook the latch and raise the door. "Yes?'' he asked impatiently.

"Can I turn this boat around yet?''

"Not yet!'' Jessica shouted.

"Give us a few more minutes,'' Damian added.

Evan chuckled. "Just promise me one thing,'' he insisted. "No, make that two.''

"All right,'' Damian said, apparently in a generous mood.

"First, I insist on being best man at the wedding.''

"Wedding,'' Jessica repeated slowly.

Damian nodded insistently. "The sooner the better. I've been waiting for you far too long already.''

"Am I going to be best man or not?'' Evan demanded.

"There's no one else I'd even consider, little brother.''

"And second,'' Evan said with a hearty sigh, "I want to be there when you tell Mom and Dad Jessica's marrying you, instead of me.''

Ten

"I'd feel better if you kissed me first," Jessica murmured, looking up at Damian. They'd called the Drydens from the marina and asked Lois to invite the Kellermans over, as well.

"If you don't kiss her, I will," Evan teased, eyeing his older sibling.

"Not this time, little brother." Damian wrapped his arm around Jessica's shoulders and gently kissed her. It would have been easy to continue had they been elsewhere. Being held and kissed by Damian was the closest Jessica had ever come to paradise, and it was difficult to break away from the tender shelter of his arms.

"I don't know why I'm so nervous," Jessica said as they headed, hand in hand, toward the parking lot.

"I do." Of late, Evan seemed to be the one with all the answers. "Both sets of parents think you're marrying me." He laughed cheerfully. Clearly he was looking forward to this meeting.

Evan had been the one who insisted they talk to all four parents immediately. Damian and Jessica had agreed, but now Jessica wished she'd suggested they return to her apartment first. She needed to change clothes. Her hair was wind-tossed, and her face was red from the sun and wind.

But Damian seemed eager for this meeting, as if he, too, wanted the matter cleared with both sets of parents. He raised Jessica's hand to his mouth and brushed his lips over her knuckles.

"Don't look so worried. Mom and Dad are going to be ecstatic."

She wasn't concerned about his parents' reaction, or hers for that matter. Neither set would object to her marrying Damian. They'd be thrilled. It was just that the idea of Damian's loving her was still so new she was afraid it wasn't real.

Jessica rode with Damian, and Evan followed in his car. They got separated on the freeway, and when they pulled into the long winding drive that led to Whispering Willows, Jessica noticed Evan's car was already parked out front.

"The speed demon," Damian commented with a chuckle. He parked behind his brother, turned off the ignition and reached for Jessica, kissing her soundly. "Are you ready to walk into the dragons' den?"

She smiled and nodded, thinking she'd follow Damian anywhere.

He helped her out of the car, tucking her hand in the bend in his arm, and they walked together into the family home. The elder Drydens and Kellermans stared back at them with a look of anxious interest.

"Hello, everyone," Damian said, leading Jessica to a chair in the massive living room. He seated her and then stood directly behind her, his hands resting on her shoulders. She raised her fingers and placed them over his.

"I imagine you're wondering why we asked you here," Jessica said to her parents. Her mother sat studying Jessica as if trying to figure out what was wrong with this picture.

"Hold on!" Evan shouted from the kitchen. "Don't say another word until I get there."

"Son?" Walter Dryden gave Damian a puzzled look. "What's the meaning of this?"

"Okay, now," Evan instructed breathlessly, carrying in a silver tray with seven crystal flutes and two bottles of champagne.

"I've asked you to be here, Mr. and Mrs. Kellerman," Damian began formally, "to request the honor of marrying your daughter."

Hamilton Kellerman's face wrinkled with confusion as he turned to his wife. "You told me she was marrying Evan."

"She's—I mean, we hoped—" Joyce stammered.

"I'm in love with Damian," Jessica broke in.

Her father scratched his head. "That's not the way I remember it. You were crazy over Evan for years. Last I heard, you were making a damned nuisance of yourself."

"Daddy, that was years ago."

"She's crazy about *me* now," Damian interjected, lightly squeezing her shoulders. "And I feel the same way about her."

"Oh, Damian." Lois Dryden covered her mouth with her fingers. "We're delighted. Just delighted. Joyce, think of it, we'll be sharing grandchildren, after all."

The two women were hugging each other and dancing around in circles as Evan passed out champagne glasses to the silent confused fathers.

"You know what this is all about, Walter?"

"Can't say that I do, Ham."

"You object?"

"Hell, no. I haven't seen that much life in Lois in fifteen years. What about you? Would you rather Jessica married someone else?"

"Heavens, no." Hamilton shook his head as if he didn't know what to think. "The wife's been talking about a union between our two families all summer, only she thought it would be between Jessica and Evan. The way I figure it, a union is a union, and the two of them certainly look to be in love."

"Yes, they undoubtedly have the look," Walter said, smiling at them.

The sound of an exploding cork echoed about the room as Evan uncorked a bottle of champagne. "I'd like to propose a toast," he said, walking from person to person filling the flutes. "To Jessica and Damian," he said, setting the bottle aside and holding up his glass. "May their lives always be filled with happy surprises, and may their love endure for all time."

"Evan, how sweet," Lois said, dabbing the corner of her eye.

"For all time," Joyce agreed.

Everyone raised their glasses, then took a sip of champagne.

"Now, let's talk about the wedding," Lois said, prepared then and there to square away the details. She sat on the sofa next to her husband.

"It'll have to be after the November election," Joyce commented thoughtfully.

"We need to make it through the September primary first," Lois said. "I can't see delaying the wedding when we don't know for certain Walter will be in contention for the Senate."

"Nonsense. Of course he'll be on the ballot."

"Does any of this matter to you?" Damian asked Jessica, leaning so that his lips were close to her ear. A warm tingling sensation raced down her arms.

She smiled softly and shook her head. Nothing mattered except Damian and his love. "I'd marry you tomorrow if we could arrange it."

Damian drew in a deep breath. "Don't tempt me, sweetheart."

"Or in six months, if that's necessary. I've waited for you all my life, Damian. A few more weeks isn't going to matter."

Their mothers would have it all arranged within the hour, Jessica guessed. Their fathers were talking, too, working out schedules and other necessary details. The two families had been friends through all the seasons of their lives. The same way their own love—hers and Damian's—would last, weathering all the ups and downs the years would bring.

Jessica felt as though she'd come to the end of a long journey. She was home now, secure in Damian's love.

Epilogue

As Evan Dryden set aside the brief he was preparing and pinched the bridge of his nose, there was a knock on his door. Glad of the interruption, he called, "Come in."

His brother entered. The changes in Damian in the months since he'd married Jessica were many. Evan remembered a time when practicing law ruled Damian's life. He worked after hours and weekends, rarely taking time away. But now his brother looked younger, happier and so damn much in love Evan couldn't help a twinge of jealousy.

Witnessing the changes in Damian caused him to wonder what his own life would have been like if he'd married Mary Jo. They'd have started a family by now. The glimpse he'd caught of her almost a year ago at the Red Sox game drifted into his mind, and with it came a stab of pain.

Loving her as he did, even now, it was impossible to want anything but the best for her. He tried not to think about Mary Jo, tried to place her firmly in the back of his mind, but every now and again, the memory of her escaped to taunt him with the might-have-beens.

It had been nearly eighteen months since they'd parted, and she still had the power to move him. He'd dated now and again, but there wasn't anyone he'd gotten serious about. He wished he knew what it was about Mary Jo that he couldn't forget.

Evan envied his brother the happiness he'd found and didn't expect to find the same happiness himself. He could see himself thirty years down the road with white hair, dressed in a smoking jacket, sitting in front of a fireplace smoking a pipe. A black Labrador would lie snoozing at his feet....

"You're looking thoughtful," Damian said, helping himself to a chair.

"Just wool-gathering."

Damian was more relaxed these days, Evan noted. His brother leaned back in the chair and rested one ankle over the other knee. "Remember last month when Jessica phoned from the doctor's office?"

Evan chuckled. "I'm not likely to forget." Nor would anyone else in the office. Rarely had he seen his brother so excited, so elated. For days he'd walked around grinning like a mad fool. It wasn't every day, he said, a man learned he was going to be a father.

Funny, Evan thought, his brother was wearing a similar grin now. "What's going on now?" he asked. "Did you just learn Jessica's carrying twins?"

"Not quite. I've been approached by the bar about an appointment as a judge."

"Damian!" Evan rose from his chair. This shouldn't come as a surprise; it was Damian's destiny, just as marrying Jessica had been. He walked around his desk. Damian stood and the two brothers embraced.

"You're going to accept." Evan didn't put the words into a question. It went without saying Damian would and should.

"Yes, if Jessica concurs."

"She will." Evan had no doubts about that, either. "Are you going out tonight to celebrate?"

"As a matter of fact we are. Cathy Hudson, Jessica's friend, is starring in a new play that's opening tonight. Did I mention she recently got engaged to some director friend of hers?"

Before Evan could respond, his intercom buzzed and he reached for the button. "The receptionist called," Mrs. Sterling informed him, "and said Earl Kress is here to see you, Mr. Dryden."

"Earl?" Evan said with surprise. He hadn't heard from him in six months or more. "Send him in."

"We'll talk later," Damian said as he walked out of the office. "Give my regards to Earl, will you?"

Evan went with him, meeting Earl in the hallway outside. The two exchanged hearty handshakes. Evan slapped the younger man on the back as he led him into his office and closed the door.

"It's good to see you," Evan said, motioning toward the chair. "Sit down and make yourself comfortable."

"I can't stay long," Earl said, sitting on the edge of the chair. "I probably should have called, but I was in the neighborhood..."

"I'm glad you stopped in. How's school?"

"Good. I got my general equivalency diploma not long ago," he announced proudly.

"Congratulations." Evan experienced a surge of pride at the younger man's progress.

"I have a lot of people to thank for that, but you're the one who started it all. I don't think you ever realized how afraid I was of having the world know I couldn't read or write. It's humiliating to admit something like that."

"I realized at the time how difficult it was for you."

"Without your support, I don't think I could have gone through with the trial."

"I'm sure glad you did."

"Yeah, me, too," Earl said with a hearty laugh. "My life would certainly be different if I hadn't. Listen, I didn't mean to take up your time, but I wanted you to know how grateful I am for all your help."

"No problem, Earl."

"I'm working as a volunteer myself now with grade-school kids, helping out in the slow-reader program. I wouldn't have grown up illiterate if I'd gotten help while I was in the elementary grades."

Evan smiled broadly. "That's great, Earl."

"By the way, I ran across a friend of yours the other day— another volunteer."

"Oh?"

"At least I assume you two know one another. Her name's Mary Jo Summerhill."

"Mary Jo." Evan realized he breathed her name more than spoke it.

"Funny, she reacted the same way when I mentioned you."

"I thought she was married," Evan said.

"Not as far as I know." Earl stood and held out his hand. "Anyway, I won't keep you. I just wanted to stop in and update you about what's been going on in my life."

"I'm happy you did," Evan said, walking his former client to the door. He stood there for a moment, his mind spinning.

A few minutes later Damian strolled into his office again.

"What did Earl have to say?" he asked.

"Mary Jo isn't married." He said it out loud just to hear the sound of it. Damian wouldn't fully understand the significance of those words, but it didn't matter.

"I see," his brother said thoughtfully. "What are you going to do about it?"

Evan thought long and hard, then a slow smile spread across his features.

Ready for Marriage

Dedicated to
Carole Grande and her family
for their loving support
through the years

One

She could always grovel at Evan's feet. Knowing him as well as she did, Mary Jo Summerhill figured he'd probably like that. The very fact that she'd made this appointment—and then had the courage to show up—proved how desperate she was. But she'd had no choice; her parents' future rested in her hands and she knew of no better attorney to help with this mess than Evan Dryden.

If he'd only *agree* to help her…

Generally, getting in touch with an old boyfriend wouldn't raise such anxiety, but Evan was more than just someone she'd dated a few times.

They'd been in love, deeply in love, and had planned to marry. In ways she had yet to fully appreciate, Mary Jo still loved him. Terminating their relationship had nearly devastated her.

And him.

Mary Jo wasn't proud of the way she'd ended it. Mailing him back the beautiful pearl engagement ring had been cowardly, but she'd known she couldn't tell him face-to-face. She should have realized Evan would never leave it at that. She'd been a fool to believe he'd take back the ring without confronting her.

He'd come to her angry and hurt, demanding an explanation. It quickly became apparent that he wouldn't accept the truth, and given no option, Mary Jo concocted a wild story about meeting another teacher and falling in love with him.

Telling such a bold-faced lie had magnified her guilt a hundredfold. But it was the only way she could make Evan believe her. The only way she could extricate herself from his life.

Her lie had worked beautifully, she noted with a twinge of pain. He'd recovered—just the way his mother had said he would. He hadn't wasted any time getting on with his life, either.

Within a matter of months he was dating again. Pictures of Evan, with Jessica Kellerman at his side, had appeared regularly in the newspaper society pages. Unable to resist knowing more, Mary Jo had researched the Kellerman family. Her investigation had told her everything she needed to know. Jessica would make the perfect Dryden wife. The Kellermans were wealthy and established, unlike the Summerhills, who didn't rate so much as a mention in Boston's social register.

Later the same year, Mary Jo had heard rumors of the extravagant Dryden family wedding. She been out of town that week at a teaching seminar, so she'd missed the newspaper coverage, but talk of the wedding and huge reception that followed had lingered for months. It was called the social event of the year.

That was nearly three years ago. Evan and Jessica were an old married couple by now. For all she knew, they might have already started a family. The twinge of regret became a knot in her stomach. Evan would make a wonderful father. They'd talked of a family, and she remembered how eager he was for children.

This wasn't exactly the best time for her to reenter his life, but she had no alternative. Her parents' future depended on Evan.

"Mr. Dryden will see you now," the receptionist said, breaking into Mary Jo's thoughts.

Her head shot up and she nearly lost her nerve right then and there. Her heart pounded furiously. In a dead panic she tightened her hold on her purse strap, fighting the urge to dash straight out of her chair and out of the office.

"If you'll come this way."

"Of course," Mary Jo managed, although the words came out in gurglelike sounds, as if she were submerged in ten feet of water.

She followed the receptionist down a wide, plush-carpeted hallway to Evan's office. His name was on the door, engraved on a gold plate. The receptionist ushered her in, and left.

Mary Jo recognized Evan's secretary immediately, although they'd never met. Mrs. Sterling was exactly the way he'd described her. Late middle-age. Short and slim, with the energy of a Tasmanian devil. Formidably efficient. He'd claimed that the woman could easily reorganize the world if she had to, and that she'd willingly take on any project he asked of her. She was loyal to a fault.

"Evan asked me to send you right in," Mrs. Sterling said, leading the way to the closed inner door. She opened it, then asked, "Can I get you a cup of coffee?" Her tone was friendly but unmistakably curious.

"No, thank you." Mary Jo stepped over the threshold, her heart in her throat. She wondered how she'd feel seeing Evan again after all this time. She'd already decided that a facade was necessary. She planned to approach him as if they were long-lost friends. Casual friends. With a smile, she'd shake his hand, inquire about Jessica and catch up on events in his life.

Now that only a few feet stood between her and the man she loved, Mary Jo found she couldn't move, barely even breathe.

Nothing, she realized, could have prepared her for the force of these emotions. Within seconds she was drowning in feelings she didn't know how to handle. She felt swamped and panicky, as if she were going down for the third time.

She conjured up Gary's face, the man she'd dated off and on for the past few months, but that didn't help. Next she struggled to come up with some clever comment, some joke, anything. Instead, all she could remember was that the man she'd loved three years ago, loved now, was married to someone else.

Evan sat at his desk, writing; only now did he look up. Their eyes met and for the briefest moment, he seemed to experience the same sense of loss and regret she was feeling. He blinked and the emotion disappeared, wiped out with a mere movement of his eyes.

"Hello, Evan," she said, amazed at how casual she sounded. "I imagine it's a surprise to see me after all this time."

He stood and extended his hand for a perfunctory shake, and when he spoke his voice was crisp and professional. "Mary Jo. It's good to see you."

Mary Jo nearly laughed out loud. Evan never did know how to tell a good lie. He was anything but pleased to see her again.

He motioned toward the chair on the other side of his desk. "Sit down."

She did, gratefully, uncertain how much longer her knees would support her. She set her purse on the carpet and waited for her heart rate to return to normal before she told him the purpose of her visit.

"Did Mary offer you a cup of coffee?"

"Yes. I'm fine, thank you," she said hurriedly. Her hands were trembling.

Evan sat down again and waited.

"I—guess you're wondering why I'm here...."

He leaned back in his chair, looking cool and composed. It'd been three long years since she'd last seen him. He hadn't changed, at least not outwardly. He remained one of the handsomest men she'd ever seen. His hair was as dark as his eyes, the color of rich Swiss chocolate. His features were well defined, almost chiseled, but that was too harsh a word for the finely cut, yet pronounced lines of his face. Walter Dryden, Evan's father, was a Massachusetts senator, and it was commonly accepted that Evan would one day enter politics himself. He certainly had the smooth, clean-cut good looks for such a calling.

What had made him fall in love with Mary Jo? She'd always wondered, always been fascinated by that question. She suspected it had something to do with being different from the other women he'd dated. She'd amused him, hadn't taken him too seriously, made him laugh.

"You have something you wanted to discuss with me?" he prompted, his tone revealing the slightest hint of irritation.

"Yes...sorry," she said, quickly returning her attention to the matter at hand. "My parents...actually, my father...he retired not long ago," she said, rushing the words together, "and he invested his savings with a financial company, Adison Investments. Have you ever heard of the firm?"

"No, I can't say that I have."

This didn't surprise Mary Jo. Wealthy men like Evan had huge financial portfolios with varied and multiple investments. Her father had taken his life's savings and entrusted it to a man he'd met and trusted completely.

"Dad invested everything he had with the company," she continued. "According to the terms of the agreement, he was to receive monthly interest checks. He hasn't. At first there were a number of plausible excuses, which Dad readily accepted. He wanted to believe this Bill Adison so much that it was easier to accept the excuses than face the truth.''

"Which is?'' Evan asked.

"I...I don't know. That's why I'm here. My father's worked thirty-five years as a construction electrician. He's raised six children, scrimped and saved all that time to put something extra away for his retirement. He wanted to be able to travel with Mom. They've dreamed of touring the South Pacific, and now I'm afraid they're going to be cheated out of everything.''

Evan scribbled down a few notes.

"I'm coming to you because I'm afraid my brothers are about to take things into their own hands. Jack and Rich went to Adison's office last week and made such a fuss they were almost arrested. It'd destroy my parents if my brothers ended up in jail over this. As far as I can see, the only way to handle it is through an attorney.''

Evan made another note. "Did you bring the papers your father signed?''

"No. I didn't tell anyone I was coming to see you. I thought if I could convince you to accept this case for my family, I'd bring my parents in and you could discuss the details with them. You need to understand that it's more than the money. My dad's embarrassed that he could have trusted such a man. He feels like an old fool.'' Her father had become very depressed. Adison Investments had robbed him of far more than his retirement savings. They'd taken his self-confidence and left him feeling vulnerable and inept.

"There are strict laws governing investments in this state.''

Anxious to hear what he had to say, Mary Jo leaned forward in her chair. This was the very reason she'd swallowed her pride and come to Evan. He had the knowledge and political clout to be effective in ways her family never could.

"Then you can help us?'' she asked eagerly. Evan's hesitation sent her heart plummeting. "I'll be happy to pay you whatever your fee is,'' she added, as if that was his sole concern. "I wouldn't expect you to charge less than you'd receive from anyone else.''

Evan stood and walked over to the window, his back to her. "Our firm specializes in corporate law."

"That doesn't mean you can't take this case, does it?"

Evan clenched his hands at his sides, then flexed his fingers. "No, but these sorts of cases have a tendency to become involved. You may end up having to sue."

"My family is willing to do whatever to takes to settle this matter," she said with a stubborn tilt to her jaw.

"Lawsuits don't come cheap," he warned, turning around to face her.

"I don't care and neither do my brothers. True, they don't know I made an appointment to see you, but once I tell them, I'm sure they'll be willing to chip in whatever they can to cover your fee." They wouldn't be able to afford much. Mary Jo was the youngest of six and the only girl. Her brothers were all married and raising young families. There never seemed to be enough money to go around. The burden of the expense would fall on her shoulders, but Mary Jo readily accepted that.

"You're sure you want me to handle this?" Evan asked, frowning.

"Positive. There isn't anyone I trust more," she said simply. Her eyes met his and she refused to look away.

"I could recommend another attorney, someone far more qualified in the area of investment fraud—"

"No," she broke in. "I don't trust anyone but you." She hadn't meant to tell him that and, embarrassed, quickly lowered her gaze.

He didn't say anything for what seemed like a very long time. Mary Jo held her breath, waiting. If he expected her to plead, she'd do it willingly. It was fair compensation for the appalling way she'd treated him. "Please," she added, her voice low and trembling.

Evan's shoulders lifted with a drawn-out sigh. "Before I decide, fill me in on what you've been doing for the past three years."

Mary Jo hadn't anticipated this, wasn't prepared to detail her life. "I'm still teaching."

"Kindergarten?"

"Yes," she said enthusiastically. She loved her job. "Five-year-olds are still my favorites."

"I notice you're not wearing a wedding band."

Her gaze automatically fell to her ring finger, and she pinched her lips tightly together.

"So you didn't marry lover boy, after all."

"No."

"What happened?" he asked. He seemed almost to enjoy questioning her. Mary Jo felt as though she were on the witness stand being cross-examined.

She shrugged, not wanting to become trapped in a growing web of untruths. She'd regretted that stupid lie every day for the past three years.

"It didn't work out?" he suggested.

This was agony for her. "You're right. It didn't work out."

He grinned then, for the first time, as if this information delighted him.

"Are you seeing someone now?"

"I don't believe that information's necessary to the case. You're my attorney, not my confessor."

"I'm nothing to you," he said and his words were sharp. "At least not yet."

"Will you take the case or won't you?" she demanded.

"I haven't decided yet."

He did want her to grovel. And they said hell hath no fury like a *woman* scorned. Apparently women didn't hold the patent on that.

"Gary Copeland," she said stiffly, without emotion. "Gary and I've been seeing each other for several months."

"Another teacher?"

"He's a fireman."

Evan nodded thoughtfully.

"Will you or won't you help my parents?" she asked again, growing tired of this silly game.

He was silent for a moment, then said abruptly, "All right. I'll make some inquiries and learn what I can about Adison Investments."

Mary Jo was so relieved and grateful she sagged in her chair.

"Make an appointment with Mrs. Sterling for next week, and

bring your father in with you. Friday would be best. I'll be in court most of the week.''

''Thank you, Evan,'' she whispered, blinking rapidly in an effort to fight back tears.

She stood, eager now to escape. Resisting the urge to hug him, she hurried out of his office, past Mrs. Sterling and into the hallway. She was in such a blind rush she nearly collided with a woman holding a toddler in her arms.

''Oh, I'm so sorry,'' Mary Jo said, catching herself. ''I'm afraid I wasn't watching where I was going.''

''No problem,'' the other woman said with a friendly smile. She held the child protectively against her hip. The little boy, dressed in a blue-and-white sailor suit, looked up at her with eyes that were dark and solemn. Dark as rich Swiss chocolate.

Evan's eyes.

Mary Jo stared at the tall lovely woman. This was Jessica, Evan's wife, and the baby in her arms was Evan's son. The flash of pain nearly paralyzed her.

''I shouldn't have been standing so close to the door,'' Jessica went on to say. ''My husband insisted he was taking us to lunch, and asked me to meet him here.''

''You must be Jessica Dryden,'' Mary Jo said, finding the strength to offer her a genuine smile. She couldn't take her eyes off Evan's son. He now wore a cheerful grin and waved small chubby arms. If circumstances had been different, this child might have been her own. The void inside her widened; she'd never felt so bleak, so empty.

''This is Andy.'' Jessica did a small curtsy with her son in her arms.

''Hello, Andy.'' Mary Jo gave him her hand, and like a proper gentleman, he took it and promptly tried to place it in his mouth.

Jessica laughed softly. ''I'm afraid he's teething. Everything goes to his mouth first.'' She walked with Mary Jo toward the exit, bouncing the impatient toddler against her hip. ''You look familiar,'' she said casually. '' Do I know you?''

''I don't think so. My name's Mary Jo Summerhill.''

Jessica's face went blank, then recognition swept into her eyes as her smile slowly evaporated. Any censure, however, was quickly disguised.

"It was nice meeting you," Mary Jo said quickly, speeding up as they neared the door.

"Evan's mentioned you," Jessica said.

Mary Jo stopped suddenly. "He has?" She couldn't help it. Curiosity got the better of her.

"Yes. He...thought very highly of you."

That Jessica used the past tense didn't escape Mary Jo. "He's a top-notch attorney."

"He's wonderful," Jessica agreed. "By the way, I understand we have a mutual friend. Earl Kress."

Earl had been a volunteer at Mary Jo's school. He'd tutored slow readers, and she'd admired his patience and persistence, and especially his sense of humor. The children loved him.

Earl mentioned Evan's name at every opportunity. He seemed to idolize Evan for taking on his civil suit against the school district—and winning.

Earl had graduated from high school functionally illiterate. Because he was a talented athlete, he'd been passed from one grade to the next. Sports were important to the schools, and the teachers were coerced into giving him passing grades. Earl had been awarded a full-ride college scholarship but suffered a serious knee injury in football training camp two weeks after he arrived. Within a couple of months, he'd flunked out of college. In a landmark case, Earl had sued the school district for his education. Evan had been his attorney.

The case had been in the headlines for weeks. During the trial, Mary Jo had been glued to the television every night, anxious for news. As a teacher, she was, of course, concerned with this kind of crucial education issue. But in all honesty, her interest had less to do with Earl Kress than with Evan. Following the case gave her the opportunity to see him again, even if it was only on a television screen and for a minute or two at a time.

She'd cheered when she heard that Earl had won his case.

In the kind of irony that life sometimes tosses, Mary Jo met Earl about a year later. He was attending college classes and volunteering part-time as a tutor at the grade school. They'd become quick friends. She admired the young man and missed him now that he'd returned to the same university where he'd once failed. Again he'd gone on a scholarship, but this time it was an academic one.

"Yes, I know Earl," Mary Jo said.

"He mentioned working with you to Evan. We were surprised to learn you weren't married."

Evan knew! He'd made her squirm and forced her to tell him the truth when all along he'd been perfectly aware that she was still single. Mary Jo's hands knotted at her sides. He'd taken a little too much delight in squeezing the information out of her.

"Darling," a husky male voice said from behind Mary Jo. "I hope I didn't keep you waiting long." He walked over to Jessica, lifted Andy out of her arms and kissed her on the cheek.

Mary Jo's jaw fell open as she stared at the couple.

"Have you met my husband?" Jessica asked. "Damian, this is Mary Jo Summerhill."

"How…hello." Mary Jo was so flustered she could barely think.

Evan wasn't married to Jessica. His *brother* was.

Two

"Can you help us?" Norman Summerhill asked Evan anxiously.

Mary Jo had brought both her parents. Evan was reading over the agreement her father had signed with Adison Investments. With a sick feeling in the pit of her stomach, she noticed he was frowning. The frown deepened the longer he read.

"What's wrong?" Mary Jo asked.

Her mother hands were clenched so tightly that her fingers were white. Financial affairs confused and upset Marianna Summerhill. From the time Marianna had married Norman, she'd been a house-wife and mother, leaving the financial details of their lives to her husband.

Mary Jo was fiercely proud of her family. Her father might not be a United States senator, but he was an honest and honorable man. He'd dedicated his life to his wife and family, and worked hard through the years to provide for them. Mary Jo had been raised firmly rooted in her parents' love for each other and for their children.

Although close to sixty, her mother remained a beautiful woman, inside and out. Mary Jo had inherited her dark hair and brown eyes and her petite five-foot-four-inch frame. But the prominent high cheekbones and square jaw were undeniably from her father's side of the family. Her brothers towered above her and, like her parents, were delighted their youngest sibling was a girl.

That affection was returned. Mary Jo adored her older brothers, but she knew them and their quirks and foibles well. Living with five boys—all very different personalities—had given her plenty of practice in deciphering the male psyche. Evan might have come from a rich, upper-crust family, but he was a man, and she'd been able to read him like a book from the first. She believed that her ability to see through his playboy facade was what had originally attracted her to him. That attraction had grown and blossomed until…

"Come by for Sunday dinner. We eat about three, and we'd enjoy getting to know you better," her mother was saying. "It'd be an honor to have you at our table."

The words cut into Mary Jo's thoughts like a scythe through wheat. "I'm sure Evan's too busy for that, Mother," she blurted out.

"I appreciate the invitation," Evan said, ignoring Mary Jo.

"You're welcome to stop off at the house any time you like, young man," her father added, sending his daughter a glare of disapproval.

"Thank you. I'll keep it in mind," Evan said absently as he returned his attention to the investment papers. "If you don't object, I'd like an attorney friend of mine to read this over. I should have an answer for you in the next week or so."

Her father nodded. "You do whatever you think is necessary. And don't you worry about your fee."

"Dad, I already told you! I've talked to Evan about that. This is my gift to you."

"Nonsense," her father argued, scowling. "I was the one who was fool enough to trust this shyster. If anyone pays Evan's fee, it'll be me."

"We don't need to worry about that right now," Evan interjected smoothly. "We'll work out the details of my bill later."

"That sounds fair to me." Norman Summerhill was quick to agree, obviously eager to put the subject behind him. Her father had carried his own weight all his life and wouldn't take kindly to Mary Jo's accepting responsibility for this debt. She hoped she could find a means of doing so without damaging his formidable pride.

"Thank you for your time," she said to Evan, desperate to be on her way.

"It was good to see you again, young man," Norman said expansively, shaking hands with Evan. "No need to make yourself scarce. You're welcome for dinner any Sunday of the year."

"Daddy, please," Mary Jo groaned under her breath. The last thing she wanted was to have Evan show up for Sunday dinner with her five brothers and their assorted families. He wasn't accustomed to all the noise and chatter that invariably went on during meals. Her one dinner with his family had sufficiently pointed out the glaring differences between their upbringings.

"Before you leave," Evan said to Mary Jo, "my brother asked me to give you this. I believe it's from Jessica." He handed her a sealed envelope.

"Thank you," Mary Jo mumbled. For the better part of their meeting, he'd avoiding speaking to her. He hadn't been rude or tactless, just businesslike and distant. At least toward her. With her parents, he'd been warm and gracious. She doubted they'd even recognized the subtle difference between how he treated them and how he treated her.

Mary Jo didn't open the envelope until after she'd arrived back at her cozy duplex apartment. She stared at it several moments, wondering what Jessica Dryden could possibly have to say to her.

No need to guess, she decided, and tore open the envelope.

Dear Mary Jo,

I just wanted you to know how much I enjoyed meeting you. When I asked Evan why you were in to see him, he clammed right up. I should have known better—prying information out of Evan is even more difficult than it is with Damian.

From your reaction the other day, I could tell you assumed I was married to Evan. Damian and I got quite a chuckle out of that. You see, just about everyone tried to match me up with Evan, but I only had eyes for Damian. If you're free some afternoon, give me a call. Perhaps we could have lunch.

Warmest regards,
Jessica

Jessica had written her telephone number beneath her signature. Mary Jo couldn't understand why Damian's wife would seek her out. They were virtual strangers. Perhaps Jessica knew something

Mary Jo didn't—something about Evan. The only way to find out was to call.

Although Mary Jo wasn't entirely sure she was doing the right thing, she reached for the phone.

Jessica Dryden answered almost immediately.

"Mary Jo! Oh, I'm so glad to hear from you," she said immediately. "I wondered what you'd think about my note. I don't usually do that sort of thing, but I was just so delighted you'd been to see Evan."

"You said he's mentioned me?"

"A number of times. Look, why don't you come over one afternoon soon and we can talk? You're not teaching right now, are you?"

"School let out a week ago," Mary Jo concurred.

"That's what I thought. Could you stop by next week? I'd really enjoy talking to you."

Mary Jo hesitated. Her first introduction to Evan's family had been a catastrophe, and she'd come away knowing their love didn't stand a chance. A second sortie might prove equally disastrous.

"I'd like that very much," Mary Jo found herself saying. If Evan had been talking about her, she wanted to know what he'd said.

"Great. How about next Tuesday afternoon? Come for lunch and we can sit on the patio and have a nice long chat."

"That sounds great," Mary Jo said.

It wasn't until later that evening, when she was filling a croissant with a curried shrimp mixture for dinner, that Mary Jo stopped to wonder exactly *why* Jessica was so eager to "chat" with her.

She liked Gary. She really did. Though why she felt it was necessary to remind herself of this, she didn't know. She didn't even *want* to know.

It had been like this from the moment she'd broken off her relationship with Evan. She'd found fault with every man she'd dated. No matter how attractive he was. Or how successful. How witty, how considerate...it didn't matter.

Gary was very *nice,* she repeated to herself.

Unfortunately he bored her to tears. He talked about his golf game, his bowling score and his prowess on the handball court. Never anything that was important to her. But his biggest fault, she'd realized early on in their relationship was that he wasn't Evan.

They'd dated infrequently since the beginning of the year. To be honest, Mary Jo was beginning to think that, to Gary, her biggest attraction was her mother's cooking. Invariably, Gary stopped by early Sunday afternoon, just as she was about to leave for her parents' home. It'd happened three out of the past five weeks. She strongly suspected he'd been on duty at the fire hall the two weeks he'd missed.

"You look especially lovely this afternoon," he said when she opened her front door to him now. He held out a bouquet of pink carnations, which she took with a smile, pleased by his thoughtfulness.

"Hello, Gary."

He kissed her cheek, but it seemed perfunctory, as if he felt some display of affection was expected of him. "How've you been?" he muttered, easing himself into the old rocking chair next to the fireplace.

Although Mary Jo's rooms were small, she'd thoughtfully and carefully decorated each one. The living room had an Early American look. Her brother Lonny, who did beautiful woodwork, had carved her an eagle for Christmas, which she'd hung above the fireplace. In addition to her rocking chair, she had a small sofa and an old oak chest that she'd restored herself. Her mother had crocheted an afghan for the back of the sofa in a patriotic blend of red, white and blue.

Her kitchen was little more than a wide hallway that led to a compact dining space in a window alcove. Mary Jo loved to sit there in the morning sunshine with a cup of coffee and a book.

"You're lucky, you know," Gary said, looking around as if seeing the room for the first time.

"How do you mean?"

"Well, first off, you don't have to work in the summer."

This was an old argument and Mary Jo was tired of hearing it. True, school wasn't in session for those two and a half months, she didn't spend them lolling on a beach. This was the first time in years that she wasn't attending courses to upgrade her skills.

"You've got the time you need to fix up this place the way you want it," he went on. "You have real decorating talent, you know. My place is a mess, but then I'm only there three or four days out of the week, if that."

If he was hinting that he'd like her to help him decorate his place, she refused to take the bait.

"Are you going over to your parents' this afternoon?" Gary asked cheerfully. "I don't mean to horn in, but your family doesn't seem to mind, and the two of us have an understanding, don't we?"

"An understanding?" This was news to Mary Jo.

"Yeah. We're...I don't know, going together I guess."

"I thought we were friends." That was all Mary Jo intended the relationship to be.

"Just friends." Gary's face fell. His gaze wandered to the carnations he'd brought with him.

"When was the last time we went out on a date?" she asked, crossing her arms. "A real date."

"You mean to the movies or something?"

"Sure." Surveying her own memory, she could almost count one hand the number of times he'd actually spent money taking her out. The carnations were an exception.

"We went to the Red Sox game, remember?"

"That was in April," she reminded him.

Gary frowned. "That long ago? Time certainly flies, doesn't it?"

"It sure does."

Gary rubbed his face. "You're right, Mary Jo. I've taken you for granted, haven't I?"

She was about to say they really didn't have much of an understanding, after all, did they. Yet a serious relationship with Gary didn't interest her and, difficult as it was to admit now, never had. She'd used him to block out the loneliness. She'd used him so her parents wouldn't worry about her. They firmly believed that a woman, especially a young woman, needed a man in her life, so she'd trotted out Gary in order to keep the peace. She wasn't exactly proud of her motives.

Gary reached for her hand. "How about a movie this afternoon?" he suggested contritely. "We'll leave right after dinner at your parents'. We can invite anyone who wants to come along, as well. You wouldn't mind, would you?"

Gary was honestly trying. He couldn't help it that he wasn't Evan Dryden. The thought slipped uncensored into her mind.

"A movie sounds like a great idea," she said firmly. She was going, and furthermore, she was determined to have a wonderful time. Just because Evan Dryden had briefly reentered her life was no reason to wallow in the impossible. He was way out of her league.

"Great." A smile lighted his boyish face. "Let's drive on over to your mom and dad's place now."

"All right," Mary Jo said. She felt better already. Her relationship with Gary wasn't ideal—it wasn't even close to ideal—but he was her friend. Love and marriage had been built on a whole lot less.

Before they left the house, Gary reached for the bouquet of carnations. Mary Jo blinked in surprise, and he hesitated, looking mildly chagrined. "I thought we'd give these to your mother. You don't mind, do you?"

"Of course not," she mumbled, but she did, just a little.

Gary must have realized it because he added, "Next time I'll bring some just for you."

"You owe me one, fellow."

He laughed good-naturedly and with an elaborate display of courtesy, opened the car door for her.

Mary Jo slid into the seat and snapped her seat belt into place. During the brief drive to her parents' house, less than two miles away she and Gary didn't speak; instead, they listened companionably to part of a Red Sox game.

Her nephews and nieces were out in the huge side yard, playing a rousing game of volleyball when they arrived. Gary parked his car behind her oldest brother's station wagon.

"I get a kick out of how much fun your family has together," he said a bit wistfully.

"We have our share of squabbles, too." But any disagreement

was rare and quickly resolved. Three of her brothers, Jack, Rich and Lonny, were construction electricians like their father. Bill and Mark had both become mechanics and had opened a shop together. They were still struggling to get on their feet financially, but both worked hard. With time, they'd make a go of it; Mary Jo was convinced of that.

"I wonder what your mother decided to cook today," Gary mused, and Mary Jo swore he all but licked his chops.

Briefly she wondered if Gary bothered to eat during the week, or if he stored up his appetite for Sunday dinners with her family.

"I've been introduced to all your brothers, haven't I?" he asked, frowning slightly as he helped her out of the car.

Mary Jo had to think about that. He must have been. Not every brother came every Sunday, but over the course of the past few months surely Gary had met each of her five brothers.

"I don't recognize the guy in the red sweatshirt," he said as they moved up the walk toward the house.

Mary Jo was distracted from answering by her mother, who came rushing down the porch steps, holding out her arms as if it'd been weeks since they'd last seen each other. She wore an apron and a smile that sparkled with delight. "Mary Jo! I'm so glad you're here." She hugged her daughter close for a long moment, then turned toward Gary.

"How sweet," she said, taking the bouquet of carnations and kissing his cheek.

Still smiling, Marianna gestured her attention to her daughter. "You'll never guess who stopped by!"

It was then that Mary Jo noticed Evan walking toward them. Dressed in jeans and a red sweatshirt, he carried Lenny, her six year old nephew, tucked under one arm, and Robby, his older brother by a year, under the other. Both boys were kicking and laughing.

Evan stopped abruptly when he saw Mary Jo and Gary. The laughter drained out of his eyes.

"Hello," Gary said, stepping forward. "You must be one of Mary Jo's brothers. I don't believe we've met. I'm Gary Copeland."

Three

"What are you *doing* here?" Mary Jo demanded the minute she could get Evan alone. With a house full of people, it had taken her the better part of two hours to corner him. As it was, they were standing in the hallway and could be interrupted at any moment.

"If you'll recall, your mother invited me."

"The only reason you're here is to embarrass me." The entire meal had been an exercise in frustration for Mary Jo. Evan had been the center of attention and had answered a multitude of questions from her parents and brothers. As for the way he'd treated Gary—every time she thought about it, she seethed. Anyone watching them would think Evan and Gary were old pals. Evan had joked and teased with Gary, even going so far as to mention that Mary Jo's ears grew red whenever she was uncomfortable with a subject.

The second he'd said it, she felt the blood rush to her ears. Soon they were so hot she was afraid Gary might mistake them for a fire engine.

What upset her most was the way Evan had her family eating out of his hand. Everyone acted as though he was some sort of celebrity! Her mother had offered him the first slice of chocolate cake, something Mary Jo could never remember happening. No matter who was seated at the dinner table, her father had always been served first.

"I didn't mean to make you uncomfortable," Evan said now, his eyes as innocent as a preschooler's.

Mary Jo wasn't fooled. She knew why he'd come—to humiliate her in front of her family. Rarely had she been angrier. Rarely had she felt more frustrated. Tears filled her eyes and blurred her vision.

"You can think what you want of me, but don't *ever* laugh at my family," she said between gritted teeth. She whirled away and had taken all of two steps when he caught hold of her shoulder and yanked her around.

Now he was just as angry. His dark eyes burned with it. They glared at each other, faces tight, hands clenched.

"I would never laugh at your family," he said evenly.

Mary Jo straightened her shoulders defiantly. "But you look forward to make a laughingstock out of *me*. Let me give you an example. You knew I wasn't married, yet you manipulated me into admitting it. You *enjoy* making me uncomfortable!"

He grinned then, a sly off-center grin. "I figured you owed me that much."

"I don't owe you anything!" she snapped.

"Perhaps not," he agreed. He was laughing at her, had been from the moment she stepped into his high-priced office. Like an unsuspecting fly, she'd carelessly gotten caught in a spider's web.

"Stay out of my life," she warned, eyes narrowed.

Evan glared back at her. "Gladly."

Just then Sally, one of Mary Jo's favorite nieces, came skipping down the hallway as only a five-year-old can, completely unaware of the tension between her and Evan. Sally stopped when she saw Mary Jo with Evan.

"Hi," she said, looking up at them.

"Hello, sweetheart," Mary Jo said, forcing herself to smile. Her mouth felt as if it would crack.

Sally stared at Evan, her eyes wide with curiosity. "Are you going to be my uncle someday?"

"No," Mary Jo answered immediately, mortified. It seemed that even her own family had turned against her. "Why not?" Sally wanted to know. "I like him better than Gary, and he likes you, too. I can tell. When we were eating dinner, he kept looking at you. Like Daddy looks at Mommy sometimes."

"I'm dating Gary," Mary Jo insisted, "and he's taking me to a movie. You can come if you want."

Sally shook her head. "Gary likes you, but he doesn't like kids very much."

Mary Jo's heart sank as though it were weighted down with cement blocks. She'd noticed that about Gary herself. He wasn't accustomed to small children; they made him uncomfortable. Kid noise irritated him. Evan, on the other hand, was an instant hit with both the adults and the kids. Nothing her nieces or nephews said or did seemed to bother him. If anything, he appeared to enjoy himself. He'd played volleyball and baseball with her brothers, chess with her father, and wrestled with the kids—ten against one.

"I hope you marry Evan," Sally said, her expression serious. Having stated her opinion, she skipped on down to the end of the hallway.

"Mary Jo."

Before she could say anything else to Evan—although she didn't know what—Gary came looking for her. He stopped abruptly when he saw who she was with.

"I didn't mean to interrupt anything," he said, burying his hands in his pockets, obviously uncomfortable.

"You didn't," Mary Jo answered decisively. "Now, what movie do you think we should see?" She turned her back on Evan and walked toward Gary, knowing in her heart that Sally was right. Evan was the man for her. Not Gary.

"I'm absolutely delighted you came," Jessica Dryden said, opening the front door. Mary Jo stepped into the Dryden home, mildly surprised that a maid or other household help hadn't greeted her. From what she remembered of the older Drydens' home, Whispering Willows, the domestic staff had been with them for nearly thirty years.

"Thank you for inviting me," Mary Jo said, looking around. The house was a sprawling rambler decorated with comfortable modern furniture. An ocean scene graced the wall above the fireplace, but it wasn't by an artist Mary Jo recognized. Judging by the decor and relaxed atmosphere, Damian and Jessica seemed to be a fairly typical young couple.

"I fixed us a seafood salad," Jessica said, leading Mary Jo into the large, spotless kitchen. She followed, her eyes taking in everything around her. Jessica and Damian's home was spacious and attractive, but it was nothing like Whispering Willows.

"You made the salad yourself?" Mary Jo asked. She didn't mean to sound rude, but she'd assumed Jessica had kitchen help.

"Yes," Jessica answered pleasantly. "I'm a fairly good cook. At least Damian hasn't complained. Much," she added with a dainty laugh. "I thought we'd eat on the patio. That is, if you don't mind. It's such a beautiful afternoon. I was working in the garden earlier and I cut us some roses. They're so lovely this time of year."

Sliding glass doors led to a brick-lined patio. A round glass table, shaded by a brightly striped umbrella, was set with two pink placemats and linen napkins. A bouquet of yellow roses rested in the middle.

"Would you like iced tea with lunch?" Jessica asked next.

"Please."

"Sit down and I'll bring everything out."

"Let me help." Mary Jo wasn't accustomed to being waited on and would have been uncomfortable letting Jessica do all the work. She followed her new friend into the kitchen and carried out the pitcher of tea while Jessica brought the seafood salad.

"Where's Andy?" Mary Jo asked.

"Napping." She set the salad bowl and matching plates on the table and glanced at her watch. "We'll have a solid hour of peace. I hope."

They sat down together. Jessica gazed at her earnestly and began to speak. "I realize you must think I'm terribly presumptuous to have written you that note, but I'm dying to talk to you."

"I'll admit curiosity is what brought me here," Mary Jo confessed. She'd expected to feel awkward and out of place, but Jessica was so easygoing and unpretentious Mary Jo felt perfectly at ease.

"I've known Evan from the time I was a kid. We grew up next door to each other," Jessica explained. "When I was a teenager I had the biggest crush on him. I made an absolute fool of myself." She shook her head wryly.

Mary Jo thought it was no wonder she found herself liking Jessica so much. They obviously had a great deal in common—especially when it came to Evan!

"As you may be aware, I worked with Evan when he represented

Earl Kress. Naturally we spent a good deal of time together. Evan and I became good friends and he told me about you.''

Mary Jo nervously smoothed the linen napkin across her lap. She wasn't sure she wanted to hear what Jessica had to say.

''I hurt him deeply, didn't I?'' she asked, keeping her head lowered.

''Yes.'' Apparently Jessica didn't believe in mincing words. ''I don't know what happened between you and the man you left Evan for, but clearly it didn't work out the way you expected.''

''Few things in life happen the way we expect them to, do they?'' Mary Jo answered cryptically.

''No.'' Jessica set down her fork. ''For a while I was convinced there wasn't any hope for Damian and me. You see, I loved Damian, but everyone kept insisting Evan and I should be a couple. It gets confusing, so I won't go into the details, but Damian seemed to think he was doing the noble thing by stepping aside so I could marry Evan. It didn't seem to matter that I was in love with him. Everything was complicated even more by family expectations. Oh, my heavens,'' she said with a heartfelt sigh, ''those were bleak days.''

''But you worked everything out.''

''Yes,'' Jessica said with a relaxed smile. ''It wasn't easy, but it was sure worth the effort.'' She paused, resting her hands in her lap. ''This is the reason I asked you to have lunch with me. I realize that what happens between you and Evan is none of my business. And knowing Evan, he'd be furious with me if he realized I was even speaking to you, but...'' She stopped and took in a deep breath. ''You once shared something very special with Evan. I'm hoping that with a little effort on both your parts you can reclaim it.''

A cloak of sadness seemed to settle over Mary Jo's shoulders, and when she spoke her words were little more than a whisper. ''It isn't possible anymore.''

''Why isn't it? I don't know why you've come to Evan. That's none of my affair. But I do realize how much courage it must have taken. You're already halfway there, Mary Jo. Don't give up now.''

Mary Jo wished she could believe that, but it was too late for her and Evan now. Whatever chance they'd had as a couple had been destroyed long ago.

By her own hand.

Her reasons for breaking off the relationship hadn't changed. She'd done it because she had to, and she'd done it in such a way that Evan would never forgive her. That was part of her plan—for his own sake.

"In some ways I think Evan hates me," she murmured. Speaking was almost painful; there was a catch in her voice.

"Nonsense," Jessica insisted. "I don't believe that for a moment."

Mary Jo wished she could accept her friend's words, but Jessica hadn't been there when Evan suggested she hire another attorney. She hadn't seen the look in Evan's eyes when she'd confronted him in the hallway of her family home. Nor had she been there when Mary Jo had introduced him to Gary.

He despised her, and the ironic thing was she couldn't blame him.

"Just remember what I said," Jessica urged. "Be patient with Evan, and with yourself. But most of all, don't give up, not until you're convinced it'll never work. I speak from experience, Mary Jo—the rewards are well worth whatever it costs your pride. I can't imagine my life without Damian and Andy."

After a brief silence, Mary Jo resolutely changed the subject, and the two women settled down to their meal. Conversation was light-hearted—books and movies they'd both enjoyed, anecdotes about friends and family, opinions about various public figures.

They were continuing a good-natured disagreement over one of the Red Sox pitchers as they carried their plates back inside. Just as they reached the kitchen, the doorbell chimed.

"I'll get that," Jessica said.

Smiling, Mary Jo rinsed off the plates and placed them in the dishwasher. She liked Jessica very much. Damian's wife was open and natural and had a wonderful sense of humor. She was also deeply in love with her husband.

"It's Evan," Jessica said, returning to the kitchen. Her voice was strained and tense. Evan stood stiffly behind his sister-in-law. "He dropped off some papers for Damian."

"Uh, hello, Evan," Mary Jo said awkwardly.

Jessica's gaze pleaded with her to believe she hadn't arranged this accidental meeting.

Andy let out a piercing cry, and Mary Jo decided the toddler had the worst sense of timing of any baby she'd ever known.

Jessica excused herself, and Mary Jo was left standing next to the dishwasher, wishing she were anyplace else in the world.

"What are you doing here?" he demanded the minute Jessica was out of earshot.

"You showed up at *my* family's home. Why is it so shocking that I'm at your brother's house?"

"I was invited," he reminded her fiercely.

"So was I."

He looked for a moment as if he didn't believe her. "Fine. I suppose you and Jessica have decided to become bosom buddies. That sounds like something you'd do."

Mary Jo didn't have a response to such a patently unfair remark.

"As it happens," Evan said in a clear effort to put his anger behind him, "I was meaning to call you this afternoon, anyway."

"About my parents' case?" she asked anxiously.

"I've talked with my colleague about Adison Investments, and it looks as if it'll involve some lengthy litigation."

Mary Jo leaned against the kitchen counter. "Lengthy is another word for expensive, right?"

"I was prepared to discuss my fee with you at the same time," he continued in a businesslike tone.

"All right," she said, tensing.

"I can't see this costing anything less than six or seven thousand."

She couldn't help a sharp intake of breath. That amount of money was a fortune to her parents. To her, too.

"It could go even higher."

Which was another way of saying he wasn't willing to handle the case. Mary Jo felt the sudden need to sit down. She walked over to the table, pulled out a chair and plunked herself down.

"I'd be willing to do what I can, but—"

"Don't lie to me, Evan," she said, fighting back her hurt and frustration. She'd come to him because he had the clout and the influence to help her family. Because he was a damn good attorney. Because she'd trusted him to be honest and ethical.

"I'm not lying."

"Six or seven thousand dollars is far beyond what my parents or I can afford. That may not be a lot of money to you or your family, but there's no way we could hope to raise that much in a short amount of time."

"I'm willing to take payments."

How very generous of him, she mused sarcastically.

"There might be another way," he said.

"What?"

"If you agree, of course."

Mary Jo wasn't sure she liked the sound of this.

"A summer job. You're out of school, aren't you?"

She nodded.

"My secretary, Mrs. Sterling, is taking an extended European vacation this summer. I'd intended to hire a replacement, but as I recall your typing and dictation skills are excellent."

"My typing skills are minimal and I never took shorthand."

He grinned as if that didn't matter. Obviously, what did matter was making her miserable for the next two months.

"But you're a fast learner. Am I right or wrong?" he pressed.

"Well...I do pick up things up fairly easily."

"That's what I thought." He spread out his hands. "Now, do you want the job or not?"

Four

"Mr. Dryden's a real pleasure to work for. I'm sure you won't have any problems," Mrs. Sterling said, looking absolutely delighted that Mary Jo would be substituting for her. "Evan's not the least bit demanding, and I can't think of even one time when he's been unreasonable."

Mary Jo suspected that might not be the case with her.

"I could have retired with my husband, but I enjoy my job so much I decided to stay on," Mrs. Sterling continued. "I couldn't bear leaving that young man. In some ways, I think of Evan as my own son."

"I'm sure he reciprocates your feelings," Mary Jo said politely. She didn't know how much longer she could endure listening to this list of Evan's finer qualities. Not that she doubted they were true. For Mrs. Sterling.

Thus far, Evan had embarrassed her in front of her family and blackmailed her into working for him. She had a problem picturing him as Prince Charming to her Cinderella. As for his being a "real pleasure" to work for, Mary Jo entertained some serious reservations.

"I'm glad you've got the opportunity to travel with your husband," Mary Jo added.

"That's another thing," Evan's secretary gushed. "What boss would be willing to let his secretary go for two whole months like this? It's a terrible inconvenience to him. Nevertheless, Mr. Dryden encouraged me to take this trip with Dennis. Why, he *insisted* I go. I promise you, they don't come any better than Mr. Dryden. You're going to thoroughly enjoy your summer."

Mary Jo's smile was weak at best.

Evan wanted her under his thumb, and much as she disliked

giving in to the pressure, she had no choice. Six or seven thousand dollars would financially cripple her parents. Evan knew that. He was also well aware that her brothers weren't in any position to help.

With the slump in the economy, new construction starts had been way down. Jack, Rich and Lonny had collected unemployment benefits most of the winter and were just scraping by now. Bill and Mark's automotive business was barely on its feet.

She was the one who'd gone to Evan for help, and she was the one who'd accepted the financial responsibility. When she'd told her parents she'd be working for Evan, they were both delighted. Her mother seemed to think it was the perfect solution. Whether Evan had planned it this way or not, his employing her had helped smooth her father's ruffled feathers about Evan's fee. Apparently, letting her pick up any out-of-pocket expenses was unacceptable to Norman Summerhill, but an exchange of services, so to speak, was fine.

Evan, who could do no wrong as far as her parents were concerned, came out of this smelling like a rose, to use one of her dad's favorite expressions.

Mary Jo wondered if she was being unfair to assume that Evan was looking for vengeance, for a means of making her life miserable. Perhaps she'd misjudged him.

Perhaps. But she sincerely doubted it.

"I'm taking my lunch now," Mrs. Sterling said, pulling open the bottom drawer of her desk and taking out her handbag. She hesitated. "You will be all right here by yourself, won't you?"

"Of course." Mary Jo made an effort to sound infinitely confident, even if she wasn't. Evan's legal assistant, Peter McNichols, was on vacation for the next couple of weeks, so she'd be dealing with Evan entirely on her own.

Mary Jo wasn't sure she was emotionally prepared for that just yet. The shaky, unsure feeling in the pit of her stomach reminded her of the first time she'd stood in front of a classroom filled with five-year-olds.

No sooner had Mrs. Sterling left when Evan summoned Mary

Jo. Grabbing a pen and pad, she hurried into his office, determined to be the best substitute secretary he could have hired.

"Sit down," he instructed in a brisk, businesslike tone.

Mary Jo complied, sitting on the very edge of the chair, her back ramrod-straight, her shoulders stiff.

He reached for a small, well-worn black book and flipped through the flimsy pages, scrutinizing the names. Mary Jo realized it had to be the typical bachelor's infamous "black book." She knew he had a reputation, after all, as one of Boston's most eligible bachelors. Every six months or so, gossip columns speculated on Evan Dryden's current love interest. A little black book was exactly what she expected of him.

"Order a dozen red roses to be sent to Catherine Moore," he said, and rattled off the address. Mary Jo immediately recognized it as being in a prestigious neighborhood. "Suggest we meet for lunch on the twenty-fifth. Around twelve-thirty." He mentioned one of Boston's most elegant restaurants. "Have you got that?" he asked.

"I'll see to it immediately," Mary Jo said crisply, revealing none of her feelings. Evan had done this on purpose. He was having her arrange a lunch date with one of his many conquests in order to humiliate her, to teach her a lesson. It was his way of telling her that he'd recovered completely from their short-lived romance. There were any number of women who would welcome his attentions.

Well, Mary Jo got the message, loud and clear. She stood, ready to return to her desk.

"There's more," Evan said.

Mary Jo sat back down and was barely able to keep up with him as he listed name after name, followed by phone number and address. Each woman was to receive a dozen red roses and an invitation to lunch, with time and place suggested.

When he'd finished, Mary Jo counted six names, each conjuring up a statuesque beauty. No doubt every one of them could run circles around her in looks, talent and, most important, social position.

Mary Jo didn't realize one man could find that many places to eat with so many different women, but she wisely kept her opinion to herself. If he was hoping she'd give him the satisfaction of a response, he was dead wrong.

She'd just finished ordering the flowers when Damian Dryden stepped into the office.

"Hello," he said. His eyes widened with surprise at finding her sitting at Mrs. Sterling's desk.

Mary Jo stood and extended her hand. "I'm Mary Jo Summerhill. We met briefly last week." She didn't mention the one other time she'd been introduced to Damian, certain he wouldn't remember.

It was well over three years ago. Evan and Mary Jo had been sailing, and they'd run into Damian at the marina. Her first impression of Evan's older brother was that of a shrewd businessman. Damian had seemed stiff and somewhat distant. He'd shown little interest in their cheerful commentary on sailing and the weather. From conversations she'd previously had with Evan regarding his brother, she'd learned he was a serious and hardworking lawyer, and that was certainly how he'd struck her—as someone with no time for fun or frivolity. Currently, he was a Superior Court judge, but he often stopped in at the family law firm. Apparently the two brothers were close friends, as well as brothers.

The man she'd met on the dock that day and the one who stood before her now might have been two entirely different men. Damian remained serious and hardworking, but he was more relaxed now, more apt to smile. Mary Jo was convinced that marriage and fatherhood had made the difference, and she was genuinely happy for him and for Jessica. They seemed perfect for each other.

"You're working for the firm now?" Damian asked.

"Mrs. Sterling will be traveling in Europe this summer," Mary Jo explained, "and Evan, uh, offered me the job." Which was a polite way of saying he'd coerced her into accepting the position.

"But I thought—" Damian stopped abruptly, then grinned. "Is Evan in?"

"Yes. I'll tell him you're here." She reached for the intercom switch and announced Damian, who walked directly into Evan's office.

Mary Jo was acquainting herself with the filing system when she heard Evan burst out laughing. It really wasn't fair to assume it had something to do with her, but she couldn't help believing that was the case.

Damian left a couple of minutes later, smiling. He paused in front of Mary Jo's desk. "Don't let him give you a hard time," he said pleasantly. "My wife mentioned having you over for lunch last week, but she didn't say you'd accepted a position with the firm."

"I...I didn't know it myself at the time," Mary Jo mumbled. She hadn't actually agreed to the job until much later, after she'd spent a few days sorting through her limited options.

"I see. Well, it's good to have you on board, Mary Jo. If you have any questions or concerns, don't hesitate to talk to Evan. And if he does give you a hard time, just let me know and I'll straighten him out."

"Thank you," she said, and meant it. Although she couldn't very well see herself complaining to one brother about the other....

She decided to change her attitude about the whole situation. She'd forget about Evan's probable motives and, instead, start looking at the positive side of this opportunity. She'd be able to help her parents now, without dipping into her own savings. Things could definitely be worse.

Mary Jo didn't learn just how *much* worse until Wednesday— the first day she was working on her own. Mrs. Sterling had spent the first two days of the week acquainting Mary Jo with office procedures and the filing system. She'd updated her on Evan's current cases, and Mary Jo felt reasonably confident she could handle whatever came up.

He called her into his office around eleven. "I need the William Jenkins file."

"I'll have it for you right away," she assured him. Mary Jo returned to the outer office and the filing cabinet, and sorted through the colored tabs. She located three clients named Jenkins, none of whom was William. Her heart started to pound with dread as she hurried to another filing drawer, thinking it might have been misfiled.

Five minutes passed. Evan came out of his office, his movements as brusque and irritated as his voice. "Is there a problem?"

"I...can't seem to find the William Jenkins file," she said, hurriedly riffling through the files one more time. "Are you sure it isn't on your desk?"

"Would I have asked you to find it if I had it on my desk?" She could feel his cold stare directly between the shoulder blades.

"No, I guess not. But it isn't out here."

"It has to be. I distinctly remember giving it to Mrs. Sterling on Monday."

"She had me replace all the files on Monday," Mary Jo admitted reluctantly.

"Then you must have misfiled it."

"I don't recall any file with the name Jenkins," she said stubbornly. She didn't want to make an issue of this, but she'd been extremely careful with every file, even double-checking her work.

"Are you telling me I *didn't* return the file? Are you calling me a liar?"

This wasn't going well. "No," she said in a slow, deliberate voice. "All I'm saying is that I don't recall replacing any file with the name Jenkins on it." Their gazes met and locked in silent battle.

Evan's dark eyes narrowed briefly. "Are you doing this on purpose, Mary Jo?" he asked, crossing his arms over his chest.

"Absolutely not." Outraged, she brought her chin up and met his glare. "You can think whatever you like of me, but I'd never do anything so underhanded as hide an important file."

She wasn't sure if he believed her or not, and his lack of trust hurt her more than any words he might have spoken. "If you honestly suspect I'd sabotage your office, then I suggest you fire me immediately."

Evan walked over to the cabinet and pulled open the top drawer. He was searching through the files, the same way she had earlier.

Silently Mary Jo prayed she hadn't inadvertently missed seeing the requested file. The humiliation of having him find it would be unbearable.

"It isn't here," he murmured, sounding almost surprised.

Mary Jo gave an inward sigh of relief.

"Where could it possibly be?" he asked impatiently. "I need it for an appointment this afternoon."

Mary Jo edged a couple of steps toward him. "Would you mind if I looked in your office?"

He gestured toward the open door. "By all means."

She sorted through the stack of files on the corner of his desk and leafed through his briefcase, all to no avail. Glancing at the clock, she groaned inwardly. "You have a luncheon appointment," she reminded him.

"I need that file!" he snapped.

Mary Jo bristled. "I'm doing my best."

"Your best clearly isn't good enough. *Find that file.*"

"I'll do a much better job of it if you aren't here breathing down my neck. Go and have lunch, and I'll find the Jenkins file." She'd dismantle the filing cabinets one by one until she'd located it, if that was what it took.

Evan hesitated, then glanced at his watch. "I won't be long," he muttered, reaching for his jacket and thrusting his arms into the sleeves. "I'll give you a call from the restaurant."

"All right."

"If worse comes to worst, we can reschedule the client," he said as he buttoned the jacket. Evan had always been a smart dresser, she reflected irrelevantly. No matter what the circumstances, he looked as if he'd just stepped off a page in *Esquire* or *G.Q.*

"Look" Evan said, pausing at the door. "Don't worry about it. The file has to surface sometime." He seemed to be apologizing, however indirectly, for his earlier bout of bad temper.

She nodded, feeling guilty although she had no reason. But the file was missing and she felt responsible, despite the fact that she'd never so much as seen it.

Since she'd brought her lunch with her to work, Mary Jo nibbled at it as she sorted through every single file drawer in every single cabinet. Mrs. Sterling was meticulously neat, and not a single file had been misplaced.

Mary Jo was sitting on the carpet, files spread around her, when Evan phoned.

"Did you find it?"

"No, I'm sorry, Evan...Mr. Dryden," she corrected quickly.

His lengthy pause added to her feelings of guilt and confusion. She'd been so determined to be a good replacement. By heaven, she'd vowed, she was going to give him his money's worth. Yet here it was—her day of working alone—and already she'd failed him.

By the time Evan was back at the office, she'd reassembled everything. He made the call to reschedule the appointment with William Jenkins, saving her the task of inventing an excuse.

At three o'clock her phone rang. It was Gary, and the instant she recognized his voice, Mary Jo groaned inwardly.

"How'd you know where to reach me?" she asked, keeping her voice low. Evan was sure to frown on personal phone calls, especially from a male friend. After their confrontation that morning, she felt bad enough.

"Your mom told me you were working for Daddy Warbucks now."

"Don't call him that," she said heatedly, surprised at the flash of anger she experienced.

Gary was silent, as if he, too, was taken back by her outburst. "I apologize," he said, sounding genuinely contrite. "I didn't phone to start an argument. I wanted you to know I've taken our talk last Sunday to heart. How about dinner and dancing this Saturday? We could go to one of those all-you-can-eat places that serve barbecued ribs, and shuffle our feet a little afterward."

"Uh, maybe we could talk about this later."

"Yes or no?" Gary cajoled. "Just how difficult can it be? I thought you'd be pleased."

"It isn't a good idea to call me at the office, Gary."

"But I'll be at the fire station by the time you're off work," he explained. "I thought you wanted us to spend more time together. That's what you said, isn't it?"

Was that what she'd said? She didn't think so. Not exactly. "Uh, well..." Why, oh why, was life so complicated?

"I'm glad you spoke up," Gary continued when she didn't, "because I tend to get lazy in a relationship. I want you to know how much I appreciate your company."

"All right, I'll go," she said ungraciously, knowing it was the only way she was likely to get him off the phone quickly. "Saturday evening. What time?"

"Six okay?. I'll pick you up."

"Six is fine."

"We're going to have a great time, Mary Jo. Just you wait and see."

She wasn't at all convinced of that, but she supposed she didn't have any right to complain. Eager to please, Gary was doing exactly what she'd asked of him. And frankly, dinner with Gary was a damn sight better than sitting home alone.

No sooner had she hung up the phone when Evan opened his door and stared at her, his look hard and disapproving. He didn't say a word about personal phone calls. He didn't have to. The heat radiated from her cheeks.

"Th-that was Gary," she said, then wanted to kick herself for volunteering the information. "I explained that I can't take personal phone calls at the office. He won't be phoning again."

"Good," he said, and closed the door. It clicked sharply into place, as if to underline his disapproval. She returned to the letter she was typing into the computer.

Just before five, Mary Jo collected the letters that required Evan's signature and carried them to his office. He was reading over a brief, and momentarily glanced up when she knocked softly and entered the room.

"Is there anything else you'd like me to do before I leave?" she asked, depositing the unsigned letters onto the corner of his desk.

He shook his head. "Nothing, thank you. Good night, Ms. Summerhill."

He sounded so stiff and formal. As if he'd never held her, never kissed her. As if she'd never meant anything to him and never would.

"Good night, Mr. Dryden." She turned quickly and walked out of the office.

After their brief exchange regarding the missing file, they'd been coolly polite to each other during the rest of the day.

If his intention was to punish her, he couldn't have devised a more effective means.

Because she loved Evan. She'd never stopped loving him, no matter how she tried to convince herself otherwise. Being with him every day and maintaining this crisp, professional facade was the cruelest form of punishment.

Once she was home, Mary Jo kicked off her low heels, slumped into the rocking chair and closed her eyes in a desperate attempt to relax. She hadn't worked for Evan a full week yet, and already she wondered if she could last another day.

The rest of the summer didn't bear thinking about.

"What I don't understand," Marianna Summerhill said as she chopped up chicken for the summer salad, "is why you and Evan ever broke up."

"Mom, please, it was a long time ago."

"Not so long. Two, three years."

"Do you want me to set the table?" Mary Jo asked, hoping to distract her mother. That she hadn't seen through this unexpected dinner invitation only showed how weary she was, how low her defenses. Her mother had phoned only the evening before, when Mary Jo was still recovering from working on her own with Evan; she'd insisted Mary Jo join them for dinner and "a nice visit."

"So, how's the job going?" her father asked, sitting down at the kitchen table. The huge dining room table was reserved for Sunday dinners with as many of the family that could come.

"Oh, just great," Mary Jo said, working up enough energy to offer him a reassuring smile. She didn't want her parents to know what the job was costing her emotionally.

"I was just saying to Mary Jo what a fine young man Evan Dryden is." Her mother set the salad in the center of the table and pulled out a chair.

"He certainly is a decent sort. You were dating him a while back, weren't you?"

"Yes, Dad."

"Seems to me the two of you were real serious." When she didn't immediately answer, he added, "As I recall, he gave you an engagement ring, didn't he? You had him come to dinner that one time. Whatever happened, Mary Jo? Did our family scare him off?''

Mary Jo was forever bound to hide the truth. Evan had been an instant hit with her family. They'd thrown open their arms and welcomed him, delighted that Mary Jo had found a man to love. Not for the world would she let her parents be hurt. Not for the world would she tell them the truth.

How could she possibly explain that their only daughter, whom they adored, wasn't good enough for the high-and-mighty Drydens? The minute Mary Jo met Evan's mother, she sensed the older woman's disappointment in her. Lois Dryden was looking for more in a daughter-in-law than Mary Jo could ever be.

Their private chat after dinner had set the record straight. Evan was destined for politics and would need a certain type of wife, Mrs. Dryden had gently explained. Mary Jo didn't hear much beyond that.

Mrs. Dryden had strongly implied that Mary Jo would hinder Evan's political aspirations. She might very well ruin his life. There'd been some talk about destiny and family expectations and the demands on a political wife—Mary Jo's memories of the conversation were vague. But her understanding of Mrs. Dryden's message had been anything but.

Evan needed a woman who would be an asset—socially and politically. As an electrician's daughter, Mary Jo couldn't possibly be that woman. End of discussion.

"Mary Jo?"

Her mother's worried voice cut into her thoughts. She shook her head and smiled. "I'm sorry, Mom, what were you saying?"

"Your father asked you a question."

"About you and Evan," Norman elaborated. "I thought you two were pretty serious."

"We were serious at one time," she admitted, seeing no other way around it. "We were even engaged. But we...drifted apart. Those things happen, you know. Luckily we realized that before it was too late."

"But he's such a dear boy."

"He's a charmer, Mom," Mary Jo said, making light of his

appeal. "But he's not the man for me. Besides, I'm dating Gary now."

Her parents exchanged meaningful glances.

"You don't like Gary?" Mary Jo prodded.

"Of course we like him," Marianna said cautiously. "It's just that...well, he's very sweet, but frankly, Mary Jo, I just don't see Gary as the man for you."

Frankly, Mary Jo didn't, either.

"It seems to me," her father said slowly while he buttered a slice of bread, "that your young man's more interested in your mother's cooking than he is in you."

So the family had noticed. Not that Gary'd made any secret of it. "Gary's just a friend, Dad. You don't need to worry—we aren't really serious."

"What about Evan?" Marianna studied Mary Jo carefully, wearing the concerned expression she always wore whenever she suspected one of her children was ill. An intense, narrowed expression—as if staring at Mary Jo long enough would reveal the problem.

"Oh, Evan's a friend, too," Mary Jo said airily, but she didn't really believe it. She doubted they could ever be friends again.

Late FRiday afternoon, just before she began getting ready to leave for the weekend, Evan called Mary Jo into his office. He was busy writing, and she waited until he'd finished before she asked, "You wanted to see me?"

"Yes," he said absently, reaching for a file folder. "I'm afraid I'm going to need you tomorrow."

"On Saturday?" She'd assumed the weekends were her own.

"I'm sure Mrs. Sterling mentioned I might occasionally need you to travel with me."

"No, she didn't," Mary Jo said, holding her shoulders rigid. She could guess what was coming. Somehow he was going to keep her from seeing Gary Saturday night. A man who lunched with a different woman every day of the week wanted to cheat her out of one dinner date with a friend.

"As it happens, I'll need you tomorrow afternoon and evening. I'm driving up to—"

"As it happens I already have plans for tomorrow evening," she interrupted defiantly.

"Then I suggest you cancel," he said impassively. "According to the terms of our agreement, you're to be at my disposal for the next two months. I need you this Saturday afternoon and evening."

"Yes, but—"

"May I remind you, that you're being well compensated for your time?"

It would take more than counting to ten to cool Mary Jo's rising temper. She wasn't fooled. Not for a second. Evan was doing this on purpose. He'd overheard her conversation with Gary.

"And if I refuse?" she asked, her outrage and defiance evident in every syllable.

Evan shrugged, as if it wasn't his concern one way or the other. "Then I'll have no choice but to fire you."

The temptation to throw the job back in his face was so strong she had to close her eyes to control it. "You're doing this intentionally, aren't you?" she asked between gritted teeth. "I have a date with Gary Saturday night—you know I do—and you want to ruin it."

Evan leaned forward in his black leather chair; he seemed to weigh his words carefully. "Despite what you might think, I'm not a vindictive man. But, Ms. Summerhill, it doesn't really matter *what* you think."

She bit down so hard, her teeth hurt. "You're right, of course," she said quietly. "It doesn't matter what I think." She whirled around and stalked out of his office.

The force of her anger was too great to let her sit still. For ten minutes, she paced the office floor, then slumped into her chair. Resting her elbows on the desk, she buried her face in her hands, feeling very close to tears. It wasn't that this date with Gary was so important. It was that Evan would purposely ruin it for her.

"Mary Jo."

She dropped her hands to find Evan standing in front of her desk. They stared at one another for a long, still moment, then Mary Jo looked away. She wanted to wipe out the past and find the man she'd once loved. But she knew that what *he* wanted was to hurt her, to pay her back for the pain she'd caused him.

"What time do you need me?" she asked in an expressionless voice. She refused to meet his gaze.

"Three-thirty. I'll pick you up at your place."

"I'll be ready."

In the ensuing silence, Damian walked casually into the room. He stopped when he noticed them, glancing from Evan to Mary Jo and back again.

"I'm not interrupting anything, am I?"

"No." Evan recovered first and was quick to reassure his older brother. "What can I do for you, Damian?"

Damian gestured with the file he carried. "I read over the Jenkins case like you asked and jotted down some notes. I thought you might want to go over them with me."

The name Jenkins leapt out at Mary Jo. "Did you say *Jenkins?*" she asked excitedly.

"Why, yes. Evan gave me the file the other day and asked me for my opinion."

"I did?" Evan sounded genuinely shocked.

Damian frowned. "Don't you remember?"

"No," Evan said, "Good Lord, Mary Jo and I've been searching for that file since yesterday."

"All you had to do, little brother," Damian chided, "was ask me."

The two men disappeared into Evan's office while Mary Jo finished tidying up for the day. Damian left as she was gathering up her personal things.

"Evan would like to see you for a moment," he said on his way out the door.

Setting her purse aside, she walked into Evan's office. "You wanted to see me?" she asked coldly, standing just inside the doorway.

He stood at the window, staring down at the street far below, his hands clasped behind his back. His shoulders were slumped as if he'd grown weary. He turned to face her, his expression composed, even cool. "I apologize for the screw-up over the Jenkins file. I was entirely at fault. I did give it to Damian to read. I'm afraid it completely slipped my mind."

His apology came as a surprise. "It's no problem," she murmured.

"About tomorrow," he said next, his voice dropping slightly, "I won't be needing you, after all. Enjoy your evening with lover boy."

Five

"Is Evan coming?" Mary Jo's oldest brother, Jack, asked as he passed the bowl of mashed potatoes to his wife, Cathy.

"Yeah," Lonny piped in. "Where's Evan?"

"I heard you were working for him now," Cathy said, adding under her breath, "Lucky you."

Mary Jo's family was sitting around the big dining room table. Jack, Cathy and their three children, Lonny and his wife, Sandra, and their two kids, plus her parents—they'd all focused their attention on Mary Jo.

"Mr. Dryden doesn't tell me his plans," she said stiffly, uncomfortable with their questions.

"You call him 'Mr. Dryden?'" her father quizzed, frowning.

"I'm his employee," Mary Jo replied.

"His father is a senator," Marianna reminded her husband, as if this was important information he didn't already know.

"I thought you said Evan's your friend." Her father wasn't going to give up, Mary Jo realized, until he had the answers he wanted.

"He *is* my friend," she returned evenly, "but while I'm an employee of the law firm it's important to maintain a certain decorum." That was a good response, she thought a bit smugly. One her father couldn't dispute.

"Did you invite him to Sunday dinner, dear?" her mother wanted to know.

"No."

"Then that explains it," Marianna said with a disappointed sigh. "Next week I'll see to it myself. We owe him a big debt of thanks."

Mary Jo resisted telling her mother that a man like Evan Dryden had more important things to do than plan his Sunday afternoons around her family's dinner. He'd come once as a gesture of friendliness, but they shouldn't expect him again. Her mother would learn that soon enough.

"How's the case with Adison Investments going, M.J.?" Jack asked, stabbing his fork into a marinated vegetable. "Have you heard anything?"

"Not yet," Mary Jo answered. "Evan had Mrs. Sterling type up a letter last week. I believe she mailed Mom and Dad a copy."

"She did," her father inserted.

"From my understanding, Evan, er, Mr. Dryden, gave Adison Investments two weeks to respond. If he hasn't heard from them by then, he'll prepare a lawsuit."

"Does he expect them to answer?" Rich burst out, his dark eyes flashing with anger.

"Now, son, don't get all riled up over this. Evan and Mary Jo are handling it now, and I have complete faith that justice will be served."

The family returned their attention to their food, and when the conversation moved on to other subjects, Mary Jo was grateful. Then, out of the blue, when she least expected it, her mother asked, "How'd your dinner date go with Gary?"

Taken aback, she stopped chewing, the fork poised in front of her mouth. Why was her life of such interest all of a sudden?

"Fine," she murmured when she'd swallowed. Once again the family's attention was on her. "Why is everyone looking at me?" she demanded.

Lonny chuckled. "It might be that we're wondering why you'd date someone like Gary Copeland when you could be going out with Evan Dryden."

"I doubt very much that Evan dates his employees," she said righteously. "It's bad business practice."

"I like Evan a whole lot," five-year-old Sally piped in. "You do, too, don't you, Aunt Mary Jo?"

"Hmm...yes," she admitted, knowing she'd never get away with a lie, at least not with her own family. They knew her too well.

"Where's Gary now?" her oldest brother asked as though he'd

only just noticed that her date hadn't joined them for dinner. "It seems to me he's generally here. You'd think the guy had never tasted home cooking."

Now was as good a time as any to explain, Mary Jo decided. "Gary and I decided not to see each other anymore, Jack," she said, hoping to gloss over the details. "We're both doing different things now, and we've...drifted apart."

"Isn't that what you were telling me about you and Evan Dryden?" her father asked thoughtfully.

Mary Jo had forgotten that. Indeed, it was exactly what she'd said.

"Seems to me," her father added with a knowing parental look, "that you've been doing a lot of drifting apart from people lately."

Her mother, bless her heart, cast Mary Jo's father a frown. "If you ask me, it's the other way around." She nodded once as if to say the subject was now closed.

In some ways, Mary Jo was going to miss Gary. He was a friend and they'd parted on friendly terms. She hadn't intended to end their relationship, but over dinner Gary had suggested they think seriously about their future together.

To put it mildly, she'd been shocked. She'd felt comfortable in their rather loose relationship. Now Gary was looking for something more. She wasn't.

She realized he'd been disappointed, but he'd seemed to accept and appreciate her honesty.

"I like Evan better, anyway," Sally said solemnly. She nodded once like her grandmother had just done, and the pink ribbons on her pigtails bobbed. "You'll bring him to dinner now, won't you?"

"I don't know, sweetheart."

"I do," her mother said, smiling confidently. "A mother knows these things, and it seems to me that Evan Dryden is the perfect man for our Mary Jo."

Evan was in the office when Mary Jo arrived early Monday morning. She quickly prepared a pot of coffee and brought him a mug as soon as it was ready.

He was on the phone but glanced up when she entered his office and smiled his appreciation as he accepted the coffee. She returned to the outer office, amazed—and a little frightened—by how much one of his smiles could affect her.

Mary Jo's greatest fear was that the longer they worked together the more difficult it would be for her to maintain her guard. Without being aware of it, she might reveal her true feelings for Evan.

The phone rang and she automatically reached for it, enjoying her role as Evan's secretary. She and Evan had had their share of differences, but seemed to have resolved them. In the office, anyway.

"Mary Jo." It was Jessica Dryden on the line.

Mary Jo stiffened, fearing Evan might hear her taking a personal call. She didn't want anything to jeopardize their newly amicable relationship. The door to his office was open and he had a clear view of her from his desk.

"May I help you?" she asked in her best secretary voice.

Jessica hesitated at her cool, professional tone. "Hey, it's me. Jessica."

"I realize that."

Jessica laughed lightly. "I get it. Evan must be listening."

"That's correct." Mary Jo had trouble hiding a smile. One chance look in her direction, and he'd know this was no client she had on the line.

"Damian told me you're working for Evan now. What happened?" Jessica's voice lowered to a whisper as if she feared Evan would hear her, too.

Mary Jo carefully weighed her words. "I believe that case involved blackmail."

"Blackmail?" Jessica repeated, and laughed outright. "This I've got to hear. Is he being a real slave driver?"

"No. Not exactly."

"Can you escape one afternoon and meet me for lunch?"

"I might be able to arrange a luncheon appointment. What day would you suggest?"

"How about tomorrow at noon? There's an Italian restaurant around the corner in the basement of the Wellman building. The food's great and the people who own it are like family."

"That sounds acceptable."

Evan appeared in the doorway between his office and hers. He studied her closely. Mary Jo swallowed uncomfortably at the obvious censure in his expression.

"Uh, perhaps I could confirm the details with you later."

Jessica laughed again. "Judging by your voice, Evan's standing right there—and he's figured out this isn't a business call."

"I believe you're right," she said stiffly.

Jessica seemed absolutely delighted. "I can't wait to hear all about this. I'll see you tomorrow, and Mary Jo..."

"Yes?" she urged, eager to get off the line.

"Have you thought any more about what I said? About working things out with Evan?"

"I...I'm thinking."

"Good. That's just great. I'll see you tomorrow, then."

Mary Jo replaced the receiver and darted a look in Evan's direction. He averted his eyes and slammed the door shut. As if he was furious with her. Worse, as if she disgusted him.

Stunned, Mary Jo sat at her desk, fighting back a surge of outrage. He was being unfair. At the very least, he could have given her the opportunity to explain!

The morning, which had started out so well, with a smile and a sense of promise, had quickly disintegrated into outright hostility. Evan ignored her for the rest of the morning, not speaking except about office matters. And even then, his voice was cold and impatient. The brusque, hurried instructions, the lack of eye contact—everything seemed to suggest he could barely tolerate the sight of her.

Without a word of farewell, he left at noon for his luncheon engagement and returned promptly at one-thirty, a scant few minutes before his first afternoon appointment. Mary Jo had begun to wonder if he planned to return at all, worrying about how she'd explain his absence if anyone called.

The temperature seemed to drop perceptibly the moment Evan walked in the door. She tensed, debating whether or not to confront him about his attitude.

Evan had changed, Mary Jo mused defeatedly. She couldn't remember him ever being this temperamental. She felt as though she were walking on the proverbial eggshells, afraid of saying or doing something that would irritate him even more.

Her afternoon was miserable. By five o'clock she knew she couldn't take much more of this silent treatment. She waited until the switchboard had been turned over to the answering service; that way there was no risk of being interrupted by a phone call.

The office was quiet—presumably almost everyone else had gone home—when she approached his door. She knocked, then immediately walked inside. He was working and seemed unaware of her presence. She stood there silently until he glanced up.

"Could I speak to you for a moment?" she asked, standing stiffly in front of his desk. She heard the small quaver in her voice and groaned inwardly. She'd wanted to sound strong and confident.

"Is there a problem?" Evan asked, raising his eyebrows as if surprised—and not pleasantly—by her request.

"I'm afraid my position here isn't working out."

"Oh?" Up went the eyebrows again. "And why isn't it?"

It was much too difficult to explain how deeply his moods affected her. A mere smile and she was jubilant, a frown and she was cast into despair.

"It...it just isn't," was the best she could do.

"Am I too demanding?"

"No," she admitted reluctantly.

"Unreasonable?"

She lowered her gaze and shook her head.

"Then what is it?" he demanded.

She gritted her teeth. "I want you to know that I've never made a personal phone call from this office during working hours."

"True, but you've received them."

"I assured you Gary wouldn't be phoning me again."

"But he did," Evan inserted smoothly.

"He most certainly did not," she said righteously.

"Mary Jo," he said with exaggerated patience, as though he were speaking to a child, "I heard you arranging a luncheon date with him myself."

"That was Jessica. Damian mentioned running into me at the office and she called and suggested we meet for lunch."

"Jessica," Evan muttered. He grew strangely quiet.

"I think it might be best if I sought employment elsewhere," Mary Jo concluded. "Naturally I'll be happy to train my replacement." She turned abruptly and started to leave.

"Mary Jo." He sighed heavily. "Listen, you're right. I've behaved like a jerk all day. I apologize. Your personal life, your phone calls—it's none of my business. I promise you this won't happen again."

Mary Jo paused, unsure what to think. She certainly hadn't expected an apology.

"I want you to stay on," he added. "You've been doing an excellent job, and I've been unfair. Will you?"

She should refuse, walk out while she had the excuse to do so. Leave without regrets. But she couldn't. She simply couldn't.

She offered him a shaky smile and nodded. "You know, you're not such a curmudgeon to work for, after all."

"I'm not?" He sounded downright cheerful. "This calls for a celebration, don't you think? Do you still enjoy sailing as much as you used to?"

She hadn't been on the water since the last time they'd taken out his sailboat. "I think so," she murmured, head spinning at his sudden reversal.

"Great. Run home and change clothes and meet me at the marina in an hour. We'll take out my boat and discover if you've still got your sea legs."

The prospect of spending time with Evan was too wonderful to turn down. For her sanity's sake, she should think twice before accepting the invitation, but she didn't. Whatever the price, she'd willingly pay it—later.

"Remember when I taught you to sail?" Evan asked, his eyes smiling.

Mary Jo couldn't keep herself from smiling back. He'd been infinitely patient with her. She came from a long line of landlubbers and was convinced she'd never become a sailor.

"I still remember the first time we pulled out of the marina with me at the helm. I rammed another sailboat," she reminded him, and they both laughed.

"You'll meet me?" Evan asked, oddly intense after their moment of lightness.

Mary Jo doubted she could have refused him anything. "Just don't ask me to motor the boat out of the slip."

"You've got yourself a deal."

A few hours earlier, she'd believed she couldn't last another hour working with Evan. Now here she was, agreeing to meet him after hours for a sailing lesson.

Rushing home, she threw off her clothes, not bothering to hang them up the way she usually did. She didn't stay longer than the few minutes it took to pull on a pair of jeans, a sweatshirt and her deck shoes. Any time for reflection, and Mary Jo was afraid she'd talk herself out of going. She wanted these few hours with Evan so much it hurt.

Right now she refused to think about anything except the evening ahead of them. For this one night she wanted to put the painful past behind them—wipe out the memory of the last three lonely years.

She could see Evan waiting for her when she arrived at the marina. The wind had turned brisk, perfect for sailing. The scent of salt and sea was carried on the breeze. Grabbing her purse, she trotted across the parking lot. Evan reached for her hand as if doing so was an everyday occurrence. Unthinkingly, Mary Jo gave it to him.

Both seemed to realize in the same instant what they'd done. Evan turned to her, his eyes questioning, as if he expected her to remove her hand from his. She met his gaze evenly and offered him a bright smile.

"I brought us something to eat," he said. "I don't know about you, but I'm starved."

Mary Jo was about to make some comment about his not eating an adequate lunch, when she remembered he'd been out with Catherine Moore. Mary Jo wondered if the other woman was as elegant as her name suggested.

Evan leapt aboard, then helped her onto the small deck. He went below to retrieve the jib and mainsail, and when he emerged Mary Jo asked, "Do you want me to rig the jib sail?"

He seemed surprised and pleased by the offer.

"That was the first thing you taught me, remember? I distinctly recall this long lecture about the importance of the captain and the responsibilities of the crew. Naturally, you were the distinguished skipper and I was the lowly crew."

Evan laughed and the sound floated out to sea on the tail end of a breeze. "You remember all that, do you?"

"Like it was yesterday."

"Then have a go," he said, motioning toward the mast. But he didn't actually leave all the work to her. They both moved forward and attached the stay for the jib to the mast, working together as if they'd been partners for years. When they were finished, Evan motored the sleek sailboat out of the slot and toward the open waters of Boston Harbor.

For all her earlier claims about not being a natural sailor, Mary Jo was still astonished by how much she'd enjoyed her times on the water. Her fondest memories of Evan had revolved around the hours spent aboard his boat. There was something wildly romantic about sailing together, gliding across the open water with the wind in their faces. She would always treasure those times with Evan.

Once they were safely out of the marina, they raised the mainsail and sliced through the emerald-green waters toward Massachusetts Bay.

"So you've been talking to Jessica, have you?" he asked with a casualness that didn't deceive her.

"Mostly I've been working for you," she countered. "That doesn't leave me much time for socializing."

The wind whipped Evan's hair about his face, and he squinted into the sun. From the way he pinched his lips together, she guessed he was thinking about her date with Gary that weekend. She considered telling him it was over between her and Gary, but before she'd figured out a way of bringing up the subject, Evan spoke again.

"There's a bucket of fried chicken below," he mentioned with a knowing grin, "if you're hungry, that is."

"Fried chicken," she repeated. She had no idea why sailing made her ravenous. And Evan was well aware of her weakness for southern-fried chicken. "Made with a secret recipe of nine special herbs and spices? Plus coleslaw and french fries?"

Evan wiggled his eyebrows and smiled wickedly. "I seem to remember you had a fondness for a certain brand of chicken. There's a bottle of Chardonnay to go with it."

Mary Jo didn't need a second invitation to hurry below. She loaded up their plates, collected the bottle and two wineglasses and carefully carried everything up from the galley.

Sitting next to Evan, her plate balanced on her knees, she ate her dinner, savoring every bite. She must have been more enthusiastic than she realized, because she noticed him studying her. With a chicken leg poised in front of her mouth, she looked back at him.

"What's wrong?"

He grinned. "Nothing. I appreciate a woman who enjoys her food, that's all."

"I'll have you know I skipped lunch." But she wasn't going to tell him it was because every time she thought about him with Catherine Moore, she lost her appetite.

"I hope your employer values your dedication."

"I hope he does, too."

When they'd finished, Mary Jo carried their plates below and packed everything neatly away.

She returned and sat next to Evan. They finished their wine, then he allowed her a turn at the helm. Almost before she was aware of it, his arms were around her. She stood there, hardly breathing, then allowed herself to lean back against his chest. It was as if three painful years had been obliterated and they were both so much in love they couldn't see anything beyond the stars in their eyes.

Those had been innocent days for Mary Jo, that summer when she'd actually believed that an electrician's daughter could fit into the world of a man as rich and influential as Evan Dryden.

If she closed her eyes, she could almost forget everything that had happened since...

The wind blew more strongly and dusk settled over the water.

Mary Jo realized with intense regret that it was time for them to head back to the marina. Evan seemed to feel the same unwillingness to return to land—and reality.

They were both quiet as they docked. Working together, they removed and stowed the sails.

Once everything was locked up, Evan walked her to the dimly lighted parking area. Mary Jo stood by the driver's side of her small car, reluctant to leave.

"I had a wonderful time," she whispered. "Thank you."

"I had a good time, too. Perhaps *too* good."

Mary Jo knew what he was saying; she felt it herself. It would be so easy to forget the past and pick up where they'd left off. Without much encouragement, she could easily find herself in his arms.

When he'd held her those few minutes on the boat, she'd experienced a feeling of warmth and completeness. Of happiness.

Sadness settled over her now, the weight of it almost unbearable. "Thank you again." She turned away and with a trembling hand inserted the car key into the lock. She wished Evan would leave before she did something ridiculous, like break into tears.

"Would you come sailing with me again some time?" he asked, and Mary Jo could have sworn he sounded tentative, uncertain. Which was ridiculous. Evan was one of the most supremely confident men she'd ever known.

Mary Jo waited for an objection to present itself. Several did. But not a single one of them seemed worth worrying about. Not tonight...

"I'd enjoy that very much." It was odd to be carrying on a conversation with her back to him, but she didn't dare turn around for fear she'd throw herself into his arms.

"Soon," he suggested, his voice low.

"How soon?"

"Next Saturday afternoon."

She swallowed against the constriction in her throat and nodded. "What time?"

"Noon. Meet me here, and we'll have lunch first."

"All right."

From the light sound of his footsteps, she knew he'd moved away. "Evan," she called, whirling around, her heart racing.

He turned toward her and waited for her to speak.

"Are you sure?" Mary Jo felt as if her heart hung in the balance.

His face was half-hidden by shadows, but she could see the smile that slowly grew. "I'm very sure."

Mary Jo's hands shook as she climbed into her car. It was happening all over again and she was *letting* it happen. She was trembling so badly she could hardly fasten her seat belt.

What did she hope to prove? She already *knew* that nothing she could do would make her the right woman for Evan. Eventually she would have to face the painful truth—again—and walk away from him. Eventually she would have to look him in the eye and tell him she couldn't be part of his life.

Mary Jo didn't sleep more than fifteen minutes at a stretch that night. When the alarm sounded, her eyes burned, her head throbbed and she felt as lifeless as the dish of last week's pasta still sitting in her fridge.

She climbed out of bed, showered and put on the first outfit she pulled out of her closet. Then she downed a cup of coffee and two aspirin.

Evan was already at the office when she arrived. "Good morning," he said cheerfully as she walked in the door.

"Morning."

"Beautiful day, isn't it?"

Mary Jo hadn't noticed. She sat down at her desk and stared at the blank computer screen.

Evan brought her a cup of coffee and she blinked up at him. "I thought I was the one who was supposed to make the coffee."

"I got here a few minutes early," he explained. "Drink up. You look like you could use it."

Despite her misery, she found the strength to grin. "I could."

"What's the matter? Bad night?"

She cupped the steaming mug with both hands. "Something like that." She couldn't very well confess *he* was the reason she hadn't slept. "Give me a few minutes and I'll be fine." A few minutes to scrounge up the courage to tell him she had other plans for Saturday and couldn't meet him, after all. A few minutes to control the searing disappointment. A few minutes to remind herself she could survive without him. The past three years had proved that.

"Let me know if there's anything I can get you."

She was about to suggest an appointment with a psychiatrist, then changed her mind. Evan would think she was joking; Mary Jo wasn't so sure it *was* a joke. Who else would put herself through this kind of torture?

"I've already sorted through the mail," Evan announced. "There's something here from Adison Investments."

That bit of information perked Mary Jo up. "What did they say?"

"I haven't read it yet, but as soon as I do, I'll let you know. I'm hoping my letter persuaded Adison to agree to a refund."

"That's what you hope, not what you expect."

Evan's dark eyes were serious. "Yes."

He returned to his office but was back out almost immediately. Shaking his head, he handed Mary Jo the brief letter. She read the two curt paragraphs and felt a sinking sense of discouragement. She had to hand it to Bill Adison. He was smooth. Believable. He had to be, otherwise her father would never have trusted him. Adison reiterated that he had a signed contract and that the initial investment wouldn't be returned until the terms of their agreement had been fully met. Never mind that he hadn't upheld *his* side of the contract.

"Do you want to make an appointment with my parents?" she asked, knowing Evan would want to discuss the contents of the letter with her mother and father.

Evan took several moments to consider the question. "No. I think it'd be better for me to stop off at their house myself and explain it to them. Less formal that way."

"Fine," she said, praying he wouldn't suggest Sunday. If he arrived Sunday afternoon, one or more of her family members would be sure to tell him she'd broken up with Gary. No doubt her niece Sally would blurt out that Evan could marry her now.

"I should probably talk to them today or tomorrow."

Mary Jo nodded, trying to conceal her profound relief.

"Why don't we plan on stopping by this evening after work?" The "we" part didn't escape her.

"I'll call my folks and tell them," she said, figuring she'd set a time with them and then—later—make some plausible excuse for not joining Evan. Like a previous date. Or an emergency appointment with a manicurist. She'd break one of her nails and...

She was being ridiculous. She *should* be there. She *would* be there. She owed it to her parents. And it was business, after all, not a social excursion with Evan. Or a real date. There was nothing to fear.

Mary Jo had just arrived at this conclusion when Evan called her into his office.

"Feeling better?" he asked, closing the door behind her.

"A little." She managed a tremulous smile.

He stared at her for an uncomfortable moment. She would have walked around him and seated herself, but he blocked the way.

"I know what might help," he said after a moment.

Thinking he was going to suggest aspirin, Mary Jo opened her mouth to tell him she'd already taken some. Before she could speak, he removed the pen and pad from her unresisting fingers and set them aside.

"What are you doing?" she asked, frowning in confusion.

He grinned almost boyishly. "Mary Jo, I am, as they say in the movies, about to kiss you senseless."

Six

"You're going to kiss me?" Mary Jo's heart lurched as Evan drew her into his arms. His breath felt warm against her face, and a wonderful, wicked feeling spread through her. She sighed and closed her eyes.

Evan eased his mouth over hers and it felt so natural, so familiar. So right.

He kissed her again, and tears gathered in Mary Jo's eyes. He wrapped her tightly in his arms and took several long, deep breaths.

"I wanted to do this last night," he whispered.

She'd wanted him to kiss her then, too, yet—paradoxically—she'd been grateful he hadn't. It occurred to her now that delaying this moment could have been a mistake. They'd both thought about it, wondered how it would be, anticipated being in each other's arms again. And after all that intense speculation, their kiss might have disappointed them both.

It hadn't.

Nevertheless, Mary Jo was relieved when the phone rang. Evan cursed under his breath. "We need to talk about this," he muttered, still holding her.

The phone pealed a second time.

"We'll talk later," she promised quickly.

Evan released her, and she leapt for the telephone on his desk. Thankfully, the call was for Evan. Thankfully, it wasn't Jessica. Or her mother. Or Gary.

Mary Jo left his office and sank slowly into her chair. Closing her eyes, she tried to make sense of what had happened.

All too soon Evan was back. He sat on the edge of her desk. "All right," he said, his eyes as bright and happy as a schoolboy's on the first day of summer vacation. "We're going to have this out once and for all."

"Have this out?"

"I don't know what happened between you and the man you fell in love with three years ago. But apparently it didn't work out, which is fine with me."

"Evan, please!" She glanced desperately around. "Not here. Not now." She was shaking inside. Her stomach knotted and her chest hurt with the effort of holding back her emotions. Eventually she'd have to tell Evan there'd never been another man, but she wasn't looking forward to admitting that lie. Or her reasons for telling it.

"You're right." He sounded, reluctant as if he wanted to settle everything between them then and there. "This isn't the place. We need to be able to talk freely." He looked at his watch and his mouth tightened. "I've got to be in court this morning."

"Yes, I know." She was pathetically grateful that he'd be out of the office for a few hours. She needed time to think. She'd already made one decision, though: she refused to lie to him again. She was older now, more mature, and she recognized that, painful though it was, Evan's mother had been right. Mary Jo could do nothing to enhance Evan's career.

But she wasn't going to run away and hide, the way she had three years ago. Nor could she bear the thought of pitting Evan against his parents. The Drydens were a close family, like her own. No, she'd have to find some other approach, some other way of convincing him this relationship couldn't possibly work. Just *how* she was going to do this, she had no idea.

Pulling her thoughts back to her morning tasks, she reached for the mail and quickly became absorbed in her work. In fact, she was five minutes late meeting Jessica.

Her friend was waiting in the Italian restaurant, sitting at a table in the back. A grandmotherly woman was holding Andy, using a bread stick to entertain the toddler.

"Nonna, this is my friend Mary Jo," Jessica said when she approached the table.

"Hello," Mary Jo murmured, pulling out a chair.

"Leave lunch to me," Nonna insisted, giving Andy back to his mother, who placed him in the high chair beside her. Jessica then handed her son another bread stick, which delighted him. Apparently Andy didn't understand he was supposed to *eat* the bread. He seemed to think it was a toy to wave gleefully overhead, and Mary Jo found herself cheered by his antics.

The older woman returned with large bowls of minestrone, plus a basket of bread so fresh it was still warm. "You eat now," she instructed, waiting for them to sample the delectable-smelling soup. "Enjoy your food first. You can talk later."

"It would be impossible *not* to enjoy our food," Jessica told Nonna, who beamed with pride.

"Nonna's right, of course," Jessica said, "but we've got less than an hour and I'm dying to hear what's happening with you and Evan."

"Not much." Which was sort of the truth. For now. Mary Jo described how Evan had coerced her into working for him. She'd expected expressions of sympathy from her friend. Instead, Jessica seemed downright pleased.

"Damian said there'd been some misunderstanding about a file. He said Evan had suspected you of doing something underhanded, and when Damian showed up with it, Evan felt wretched."

"That's all behind us now." The uncertainty of their future loomed before them, and that was what concerned her most. Mary Jo weighed the decision to confide in Jessica about their kiss that morning. If Jessica were someone other than Evan's sister-in-law, she might have done so. But it would be unfair to involve his family in this.

Jessica dipped her spoon into the thick soup. "I explained earlier that Evan and I became fairly close while I was working for the firm. What I didn't mention was how often he talked about you. He really loved you, Mary Jo."

Uncomfortable, Mary Jo lowered her gaze.

"I'm not saying this to make you feel guilty, but so you'll know that Evan's feelings for you were genuine. You weren't just a passing fancy to him. In some ways, I don't believe he's ever gotten over you."

Mary Jo nearly choked on her soup. "I wish that was true. I've arranged no less than six luncheon appointments for him. All the names came directly out of his little black book. The invitations were accompanied by a dozen red roses.'' Until that moment, Mary Jo hadn't realized how jealous she was, and how much she'd been suffering while he'd wined and dined his girlfriends.

''Don't get me wrong,'' Jessica said. ''Evan's dated. But there's never been anyone serious.''

Mary Jo energetically ripped off a piece of bread. ''He's gone out of his way to prove otherwise.''

''What were these women's names?''

Nonna returned to the table with a large platter heaped with marinated vegetables, sliced meats and a variety of cheeses. Andy stretched out his hand, wanting a piece of cheese, which Jessica willingly gave him.

''One was Catherine Moore.''

A smile hovered at the edges of Jessica's mouth. ''Catherine Moore is close to seventy and she's his great-aunt.''

Shocked, Mary Jo jerked up her head. ''His great-aunt? What about...'' and she rolled off the other names she remembered.

''All relatives,'' Jessica said, shaking her head. ''The poor boy was desperate to make you jealous.''

Mary Jo had no intention of admitting how well his scheme had worked. ''Either that, or he was being thoughtful,'' she suggested offhandedly—just to be fair to Evan. She wanted to be angry with him, but found she was more amused.

''Trust me,'' Jessica said, smiling broadly. ''Evan was desperate. He's dated, true, but he seldom goes out with the same woman more than three or four times. His mother's beginning to wonder if he'll ever settle down.''

At the mention of Lois Dryden, Mary Jo paid close attention to her soup. ''It was my understanding that Evan was planning to go into politics.''

''I believe he will someday,'' Jessica answered enthusiastically. ''In my opinion, he should. Evan has a generous, caring heart. He genuinely wants to help people. More important, he's the kind of man who's capable of finding solutions and making a difference.

''He's a wonderful diplomat, and people like him. It doesn't matter what walk of life they're from either. The best way I can describe it is that Evan's got charisma.''

Mary Jo nodded. It was the truth.

"Although he went into corporate law," Jessica continued, "I don't think his heart has ever really been in it. You should have seen him when he represented Earl Kress. He was practically a different person. No, I don't think he's at all happy as a corporate attorney.''

"Then why hasn't he decided to run for office?''

"I don't know," Jessica answered thoughtfully. "I assumed, for a while, that he was waiting until he was a bit older, but I doubt that's the reason. I know his family encourages him, especially his mother. Lois has always believed Evan's destined for great things.''

"I...got that impression from her, as well.''

"Evan and Damian have had long talks about his running for office. Damian's encouraged him, too, but Evan says the time's not right.''

Mary Jo's heart felt heavy. Everything Jessica said seconded Lois Dryden's concerns about the role Evan's wife would play in his future.

"You're looking thoughtful.''

Mary Jo forced a small smile. "I never understood what it was about me that attracted Evan.''

"I know exactly what it was," Jessica said without a pause. "He told me himself, and more than once. He said it was as though you knew him inside and out. Apparently you could see right through his schemes. I suspect it has something to do with the fact that you have five older brothers.''

"Probably.''

"Evan's been able to charm his way around just about everyone. Not you. You laughed at him and told him to save his breath on more than one occasion. Am I right?''

Mary Jo nodded, remembering the first day they'd met on the beach. He'd tried to sweet-talk her into a dinner date, and she'd refused. It didn't take much for her to realize that Evan Dryden didn't know how to accept no for an answer. In the end they'd compromised. They'd built a small fire, roasted hot dogs and marshmallows and sat on the beach talking until well past midnight.

They saw each other regularly after that. Mary Jo knew he was wealthy by the expensive sports car he drove, the kind of money he flashed around. In the beginning she'd assumed it was simply because he was a high-priced attorney. Fool that she'd been, Mary Jo hadn't even recognized the name.

It wasn't until much later, after she was already head over heels in love with him, that she learned the truth. Evan was more than wealthy. He came from a family whose history stretched back to the *Mayflower*.

"You were different from the other women he'd known," Jessica was saying. "He could be himself with you. One time he told me he felt an almost spiritual connection with you. It was something he never expected to find with anyone else."

"Evan told you all that?" Mary Jo asked breathlessly.

"Yes, and much more," Jessica said, leaning forward. "You see, Mary Jo, I know how much Evan loved you—and still loves you."

Mary Jo felt as if she was about to break into deep, racking sobs. She loved Evan, too. Perhaps there *was* hope for them. Jessica made her feel they might have a future. She seemed to have such faith that, whatever their problems, love and understanding could work them out.

Mary Jo returned to the office, her heart full of hope. She'd been wrong not to believe in their love, wrong not to give them a chance. Her insecurities had wasted precious years.

When Evan walked in, it was close to five o'clock. Mary Jo resisted the urge to fly into his arms, but immediately sensed something was wrong. He was frowning and every line of his body was tense.

"What happened?" she asked, following him into his office.

"I lost," he said pacing. "You know something? I'm a damn poor loser."

She *had* noticed, but he hadn't experienced losses often enough to grow accustomed to accepting them. "Listen, it happens to the best of us," she assured him.

"But it shouldn't have in this case. We were in the right."

"You win some and you lose some. That's the nature of the legal game."

He glared at her and she laughed outright. He reminded her of one of her brothers after a highly contested high-school basketball game. Mark, the youngest, had always loved sports and was fiercely competitive. He'd had to be in order to compete against his four brothers. In many ways, Evan reminded her of Mark.

"I can always count on you to soothe my battered ego, can't I?" he asked, his tone more than a little sarcastic.

"No. You can always count on me to tell you the truth." *Almost always,* she amended sadly, recalling her one lie.

"A kiss would make me feel better."

"Certainly not," she said briskly, but it was difficult to refuse him anything. "Not here, anyway."

"You're right," he admitted grudgingly, "but at least let me hold you." She wasn't given the opportunity to refuse, not that she would have found the strength to do so.

He brought her into his arms and held her firmly against him, breathing deeply as if to absorb everything about her. "I can't believe I'm holding you like this," he whispered.

"Neither will anyone else who walks into this room." But she didn't care who saw them. She burrowed deeper into his embrace and rested her head against the solid strength of his chest.

He eased himself away from her and framed her face with his hands. His eyes were intense as he gazed down on her. "I don't care about the past, Mary Jo. It's water under the bridge. None of it matters. The only thing that matters is *right now.* Can we put everything else behind us and move forward?"

She bit her lower lip, her heart full of a new confidence. Nothing in this world would ever stand between them again. She would have said the words, but couldn't speak, so she nodded her head in abrupt little movements.

She found herself pulled back in his arms, the embrace so hard it threatened to cut off her breath, but she didn't care. Breathing hardly seemed necessary when Evan was holding her like this. She wanted to laugh and to weep both at once, to throw back her head and shout with a free-flowing joy that sprang from her soul.

"We'll go to your parents' place," Evan said, "talk to them about Adison's response, and then I'll take you to dinner and from there—"

"Stop," Mary Jo said, breaking free of his hold and raising her right hand. "You'll take me to dinner? Do you honestly believe we're going to escape my mother without being fed?"

Evan laughed and pulled her back into the circle of his arms. "I suppose not."

Evan was, of course, welcomed enthusiastically by both her parents. He and Norman Summerhill discussed the Adison situation, while Mary Jo helped her mother prepare a simple meal of fried chicken and a pasta and vegetable salad. Over dinner, the mood was comfortable and light-hearted.

As it turned out, though, the evening included a lot more than just conversation and dinner. Her brothers all played on a softball team. They had a game scheduled for that evening, and one of the other players had injured his ankle in a fall at work. The instant Evan heard the news, he volunteered to substitute.

"Evan," Mary Jo pleaded. "This isn't like handball, you know. These guys take their game seriously."

"You think handball isn't serious?" Evan kissed her on the nose and left her with her parents while he hurried home to change clothes.

Her mother watched from the kitchen, looking exceptionally pleased. She wiped her hands on her apron skirt. "I think you did a wise thing breaking up with Gary when you did."

"I'm so happy, Mom," Mary Jo whispered, grabbing a dish towel and some plates to dry.

"You love him."

Mary Jo noticed it wasn't a question.

"I never stopped loving him."

Her mother placed one arm around Mary Jo's slender shoulders. "I knew that the minute I saw the two of you together again." She paused, apparently considering her next words. "I've always known you loved Evan. Can you tell me what happened before— why you broke it off?"

"I didn't believe I was the right woman for him."

"Nonsense! Anyone looking at the two of you would realize you're perfect for each other. Who would say such a thing to you?"

Mary Jo was intelligent enough not to mention Lois Dryden. "He's very wealthy, Mom."

"You can look past that."

Mary Jo's laugh was spontaneous. Her sweetheart of a mother saw Evan's money as a detriment—and in some ways, it was.

"His father's a senator."

"You think his money bought him that position?" Marianna scoffed. "If you do, you're wrong. He was elected to that office because he's a decent man with an honest desire to help his constituents."

Her mother had a way of making the impossible sound plausible. Mary Jo wished she could be more like her.

"Now, freshen up," Marianna said, untying the apron, "or we'll be late for your brothers' softball game."

Evan was already in the outfield catching fly balls when Mary Jo and her parents arrived. He looked as if he'd been a member of the team for years.

The game was an exciting one, with the outcome unpredictable until the very end of the ninth inning. Mary Jo, sitting in the bleachers with her family—her parents, a couple of sisters-in-law, some nieces and nephews—screamed herself hoarse. Their team lost by one run, but everyone took the defeat in stride—including Evan, who'd played as hard as any of them.

Afterward, the team went out for pizza and cold beer. Mary Jo joined Evan and the others, while her parents returned to the house, tired out from the excitement.

Evan threw his arm over her shoulders and she wrapped her own arm around his waist.

"You two an item now or something?" her brother Bill asked as they gathered around a long table at the pizza parlor.

"Yeah," Rich chimed in. "You two look awful chummy all of a sudden. What's going on?"

"Yeah, what about good ol' Gary?" Mark wanted to know.

Evan studied her, eyebrows raised. "What *about* Gary?" he echoed.

"You don't need to worry about him anymore," Jack explained, carrying a pitcher of ice-cold beer to the table. "M.J. broke up with him over the weekend."

"You did?" It was Evan who asked the question.

"Yup." Once more her brother was doing the talking for her. "Said they were drifting in opposite directions or some such garbage. No one believed her. We know the *real* reason she showed Gary the door."

"Will you guys *please stop?*" Mary Jo insisted, her ears growing redder by the minute. "I can speak for myself, thank you very much."

Jack poured them each a glass of beer and slid them down the table. "You know M.J. means business when she says *please stop.* Uh-oh—look at her ears. Let's not embarrass her anymore, guys, or there'll be hell to pay later."

Evan barked with laughter, and her brothers looked on approvingly. He fit in with her family as if he'd been born into it. This was his gift, Mary Jo realized. He was completely at ease with her brothers—as he would be with a group of government officials or lawyers or "society" people. With *anyone.* He could drink beer and enjoy it as much as expensive champagne. It didn't matter to him if he ate pizza or lobster.

But Mary Jo was definitely more comfortable with the pizza-and-beer way of life. Hours earlier she'd been utterly confident. Now, for the first time that night, her newfound resolve was shaken.

Evan seemed to notice it, although he didn't say anything until later, when they were alone, driving to her place. Reluctant for the evening to end, Mary Jo gazed at the oncoming lights of the cars zooming past. She couldn't suppress a sigh.

Evan glanced over at her. "Your family's wonderful," he said conversationally. "I envy you coming from such a large, close-knit group."

"You're close to your brother, too."

"True. More so now that we're older." He reached for her hand and squeezed it gently. "Something's troubling you."

She stared out the side window. "You're comfortable in my world, Evan, but I'm not comfortable in yours."

"World? What are you talking about? In case you haven't noticed, we're both right here in the same world—earth."

She smiled, knowing he was making light of her concerns. "If we'd been with your family, do you seriously think we'd be having pizza and beer? More than likely it'd be expensive French wine, baguettes and Brie."

"So? You don't like baguettes and Brie?"

"Yes, but..." She paused, knowing it wouldn't do any good to argue. He didn't understand her concerns, because he didn't share them. "We're different, Evan."

"Thank goodness. I'd hate to think I was attracted to a clone of myself."

"I'm an electrician's daughter."

"A very lovely one, too, I might add."

"Evan," she groaned. "Be serious."

"I *am* serious. It'd scare the socks off you if you knew *how* serious."

He exited the freeway and headed down the street toward her duplex. As he parked, he said, "Invite me in for coffee."

"Are you really interested in coffee?"

"No."

"That's what I thought," she said, smiling softly to herself.

"I'm going to kiss you, Mary Jo, and frankly, I'm a little too old to be doing it in a car. Now invite me inside—or suffer the consequences."

Mary Jo didn't need a second invitation. Evan helped her out of the car and took her arm as they walked to her door. She unlocked it but didn't turn on the lights as they moved into her living room. The instant the door was closed, Evan turned her in his arms so that her back was pressed against it.

Her lips trembled as his mouth sought hers. It was a gentle caress rather than a kiss, and she moaned, wanting, *needing* more of him.

Evan's hand curved around the side of her neck, his fingers stroking her hair. His mouth hovered a fraction of an inch from hers, as if he half expected her to protest his kiss. Instead, she raised her head to meet his lips again.

Groaning, Evan kissed her with a passion that left her breathless and weak-kneed.

Mary Jo wound her arms around his neck and stood on the tips of her toes as his mouth worked hungrily over hers. They exchanged a series of long kisses, then Evan buried his head in her shoulder and shuddered.

Mary Jo was convinced that if he hadn't been holding her upright, she would have slithered to the floor.

"We'd better stop while I have the strength," Evan whispered, almost as if he was speaking more to himself than to her. His breathing was ragged and uneven. He moved away from her, and in the dark stillness of her living room, illumined only by the glow of a streetlight, she watched him rake his hands through his thick, dark hair.

"I'll make us that coffee," she said in a purposeful voice. They both squinted when she flipped on the light.

"I really don't need any coffee," he told her.

"I know. I don't, either. It's a convenient excuse for you to stay."

Evan followed her into the kitchen and pulled out a chair. He sat down and reached for her, wrapping his arms around her waist, pulling her down onto his lap. "We have a lot of time to make up for."

Unsure how to respond, Mary Jo rested her hands lightly on his shoulders. It was so easy to get caught up again in the intensity of their attraction and renewed love. But despite her earlier optimism, she couldn't allow herself to ignore the truth. Except that she didn't know how to resolve this, or even if she could.

Evan left soon afterward, with a good-night kiss and the reminder that they'd be together again in the morning.

Mary Jo sat in her rocking chair in the dark for a long time, trying to sort out her tangled thoughts. Loving him the way she did, it was so tempting to let her heart go where it wanted to. So tempting to throw caution to the winds, to ignore all the difficult questions.

Evan seemed confident that their love was possible. Jessica did, too. Mary Jo desperately wanted to believe them. She wanted to overlook every objection. She wanted what she would probably never receive—his family's approval. Not Damian and Jessica's; she had that. His mother and father's.

Sometimes loving someone wasn't enough. Mary Jo had heard that often enough and she recognized the truth of it.

Too tired to think clearly, she stood, setting the rocker into motion, and stumbled into her bedroom.

Saturday, Mary Jo met Evan at the yacht club at noon. They planned to sail after a leisurely lunch. She'd been looking forward to this from the moment Evan had invited her on Wednesday.

The receptionist ushered her to a table outside on the patio where Evan was waiting for her. There was a festive, summery atmosphere—tables with their striped red-yellow-and-blue umbrellas, the cheerful voices of other diners, the breathtaking view of the marina. Several sailboats with multicolored spinnakers could be seen against a backdrop of bright blue sky and sparkling green sea.

Evan stood as she approached and pulled out her chair. "I don't think you've ever looked more beautiful."

It was a line he'd used a thousand times before, Mary Jo was sure of that, although he sounded sincere. "You say that to all your dates," she chided lightly, reaching for the menu.

"But it's true," he returned with an injured air.

Mary Jo laughed and spread the linen napkin across her lap. "Your problem is that you're a wonderful liar. You'd be perfect in politics since you lie so convincingly." She'd been teasing, then suddenly realized how rude that sounded. His father was a politician!

"Oh, Evan, I'm sorry. That was a terrible thing to say." Mary Jo felt dreadful, and realized anew that she was the type of person who could offend someone without ever being aware of it. She simply wasn't circumspect enough.

He chuckled and brushed off her apology. "Dad would get a laugh out of what you said."

"Promise me you won't ever tell him."

"That depends," he said, paying exaggerated attention to his menu.

"On what?" she demanded.

He wiggled his eyebrows. "On what you intend to offer me for my silence."

She smiled and repeated a line her brothers had often used on her. "I'll let you live."

Evan threw back his head and laughed boisterously.

"Evan?" The woman's voice came from behind Mary Jo. "What a pleasant surprise to find you here."

"Mother," Evan said, standing to greet Lois Dryden. He kissed her on the cheek. "You remember Mary Jo Summerhill, don't you?"

Seven

"Of course I remember Mary Jo," Lois Dryden said cheerfully. "How nice to see you again."

Mary Jo blinked, wondering if this was the same woman she'd had that painful heart-to-heart chat with all those years ago. The woman who'd suggested that if Mary Jo really loved Evan she would call off their engagement. Not in those words exactly. Mrs. Dryden had been far too subtle for that. Nevertheless, the message had been there, loud and clear.

"I didn't know you two were seeing each other again," Lois continued. "This is a...surprise."

Mary Jo noticed she didn't say it was *pleasant* surprise. Naturally, Evan's mother was much too polite to cause even a hint of a scene. Not at the yacht club, at any rate. Now, if she'd been at Whispering Willows, the Dryden estate, she might swoon or have a fit of vapors, or whatever it was wealthy women did to reveal their shock and displeasure. Mary Jo realized she was being cynical, but couldn't help herself.

Evan reached for her hand and clasped it in his own. His eyes smiled into hers. "Mary Jo's working for me this summer."

"I...I didn't know that."

"Would you care to join us?" Evan asked, but his eyes didn't waver from Mary Jo's. Although he'd issued the invitation, it was obvious that he expected his mother to refuse. That he *wanted* her to refuse.

"Another time, perhaps. I'm lunching with Jessica's mother. We're planning a first-birthday party celebration for Andrew, and, well, you know how the two of us feel about our only grandchild."

Evan chuckled. "I sure do. It seems to me that either Damian or I should see about adding another branch to the family tree."

Mary Jo felt the heat of embarrassment redden her ears. Evan couldn't have been more blatant. He'd all but announced he intended to marry her. She waited for his mother to comment.

"That would be lovely, Evan," Lois said, but if Evan didn't catch the tinge of disapproval in his mother's voice, Mary Jo did. Nothing had changed.

The lines were drawn.

Lois made her excuses and hurried back into the yacht club. Mary Jo's good mood plummeted. She made a pretense of enjoying her lunch and decided to put the small confrontation behind her. Her heart was set on enjoying this day with Evan. She loved sailing as much as he did, and as soon as they were out in the bay, she could forget how strongly his mother disapproved of her. *Almost* forget.

They worked together to get the sailboat in motion. Once the sails were raised, she sat next to Evan. The wind tossed her hair about her face, and she smiled into the warm, cheerful sunshine. They tacked left and then right, zigzagging their way through the water.

"Are you thirsty?" Evan asked after they'd been out for about an hour.

"A cold soda sounds good."

"Great. While you're in the galley, would you get one for me?"

Laughing, she jabbed him in the ribs for the clever way he'd tricked her into getting his drink. She went below and brought back two sodas. She handed him his, then reclaimed her spot beside him.

Evan eased his arm around her shoulder and soon she was nestled against him, guiding the sailboat, with Evan guiding her. When she veered off course and the sails slackened, he placed his hand over hers and gently steered them back on course.

Mary Jo had found it easy to talk to Evan from the moment they'd met. He was easygoing and congenial, open-minded and witty. But this afternoon he seemed unusually quiet. She wondered if he was thinking about the unexpected encounter with his mother.

"It's peaceful, isn't it?" Mary Jo said after several long moments of silence.

"I think some of the most profound moments of my life have

been spent aboard this boat. I've always come here to find peace, and I have, though it's usually been hard won.''

"I'm grateful you introduced me to sailing."

"I took the boat out several times after...three years ago." His hold on her tightened slightly. "I've missed you, Mary Jo," he whispered, and rubbed the side of his jaw against her temple. "My world felt so empty without you."

"Mine did, too," she admitted softly, remembering the bleak, empty months after their breakup.

"Earl Kress stopped off at the office a while back, and I learned you weren't married. Afterward, I couldn't get you out of my mind. I wondered what had happened between you and this teacher you loved. I wanted to contact you and find out. I must have come up with a hundred schemes to worm my way back into your life."

"W-why didn't you?" She felt comfortable and secure in his arms, unafraid of the problems that had driven them apart. She could deal with the past; it was the future that terrified her.

"Pride mostly," Evan said quietly. "A part of me was hoping you'd eventually come back to me."

In a way she had, on her knees, needing him. Funny, she couldn't have approached him for herself, even though she was madly in love with him, but she'd done it for her parents.

"No wonder you had that gleeful look in your eye when I walked into your office," she said, hiding a smile. "You'd been waiting for that very thing."

"I wanted to punish you," he told her, and she heard the regret in his voice. "I wanted to make you suffer the way I had. That was the reason I insisted you work for me this summer. I'd already hired Mrs. Sterling's replacement, but when I had the opportunity to force you into accepting the position, I couldn't resist."

This wasn't news to Mary Jo. She'd known the moment he'd offered her the job what his intention was. He wanted to make her as miserable as she'd made him. And his plan worked those first few days. She'd gone home frustrated, mentally beaten and physically exhausted.

"A woman of lesser fortitude would have quit the first day, when you had me ordering roses and booking luncheon dates."

"Those weren't any love interests," he confessed. "I'm related to each one."

"I know." She tilted back her head and kissed the underside of his jaw.

"How?" he asked, his surprise evident.

"Jessica told me."

"Well, I certainly hope you were jealous. I went through a great deal of unnecessary trouble if you weren't."

"I was green with it." She could have downplayed her reaction, but didn't. "Every time you left the office for another one of your dates, I worked myself into a frenzy. Please, Evan, don't ever do that to me again."

"I won't," he promised, and she could feel his smile against her hair. "But you had your revenge several times over, throwing Gary in my face. I disliked the man from the moment we met. Here I was, hoping to catch you off guard by showing up at your parents' for dinner, and my plan immediately backfires when you arrive with your boyfriend in tow."

"You didn't like Gary?"

"He's probably a nice guy, but not when he's dating *my* woman."

"But you acted like Gary was an old pal! I was mortified. My entire family thought it was hilarious. You had more to say to Gary than to me."

"I couldn't let you know how jealous I was, could I?"

Mary Jo snuggled more securely in his arms. A sea gull's cry sounded from overhead, and she looked into the brilliant blue sky, reveling in the sunshine and the breeze and in the rediscovery of their love.

"Can we ever go back?" Evan asked. "Is it possible to pretend those years didn't happen and take up where we left off?"

"I ...I don't know," Mary Jo whispered. Yet she couldn't keep her heart from hoping. She closed her eyes and felt the wind on her face. Those years had changed her. She was more confident now, more sure of herself, emotionally stronger. This time she'd fight harder to hold on to her happiness.

One thing was certain. If she walked out of Evan's life again, it wouldn't be in silence or in secrecy.

She remembered the pain of adjusting to her life without Evan. Pride had carried her for several months. She might not come from old Boston wealth, but she had nothing to be ashamed of. She was proud of her family and refused to apologize because they were working class.

But pride had only taken her so far, and when it had worn down, all that was left was the emptiness of her dreams and a life that felt hollow.

Like Evan, she'd forced herself to go on, dragging from one day to the next, but she wasn't fully alive and hadn't been until a few days ago, when he'd taken her in his arms and kissed her. Her love for him, her regret at what she'd lost, had refused to go away.

"I want to give us another chance," Evan murmured. The teasing had gone out of his voice. "Do you?"

"Yes. Oh, yes," Mary Jo said ardently.

He kissed her then, with a passion and a fervor she'd never experienced before. She returned his kiss in full measure. They clung tightly to each other until the sails flapped in the breeze and Evan had to grip the helm and steer them back on course.

"I love you, Mary Jo," Evan said. "Heaven knows, I tried not to. I became…rather irresponsible after we split up, you know. If it hadn't been for Damian, I don't know what I would have done. He was endlessly patient with me, even when I wouldn't tell him what was wrong. My brother isn't stupid. He knew it had something to do with you. I just couldn't talk about it. The only relief I found was here on the water."

Turning, Mary Jo wrapped her arms around his middle and pressed her face against his chest, wanting to absorb his pain.

"When you told me you'd fallen in love with another man, I was left with no recourse but to accept that it was over. I realized the moment you told me how difficult it was for you. Loving him while you were still engaged to me must have been hell."

A sob was trapped in her throat. This was the time to admit there'd never been another man, that it was all a lie….

"Can you tell me about him?"

"No." She jerked her head from side to side in adamant refusal. She couldn't do it, just couldn't do it. She was continuing the lie, Lord help her, but telling him would mean betraying his mother's part in all this. She wouldn't do that.

His free arm cradled her shoulders, his grip tight.

"I'd more or less decided that if I couldn't marry you," Evan said after a lengthy pause, "I wasn't getting married at all. Can't you just see me twenty years down the road sitting by a roaring fireplace in a smoking jacket with my ever-faithful dog sleeping at my side?"

The mental picture was so foreign to the devil-may-care image she'd had of him these past few years that she laughed out loud. "You in a smoking jacket? Never. You don't even smoke."

"What about me living in a huge, seven-bedroom house all by myself?"

"I can't picture that, either."

"What about fatherhood? Can you picture me as a father?"

"Easily." After watching him with Andrew and her own nieces and nephews, she realized Evan was a natural with children.

"Then it's settled," he said, sounding greatly relieved.

"What's settled?" she asked, cocking her head to one side to look up at him. His attention was focused straight ahead as he steered the sailboat.

"We're getting married. So, sweetheart, prepare yourself, because we're making up for lost time."

"Evan—"

"If you recall, when I first gave you the engagement ring, we planned our family. Remember? Right down to the timing of your first pregnancy."

Mary Jo could hardly manage a nod. Those were memories she'd rarely allowed herself to take out and examine.

"We both thought it was important to wait a couple of years before we started our family. You were supposed to have our first baby this year. Hey, we're already behind schedule! It seems to me we'd better take an extended honeymoon."

Mary Jo laughed, the wind swallowing the sound the moment it escaped her lips.

"Two, three months at the very least," Evan continued, undaunted. "I suggest a South Pacific island, off the tourist track. We'll rent a bungalow on the beach and spend our days walking along the shore and our nights making love."

He was going much too fast for her. "Do you mind retracing a few steps?" she asked. "I got lost somewhere between you sitting by a roaring fire with your faithful dog and us running into Gauguin's descendants on some South Pacific beach."

"First things first," Evan countered. "We agreed on four children, didn't we?"

"Evan!" She couldn't keep from laughing, her happiness spilling over.

"These details are important, and I want them settled before we get involved in another subject. I wanted six kids, remember. I love big families. But you only wanted two. If you'll think back, it took some fast talking to get you to agree to a compromise of four. You did agree, remember?"

"What I remember was being railroaded into a crazy conversation while you went on about building us this mansion."

"Ah, yes, the house. I'd nearly forgotten. I wanted one large enough for all the kids. With a couple of guest rooms. That, my beautiful Mary Jo, isn't a mansion."

"It is when you're talking seven bedrooms and six thousand square feet."

"But," Evan said, his eyes twinkling, "you were going to have live-in help with the children, especially while they're younger, and I wanted to be sure we had a place to escape and relax at the end of the day."

"I found an indoor swimming pool, hot tub and exercise room a bit extravagant." Mary Jo had thought he was teasing when he'd showed her the house plans he'd had drawn up, but it had soon become apparent that he was completely serious. He was serious now, too.

"I still want to build that home for us," he said, his intense dark eyes searching hers. "I love you. I've loved you for three agonizing years. I want us to be married, and soon. If it were up to me, we'd already have the marriage license."

"You're crazy." But it was a wonderful kind of crazy.

"You love me."

Tears glistened in her eyes as she nodded. "I do. I love you so much, Evan." She slid her arms around his neck. "What am I going to do with you?"

"Marry me and put me out of my misery."

He made it sound so easy and she was caught up in the tide of his enthusiasm, but she couldn't agree. Not yet. Not until she was convinced she was doing the right thing for both of them.

"Listen," Evan said as though struck by a whole new thought. "I have a judge in the family who can marry us as soon as I make the necessary arrangements. We can have a private ceremony in, say, three days' time."

"My parents would shoot us both, Evan. I know for a fact that my father would never forgive us if we cheated him out of the pleasure of escorting me down the aisle."

Evan grimaced. "You're right. My mother's the same. She actually enjoys planning social events. It's much worse now that my dad's a senator. She's organized to a fault—takes care of even the most minute details." He grinned suddenly, as if he found something amusing. "My father made a wise choice when he married Mom. She's the perfect politician's wife."

The words cut through Mary Jo like an icy wind. They reminded her that she would be a liability to Evan should he ever decide to run for political office.

Often the candidates' spouses were put under as much scrutiny as the candidates themselves. The demands placed on political wives were often no less demanding than those placed on the politicians.

"Evan," she said, watching him closely. "I'm not anything like your mother."

"So? What's that got to do with our building a mansion and filling all those bedrooms with children?"

"I won't make a good politician's wife."

He looked at her as if he didn't understand what she was saying.

Mary Jo had no option but to elaborate. "I've heard, from various people, that you intend to enter politics someday yourself."

"Someday. I'm in no rush. My family, my mother especially, seems to think I have a future in that area, but it isn't anything that's going to happen soon. When and if the time comes, the two of us will decide it together. But for now it's a moot point."

Mary Jo wasn't willing to accept that. "Evan, I'm telling you here and now that I'd hate that kind of life. I'm not suited for it. Your mother enjoys arranging spectacular society events and giving interviews and living her life a certain way, but I don't. I'm the kind of person who's uncomfortable in a roomful of strangers— unless they're five-year-olds."

"All right," Evan said with an amused air. "Then I won't enter politics. My mother has enough to keep her busy running my father's career. You're far more important to me than some elected position. Besides, I have the feeling Mother would have driven me crazy."

His words should have reassured her, but didn't. It seemed ludicrous to pin their future together on something as fleeting as this promise, so lightly made. Her greatest fear was that Evan would change his mind and regret ever marrying her.

"Let's go talk to your parents," Evan said, apparently unaware of the turmoil inside her.

"About what?"

His head went back and he frowned at her. "Making the arrangements for the wedding, what else? My mother will put up a fight, but I believe a small, private ceremony with just our immediate families would be best."

"Oh, Evan, please, don't rush me," Mary Jo pleaded. "This is the most important decision of our lives. We both need to think this through very carefully."

He gaze narrowed. "What's there to think about? I love you, and you love me. That's all that matters."

How Mary Jo wished that were true.

It demanded far more courage to drive over to Whispering Willows than Mary Jo anticipated. She'd spent most of the night alternating between absolute delight and abject despair. She awoke

Sunday morning convinced she'd never find the answers she needed until she'd talked to Evan's mother.

That was how Mary Jo came to be standing outside the Drydens' front door shortly before noon. With a shaking hand, she rang the bell.

She'd expected one of the household staff to answer. Instead, Lois Dryden herself appeared at the door. The two women stared at each other.

Mary Jo recovered enough to speak first. "I'm sorry to disturb you, Mrs. Dryden, but I was wondering if I could have a few minutes of your time."

"Of course." The older woman stepped aside to let Mary Jo enter the lavish house. The foyer floor was of polished marble, and a glittering crystal chandelier hung from the ceiling, which was two and a half stories high.

"Perhaps it would be best if we talked in my husband's office," Lois Dryden said, ushering Mary Jo's to the darkly paneled room down the hall. This was the room Evan had described in his absurd scenario of lonely bachelor sitting by the fire with his dog.

"Would you like some something cold to drink? Or perhaps coffee?"

"No, thank you," Mary Jo answered. She chose the dark green leather wing chair angled in front of the fireplace. Mrs. Dryden sat in its twin.

"I realize you were surprised to see me with Evan yesterday."

"Yes," Lois agreed, her hands primly folded in her lap, "but who my son chooses to date is really none of my concern."

"That's very diplomatic of you. But I suspect you'd rather Evan dated someone other than me."

"Mary Jo, please. I feel we got started on the wrong foot all those years ago. It was entirely my fault, and I've wished many times since that I'd been more thoughtful. I have the feeling I deeply offended you and, my dear girl, that wasn't my intention."

"I'm willing to put the past behind us," Mary Jo suggested, managing a small smile. "That was three years ago, and I was more than a little overwhelmed by your family's wealth and position. If there's anyone at fault, it was me."

"That's very gracious of you, my dear." Mrs. Dryden relaxed in her chair and demurely crossed her ankles.

"I love Evan," Mary Jo said, thinking it would be best to be as forthright as possible. "And I believe he loves me."

"I'm pleased for you both." No telltale emotion sounded in her voice. They could have been discussing the weather for all the feeling her words revealed.

"Evan has asked me to marry him," she announced, carefully watching the woman who sat across from her for any signs of disapproval.

"I'm very pleased." A small and all-too-brief smile accompanied her statement. "Have you set the date? I hope you two realize we'll need at least a year to plan the wedding. This type of event takes time and careful preparation."

"Evan and I have decided on a small, private ceremony."

"No," Lois returned adamantly. "That won't be possible."

"Why not?" Mary Jo asked, taken aback by the vehemence in the older woman's voice.

"My husband is a senator. The son of a man in my husband's position does not sneak away and get married in...in secret."

Mary Jo hadn't said anything about sneaking away or secrecy, but she wasn't there to argue. "I come from a large family, Mrs. Dryden. We—"

"There were ten of you or some such, as I recall." Her hands made a dismissive motion.

Mary Jo bristled. The woman made her parents sound as if they'd produced a warren of rabbits, instead of a large, happy family.

"My point," Mary Jo said, controlling her irritation with some difficulty, "is that neither my parents nor I could afford a big, expensive wedding."

"Of course," Lois said, sounding relieved. "We wouldn't expect your relatives to assume the cost of such an elaborate affair. Walter and I would be more than happy to foot the bill."

"I appreciate the offer, and I'm sure my parents would, too, but I'm afraid we could never accept your generosity. Tradition says that the bride's family assumes the cost of the wedding, and my father is a very traditional man."

"I see." Mrs. Dryden gnawed her lower lip. "There must be some way around his pride. Men can be such sticklers over things like this." For the first time she sounded almost friendly. "I'll think of something. Just leave it to me."

"There's something you don't understand. An ostentatious wedding isn't what I want, either."

"But you must. I've already explained why it's necessary. We wouldn't want to create even a breath of scandal with some hushed-up affair. Why, that could do untold damage to my husband and to Evan's political future."

"Breath of *scandal?*"

"My dear girl, I don't mean to be rude, and please forgive me if I sound like an old busybody, but there are people who'd delight in finding the least little thing to use against Walter."

"But I'm marrying Evan, not Walter."

"I realize that. But you don't seem to understand that these matters have to be handled...delicately. We must start planning immediately. The moment the announcement is made, you and your family will be the focus of media attention."

Mary Jo's head started to spin. "I'm sure you're mistaken. Why should anyone care about me or my family?"

Lois had begun wringing her hands. "I don't suppose it does any harm to mention it, although I must ask you not to spread this information around. Walter has been contacted by a longtime friend who intends to enter the presidential campaign this coming year. This friend has tentatively requested Walter to be his running mate, should he garner the party's nomination."

Mary Jo developed an instant throbbing headache.

"My husband and I must avoid any situation that might put him in an unflattering light."

"We could delay the wedding." She'd been joking, but Evan's mother looked greatly relieved.

"Would you?" she asked hopefully.

"I'll talk to Evan."

At the mention of her youngest son, Lois Dryden frowned. "Shouldn't he be here with you? It seems a bit odd that you'd tell me about your engagement without him."

"I wanted the two of us to chat first," Mary Jo explained.

"An excellent idea," Lois said with a distinct nod of her head. "Men can be so difficult. If you and I can agree on cer- tain...concerns before we talk to Evan and my husband, I feel sure we can work everything out to our mutual satisfaction."

"Mrs. Dryden, I'm a kindergarten teacher. I think you should know I feel uncomfortable with the idea of becoming a media fig- ure."

"I'll do whatever I can to help you, Mary Jo. I realize it's a lot to have thrust on you all at once, but if you're going to marry my son, you have to learn how to handle the press. I'll teach you how to use them to your advantage and how to turn something negative into a positive."

Mary Jo's headache increased a hundredfold. "I don't think I've been clear enough, Mrs. Dryden. I'm more than uncomfortable with this—I refuse to become involved in it."

"Refuse?" She repeated the word as if unsure of the meaning.

"I've already explained my feelings to Evan," Mary Jo contin- ued. "I love your son so much..." Her voice shook and she stopped speaking for a moment. "I'm not like you or your husband, or Evan for, that matter. Nor do I intend to be. When Evan asked me to marry him, I told him all this."

A frown creased Lois Dryden's brow. "I'm not sure I under- stand."

"Perhaps I'm not explaining it right. Basically, I refuse to live my life seeking the approval of others. I want a small, private wed- ding and Evan has agreed."

"But what about the future, when Evan decides to enter politics? Trust me, Mary Jo, the wife's position is as demanding as that of her husband."

"I'm sure that's true. But I'd hate the kind of life you're de- scribing. Evan knows that and understands. He's also agreed that as long as I feel this way, he won't enter politics."

His mother vaulted out of her chair. "But you can't do this! Politics is Evan's destiny. Why, from the time he was in grade school his teachers have told me what a natural leader he is. He was student-body president in high school *and* in college. From his early twenties on, he's been groomed for this very thing. I can well visualize my son in the White House someday.''

His mother had lofty plans indeed. "Is this what Evan wants?"

''Of course it is,'' she said vehemently. "Ask him yourself. His father and brother have had countless conversations with him about this. If my son were to marry a woman who didn't appreciate his abilities or understand his ambitions, it might ruin him.''

If the words had come from anyone other than Lois Dryden, Mary Jo would have thought them absurd and melodramatic. But this woman believed implicitly what she said.

"Evan's marrying the right kind of woman is crucial to your plans for his future, isn't it?" Mary Jo asked with infinite sadness.

Mrs. Dryden looked decidedly uncomfortable. "Yes."

"I'm not that woman."

The older woman sighed. "I realize that. The question is, what do you intend to do about it?"

Eight

"I love Evan," Mary Jo insisted again, but even as she spoke, she realized that loving him wasn't enough. Although she'd matured and wasn't the skittish, frightened woman she'd been three years earlier, nothing had really changed. If she married Evan, she might ruin his promising career. It was a heavy burden to carry.

Mary Jo couldn't change who and what she was; nor should she expect Evan to make all the concessions, giving up his future.

"I'm sure you do love my son," Lois said sincerely.

"And he loves me," Mary Jo added, keeping her back straight and her head high. She angled her chin at a proud, if somewhat defiant, tilt, unwilling to accept defeat. "We'll work this out somehow," she said confidently. "There isn't anything two people who love each other can't resolve. We'll find a way."

"I'm sure you will, my dear." Lois Dryden's mouth formed a sad smile that contradicted her reassurances. "In any case, you're perfectly right. You should discuss this all with Evan and reach a decision together."

The older woman smoothed an invisible wrinkle from her dove-gray skirt. "Despite what you may think, Mary Jo, I have no personal objections to your marrying my son. When the two of you separated some time ago, I wondered if it had something to do with our little talk. I don't mind telling you I suffered more than a few regrets. I never intended to hurt you, and if I did, I beg your forgiveness."

"You certainly opened my eyes," Mary Jo admitted. Evan's mother had refined that talent over the past few years, she noted silently.

"I might sound like a interfering old woman, but I do hope you'll take our little talk to heart. I trust you'll seriously consider what we've discussed." She sighed. "I love Evan, too. God has blessed me with a very special family, and all I want is what's best for my children. I'm sure your parents feel the same way about you."

"They do." The conversation was becoming more and more unbearable. Mary Jo wanted desperately to leave. And she needed to talk to Evan, to share her concerns and address their future. But deep down she'd caught a fearful glimpse of the truth.

Mary Jo stood up abruptly and offered Mrs. Dryden her hand. "Thank you for your honesty and your insights. It wasn't what I wanted to hear, but I suppose it's what I needed to know. I'm sure this was just as difficult for you. We have something in common, Mrs. Dryden. We both love your son. Evan wouldn't be the man he is without your love and care. You have a right to be proud."

Evan's mother took Mary Jo's hand in both of her own and held it firmly for several moments. "I appreciate that. Do keep in touch, won't you?"

Mary Jo nodded. "If you wish."

The older woman led her to the front door and walked out to the circular driveway with her. Mary Jo climbed into her car and started the engine. As she pulled away, she glanced in her rearview mirror to find Lois Dryden's look both thoughtful and troubled.

Normally Mary Jo joined her family for their Sunday get-togethers. But not this week. Needing time and privacy to sort out her thoughts, she drove to the marina. She parked, then walked slowly to the waterfront. The wind coming off the ocean was fresh and tangy with salt. She had to think, and what better place than here, where she'd spent countless happy hours in Evan's company?

How long she sat on the bench overlooking the water she didn't know. Time seemed to be of little consequence. She gazed at the boats moving in and out of their narrow passageways. The day had turned cloudy, which suited her somber mood.

Standing, she walked along the pier, once again reviewing her conversation with Evan's mother. Her steps slowed as she realized no amount of brooding would solve the problems. She needed to talk to Evan, and soon, before she lost her nerve.

She found a pay phone, plunked in a quarter and dialed his home number.

"Mary Jo. Thank goodness! Where were you?" Evan asked. "I've been calling your place every fifteen minutes. I have some wonderful news."

"I...had an errand to run," she said, not wanting to elaborate just then. He sounded terribly excited. "What's your good news?"

"I'll tell you the minute I see you."

"Do you want to meet somewhere?" she asked.

"How about Rowe's Wharf? We can take a stroll along the pier. If you want, we can visit the aquarium. I haven't been there in years. When we're hungry we can find a seafood restaurant and catch a bite to eat." He paused and laughed at his own sorry joke. "No pun intended."

"That'll be great," she said, finding it difficult to rouse the proper enthusiasm.

"Mary Jo?" His voice rose slightly. "What's wrong? You sound upset."

"We need to talk."

"All right," he agreed guardedly. "Do you want me to pick you up?" When she declined, he said, "I'll meet you there in half an hour, okay?"

"Okay." It was ironic, Mary Jo mused, that Evan could be so happy while she felt as if her entire world was about to shatter.

When she finished speaking to Evan, Mary Jo phoned her mother and told her she wouldn't be joining them for dinner. Marianna knew instantly that something wasn't right, but Mary Jo promised to explain later.

From the marina she drove down Atlantic Avenue and found a suitable place to park. It had been less than twenty-four hours, and already she was starved for the sight of Evan. It seemed unthinkable to live the rest of her life without him.

He was standing on the wharf waiting for her when she arrived. His face lighted up as she approached, and he held out both hands to her.

Mary Jo experienced an immediate sense of comfort the moment their fingers touched. In another second, she was securely wrapped in his arms. He held her against him as though he didn't intend to

ever let her go. And she wished she didn't have to leave the protective shelter of his arms.

"I've missed you," he breathed against her temple. "Lord, how
I've missed you." He threaded his fingers lovingly through her
windblown hair.

"We spent nearly all of yesterday together," she reminded him
lightly, although she shared his feelings. Even a few hours apart
left her wondering how she'd managed to survive all those years
without him. How she'd ever do it again...

"I love you, Mary Jo. Don't forget that."

"I won't." Loving him as she did, she found his words an intense comfort. She buried her face in his neck and clung to him,
wanting to believe with everything she possessed that there was a
way for them to find happiness together.

"Now tell me your good news," she murmured. Evan eased her
out of his arms, but tucked her hand inside his elbow and pressed
it there. His eyes were shining with excitement.

"Damian and I had a long talk last evening," Evan said. "I
phoned to tell him about the two of us, and he's absolutely delighted. Jessica, too. They both send their congratulations by the
way."

"Thank them for me," she said softly. "So come on, tell me
your news." She leaned against him as they strolled leisurely down
the wharf.

"All right, all right. Damian's been in contact with a number of
key people over the past few weeks. The general consensus is that
the time for me to make my move into the political arena is now."

Mary Jo felt as though a fist had been plowed into her midsec-
tion. For a moment she remained frozen. She couldn't breathe.
Couldn't think. She was dimly aware of Evan beside her, still talking.

"Now?" she broke in. "But I thought...you said..."

"I know it probably seems way too early to be discussing next
year's elections," Evan went on to say, his face alive with energy.
"But we've got some catching up to do. I won't file for office until
after the first of the year, but there're a million things that need to
be done before then."

"What office do you intend to run for?" Her mind was awhirl with doubts and questions. The sick feeling in the pit of her stomach refused to go away. She felt both cold and feverishly hot at the same time.

"I'm running for city council. There's nothing I'd enjoy more. And, Mary Jo," he said with a broad grin, "I know I can make a difference in our city. I have so many ideas and I've got lots of time, and I don't mind working hard." He raised her hand to his lips and kissed the knuckles. "That's one of the reasons I want us to be married as soon as it can be arranged. We'll work together, side by side, the way my father and mother did when he ran for the Senate."

"I—"

"You'll need to quit your teaching job."

So many objections rose up in her she didn't know which one to address first. "Why can't I teach?"

He looked at her as if the question surprised him. "You don't have to work anymore, and besides, I'm going to need you. Don't you see, sweetheart? This is just the beginning. There's a whole new life waiting for the two of us."

"Have you talked this over with your parents?" Mrs. Dryden must have already known, Mary Jo mused.

"Dad and I discussed it this morning, and he agrees with Damian. The timing is right. Naturally, he'd like to see me run for mayor a few years down the road, and I might, but there's no need to get ahead of ourselves. I haven't been elected to city council yet."

"What did your mother have to say?"

"I don't know if Dad's had the chance to talk to her yet. What makes you ask?"

"I...visited her this morning," Mary Jo admitted, studying the water. It was safer to look out over Boston Harbor than at the man she loved.

"You spent the morning with my mother?" Evan stopped. "At Whispering Willows?"

"Yes."

His eyebrows shot straight toward his hairline. "Why would you go and visit my mother?"

Mary Jo heaved in a deep breath and held it until her chest ached. "There's something you should know, Evan. Something I should have told you a long time ago." She hesitated, finding it difficult to continue. When she did, her voice was low and strained. "When I broke our engagement three years ago, it wasn't because I'd fallen in love with another man. There was never anyone else. It was all a big lie."

She felt him stiffen. He frowned and his eyes narrowed, first with denial and then with disbelief. He shook off her hand and she walked over to the pier, waiting for him to join her.

It took him several moments.

"I'm not proud of that lie," she told him, "and I apologize for stooping to such cowardly methods. You deserved far better, but I wasn't strong enough or mature enough to confront you with the truth."

"Which was?" He was obviously making a strenuous effort to keep his voice level and dispassionate. But his fists were clenched. She could feel his anger, had anticipated it, understood it.

"Various reasons," she confessed. "I invented another love interest because I knew you'd believe me, and...and it avoided the inevitable arguments. I couldn't have dealt with a long-drawn-out debate."

"That makes no sense whatsoever." He sounded angry now, and Mary Jo couldn't blame him. "You'd better start at the beginning," he suggested after a long silence, gather his resolve. "What was it we would have argued about?"

"Our getting married."

"Okay," he said, obviously still not understanding.

"It all started the evening you took me to meet your family," Mary Jo began. "I'd realized you were wealthy, of course, but I had no idea how prominent your family was. I was naive and inexperienced, and when your mother asked me some...pertinent questions, I realized a marriage between us wouldn't work."

"What kind of 'pertinent' questions?" The words were stiff with contained fury.

"Evan, please, it doesn't matter."

"The hell it doesn't!"

Mary Jo briefly closed her eyes. "About my family and my background, and how suitable I'd be as a political wife. She stressed the importance of your marrying the right woman."

"It appears my mother and I need to have a chat."

"Don't be angry, Evan. She wasn't rude or cruel, but she brought up a few truths I hadn't faced. Afterward, I was convinced a marriage between us would never survive. We have so little in common. Our backgrounds are nothing alike, and I was afraid that in time you'd...you'd regret having married me."

He made a disgusted sound. "And so you made up this ridiculous lie and walked out of my life, leaving me lost and confused and so shaken it..." He paused as if he'd said more than he'd intended.

"I behaved stupidly—I know that. But I hurt, too, Evan. Don't think it was easy on me. I suffered. Because I loved you then and I love you still."

He sighed heavily. "I appreciate your honesty, Mary Jo, but let's put the whole mess behind us. It doesn't concern us anymore. We're together now and will be for the next fifty years. That's all that matters."

Tears blurred Mary Jo's eyes as she watched the airport shuttle boat cruise across Boston Harbor. The waters churned and foamed—like her emotions, she thought irrelevantly.

"It's quite apparent, however," Evan continued, "that I need to have a heart-to-heart with my dear, sweet, interfering mother."

"Evan, she isn't the one to blame. Breaking up, lying to you— that was *my* bad idea. But it isn't going to happen again."

"I won't let you out of my life that easily a second time."

"I don't plan on leaving," she whispered. He placed his arm around her shoulder, and Mary Jo slid her own arm around his waist. For a moment they were content in the simple pleasure of being together.

"Because of that first meeting with your mother, I felt it was important to talk to her again," Mary Jo said, wanting to explain why she'd gone to see Mrs. Dryden that morning. "She's a wonderful woman, Evan, and she loves you very much."

"Fine. But I refuse to allow her to interfere in our lives. If she doesn't understand that now, she will when I finish talking to her."

"Evan, please! She did nothing more than open my eyes to a few home truths."

"What did she have to say this morning?"

"Well...she had some of the same questions as before."

"Such as?" he demanded.

"You want us to be married soon, right?"

He nodded. "The sooner the better." Bending his head, he kissed a corner of her mouth. "As I said earlier, we have three years of lost time to make up for. Keep that house with all those empty bedrooms in mind."

Despite the ache in her heart, Mary Jo smiled. "Your mother told me that a small, private wedding might cause problems for your father."

"Whose wedding is this?" Evan cried. "We'll do this our way, sweetheart. Don't worry about it."

"It could be important, Evan," she countered swiftly. "Your father can't be associated with anything that...that could be misinterpreted."

Evan laughed outright. "In other words, she prefers to throw a large, gala wedding with a cast of thousands? That's ridiculous."

"I...think she might be right."

"That's the kind of wedding you want?" Evan asked, his eyes revealing his disbelief.

"No. It isn't what I want at all. But on the other hand, I wouldn't want to do anything to hurt your father."

"Trust me, sweetheart, you won't." He gave her an affectionate squeeze. "Now you listen. We're going to be married and we'll have the kind of wedding *we* want, and Mother won't have any choice but to accept it."

"But, Evan, what if our rushed wedding did cause speculation?"

"What if it did? Do you think I care? Or my father, either, for that matter? My mother is often guilty of making mountains out of molehills. She loves to worry. In this day and age, it's ridiculous to stew about such things."

"But—"

He silenced her with a kiss thorough enough to leave her feeling certain anything was possible. "I love you, Mary Jo. If it was up to me, we'd take the next plane to Las Vegas and be married this evening.''

"People might gossip.'' She managed to dredge up one last argument.

"Good. The more my name's in circulation, the better.''

Mary Jo's spirits had lightened considerably. She so desperately wanted to believe him she didn't stop to question what he was saying.

"It's settled, then. We'll be married as soon as we can make the arrangements. Mom can make all the fuss she wants, but it isn't going to do her any good.''

"I... There are some other things we need to talk over first.''

"There are?'' He sounded exasperated.

She leaned against the pier, knotting and unknotting her hands. "You're excited about running for city council, aren't you?''

"Yes,'' he admitted readily. "This is something I want, and I'm willing to work for it. I wouldn't run for office if I wasn't convinced I could make some positive changes. This is exactly the right way for me to enter politics, especially while Dad's in the Senate.''

She turned to study him. "What if I asked you not to run?''

Evan took several moments to mull over her words. "Why would you do that?''

"What if I did?'' she asked again. "What would you do then?''

"First, I'd need to know exactly what you objected to.''

"What if I reminded you I wasn't comfortable in the spotlight? Which, I might add, was something we discussed just yesterday. I'm not the kind of person who's comfortable living my life in a fishbowl.''

"It wouldn't be like that,'' he protested.

Her smile was sad. Evan didn't understand. He'd grown up accustomed to having people interested in his personal life. Even now, his dating habits often enough provided speculation for the society pages.

"It *would* be like that, Evan. Don't kid yourself.''

"Then you'll adjust,'' he said with supreme confidence.

"I'll adjust,'' she repeated slowly. "What if I don't? Then what happens? I could be an embarrassment to you. My family might be as well. Let me give you an example. Just recently, Jack and Rich were so upset over this investment problem my father's having that they were ready to go to Adison's office and punch him out. If we hadn't stopped them, they'd have been thrown in jail. The press would have a field day with that."

"You're overreacting."

"Maybe," she agreed grudgingly, then added with emphasis, "but I don't think so. I told you before how I feel about this. You didn't believe me, did you? You seem to think a pat on the head and a few reassurances are all I need. You've discounted everything I've said to you."

"Mary Jo, please—"

"In case you haven't noticed, I—I have this terrible habit of blushing whenever I'm the center of attention. I'm not the kind of woman your mother is. She enjoys the spotlight, loves arranging social events. She has a gift for making everyone feel comfortable and welcome. I can't do that, Evan. I'd be miserable."

Evan said nothing, but his mouth tightened.

"You may think I'm being selfish and uncaring, but that isn't true. I'm just not the right woman for you."

"Because my mother said so."

"No, because of who and what I am."

Evan sighed heavily. "I can see that you've already got this all worked out."

"Another thing. I'm a good teacher and I enjoy my job. I'd want to continue with my kindergarten class after we were married."

Evan took several steps away from her and rubbed his hand along the back of his neck. "Then there's nothing left for me to say, is there? I'll talk to Damian and explain that everything's off. I won't run for city council, not if it makes you that uncomfortable."

"Oh, Evan." She was on the verge of tears. This was exactly what she'd feared. Exactly what she didn't want. "Don't you see?" she pleaded, swallowing back a sob. "I can't marry you knowing I'm holding you back from your dreams. You may love me now, but in time you'd grow to resent me, and it would ruin our marriage."

"You're more important to me than any political office," Evan said sharply. "You're right, Mary Jo, you did tell me how you felt about getting involved in politics, and I did discount what you said. I grew up in a family that was often in the limelight. This whole thing is old hat to me. I was wrong not to have considered your feelings."

She closed her eyes in an effort to blot out his willingness to sacrifice himself. "It just isn't going to work, Evan. In the beginning you wouldn't mind, but later it would destroy us. It would hurt your family, too. This isn't only your dream, it's theirs."

"Leave my family to me."

"No. You're a part of them and they're a part of you. Politics has been your dream from the time you were a boy. You told me yourself that you believe you can make a difference to the city's future."

By now, the tears were running down her face. Impatiently she brushed them aside and forced herself to continue. "How many times are you going to make me say it? *I'm not the right woman for you.*"

"You *are* the right woman," he returned forcefully. His hands gripped her shoulders and he pulled her toward him, his eyes fierce and demanding. "I'm not listening to any more of this. We've loved each other too long. We're meant to be together."

Mary Jo closed her eyes again and hung her head. "There's someone else out there—from the right family, with the right background. A woman who'll share your ambition and your dreams, who'll work with you and not against you. A woman who'll...love you, too."

"I can't believe you're saying this." His grip tightened on her shoulder until it was almost painful, but she knew he didn't even realize it. "It's you I love. It's you I want to marry."

Mary Jo sadly shook her head.

"If you honestly believe there's another woman for me, why didn't I fall in love with someone else? I had three whole years to find this phantom woman you mention. Why didn't I?"

"Because your eyes were closed. Because you were too wrapped up in your own pain to look. For whatever reasons... I don't know..."

"Is this what you want? To walk out of my life a second time as if we meant nothing to each other?" He was beginning to attract attention from passersby, and he lowered his voice.

"No," she admitted. "This is killing me. I'd give anything to be the kind of woman you need, but I can only be me. If I ask you to accept who I am, then...I can't ask you to be something you're not."

"Don't do this," he said between clenched teeth. "We'll find a way."

How she wanted to believe that. How she wished it could be possible.

Evan drew a deep breath and released her shoulder. "Let's not make any drastic decisions now. We're both emotionally spent. Nothing has to be determined right this minute." He paused and gulped another deep breath. "Let's sleep on it and we can talk in the morning. All right?"

Mary Jo nodded. She couldn't have endured much more of this.

The following morning Evan phoned the office shortly after she'd arrived and told her he'd be in late. His voice was cool, without a hint of emotion, as he asked her to reschedule his first two appointments.

Mary Jo thought she might as well have been speaking to a stranger. She longed to ask him how he was or if he'd had any further thoughts, but it was clear he wanted to avoid speaking to her about anything personal.

With a heavy heart, she began her morning duties. Around nine-thirty, the office door opened and Damian walked in. He paused as if he wasn't sure he'd come to the right room.

"Evan won't be in until eleven this morning," she explained.

"Yes, I know." For a man she'd assumed was utterly confident, Damian appeared doubtful and rather hesitant. "It wasn't Evan I came to see. It was you."

"Me?" She looked up at Damian, finding his gaze warm and sympathetic. "Why?"

"Evan stopped by the house yesterday afternoon to talk to both Jessica and me. He was confused and..."

"Hurt," Mary Jo supplied for him. She knew exactly what Evan was feeling because she'd felt the same way.

"I don't know that my talking to you will solve anything, but I thought I should give it a try. I'm not sure my brother would appreciate my butting into his personal business, but he did it once for me. I figure I owe him one." Damian's smile was fleeting. "I don't know if this is what you want to hear, but Evan sincerely loves you."

A lump developed in her throat and she nodded. "I realize that." She sincerely loved him, too.

"From what Evan said to us, I gather he's decided against running for city council. He also told us why he felt he had to back out. Naturally, I support any decision he chooses to make."

"But..." There had to be a "but" in all this.

"But it would be a shame if he declined."

"I'm not going to let that happen," Mary Jo said calmly. "You see, I love Evan and I want what's best for him, and to put it simply, that isn't me."

"He doesn't believe that, Mary Jo, and neither do I."

She could see no reason to discuss the issue. "Where's he now?" she asked softly.

"He went to talk to our parents."

Their parents. If anyone could get him to face the truth, it was Lois Dryden. Mary Jo had approached the woman, strong and certain of her love, and walked away convinced she'd been living in a dreamworld. Lois Dryden was capable of opening Evan's eyes as no one else could.

"We both need time to think this through," Mary Jo murmured. "I appreciate your coming to me, Damian, more than I can say. I know you did it out of love, but what happens between Evan and me, well, that's our concern."

"You didn't ask for my advice, but I'm going to give it to you, anyway," Damian said. "Don't be so quick to give up."

"I won't," she promised.

Mary Jo was sitting at her desk sorting mail when Evan arrived shortly after eleven. She stood up to greet him, but he glanced past her and said tonelessly, "I can't fight both of you." Then he walked into his office and closed the door.

His action said more than his words. In her heart, Mary Jo had dared to hope that if Evan confronted his parents and came away with his convictions intact, there might be a chance for them.

But obviously that hadn't happened. One look plainly revealed his resignation and regret. He'd accepted from his parents what he wouldn't from her. The truth.

Sitting back down, Mary Jo typed out her letter of resignation and signed it. Next she phoned a temporary employment agency and made the arrangements for her replacement to arrive that afternoon.

When she'd finished, she tapped lightly on his closed door and let herself into his office.

"Yes?" Evan said.

She found him standing in front of the window, hands clasped behind his back. After a moment, he turned to face her.

With tears blocking her throat, she laid the single sheet on his desk and crossed to stand beside him.

His gaze went from the letter to her and back. "What's that?"

"My letter of resignation. My replacement will be here within the hour. I'll finish out the day—show her around and explain her duties."

She half expected him to offer a token argument, but he said nothing. She pressed her hand against the side of his face and smiled up at him. His features blurred as the tears filled her eyes.

"Goodbye, Evan," she whispered.

Nine

A week passed and the days bled into one another until Mary Jo couldn't distinguish morning from afternoon. A thousand regrets hounded her at all times of the day and night.

Blessed with a loving family, Mary Jo accepted their comfort, needed it. There was for all of them, some consolation in the news that came from Evan. Through his new secretary, he'd been in touch with her father regarding Adison Investments.

Mary Jo heard from him, too. Once. In a brief letter explaining that Adison would be forthcoming with the return of the original investment money, plus interest. Since he'd calculated his fee for an extended lawsuit, she owed him nothing.

Mary Jo read the letter several times, looking for a message. Anything. But there were only three short sentences, their tone crisp and businesslike, with no hidden meaning that she could decipher. Tears blurred her eyes as she lovingly ran her finger over his signature. She missed him terribly, felt empty and lost and this was as close as she would ever be to him again—her finger caressing his signature at the end of a letter.

Another week passed. Mary Jo was no less miserable than she'd been the first day after she'd stopped working for Evan. She knew it would take time and effort to accept the infeasibility of her love for him, but she wasn't ready. Not yet. So she stayed holed up in her apartment, listless and heartbroken.

The fact that the summer days were glorious—all sunshine and blue sky—didn't help. The least Mother Nature could have done was cooperate and match her mood with dark gray clouds and gloomy days.

She dragged herself out of bed late that morning and didn't bother to eat until early afternoon. Now she sat in front of the television dressed in her nightie and munching dry cornflakes. She hadn't been to the grocery store in weeks and had long since run out of milk. And just about everything else.

The doorbell chimed, and Mary Jo shot an accusing glance in the direction of her front door. It was probably her mother or one of her sisters-in-law, who seemed to think it was up to them to boost her spirits. So they invented a number of ridiculous excuses to pop in unexpectedly.

The love and support of her family was important, but all Mary Jo wanted at the moment was to be left alone. To eat her cornflakes in peace.

She set the bowl aside, walked over to the door and squinted through the peephole. She caught a glimpse of a designer purse, but unfortunately whoever was holding it stood just outside her view.

"Who is it?" she called out.

"Jessica."

Mary Jo pressed her forehead against the door and groaned. She was an emotional and physical wreck. The last person she wanted to see was anyone related to Evan.

"Mary Jo, please open the door," Jessica called. "We need to talk. It's about Evan."

Nothing could have been more effective. Mary Jo didn't want company. She didn't want to talk. But the minute Jessica said Evan's name, she turned the lock and opened the door. Standing in the doorway, she closed her eyes against the painfully bright sun.

"How are you?" Jessica asked, walking right in.

"About as bad as I look," Mary Jo mumbled, shutting the door behind her. "What about Evan?"

"Same as you." She strode into the room, removed a stack of papers from the rocking chair and planted herself on it as if she intended to stay for a while.

"Where's Andy?" Mary Jo asked, still holding the doorknob.

Jessica crossed her legs, rocking gently as if she had all the time in the world. "My mother has him—for the *day*."

Mary Jo noted the emphasis. Jessica intended to stay here until she got what she wanted.

"I told Mom I had a doctor's appointment, and I do—later," Jessica continued. "I think I'm pregnant again." A radiant happiness shone from her eyes.

"Congratulations." Although Mary Jo was miserable, she was pleased for her friend, who was clearly delighted.

"I know it's none of my business," Jessica said sympathetically, "but tell me what happened between you and Evan."

"I'm sure he's already explained." Mary Jo wasn't up to hauling up all the painful details. Besides, it would solve nothing.

Jessica laughed shortly. "Evan talk? You've got to be joking. He wouldn't say so much as a word. Both Damian and I've tried to get him to discuss what happened, but it hasn't done a bit of good."

"So you've come to me."

"Exactly." Jessica was obviously determined to stay until she learned what she wanted to know.

"Please don't do this, Jessica," Mary Jo said, fighting back the tears. "It's just too painful."

"But you both love each other so much."

"That's why our breakup's necessary. It isn't easy on either of us, but this is the way it has to be."

Jessica tossed her hands in the air. "You're a pair of fools. There's no talking to Evan, and you're not much better. What's it going to take to get you two back together?"

"A miracle," Mary Jo answered.

Jessica took several moments to digest this. "Is there anything I can do?"

"No," Mary Jo said sadly. There wasn't anything anyone could do. But one thing was certain: she couldn't continue like this. Sliding from one day to the next without a thought to the future. Buried in the pain of the past, barely able to live in the present.

"You're sure?"

"I'm thinking of leaving Boston," she said suddenly. The impulse had come unexpectedly, and in a heartbeat Mary Jo knew it was the right thing to do. She couldn't live in this town, this state, without constantly being bombarded with information about the Dryden family. Not a week passed that his father wasn't in the news for one reason or another, or so it seemed. It wouldn't get any better once Evan was elected to city council.

Escape seemed her only answer.

"Where would you go?" Jessica pressed.

Anywhere that wasn't here. "The Northwest," she said again, blurting out the first destination that came to mind. "Washington, maybe Oregon. I've heard that part of the country's beautiful." Teachers were needed everywhere and she shouldn't have much trouble obtaining a position.

"So far away?" Jessica seemed to breathe the question.

The farther the better. Her family would argue with her, but for the first time in two weeks, Mary Jo had found a reason to look ahead.

Her parents would tell her she was running away, and Mary Jo would agree, but sometimes running was necessary. She remembered her father's talks with her older brothers; he'd explained that there might come a day when they'd find themselves in a no-win situation. The best thing to do, he'd told them, was to walk away. Surely this was one of those times.

"Thank you for coming," Mary Jo said, looking solemnly at her friend. "I appreciate it. Please let me know when the baby's born."

"I will," Jessica said, her eyes sad.

"I'll have my mother send me the results of the election next year. My heart will be with Evan."

It would always be with him.

Jessica left soon afterward, flustered and discouraged. They hugged and, amid promises to keep in touch, reluctantly parted. Mary Jo counted Evan's sister-in-law as a good friend.

Mary Jo was suddenly filled with purpose. She dressed, made a number of phone calls, opened the door and let the sunshine pour in. By late afternoon, she'd accomplished more than she had in the entire previous two weeks. Telling her parents her decision wouldn't be easy, but her mind was made up. It was now Tuesday. First thing next Monday morning, she was packing what she could in her car and heading west. As soon as she'd settled somewhere she'd send for her furniture.

Before Mary Jo could announce her decision, her father phoned her with the wonderful news that he'd received a cashier's check returning his investment. Not only that, Evan had put him in contact with a reputable financial adviser.

"That's great," Mary Jo said, blinking back tears. Hearing the relief in her father's voice was all the reward she would ever need. Although it had ultimately broken her heart, asking Evan to help her parents had been the right thing to do. Her father had gotten far more than his investment back. In the process he'd restored his pride and his faith in justice.

"I need to talk to you and Mom," Mary Jo announced, steeling herself for the inevitable confrontation. "I'll be over in a few minutes."

The meeting didn't go well. Mary Jo hadn't expected that it would. Her parents had a list of objections that lasted nearly an hour. Mary Jo's resolve didn't waver. She was leaving Boston; she would find a new life for herself.

To her surprise, her brothers sided with her. Jack insisted she was old enough to make her own decisions. His words did more to convince her parents than hours of her own arguments.

The Friday before she was leaving, Mary Jo spent the day with her mother. Marianna was pickling cucumbers in the kitchen, dabbing her eyes now and again when she didn't think Mary Jo was looking.

"I'm going to miss you," Marianna said, putting on a brave front.

Mary Jo's heart clenched. "I'll miss you, too. But, Mom, you make it sound like you'll never hear from me again. I promise to phone at least once a week."

"Call when the rates are cheaper, understand?"

Mary Jo suppressed a smile. "Of course."

"I talked to Evan," her mother mentioned casually as she was inserting large cloves of garlic into the sterilized canning jars.

Mary Jo froze, and her breath jammed in her chest.

"I told him you'd decided to leave Boston, and you know what he said?"

"No." The word rose from her throat on a bubble of hysteria.

"Evan said you'd know what was best." She paused as if carefully judging her words. "He didn't sound like himself. I'm worried about that boy, but I'm more concerned about you."

"Mom, I'm going to be fine."

"I know that. You're a Summerhill and we're strong people."

Mary Jo followed her mother, dropping a sprig of dill weed into each of the sparkling clean jars.

"You never told me what went wrong between you and Evan, not that you had to. I've got eyes and ears, and it didn't take much for me to figure out his family had something to do with all this."

Her mother's insight didn't come as any surprise, but Mary Jo neither confirmed nor denied it.

"The mail's here," Norman Summerhill said, strolling into the kitchen. "I had one of those fancy travel agencies send us a couple of brochures on the South Pacific. When you're finished packing those jars, let's sit down and read over what they've got to say."

Marianna's nod was eager. "We won't be long."

Her father set the rest of the mail on the table. The top envelope captured Mary Jo's attention. The return address was a bankruptcy court. She didn't think anything of it until later when her father opened the envelope.

"I wonder what this is?" he mumbled, sounding confused. He stretched his arms out in front of him to read it.

"Norman, for the love of heaven, get your glasses," Marianna chastised.

"I can see fine without them." He winked at Mary Jo. "Here, you read it for me." Mary Jo took the cover letter and scanned the contents. As she did, her stomach turned. The bankruptcy court had written her parents on behalf of Adison Investments. They were to complete the attached forms and list, with proof, the amount of their investment. Once all the documents were returned, the case would be heard.

The legal jargon was difficult for Mary Jo to understand, but one thing was clear. Adison Investments hadn't returned her father's money.

Evan had.

"It's nothing, Dad," Mary Jo said, not knowing what else to say.

"Then throw it away. I don't understand why we get so much junk mail these days. You'd think the environmentalists would do something about wasting all those trees."

Mary Jo stuck the envelope in her purse, made her excuses and left soon afterward. She wasn't sure what she was going to do, but if she didn't escape soon, there'd be no hiding her tears.

Evan had done this for her family because he loved her. This was his way of saying goodbye. Hot tears blurred her eyes, and sniffling, she rubbed the back of her hand across her face.

The blast of a car horn sounded from behind her and Mary Jo glanced in the direction of the noise. Adrenaline shot through her as she saw a full-size sedan barreling toward her.

The next thing she heard was metal slamming against metal. The sound exploded in her ears and she instinctively brought her hands up to her face. The impact was so strong she felt as though she were caught in the middle of an explosion.

Her world went into chaos. There was only pain. Her head started to spin, and her vision blurred. She screamed.

Her last thought before she lost consciousness was that she was going to die.

"Why didn't you call me right away?" a gruff male voice demanded.

It seemed to come from a great distance away and drifted slowly toward Mary Jo as she floated, unconcerned, on a thick black cloud. It sounded like Evan's voice, but then again it didn't. The words came to her sluggish and slurred.

"We tried to contact you, but your secretary said you couldn't be reached."

The second voice belonged to her father, Mary Jo determined. But he, too, sounded odd, as if he were standing at the bottom of a deep well and yelling up at her. The words were distorted and they vibrated, making them difficult to understand. They seemed to take a very long time to reach her. Perhaps it was because her head hurt so badly. The throbbing was intense and painful.

"I came as soon as I heard." It was Evan again and he sounded sorry, as if he was to blame. "How seriously is she hurt?"

"Doc says she sustained a head injury. She's unconscious, but they claim she isn't in a coma."

"She'll wake up soon," her mother said in a soothing tone. "Now sit down and relax. Everything's going to be all right. I'm sure the doctor will be happy to answer any of your questions. Mary Jo's going to fine, just wait and see."

Her mother was comforting Evan as if he were one of her own children, Mary Jo realized. She didn't understand why Evan should be so worried. Perhaps he was afraid she was going to die. Perhaps she already had, but then she decided she couldn't be dead because she hurt too much.

"What have they done to her head?"

Mary Jo was anxious for that answer herself.

"They had to shave off her hair."

"Relax." It was her father speaking. "It'll grow back."

"It's just that she looks so..." Evan didn't finish the sentence.

"She'll be fine, Evan. Now sit down here by her side. I know it's a shock seeing her like this."

Mary Jo wanted to reassure Evan herself, but her mouth refused to open and she couldn't speak. Something must be wrong with her if she could hear but not see or speak. When she attempted to move, she found her arms and legs wouldn't cooperate. A sense of panic overwhelmed her and the pounding pain intensified.

Almost immediately she drifted away on the same dark cloud and the voices slowly faded. She longed to call out, to pull herself back, but she hadn't the strength. And this way, the pain wasn't nearly as bad.

The next thing Mary Jo heard was a soft thumping. It took her several moments to recognize what that particular sound meant. Someone was in her room, pacing. Whoever it was seemed impatient, or maybe anxious. She didn't know which.

"How is she?" A feminine voice that was vaguely familiar drifted soothingly toward Mary Jo. The pain in her head was back, and she desperately wanted it to go away.

"There's been no change." It was Evan who spoke. Evan was the one pacing her room. Knowing he was there filled her with a gentle sense of peace. She'd recover if Evan was with her. How she knew this, Mary Jo didn't question.

"How long have you been here?" The feminine voice belonged to Jessica, she decided.

"A few hours."

"It's more like twenty-four. I met Mary Jo's parents in the elevator. They're going home to get some sleep. You should, too. The hospital will call if there's any change."

"No."

Mary Jo laughed to herself. She'd recognize that stubborn streak of his anywhere.

"Evan," Jessica protested. "You're not thinking clearly."

"Yeah, I know. But I'm not leaving her, Jessica. You can argue if you want, but it won't do you a damn bit of good."

There was a short silence. Mary Jo heard a chair being dragged across the floor. It was coming toward her. "Mary Jo was leaving Boston, did you know?"

"I know," Evan returned. "Her mother called to tell me."

"Were you going to stop her?"

It took him a long time to answer. "No."

"But you love her."

"Jess, please, leave it alone."

Evan loved her and she loved him, and it was hopeless. A sob swelled within her chest and Mary Jo experienced an overwhelming urge to weep.

"She moved," Evan said sharply, excitedly. "Did you see it? Her hand flinched just now."

Mary Jo felt herself being pulled away once more into a black void where there was no sound. It seemed to close in around her like the folds of a dark, bulky blanket.

When Mary Jo opened her eyes, the first thing she saw was a patch of blue. It took her a moment to realize it was the sky from outside the hospital window. A scattering of clouds shimmied across the horizon. She blinked, trying to remember what she was doing in this bed, in this room.

She'd been in a car accident, that was it. She couldn't remember any details—except that she thought she was dying. Her head had hurt so badly. The throbbing wasn't nearly as intense now, but it was still there and the bright sunshine made her eyes water.

Rolling her head to the other side demanded a great deal of effort. Her mother was sitting at her bedside reading from a Bible and her father was standing on the other side of the room. He pressed his hands against the small of his back as if to relieve tired muscles.

"Mom." Mary Jo's voice was husky and low.

Marianna Summerhill vaulted to her feet. "Norman, Norman, Mary Jo's awake." Having said that, she covered her face with her hands and burst into tears.

It was very unusual to see her mother cry. Mary Jo looked at her father and saw that his eyes, too, were brimming with tears.

"So you decided to rejoin the living," her father said, raising her hand to his lips. "Welcome back."

Smiling required more strength than she had.

"How do you feel?" Her mother was dabbing at her eyes with a tissue and looking so pale that Mary Jo wondered if she'd been ill herself.

"Weird," she said hoarsely.

"The doctor said he expected you to wake up soon."

There was so much she wanted to ask, so much she had to say. "Evan?" she managed to croak.

"He was here," her mother answered. "From the moment he learned about the accident until just a few minutes ago. No one could convince him to leave."

"He's talking with some fancy specialist right now," her father explained. "I don't mind telling you, he's been beside himself with worry. We've all been scared."

Her eyes drifted shut. She felt so incredibly weak, and what energy she had evaporated quickly.

"Sleep," her mother cooed. "Everything's going to be fine."

No, no, Mary Jo protested, fighting sleep. Not yet. Not so soon. She had too many questions that needed answering. But the silence enveloped her once more.

It was night when she stirred again. The sky was dark and the heavens were flecked with stars. Moonlight softly illuminated the room.

She assumed she was alone, then noticed a shadowy figure against the wall. The still shape sat in the chair next to her bed. It was Evan, she realized, and he was asleep. His arms were braced against the edge of the mattress, supporting his head.

The comfort she felt in knowing he was with her was beyond measure. Reaching for his hand, she covered it with her own, then yawned and closed her eyes.

"Are you hungry?" Marianna asked, carrying in the hospital tray and setting it on the bedside table.

Mary Jo was sitting up for the first time. "I don't know," she said, surprised by how feeble her voice sounded.

"I talked to the doctor about the hospital menu," her mother said, giving her head a disparaging shake. "He assured me you'll survive on their cooking until I can get you home and feed you properly."

It probably wasn't all that amusing, but Mary Jo couldn't stop smiling. For the first time she really took note of her surroundings. The room was filled with fresh flowers. They covered every available surface; there were even half a dozen vases lined up on the floor.

"Who sent all the flowers?" she asked.

Her mother pointed toward the various floral arrangements. "Your brothers. Dad and I. Those two are from Jessica and Damian. Let me see—the teachers at your old school. Oh, the elaborate one is from the Drydens. That bouquet of pink carnations is from Gary."

"How sweet of everyone." But Mary Jo noticed that there were a number of bouquets her mother had skipped. Those, she strongly suspected, were from Evan.

Evan.

Just thinking about him made her feel so terribly sad. From the time she'd regained consciousness, he'd stopped coming to the hospital. He'd been there earlier, she was sure of it. The memories were too vivid not to be real. But as soon as she was out of danger, he'd left her life once more.

"Eat something," Marianna insisted. "I know it's not your mama's cooking, but it doesn't look too bad."

Mary Jo shook her head and leaned back against the pillow. "I'm not hungry."

"Sweetheart, please. The doctors won't let you come home until you've regained your strength."

Evan wasn't the only one with a stubborn streak. She folded her arms and refused to even look at the food. Eventually, she was persuaded to take a few bites, because it was clear her lack of appetite was distressing her mother.

When the tray was removed, Mary Jo slept. Her father was with her when she awoke. Her eyes met his, which were warm and tender.

"Was the accident my fault?" She had to know, she remembered so little of what had happened.

"No. The other car ran a red light."

"Was anyone else hurt?"

"No," he said, taking her hand in both of his.

"I'm sorry I worried you."

A slight smile crossed his face. "Your brothers were just as worried. And Evan."

"He was here, wasn't he?"

"Every minute. No one could get him to leave, not even his own family."

But he wasn't there now. When she really needed him.

Her father gently patted her hand, and when he spoke it was as if he'd been reading her thoughts. "Life has a way of making things right. Everything will turn out just the way it's supposed to. So don't you fret about Evan or his family or anything else. Just concentrate on getting well."

"I will." But her heart wasn't in it. Her heart was with Evan.

*   *   *

A week passed, and Mary Jo regained more of her strength each day. With her head shaved, she looked as if she'd stepped out of a science-fiction movie. All she needed were the right clothes and a laser gun and she'd be real Hollywood material.

If she continued to improve at this pace, she should be discharged from the hospital within the next couple of days. That was good news—not that she didn't appreciate the excellent care she'd received.

Mary Jo spent part of the morning slowly walking the corridors in an effort to rebuild her strength. She still tired easily and took frequent breaks to chat with nurses and other patients. After a pleasant but exhausting couple of hours, she decided to go back to bed for a while.

As she entered her room, she stopped abruptly. Lois Dryden stood by the window, looking out of place in her tailored suit.

Lois must have sensed her return. There was no disguising her dismay when she saw Mary Jo's shaved, bandaged head. She seemed incapable of speech for a moment.

Mary Jo took the initiative. "Hello, Mrs. Dryden," she said evenly.

"Hello, my dear. I hope you don't mind my dropping in like this."

"No, of course I don't mind." Mary Jo made her way to the bed and got in, conscious of her still-awkward movements.

"I was very sorry to hear about your accident."

Mary Jo adjusted the covers around her legs and leaned back against the raised mattress. "I'm well on the way to recovery now."

"That's what I understand. I heard there's a possibility you'll be going home soon."

"I hope so."

"Is there anything I can do for you?"

The offer surprised Mary Jo. "No, but thank you."

Lois walked away from the window and stood at the foot of the bed, the picture of conventional propriety with her small hat and spotless white gloves. She looked directly at Mary Jo.

"I understand Jessica has come by a number of times," she said.

"Yes," Mary Jo answered. "She's been very kind. She brought me a tape player and some books on tape." Except that Mary Jo hadn't been able to concentrate on any of the stories. No sooner would the tape begin than she'd drift off to sleep.

"I suppose Jessica told you she and Damian are expecting again."

Without warning, Mary Jo's heart contracted painfully. "Yes, I'm delighted for them."

"Naturally, Walter and I are thrilled with the prospect of a second grandchild."

It became important not to look at Evan's mother, and Mary Jo focused her gaze out the window. The tightness in her chest refused to go away, and she realized the source of the pain was emotional. She longed for a child herself. Evan's child. They'd talked about their home, planned their family. The picture of the house he'd described, with a yard full of laughing, playing children flashed into her mind.

The house would never be built now. There would be no children. No marriage. No Evan.

"Of course, Damian is beside himself with happiness."

From somewhere deep inside, Mary Jo found the strength to say, "I imagine he is."

"There'll be a little less than two years between the two children. Andrew will be twenty months old by the time the baby's born."

Mary Jo wondered why Mrs. Dryden was telling her all this and could think of nothing more to say. She found the conversation exhausting. She briefly closed her eyes.

"I...I suppose I shouldn't tire you any longer."

"Thank you for stopping by," Mary Jo murmured politely.

Lois stepped toward the door, then hesitated and turned back to the bed. Mary Jo noticed that the older woman's hand trembled as she reached out and gripped the foot of the bed.

"Is something the matter?" Mary Jo asked, thinking perhaps she should ring for the nurse.

"Yes," Evan's mother said. "Something is very much the matter—and I'm the one at fault. You came to me not long ago because you wanted to marry my son. I discouraged you, and Evan, too, when he came to speak to his father and me.''

''Mrs. Dryden, please—''

''No, let me finish.'' She took in a deep breath and leveled her gaze on Mary Jo. ''Knowing what I do now, I would give everything I have if you'd agree to marry my son.''

Ten

Mary Jo wasn't sure she'd heard Evan's mother correctly. "I don't understand."

Instinctively, she knew that Mrs. Dryden was someone who rarely revealed her feelings. She knew that the older woman rarely lost control of a situation—or of herself. She seemed dangerously close to losing it now.

"Would...would you mind if I sat down?"

"Please do." Mary Jo wished she'd thought to suggest it herself.

Lois pulled the chair closer to the bed, and Mary Jo was surprised by how delicate, how fragile, she suddenly appeared. "Before I say anything more, I must ask your forgiveness."

"Mine?"

"Yes, my dear. When you came to me, happy and excited, to discuss marrying my son, I was impressed by your...your courage. Your sense of responsibility. You'd guessed my feelings correctly when Evan brought you to dinner three or so years ago. Although you were a delightful young woman, I couldn't picture you as his wife. My son, however, was clearly enthralled with you."

Mary Jo started to speak, but Mrs. Dryden shook her head, obviously determined to finish her confession. "I decided that very night that it was important for us to talk. I'd never intended to hurt you or Evan, and when I learned you were no longer seeing each other, I realized it might have had something to do with what I'd said to you."

"Mrs. Dryden, please, this isn't necessary."

"On the contrary. It's very necessary. If you're to be my daughter-in-law, and I sincerely hope you will be, then I feel it's vital for us to...to begin afresh."

Mary Jo's pulse began to hammer with excitement. "You meant what you said earlier, then? About wanting me to marry Evan?"

"Every word. Once we know each other a little better, you'll learn I rarely say what I don't mean. Now, please, allow me to continue."

"Of course. I'm sorry."

Mrs. Dryden gave her an ironic smile. "Once we're on more familiar terms, you won't need to be so apprehensive of me. I'm hoping we can be friends, Mary Jo. After all I pray you'll be the mother of my grandchildren." She smiled again. "Half of them, anyway."

Mary Jo blinked back her tears, deeply moved by the other woman's unmistakable contrition and by her generosity.

"Now...where was I?" Oh, yes, we were talking about three years ago. You and Evan had decided not to see each other again, and frankly—forgive me for this, Mary Jo—I was relieved. But Evan seemed to take the breakup very badly. I realized then that I might have acted too hastily. For months, I contemplated calling you myself. I'm ashamed to tell you I kept putting it off. No," she said and her voice shook, "I was a coward. I dreaded facing you."

"Mrs. Dryden, it was a long time ago."

"You're right, it was, but that doesn't lessen my guilt." She paused. "Evan changed that autumn. He'd always been such a lighthearted young man. He continued to joke and tease, but it wasn't the same. The happiness had gone out of his eyes. Nothing held his interest for long. He drifted from one brief relationship to another. He was miserable, and it showed."

In those bleak, lonely months, Mary Jo hadn't fared much better, but she said nothing about that now.

"It was during this time that Walter decided to run for the Senate, and our lives were turned upside down. Our one concern was Evan. The election was important to Walter, and in some ways, Evan was a problem. Walter discussed the situation with Evan... Oh, dear. None of this applies to the present situation. I'm getting sidetracked."

"No. Go on," Mary Jo pleaded.

"I have to admit I'm not proud of what we did. Walter and I

felt strongly that Jessica Kellerman was the right woman for Evan, and we did what we could to encourage a relationship. As you know, Damian and Jessica fell in love. You'd think I'd have learned my lesson about interfering in my sons' lives, but apparently not."

Mary Jo wished she could say something to reassure Lois.

"Early this summer, Walter and I noticed a...new happiness in Evan. He seemed more like the way he used to be. Later we learned that you were working for him. I decided then and there that if you two decided to rekindle your romance, I'd do nothing to stand in your way."

"You didn't," Mary Jo said quickly.

"Then you came to me and insisted on a small, private wedding. It was obvious you didn't understand the social demands made upon a husband in politics. I could see you were getting discouraged, and I did nothing to change that. At the time it seemed for the best."

"Mrs. Dryden, you're taking on far more blame than you should."

"That's not all, Mary Jo." She clenched her purse with both gloved hands and hung her head. "Evan came to speak to Walter and me about the two of you. I don't believe I've ever seen him so angry. No other woman has ever held such power over my son. You see, Evan and I've always been close and it...pains me to admit this, but I was jealous. I told him that if you were willing to break off another engagement over the first disagreement, then you weren't the woman for him.

"I must have been more persuasive than I realized. Later Evan told me he couldn't fight both of us and that he'd decided to abide by your wishes."

"He said that to me, too," Mary Jo murmured.

"It's been several weeks now, but nothing's changed. My son still loves you very much. When you had this accident, he refused to leave the hospital. I came here myself early one morning and found Evan sitting alone in the hospital chapel." She paused and her lower lip trembled. "I knew then that you weren't some passing fancy in his life. He loves you as he's never loved another woman and probably won't again."

Mary Jo leaned forward. "I'll never be comfortable in the lime-light, Mrs. Dryden," she said urgently. "But I'm willing to do whatever it takes to be the kind of wife Evan needs."

Mrs. Dryden snapped open her purse, took out a delicate white handkerchief and dabbed her eyes. "It's time for another confes-sion, I'm afraid. I've always believed Evan would do well in pol-itics. I've made no secret of my ambitions for my son, but that's what they were—*my* ambitions. Not his. If Evan does decide to pursue a political career, it should be his decision, not mine.

"In light of what's happened between you two, I'm determined to stay out of it entirely. Whatever happens now depends on Evan. On you, too, of course," she added hurriedly, "but I promise you, I won't interfere. I've finally learned my lesson."

Unable to speak, Mary Jo reached for the other woman's hand and held it tightly.

"I'd like it if we could be friends, Mary Jo," Lois added softly. "I'll do my damnedest to stop being an interfering old woman."

"My mother learned her lessons with my oldest brother, Jack, and his wife. You might like to speak to her sometime and swap stories," Mary Jo suggested.

"I'd like that." She stood and bent to kiss Mary Jo's cheek. "You'll go to Evan, then, when you're able?"

Mary Jo grinned. "As soon as I look a bit more presentable."

"You'll look wonderful to Evan now, believe me." The older woman touched her hand softly. "Make him happy, Mary Jo."

"I'll do my very best."

"And please let me know when your mother and I can talk. We have a million things to discuss about the wedding."

Mary Jo ventured, a little hesitantly, "The wedding will be small and private."

"Whatever you decide."

"But perhaps we could have a big reception afterward and invite the people you wouldn't want to offend by excluding."

"An excellent idea." Lois smiled broadly.

"Thank you for coming to see me."

A tear formed in the corner of one of Lois's eyes. "No. Thank *you*, my dear."

* * *

From the day of Lois Dryden's visit, Mary Jo's recovery was little short of miraculous. She was discharged two days later and spent a week recuperating at her parents' home before she felt ready to confront Evan.

According to Jessica, he was frequently out on his sailboat. With her friend's help, it was a simple matter to discover when he'd scheduled an outing.

Saturday morning, the sun was bright and the wind brisk—a perfect sailing day. Mary Jo went down to the marina. Using Damian's key, she let herself in and climbed aboard Evan's boat to wait for him.

She hadn't been there long when he arrived. He must have seen her right away, although he gave no outward indication that he had.

She still felt somewhat uncomfortable about her hair, now about half an inch long. She'd tried to disguise it with a turban, but that only make her look as if she should be reading palms or tea leaves. So she left it unadorned.

"Mary Jo?"

"It hard to tell without the hair, right?" she joked.

"What are you doing here?" Evan wasn't unfriendly; nor did he seem particularly pleased to see her.

"I wanted to talk, and this is the place we do our best talking. Are you taking the boat out this morning?"

He ignored the question. "How are you?" The craft rocked gently as he climbed on deck and sat down beside her.

"Much better. A little weak, but I'm gaining more strength every day."

"When were you released from the hospital?"

Evan knew the answer as well as she did, Mary Jo was sure. Why was he making small talk at a time like this?

"You already know. Your mother told you, or Jessica." She paused. "You were at the hospital, Evan."

His mouth tightened, but he said nothing.

"There were periods when I could hear what was going on around me. I was awake, sort of, when you first got there. Another time, I heard you pacing my room, too, and I heard you again when Jessica came by once." She reached for Evan's hand and threaded her fingers through his. "One of the first times I actually woke was the middle of the night, and you were there, asleep."

"I've never been more frightened in my life," he said hoarsely, as if the words had been wrenched from his throat. He wrapped his arms around her then, but gently, with deliberate care. Mary Jo rested her head against his shoulder, and his grip on her tightened just a little. He buried his face in the delicate curve of her shoulder; she felt his warm strength. After a moment, he released her.

"I understand my parents' investment was returned to them— with interest," she said, her tone deceptively casual.

"Yes," he admitted. "They were among the fortunate few to have their money refunded."

"*Their* money?" She raised her hand to his mouth, kissing his knuckles. "Evan, I know what you did."

He frowned. He had that confused, what-are-you-talking-about expression down to an art.

"You might have been able to get away with it but, you see, the papers came."

"What papers?"

"The day of my accident my parents received a notice from the bankruptcy court—as I'm sure you know. If their investment had been returned, how do you explain that?"

He shrugged. "Don't have a clue."

"Evan, please, it's not necessary to play games with me."

He seemed to feel a sudden need to move around. He stood, stretched and moved to the far end of the sailboat. Pointedly, he glanced at his watch. "I wish I had time to chat, but unfortunately I'm meeting a friend."

"Evan, we need to talk."

"I'm sorry, but you should have let me know sooner. Perhaps we could get together some other time." He made an elaborate display of staring at the pier, then smiling and waving eagerly.

A tall, blond woman, incredibly slender and beautifully tanned, waved back. She had the figure of a fashion model and all but purred when Evan hopped out of the boat and met her dockside. She threw her arms around his neck and kissed him, bending one shapely leg at the knee.

Mary Jo was stunned. To hear his mother speak, Evan was a lost, lonely man, so in love with her that his world had fallen apart. Clearly, there was something Mrs. Dryden didn't know.

In her rush to climb out of the sailboat, Mary Jo nearly fell overboard. With her nearly bald head and the clothes that hung on her because of all the weight she'd lost, she felt like the little match girl standing barefoot in the snow. Especially beside this paragon of feminine perfection.

She suffered through an introduction that she didn't hear, made her excuses and promptly left. When she was back in her car, she slumped against the steering wheel, covering her face with both hands.

Shaken and angry, she returned her parents' place and called Jessica to tell her what had happened. She was grateful her parents were out.

She paced the living room in an excess of nervous energy until Jessica arrived, an hour later, looking flustered and disgruntled. "Sorry it took me so long, but I took a cab and it turned out to be the driver's first day on the job. We got lost twice. So what's going on? Lord, I don't know what I'm going to do with the two of you."

Mary Jo told her in great detail what had taken place, painting vivid word pictures as she described the other woman.

Jessica rolled her eyes. "And you *fell* for it?"

"Fell for what?" Mary Jo cried. "Bambi was all over him. I didn't need anyone to spell it out. I was mortified. Good grief," she said, battling down a sob, "look at me. Last week's vegetable casserole has more hair than I do."

Jessica laughed outright. "Mary Jo, be sensible. The man loves you."

"Yeah, I could tell," she muttered.

"Her name's Barbara, not that it matters. Trust me, she doesn't mean a thing to him."

The doorbell chimed and the two women stared at each other. "Are you expecting company?"

"No."

Jessica lowered her voice. "Do you think it could be Evan?"

On her way to the door, Mary Jo shook her head dismally. "I doubt it."

"Just in case, I'd better hide." Jessica backed out of the room and into the kitchen.

To her complete surprise, Mary Jo found Lois Dryden at the door.

"What happened?" the older woman demanded.

Mary Jo opened the door and let her inside. "Happened?"

"With Evan."

"Jessica," Mary Jo called over her shoulder. "You can come out now. It's a Dryden, but it isn't Evan."

"So, Jessica's here?" Lois said.

"Yes," Jessica said. "But what are *you* doing here?"

"Checking up on Mary Jo. I got a call from Damian. All he said was that he suspected things hadn't gone well with Evan and Mary Jo this morning. He said Mary Jo had phoned and Jessica had hurried out shortly afterward. I want to know what went wrong."

"It's a long story," Mary Jo said reluctantly.

"I tried calling you," Lois explained, "then realized you must still be staying with your family. I was going out, anyway, and I thought this might be an excellent opportunity to meet your mother."

"She's out just now." Mary Jo exhaled shakily and gestured at the sofa. "Sit down, please."

Her parents' house lacked the obvious wealth and luxury of Whispering Willows, but anyone who stepped inside felt immediately welcome. A row of high-school graduation pictures sat proudly on the fireplace mantel. Photos of the grandchildren were scattered about the room. The far wall was lined with bookcases, but some shelves held more trophies than books.

"I understand you went to see Evan this morning," his mother said, regarding her anxiously. "I take it the meeting was something of a disaster?"

"Evan had a *date*," Mary Jo said, glancing sharply at Jessica.

"Hey," Jessica muttered, "all you asked me to do was find out the next time he was going sailing. How was I supposed to know he was meeting another woman?"

"Who?" Lois demanded, frowning.

"Barbara," Mary Jo supplied.

Lois made a dismissive gesture with her hand. "Oh, yes, I know who she is. She's a fashion model who flies in from New York every now and again. You haven't a thing to worry about."

"A fashion model." Mary Jo spirits hit the floor.

"She's really not important to him."

"That may be so," Mary Jo pointed out, "but he certainly looked pleased to see her." Depressed, she slouched down on the sofa and braced her feet against the edge of the coffee table.

Lois's back stiffened. "It seems to me I'd better have a chat with that boy."

"Mother!" Jessica cried at the same moment Mary Jo yelped a protest.

"You promised you weren't going to interfere, remember?" Jessica reminded her mother-in-law. "It only leads to trouble. If Evan wants to make a fool of himself, we're going to have to let him."

"I disagree," Lois said. "You're right, of course, about my talking to him—that would only make matters worse—but we can't allow Mary Jo to let him think he's getting away with this."

"What do you suggest we do?" Jessica asked.

Lois bit her bottom lip. "I don't know, but I'll think of something."

"Time-out," Mary Jo said, forming a T with her hands—a technique she often used with her kindergarten class. "I appreciate your willingness to help, but I'd really like to do my own plotting, okay? Don't be offended, but..." Her words trailed off, and her expression turned to pleading.

Jessica smiled and reached for her hand. "Of course," she said.

Mary Jo looked at Lois, and the woman nodded. "You're absolutely right, my dear. I'll keep my nose out." She reached over and gave Mary Jo a hug.

"Thank you," Mary Jo whispered.

Mary Jo didn't hear from Evan at all the following week. She tried to tell herself she wasn't disappointed—but of course she was. When it became clear that he was content to leave things between them as they were, she composed a short letter and mailed it to him at his office. After all, it was a business matter.

Without elaborating, she suggested she work for him the next four summers as compensation for the money he'd given her parents.

Knowing exactly when he received his morning mail, she waited anxiously by her phone. It didn't take long. His temporary secretary phoned Mary Jo and set up an appointment for the next morning. By the time she hung up the receiver, Mary Jo was downright gleeful.

The day of her appointment, she dressed in her best suit and high heels, and arrived promptly at eleven. His secretary escorted her into his office.

Evan was at his desk, writing on a yellow legal pad, and didn't look up until the other woman had left the room.

"So, is there a problem?" she asked flatly.

"*Should* there be a problem?"

She lifted one delicate shoulder. "I can't imagine why you'd ask to see me otherwise. I can only assume it has something to do with my letter."

He leaned back in his chair and rolled a gold pen between his palms. "I don't know where you came up with this harebrained idea that I forked over twenty-five thousand dollars to your mother and father."

"Evan, I'm not stupid. I know exactly what you did. And I know why."

"I doubt that."

"I think it was very sweet, but I can't allow you to do it."

"Mary Jo—"

"I believe my suggestion will suit us both nicely. Mrs. Sterling would love having the summers free to travel. If I remember correctly, her husband recently retired, and unless she has the freedom to do as she'd like now and then, you're going to lose her."

Evan said nothing, so she went on, "I worked out all right while I was here, didn't I? Well, other than losing that one file, and that wasn't my fault. Naturally, I hope you won't continue trying to make me jealous. It almost worked, you know."

"I'm afraid I don't know what you're talking about."

"Oh, Evan," she said with an exaggerated sigh. "You must think I'm a complete fool."

He arched his thick brows. "As it happens, I do."

She ignored that. "Do you honestly believe you could convince me you're attracted to...to Miss August. I know you better than you think, Evan Dryden."

His lips quivered slightly with the beginning of a smile, but he managed to squelch it almost immediately.

"Are you agreeable to my solution?" she asked hopefully.

"No," he said.

The bluntness of his reply took her by surprise and her head snapped back. "No?"

"You don't owe me a penny."

At least he wasn't trying to get her to believe the money came from Adison Investments.

"But I can't let you do this."

"Why not?" He gave the appearance of growing bored. Slumped in his chair, he held the pen at each end and twirled it between his thumb and index finger.

"It isn't right. You don't owe them anything, and if they knew, they'd return it instantly."

"You won't tell them." Although he didn't raise his voice, the tone was determined.

"No, I won't," she admitted, knowing it would devastate her parents, "but only if you allow me to reimburse you myself."

He shook his head. "No deal."

Mary Jo knew he could be stubborn, but this was ridiculous. "Evan, please, I *want* to do it."

"The money was a gift from me to them, sent anonymously with no strings attached. And your plan to substitute for Mrs. Sterling— it didn't work out this summer. What makes you think it will in the future? As far as I'm concerned, this issue about the money is pure silliness. I suggest we drop it entirely." He set the pen down on his desk, as if signaling the end of the conversation.

Silliness. Mary Jo stiffened and reached for her purse. "Apparently we don't have anything more to say to each other."

"Apparently not," he agreed without emotion.

Mary Jo stood and, with her head high, walked out of the office. It wasn't until she got to the elevator that the trembling started.

'Are you going to tell me what's troubling you?" Marianna asked Mary Jo. They were sitting at the small kitchen table shelling fresh peas Marianna had purchased from the local farmer's market. Both women quickly and methodically removed the ripe peas from their pods and tossed them into a blue ceramic bowl.

"I'm fine," Mary Jo returned, even though she knew it was next to impossible to fool her mother. After years of raising children and then dealing with grandchildren, Marianna Summerhill had an uncanny knack of knowing when something was right or wrong with any of her family.

"Physically, yes," her mother agreed. "But you're troubled. I can see it in your eyes."

Mary Jo shrugged.

"If I was guessing, I'd say it had something to do with Evan. You haven't seen hide nor hair of him in two weeks."

Evan. The name alone was enough to evoke a flood of unhappiness. "I just don't understand it!" Mary Jo cried. "To hear his mother talk, you'd think he was fading away for want of me."

"He isn't?"

"Hardly. He's dated a different woman every night this week."

"He was mentioned in some gossip column in the paper this morning. Do you know anything about a Barbara Jackson?"

"Yes." Mary Jo clamped her lips together and stewed. If he was flaunting his romantic escapades in an effort to make her jealous, he'd succeeded.

"I imagine you're annoyed."

"'Annoyed' isn't it." She snapped a pea pod so hard, the peas scattered across the tabletop like marbles shooting over a polished hardwood floor. Her mother's smile did nothing to soothe her wounded pride. "What I don't understand," she muttered, "is why he's doing this."

"You haven't figured that out yet?" Marianna asked, her raised voice indicating her surprise. The peas slid effortlessly from the pod to the bowl.

"No, I haven't got a clue. Have *you* figured it out?"

"Ages ago," the older woman said casually.

Mary Jo jerked her head toward her mother. "What do you mean?"

"You're a bright girl, Mary Jo, but when it comes to Evan, I have to wonder."

The words shook her. "What do you mean? I *love* Evan!"

"Not so I can tell." This, too, was said casually.

Mary Jo pushed her mound of pea pods aside and stared at her mother. "Mom, how can you say that?"

"Easy. Evan isn't sure you love him. Why should he be? He—"

Mary Jo was outraged. "Not sure I love him? I can't believe I'm hearing this from my own mother!"

"It's true," Marianna continued, her fingers working rhythmically and without pause. "Looking at it from Evan's point of view, I can't say I blame him."

As the youngest in a big family, Mary Jo had had some shocking things said to her over the years, but never by her own mother. And never this calmly—as if they were merely discussing the price of fresh fruit.

Her first reaction had been defensive, but she was beginning to realize that maybe Marianna knew something she didn't. "I don't understand how Evan could possibly believe I don't love him."

"It's not so hard to understand," Marianna answered smoothly. "Twice you've claimed to love him enough to want to marry him, and both times you've changed your mind."

"But—"

"You've turned your back on him when you were confronted with any resistance from his family. You've never given him the opportunity to answer your doubts. My feeling is, Evan would have stood by you come hell or high water, but I wonder if the reverse is true."

"You make it sound so...so simple, but our situation is a lot more difficult than you know or understand."

"Possibly."

"His family is *formidable*."

"I don't doubt that for an instant," came Marianna's sincere reply. "Let me ask you one thing, though, and I want you to think before you answer. Do you love Evan enough to stand up to opposition, no matter what form it takes?"

"Yes," Mary Jo answered heatedly.

Marianna's eyes brightened with her wide smile. "Then what are you going to do about it?"

"Do?" Mary Jo had tried twice and been thwarted by his pride with each attempt. One thing was certain—Evan had no intention of making this easy for her.

"It seems to me that if you love this man, you're not going to take no for an answer. Unless, of course..." Her mother hesitated.

"Unless what?"

"Unless Evan isn't as important to you as you claim."

Eleven

Mary Jo pushed up the sleeves of her light sweater and paced the floor of her living room. Her mother's comments about the way she'd treated Evan still grated. But what bothered her most was that her mother was right!

No wonder Evan had all but ignored her. He couldn't trust her not to turn her back and run at the first sign of trouble. After all her talk of being older, wiser, and more mature, Mary Jo was forced to admit she was as sadly lacking in those qualities as she'd been three years before. And she was furious.

With herself.

What she needed now was a way to prove her love to Evan so he'd never have cause to doubt her again. One problem was that she had no idea how long it would take for that opportunity to present itself. It might be months—maybe even another three long years. Mary Jo was unwilling to wait. Evan would just have to take her at her word.

But why should he, in light of their past? If he refused, Mary Jo couldn't very well blame him. She sighed, wondering distractedly what to do next.

She could call Jessica, who'd been more than generous with advice. But Mary Jo realized that all Jessica could tell her was what she already knew. Mary Jo needed to talk to Evan herself, face-to-face, no holds barred.

Deciding there was no reason to postpone what had to be done, she carefully chose her outfit—a peach-colored pantsuit with gold buttons, along with a soft turquoise scarf and dangly gold earrings.

When she arrived at his office, Mary Jo was pleasantly surprised to find Mrs. Sterling.

"Oh, my, don't you look lovely this afternoon," the older

woman said with a delighted smile. She seemed relaxed and happy; the trip had obviously done her good.

"So do you, Mrs. Sterling. When did you get back?"

"Just this week. I heard about your accident. I'm so pleased everything turned out all right."

"So am I. Is Evan in?"

"I'm sorry, no, but I expect him any time. Why don't you make yourself at home there in his office? I'll bring you some coffee. I don't think he'll be more than a few minutes."

"Thanks, I will." Mary Jo walked into the office and sank onto the sofa. In her determination to see this matter through, she naively hadn't considered the possibility of Evan's being out of the office. And she feared the longer the wait, the more her courage would falter.

She was sipping the coffee Mrs. Sterling had brought her and lecturing herself, trying to bolster her courage, when she heard Evan arrive. Her hands trembled as she set the cup aside.

By the time Evan strolled into the room, still rattling off a list of instructions for Mrs. Sterling, Mary Jo's shoulders were tensed, as if she was bracing herself for an assault.

His secretary finished making her notes. "You have a visitor," she announced, smiling approvingly in Mary Jo's direction.

Evan sent a look over his shoulder, but revealed no emotion when he saw who it was. "Hello, Mary Jo."

"Evan." She pressed her palms over her knees, certain she must resemble a schoolgirl confronting the principal after some misdemeanor. "I'd like to talk to you, if I may."

He frowned and glanced at his watch.

"Your schedule is free," Mrs. Sterling said emphatically, and when she walked away, she closed the door.

"Well, it seems I can spare a few minutes," Evan said without enthusiasm as he walked behind his desk and sat down.

Mary Jo stood and took the chair across from him. "First I'd like to apologize."

"No," he said roughly. "There's nothing to apologize for."

"But there is," she returned. "Oh, Evan, I've nearly ruined everything."

His eyebrows rose, and his expression was skeptical. "Come now, Mary Jo."

She slid forward in her seat. "It all started that summer we met when—"

"That was years ago, and if you don't mind, I'd prefer to leave it there." He reached for his gold pen, as if he needed to hold on to something. "Rehashing it all isn't going to do either of us any good."

"I disagree." Mary Jo refused to be so easily discouraged this time. "We need to clear up the past. Otherwise once we're married—"

"It seems to me you're taking a lot for granted," he said sharply.

"Perhaps, but I doubt it."

"Mary Jo, I can't see that this will get us anywhere."

"I do," she said hurriedly. "Please listen to what I have to say, and if you still feel the same afterward, then...well, then I'll just say it another way until you're willing to accept that I love you."

His eyebrows rose again. "I have a date this evening."

"Then I'll talk fast, but I think you should know that you aren't fooling me."

"Do you think I'm lying?"

"Of course not. You may very well have arranged an evening with some woman, but it's me you love."

His handsome features darkened in a frown, but she took heart from the fact that he didn't contradict her.

Mary Jo studied her own watch. "How much time do I have before you need to leave?"

Evan shrugged. "Enough."

He wasn't doing anything to encourage her, but that was fine; she knew what she wanted, and she wasn't going to let a little thing like a bad attitude stand in her way.

It took her a few moments to arrange her thoughts and remember what she'd so carefully planned to say. Perhaps that was for the best. She didn't want to sound as if she'd practiced in front of a mirror, although she'd done exactly that.

"You were saying?" Evan pressed.

She nibbled her lower lip. "Yes. I wanted to talk to you about the house."

"What house?" he asked impatiently.

"The one with the seven bedrooms. The one we've discussed in such detail that I can see it clear as anything. The house I want to live in with you and our children."

She noticed that his eyes drifted away from hers.

"I've been doing a lot of thinking lately," Mary Jo continued. "It all started when I was feeling sorry for myself, certain that I'd lost you. I...found the thought almost unbearable."

"You get accustomed to it after a while," he muttered dryly.

"I never will," she said adamantly, "not ever again."

He leaned forward in his chair as if to see her better. "What brought about this sudden change of heart?"

"It isn't sudden. Well, maybe it is. You see, it's my mother. She—"

"Are you sure it wasn't *my* mother? She seems to have her hand in just about everything that goes on between you and me."

"Not anymore." This was something else Mary Jo wanted to correct. "According to Jessica, your mother's been beside herself wondering what's going on with us. We have to give her credit, Evan—she hasn't called or pressured me once. You see, she promised she wouldn't, and your mother's a woman of her word."

"Exactly what did she promise?"

"Not to meddle in our lives. She came to me when I was still in the hospital, and we had a wonderful talk. Some of the problems between us were of my own making. Your mother intimidated me, and I was afraid to go against her. But after our talk, I understand her a little better and she understands me."

She waited for him to make some comment, but was disappointed. From all outward appearances, Evan was merely enduring this discussion, waiting for her to finish so he could get on with his life.

"I'm not Lois's first choice for a daughter-in-law. There are any number of other women who'd be a far greater asset to you and your political future than I'll ever be."

"I'm dating one now."

The information was like a slap in the face, but Mary Jo revealed none of her feelings.

"Above and beyond anything else, your mother wants your happiness, and she believes, as I do, that our being together will provide that."

"Nice of her to confer with me. It seems the two of you—and let's not forget dear Jessica—have joined forces. You're all plotting against me."

"Absolutely not. I've talked to Jessica a number of times, but not recently. It was my mother who helped me understand what was wrong."

"And now *she's* involved." He rolled his eyes as if to say there were far too many mothers interfering in all this.

"All my mother did was show me a few home truths. If anything, we should thank her. She pointed out that you've got good reason to question the strength of my love for you. I was floored that my own mother could suggest something like that. Especially since she knew how unhappy and miserable I've been lately."

The hint of a smile lifted his mouth.

"Mom said if I loved you as much as I claim to, I would have stood by your side despite any opposition. She…she said if our situations had been reversed, you would have stood by me. I didn't, and, Evan, I can't tell you how much I regret it." She lowered her gaze to her hands. "If I could undo the past, step back three years— or even three weeks—I'd do anything to prove exactly how much I love you. I believe in you, Evan, and I believe in our love. Never again will I give you cause to doubt it. Further-more—"

"You mean there's more?" He sounded bored, as if this was taking much longer than he'd anticipated.

"Just a little," she said, and her voice wavered with the strength of her conviction. "You're going to make a wonderful member of the city council, and I'll do whatever's necessary to see that it happens. It won't be easy for me to be the focus of public attention, but in time, I'll learn not to be so nervous. Your mother's already volunteered to help me. I can do this, Evan, I know I can. Another three or four years down the road, I'll be a pro in front of the cameras. Just wait and see."

He didn't speak, and Mary Jo could feel every beat of her heart in the silence that followed.

"That's all well and good," Evan finally said, "but I don't see how any of it changes things."

"You don't?" She vaulted to her feet. "Do you or don't you love me?" she demanded.

He regarded her with a look of utter nonchalance. "Frankly, I don't know what I feel for you anymore."

In slow motion, Mary Jo sank back into her seat. She'd lost him. She could see it in his eyes, in the way he looked at her as if she was nothing to him anymore. Someone he'd loved once, a long time ago, but that was all.

"I see," she mumbled.

"Now, if you'll excuse me, I have some business I need to attend to."

"Ah..." The shock of his rejection had numbed her, and it took her a moment to get to her feet. She clutched her purse protectively to her stomach. "I...I'm sorry to have bothered you." She drew on the little that remained of her pride and dignity to carry her across the room.

"No bother," Evan said tonelessly.

It was at that precise moment that Mary Jo knew. She couldn't have explained exactly how, but she *knew*. Relief washed over her like the warm blast of a shower after a miserable day in the cold. He loved her. He'd always loved her.

Confident now, she turned around to face him.

He was busily writing on a legal pad and didn't look up.

"Evan." She whispered his name.

He ignored her.

"You love me."

His hand trembled slightly, but that was all the emotion he revealed.

"It isn't going to work," she said, stepping toward him.

"I beg your pardon?" He sighed heavily.

"This little charade. I don't know what you're trying to prove, but it isn't working. It never will. You couldn't have sat by my hospital bed all those hours and felt nothing for me. You couldn't have given my parents that money and not cared for me.''

"I didn't say I didn't care. But as you said yourself, sometimes love isn't enough.''

"Then I was wrong,'' she muttered. "Now listen. My mother and yours are chomping at the bit to start planning our wedding. What do you want me to tell them? That the whole thing's off and you don't love me anymore? You don't honestly expect anyone to believe that, do you? *I* don't.''

"Believe what you want.''

Briefly, she closed her eyes. "You're trying my patience, Evan, but you have a long way to go if you think you can get me to change my mind.'' She moved closer. There was more than one way of proving her point. More than one way to kick the argument out from under him. And she wasn't going to let this opportunity pass.

She stepped over to his desk and planted both hands on it, leaning over the top so that only a few inches separated their faces. "All right, Dryden, you asked for this.''

His eyes narrowed, as she edged her way around the desk. His head followed her movements. He turned in his chair, eyeing her speculatively.

At that moment, she threw herself on his lap, wrapped her arms around his neck and kissed him. She felt his surprise and his resistance, but the latter vanished almost the instant her mouth settled over his.

It'd been so long since they'd kissed. So long since she'd experienced the warm comfort of his embrace.

Groaning, Evan kissed her back. His mouth was tentative at first, then hard and intense. His hold tightened and a frightening kind of excitement began to grow inside her. As she clung to him, she could feel his heart beating as fast as hers, his breathing as labored.

Cradling his face with her hands, she spread eager, loving kisses over his mouth, his jaw, his forehead. "I love you, Evan Dryden.''

"This isn't just gratitude?''

She paused and lifted her head. "For what?''

"The money I gave your family.''

"No," she said, teasing a corner of his mouth with the tip of her tongue. "But that *is* something we need to discuss."

"No, we don't." He tilted her so that she was practically lying across his lap. "I have a proposition to make."

"Decent or indecent?" she asked with a pretended leer.

"That's for you to decide."

She looped her arms around his neck, hoisted herself upright and pressed her head against his shoulder.

"You'll marry me?" he asked.

"Oh, yes—" she sighed with happiness "—and soon. Evan, let's make this the shortest engagement on record."

"On one condition. You never mention that money again."

"But—"

"Those are my terms." He punctuated his statement with a kiss so heated it seared her senses.

When it ended, Mary Jo had difficulty breathing normally. "Your terms?" she repeated in a husky whisper.

"Do you agree, or don't you?"

Before she could answer, he swept away her defenses and any chance of argument with another kiss. By the time he'd finished, Mary Jo discovered she would have concurred with just about anything. She nodded numbly.

Evan held her against him and exhaled deeply. "We'll make our own wedding plans, understood?"

Mary Jo stared at him blankly.

"This is our wedding and not my mother's—or your mother's."

She smiled softly and lowered her head to his shoulder. "Understood."

They were silent for several minutes, each savoring the closeness.

"Mom was right, wasn't she?" Mary Jo asked softly. "About how I needed to prove that my love was more than words."

"If you'd walked out that door, I might always have wondered," Evan confessed, then added, "You wouldn't have gotten far. I would've come running after you, but I'm glad I didn't have to."

"I've been such a fool." Mary Jo lovingly traced the side of his neck with her tongue.

"I'll give you fifty or sixty years to make it up to me, with time off for good behavior."

The happiness on her face blossomed into a full-blown smile. She raised her head and waited until their eyes met before she lowered her mouth to his. The kiss was long, slow and thorough. Evan drew in a deep, stabilizing breath when they'd finished.

"What was that for?"

"To seal our bargain. From this day forward, Evan Dryden, we belong to each other. Nothing will ever get between us again."

"Nothing," he agreed readily.

The door opened and Mrs. Sterling poked her head in. "I just wanted to check and make sure everything had worked itself out," she said, smiling broadly. "I can see that it has. I couldn't be more pleased."

"Neither could I," Mary Jo said.

Evan drew her mouth back to his and Mary Jo heard the office door click softly shut in the background.

Epilogue

Three years later.

'Andrew, don't wake Bethanne!" Jessica called out to her four-year-old son.

Mary Jo laughed as she watched the child bend over to kiss her newborn daughter's forehead. "Look, they're already kissing cousins."

"How are you feeling?" Jessica asked, carrying a tall glass of iced tea over to Mary Jo, who was sitting under the shade of the patio umbrella.

"Wonderful."

"Evan is delighted with Bethanne, isn't he?"

"Oh, yes. He reminded me of Damian when you had Lori Jo. You'd think we were the only two women on earth to have ever given birth."

Jessica laughed and shook her head. "And then the grandparents…"

"I don't know about you," Mary Jo teased, "but I could become accustomed to all this attention."

Jessica eyed her disbelievingly.

"All right, all right. I'll admit I was a bit flustered when the mayor paid me a visit in the hospital. And it was kind of nice to receive flowers from all those special-interest groups—the ones who think Evan is easily influenced. Clearly, they don't know my husband."

Jessica sighed and relaxed in her lounge chair. "You've done amazingly well with all this. Evan's told Damian and me at least a hundred times or more that you as much as won that council position for him.''

Mary Jo laughed off the credit. ''Don't be silly.''

''You were the one who walked up to the microphone at that rally and said if anyone believed Evan wasn't there for the worker, they should talk to you or your family.''

Mary Jo remembered the day well. She'd been furious to hear Evan's opponent state that Evan didn't understand the problems of the everyday working person. Evan had answered the accusation, but it was Mary Jo's fervent response that had won the hearts of the audience. As it happened, television cameras had recorded the rally and her impassioned reply had been played on three different newscasts. From that point on, Evan's popularity had soared.

Bethanne stirred, and Mary Jo reached for her daughter, cradling the infant in her arms.

A sound in the distance told her that Evan and his brother were back from their golf game.

''That didn't take long,'' Jessica said when Damian and Evan strolled onto the patio. Damian poured them each a glass of iced tea.

Evan took the seat next to his wife. ''How long has it been since I told you I loved you?'' he asked in a low voice.

Smiling, Mary Jo glanced at her watch. ''About four hours.''

''Much too long,'' he said, kissing the side of her neck. ''I love you.''

''Look at that pair,'' Damian said to his wife. ''You'd think they were still on their honeymoon.''

''So? What's wrong with that?'' Jessica reached over and squeezed his hands.

He smiled at her lovingly. ''Not a thing, sweetheart. Not a damn thing.''

CARLA NEGGERS

Fun and a little hard work was all Tess Haviland had in mind when she purchased the run-down, nineteenth-century carriage house on Boston's North Shore. She never anticipated getting involved with the local residents, and never imagined what it would be like to own a house rumored to be haunted.

Then Tess discovers a skeleton in the dirt cellar—human remains that suddenly go missing. And she begins to ask questions about the history of her house…and the wealthy, charismatic man who planned to renovate it, until he disappeared a year before. Questions a desperate killer will do anything to silence before the truth exposes that someone got away with murder.

THE CARRIAGE HOUSE

"When it comes to romance, adventure and suspense, nobody delivers like Carla Neggers."
—Jayne Ann Krentz

On sale Febraury 2001
wherever paperbacks are sold!

JAYNE ANN KRENTZ

Jamie Garland had fallen in love…with a lie. Cade Santerre had pretended to be someone he wasn't. Worse, he'd used her in his elaborate attempt to catch a man he believed was a criminal.

Though his suspect had escaped, Cade was still around, masculine and overwhelming. He had some unfinished business and he needed Jamie's help. But Jamie had some unfinished business, as well: to find out if the man she'd fallen in love with really existed.

TRUE COLORS

"Nobody does it better!"
—Romantic Times